MORE PRAI[SE]

Killer Listing

"Sexy, savvy, and entertaining, real estate agent Darby Farr solves the crime, nets the commission, and looks great doing so. Vicki Doudera displays a deft hand with story and characters. *Killer Listing* is a real showcase."

—Julia Spencer-Fleming author of *One Was a Soldier*

"A hot property! Multi-million dollar deals, mojitos, and murder—real estate brings real trouble to this smart and savvy heroine. Scheming, speculation, and a scary bad guy will keep you turning the pages of this suspenseful and cleverly plotted mystery. Readers beware: though the setting is sunny, there's a twist around every corner."

—Hank Phillippi Ryan, Anthony, Agatha, and
Macavity award-winning author

House to Die For

"[Doudera] expertly weaves a tale of suspense on a Maine island, where murder and real estate are an explosive combination."

—Tess Gerritsen, bestselling author of the *Rizzoli & Isles* novels

"The cutthroat world of luxury real estate is the perfect setting for a murder mystery, and Vicki Doudera's *A House to Die For* doesn't disappoint. Here's a fast-paced and well-told story with a smart, savvy real estate agent as the heroine, solving crimes while making sales. Bring on the next one!"

—Barbara Corcoran, real estate contributor for NBC's *Today Show*

"An appealing debut . . . the author does a good job portraying Darby in her efforts to make peace with her childhood past and solve a murder on a picturesque Maine island."

—*Publishers Weekly*

"A superb prologue, wonderful story, atmospheric with a good plot."

—*Crimespree Magazine*

KILLER
LISTING

ALSO BY VICKI DOUDERA

A House to Die For

KILLER LISTING

A Darby Farr Mystery

Vicki Doudera

MIDNIGHT INK
WOODBURY, MINNESOTA

FIRST EDITION
First Printing, 2011

Book design by Donna Burch
Cover design by Lisa Novak
Cover illustration © Dominick Finelle/The July Group
Edited by Connie Hill

Midnight Ink, an imprint of Llewellyn Worldwide Ltd.

Library of Congress Cataloging-in-Publication Data

Doudera, Vicki, 1961–
   Killer listing : A Darby Farr mystery / Vicki Doudera.— 1st ed.
      p.   cm.
   ISBN 978-0-7387-1979-5
   1. Women real estate agents—Fiction. 2. Murder—Investigation—Fiction.
   3. Real estate busines—Fiction. 4. Florida—Fiction. I. Title.

   PS3604.O895K55   2011
   813'.6—dc22   2010045347

Midnight Ink
Llewellyn Worldwide Ltd.
2143 Wooddale Drive
Woodbury, MN 55125-2989
www.midnightinkbooks.com

Printed in the United States of America

ACKNOWLEDGMENTS

I am grateful to Gloria and Arthur Doudera for introducing me to the perfect spot in which to set *Killer Listing*—the Gulf Coast of Florida. Thnks also to Lucy Morgan for an inspiring stay in her beautiful "to die for" home on Siesta Bay.

For specialized asistance when I needed it, thank you to the Florida Association of REALTORS, rum expert Will Clemente, wine connoisseur Rich Beauchesne, SCUBA divemaster Matt Doudera, and William J. Albany, Chief of Police, Limerick Township, Pennsylvania.

Thank you to my manuscript readers, Lynda Chilton, Ed Doudera, and Jane Lafleur. I appreciate your skill and time.

Thank you to my literary agent, Tris Coburn, and to all the good people at Midnight Ink, including Marissa Pederson, Steven Pomije, Connie Hill, and Terri Bischoff. Thanks to Lisa Novak and Donna Burch for another great-looking book.

I appreciate the support of my fellow real estate brokers in Camden and beyond, and all of the new friends I have made in the world of mystery since Darby Farr's debut.

Finlly, this book would not have been possible without the help, love, and encouragement of my friends and family. Special thanks to my "killer" crew of Matt, Nate, Lexi, and Ed.

PROLOGUE

KYLE CAMERON LET OUT a long moan of pleasure as her massage therapist gave one more long gliding stroke to her lightly tanned shoulders.

"Like sex, only better, eh?" asked Sassa Jorgensen, smiling with satisfaction at her client's inert form.

"Ummmm … way better." Kyle lay motionless for a few precious moments, savoring the feeling of total relaxation she always experienced after her weekly session with the talented practitioner.

"You are the best, Sassi." She inhaled deeply, the faint scent of sandalwood filling her nostrils, and pulled the soft terry towel over her torso. She didn't care if the older woman saw her naked—she'd done so many times and besides, Kyle was justifiably proud of her firm, forty-two-year-old body—but the towel was warm and soft, and the temperature in the air-conditioned condominium was beginning to feel chilly.

Sassa capped the multivitamin lotion she'd slathered on Kyle's skin and placed it in her satchel. She gave a sly smile, the corners of her eyes crinkling with mischief. "Your Sassi can make you feel as good as your big-shot boyfriend, eh?" she teased, handing Kyle her plush terry robe. "Even with his fancy dinners, private jet, and undoubtedly large—"

"Now that's enough," Kyle interrupted, laughing. "I've told you before, there's no competition between you and any of my lovers. Are you this probing with all of your clients?"

Sassa shooed Kyle off her massage table and began folding it up. "Just the ones I worry about." She leaned the folded table against the hallway wall and reached for her satchel, her air of lightheartedness suddenly gone.

"What is it?" Kyle asked, hugging the robe closer to her body, longing for the hot shower she always took after one of Sassa's sessions. She glanced at the masseuse's frowning face and felt a trickle of irritation. "You're giving me the creeps."

The older woman waited a moment before speaking. "It's that man McFarlin, the one you are seeing. He's always in the papers. This party, that party... with a blonde woman on his arm..."

"His wife?" Kyle gave a harsh laugh. She ran a hand through her tousled chestnut hair. "That's Lieutenant Governor Howe, Sassa. An old friend of mine." The bitterness in her voice was hard to ignore. "He doesn't love her anymore than she cares for him. It's just convenient."

"Then it is convenient also that he has your warm bed, eh?" Sassa glanced up quickly, hoping she had not overstepped her bounds with her best-paying client. To her relief, she saw that Kyle's countenance was once again serene. The therapist bit her lip and continued. "I have a bad feeling about him. I've warned you before..."

"I know," Kyle interjected, trying to keep her tone light. "You think he's using me. I wasn't born yesterday, Sassa, and I'm not some silly twenty-year-old who's gaga over him and his billions." She paused and tilted her chin in defiance. "I enjoyed what Foster could give me, it's true, and I liked the 'no strings attached' nature of our relationship. And being his exclusive listing agent is how I've paid for all of this—and you." She glanced at her perfectly manicured nails and frowned. "Truthfully, I've used him as much as he's used me."

"You talk almost as if…"

"As if it's over between us?" Kyle gave a quick grin, raising her expertly arched eyebrows. "Yes, you little Swedish worrywart. Romantically at least, I'm finished with Foster McFarlin, and he knows it. We had it all out last night." She rose and reached for a soft leather clutch, one of the few items out of place in the immaculate room, and opened it. Handing the masseuse a check that included a generous tip, she smiled again. "Here you go. Next week you'll need something else to pester me about."

Sassa Jorgensen smiled. *So then it isn't too late*, she thought, trying to dismiss the feeling of foreboding she'd possessed since entering Kyle's condo. She nodded briskly and picked up her massage table. "I am glad," she said simply, moving down the hallway to the door. "Until next Monday, then."

Kyle locked the door behind Sassa and padded down the hallway, past her carefully chosen furnishings. She paused before a carved table, upon which was an exquisite cut glass bowl filled with water. Inside the bowl swam a solitary goldfish.

"Hey, Buddy. How many laps are you up to today?" The scales on the fish flashed brilliantly as the little creature completed another circle, seeming to swim even faster with an audience. "Don't overdo it, huh?" Kyle opened a drawer and pulled out a small box. Was it her imagination, or did Buddy seem to notice that it was lunchtime? She pinched a small amount of the flakes and sprinkled them on the surface. Immediately, the fish streaked to the food, gobbling up a slowly sinking morsel or two and darting back down, only to repeat the process until all of it was eaten.

Kyle chuckled and replaced the box in the drawer. She'd purchased Buddy when she moved into the condo, going on two years now, and was amazed at his longevity. No fancy aquarium, no special water, and yet he seemed to be thriving. *He's got straightforward—but expensive—taste in property*, she thought. *Real estate applies even to fish.*

The bowl had been one of her grandmother's most treasured possessions, one of the few things she'd managed to remove from her elegant Warsaw apartment while fleeing the Nazis. Kyle imagined the elderly woman's delighted expression if she'd lived to see her Lalique crystal inhabited by a goldfish. "She'd have welcomed you with open arms," Kyle said. The fish seemed to slow his swimming to ponder Kyle's words.

Warm-hearted Grandma Anna was without a doubt the biggest influence in Kyle Cameron's life. When she was five, her mother disappeared after going on a particularly long drinking binge, and in her place appeared a silver-haired angel who announced she was Kyle's grandmother. She took the entranced child to her apartment at the Sunshine Senior Home in Sarasota, Florida, and made her a snug little room out of an oversized closet. The presence of a precocious little girl, along with the excitement of duping the Sunshine staff (there were rules about roommates, and grandchildren were totally forbidden) buoyed Anna's and all the rest of the residents' spirits immeasurably. Kyle grew up surrounded by dozens of loving grandparents, always eager to assist with her homework, teach her Canasta, or read her a story. Despite her mother's disappearance and her lack of knowledge of her father, Kyle's was a blissful—if somewhat unorthodox—childhood.

Sighing at the memory of Anna Slivicki, Kyle turned on the shower and reflected on the rest of her day's schedule. Her Esperanza Shores open house at noon was first and foremost on her agenda. Following that, she had several appointments, as well as a cocktail party on the very chic St. Andrew's Isle, home of the PGA's leading golfer. She stepped into the steaming shower and pondered her wardrobe, knowing there would be no time to change once she left her condo. Professional attire was needed for most of the day, with something classy for the party. She pictured her navy blue suit with the pencil skirt. If she paired it with a cream-colored sleeveless cashmere shell and pearls, she could remove the jacket at the party and look properly elegant. *I'll bring my new Marc Jacobs clutch for the cocktail party,* she decided, uncapping her lightly-scented lavender shampoo.

Everything she needed for the open house—business cards, flyers, several signs—was already stashed in her Miata. Idly she wondered who would show up on a hot July Monday. Open houses always brought out curious neighbors, eager for free food, as well as the "ladies who lunch" crowd, looking for a peek into the Sunshine Coast's finest properties. On occasion, the events brought out true home buyers as well—making the work, expense, and lost time worth the effort. *Not only is it excellent publicity for the project,* Kyle reminded herself, *but it will give me something positive to report to Foster.*

Kyle rinsed her hair and let her thoughts drift back to the previous night's breakup with Florida's largest developer. Neither one of them had seemed truly surprised, nor were they overly regretful. Their affair had run its course, the passion and intensity waning over the weeks as both realized there was nothing more to be gained than an hour of illicit pleasure once or twice a week. Even if he had been single, Kyle was not interested in marrying Foster McFarlin. After being wined, dined, and eventually seduced by the man, Kyle had nothing more to gain by continuing the liaison, and had gently initiated the discussion following a hop to Miami in Foster's private jet.

McFarlin had taken the news well, seeming to share Kyle's feelings that it was time for their love affair to end. It was as if he'd achieved his conquest of the desirable and driven Kyle Cameron— a goal he'd been trying to achieve since college—and with that mission accomplished, was only too happy to part romantic ways. *He agreed we'd keep our professional relationship cordial, and today will be the test.*

Two years earlier, she'd secured his business, chiefly several large and extremely lucrative real estate projects for which Kyle was the exclusive agent. Sales of Foster McFarlin's properties thus far had made her very wealthy, and if she could manage to weather the economic slowdown and remain his agent, she knew her good fortune would continue. *My life is changing, and I'll need those listings. I've got to safeguard them at all costs.*

Half an hour later, Kyle put all thoughts of Foster McFarlin out of her mind and was dressed and ready to leave. Her makeup was expertly applied, the navy blue suit clung perfectly in all the right places, and her new purse was ready for its evening tour of duty. She glanced critically at her reflection in the full-length mirror. Her chin-length bob looked chic and professional, her chestnut hair shiny and smooth. But something was needed to offset the pearls…

Her jewelry box yielded nothing satisfactory and Kyle was about to give up when she noticed a small red box tucked behind some beads. With a stab of recognition, she opened the velvet lid and removed the ring inside. It was an unusual little piece: antique rose gold with six sapphires set three on either side of an old European cut diamond. The design was unique. Rather than a circular setting, the sapphires formed a long oval that accentuated Kyle's tapered fingers. It was striking: old-fashioned, and yet strangely modern too, and never failed to elicit compliments.

Kyle slipped the ring on her little finger and thought once more of Grandma Anna. This had been her treasured cocktail ring, one of her favorite pieces of jewelry, the ring that had bought her way out of danger more than once. Kyle sighed and closed the box. Moments later she gathered up her Smartphone, clutch, and briefcase, and strode out the door.

Her blue Miata waited outside the condo, parked under a striking fan palm, and Kyle noted with annoyance that it needed a wash. No time for that now, she thought as she revved the engine and sped down the streets of the development. She glanced at the neighboring properties with the practiced eye of a real estate agent. Green, well-watered lawns dotted with palm trees, pedestrian-friendly sidewalks, and ample street lighting: it all added up to a feeling of well-being and security. Somerset Sound, one of Foster McFarlin's earliest projects, was aging well.

Kyle drove by one of two inviting pools, the scent of chlorine and suntan lotion taking her back to childhood days at a much smaller pool, presided over by her grandmother. Passing by the Somerset Sound gatehouse, Kyle waved to the uniformed man on duty, who gave a friendly smile and waved back. She sped out onto the two-lane highway, cruising past a few shopping centers with liquor stores, Chinese food, and pet supply centers, relieved to see that the late morning traffic was light. Driving through several small beach towns, she went over a causeway and onto Serenidad Key. She smiled as she drove by the trim little office of Near & Farr Realty. Her appointment with the firm's owner was later in the day; "cocktail hour" as Helen Near called it, and Kyle knew there would be some sort of frothy—and alcoholic—beverage waiting when she arrived.

Esperanza Shores was at the end of the key, tucked onto a gently curving swath of waterfront land McFarlin had purchased twenty years ago. Construction was nearly complete, but the project was not the blazing success its creators had hoped. Out of 48 condominium units, only a dozen were sold and occupied. Esperanza Plaza, in the center of the development, had promised several boutiques and a four-star restaurant—none of which were finished, much less open for business. Kyle tried not to think of the many lawsuits against McFarlin and whether she, also, would come under investigation. What was the point in worrying? Better to focus on staying positive. "Don't let your mind dwell on bad thoughts," Grandma Anna would have said. Kyle turned into the model unit and began unloading the Miata. Perhaps today's open house would mark the end of Foster McFarlin's streak of bad luck.

————

The humidity was stifling, and as Kyle emerged from the Miata, she felt it envelop her like a wet blanket. She grabbed the open house signs and set them at the foot of the driveway, knowing she wouldn't want to venture into the heat again once she was back inside an air-conditioned space. She took her cards and flyers out of the Miata and locked it. Trying to stay cool, she forced herself to walk slowly to the condo, watching a few geckos scatter into the bushes as she passed. She unlocked the door, flipped off the alarm, and set the publicity materials on a circular table just inside the door.

She glanced quickly at the living room and down the hallway to the bedrooms. Everything was neat and clean, furnished tastefully but rather blandly. She checked the bathrooms and the upstairs suite, turning on lights as she entered the rooms. Satisfied with what she saw, Kyle nodded. All was fine.

The condo's kitchen smelled faintly of lemons. Kyle knew the cleaning staff had been by earlier to spruce it up and let in the catering company. On one of the granite counters were several plastic bags of finger rolls along with a small stack of white plates and napkins embossed with the Esperanza Shores logo. Kyle opened the refrigerator. The appliance's sparkling clean shelves held two trays of sliced deli meats, a plate of artfully arranged fruits, and an array of bottled waters. Kyle glanced at her watch. Eleven fifteen. She had plenty of time to put out the caterer's fare before anyone arrived. First, she wanted to put on some background music.

She turned on the condo's stereo system and located a radio station that played light jazz. Nothing crazy or discordant—just pleasant music that would soothe and provide a mellow backdrop. With that accomplished, she straightened and contemplated opening more blinds. She had started down the hallway when she heard the click of a door opening.

Kyle frowned. The open house didn't start for forty-five minutes, but apparently some of the neighbors couldn't wait. *My fault*, she thought. *I did put out the signs…*

"Hello," she called out, backtracking down the hall to the foyer.

"Hello?" The house was still. Kyle shrugged. Perhaps someone had been about to enter and decided to wait. She glanced out the living room's picture window. No cars, no people. And yet she knew she had heard *something*.

Kyle felt her first frisson of fear. That door had opened, she knew it had, but where was the person who had opened it? If they were outside, wouldn't she have seen them in the driveway? Perhaps they had ducked to the side of the building and had been out of Kyle's line of vision. She took a shallow breath. That explanation made sense. An early visitor to the open house had decided to walk around the property first.

But there was another explanation. Someone was inside, somewhere in the condo…

My cell, she thought. She'd left it on the counter, next to the refrigerator, with her purse. She walked slowly to the kitchen, listening intently. Nothing but the calming sounds of the jazz, and her heart pounding in her ears.

Kyle exhaled as she entered the kitchen, seeing nothing out of place. She grabbed her cell and turned to go back to the window.

No doubt she'd see someone outside, coming from the other side of the property, any second now. There was no need to panic.

She walked out of the kitchen feeling less frightened. Turning to look out the living room window, she saw a dark shape in the corner of her eye. She wheeled around, ready to scream, until she saw who it was.

"Shit! You scared the hell out of me."

"Sorry."

"I didn't expect to see you here. Are you checking up on me?"

A blow across the face caught Kyle Cameron completely unprepared, the force of it pushing her back against the picture window with a resounding crack. She gasped, her dark eyes wide with fear, and saw the glint of a long knife as it arced down through the air and straight toward her heart. Before she could move she felt a piercing pain, heard the crack of bone, and then a whooshing sound as the knife was retracted.

Kyle opened her mouth to scream. Instead she sucked in air, desperate to make a sound, but able only to gasp. She tried to understand what was happening, but the sensations were all around her, pounding at her: the smell of something thick and rusty, the feeling that she was emptying from her core out, the knowledge that she could not escape whatever was going to happen next. Still on her feet, she staggered, then sagged against the picture window, sinking downward until she was crumpled on the butter-yellow wood floors. The blade was coming close again, slicing through her cashmere sweater, now soaked crimson with blood. She did not see it penetrate her sternum, nor did she see it rise once more to begin its downward descent into her throat. Deep darkness was all she could see, a black hole bereft of pain into which she mercifully fell.

ONE

Darby Farr pulled her long black hair into a quick ponytail and surveyed the map of Serenidad Key, Florida. About an hour earlier, she'd picked up a sporty black Mustang convertible at the airport, promptly setting the car's air conditioner to full blast. According to the dashboard thermometer it was ninety-five degrees Farenheit, and all Darby could think about was a tall glass of lemony iced tea. Yes, it was hot, but then it was the middle of a July afternoon and she was on the Gulf Coast of Florida.

She consulted her directions, found the street she needed and pulled back into traffic, counting two traffic lights and then turning right, toward the Gulf of Mexico. A quick left and she was on Driftwood, a street of modest homes with glimpses of blue water through the backyards. Seconds later she was parked at her destination, a trim Caribbean style home with a porch framed by two massive coconut palm trees.

The front door opened and the tanned face of Helen Near broke into a wide grin. "You made it! Come on in out of this heat. Must feel especially brutal to a Northerner!"

Darby smiled. She didn't think of herself as being from the North, although she had been raised on an island off the coast of Maine.

"I'm from southern California, remember?" She grabbed her purse and slammed the door of the Mustang. She stepped onto the porch and gave the older woman a damp hug, inhaling the faint scent of coconut. "Helen, you look terrific."

"Why thank you, sweetie. You are just as pretty as when I saw you in Maine." The two women shared a quick smile at the memory of their first meeting the month before at the memorial service for Darby's aunt. Darby had been impressed with the kindness and common sense of her aunt's business partner, this tall and sensible woman in her late sixties with short silver hair and an athlete's figure. "For goodness sakes, come on in where it's not an oven." The older woman paused and gestured toward the Mustang. "I like your fancy car. Better lock it up. This isn't Hurricane Harbor, you know."

Darby acquiesced, hearing the soft beep of the automatic key lock, and entered the cool interior, feeling her body temperature lower in relief. She looked around the sunny spaces, furnished in a relaxed cottage style, and smiled.

"What a great house." She took in the original light woodwork, the pleasing symmetrical proportions, and laid-back beach style. "I'm guessing 1850?"

"Damn close. 1845. I've researched the house's lineage to a local shipping captain who was captivated by the Bahamas. Even married a Bahamian woman, which wasn't exactly legal in those days. He bought the land in 1843 and had local craftsmen build this place from a sketch drawn on a piece of bark. It's the only Caribbean style house—well, original that is—in the county. They're quite popular on Key West where they call them 'conch' houses, but you don't usually see them on this coast."

Darby nodded. "I've heard of the unique architecture on the Keys, but never seen it myself. Someday I'd love to get down there."

"Key West is quite a distance from here, but growing up in Miami I went there all the time. They've changed—well everything has—but there is still something special about those colorful little bungalows, Papa Hemingway's adventures, and that feeling of being suspended out in the ocean." She gave Darby a kind smile. "Now, didn't you tell me that you own a bungalow as well?"

"That's right. Near San Diego, a small town called Mission Beach. Why is it that those of us in real estate seem to gravitate toward smaller homes?"

"Because we know it's grand to sell big places and get big fat commission checks, but way easier to live in something small!" Helen gave a booming laugh. "What the hell am I doing, not giving you a drink? What kind of Southern hostess am I, anyway?" She beckoned to Darby. "Come and see my kitchen. If you're a small house person, you're going to love it."

Darby followed Helen through a tidy little dining room with a built-in china cabinet, catching a whiff of something citrus on the air. "Don't tell me you have grapefruit trees?"

Helen smiled. "That's right. Just as sweet as oranges, they are. Lemons, too. You help yourself, Darby. Pick 'em right off the branches. Live the real Florida life while you're here."

The kitchen was tucked in the back of the cottage. Neat little cabinets and shelves made from the same light-colored wood were a pleasing counterpoint to yellow walls and a cheerful café curtain in a vintage cherry pattern. A small collection of Fiestaware pitchers filled several shelves, looking right at home. Wide windows looked out onto a small stone patio framed by blooming bougainvilleas in the same colorful hues as the china.

"That's my oasis," said Helen, waving a tanned hand toward the patio. "When it's not so blazing hot, we'll go out there. In the meantime, something to cool you down. One of my personal favorites—a Mojito."

Darby accepted the tall glass, verdant with crushed mint, and took a sip. It was the perfect antidote for the cloying humidity: fresh, clean, and bracing, like a cool breeze.

"Delicious."

"Lime, mint, sugar, and white rum. The secret to making a good one is all in the muddling."

"Muddling?"

"The pressing of the mint. Most people use only the leaves, but that's not how you get the best flavor." She picked up a sprig of the aromatic herb and waved it. "The stems are where all the juice is, so that's what you gently crush. The leaves need to remain untouched, as they have the oils for that wonderful aroma." She smiled. "Good rum doesn't hurt, either."

Darby took another sip. "Is this triple distilled Matusalem?"

Helen gave her an incredulous look and reached behind her for the bottle. She glanced at the label and shook her head. "You're right. How in the world did you know that?"

"It's legendary—one of the highest rated white rums around. I tasted it at the San Francisco Spirits competition a few years ago, and I believe it won several awards." She smiled at the older woman, whose look of disbelief still lingered. "Some people liken the taste of high-quality platino rums like this to Sake, but I can't quite make that comparison. I do love its crispness … the hints of vanilla, molasses, and roasted coconut." She took another sip of the Mojito. "And you're a Miami girl. So you'd never buy rum that wasn't steeped in the Cuban tradition."

Helen's smile was wide. "You've got me there. I've always said, it's a crime to make one of Cuba's most famous drinks with just any old rum." She picked up a yellow Fiestaware pitcher and a stirrer and signaled for Darby to follow her to the living room. She placed the pitcher on a glass-topped coffee table, sat down on a rattan arm chair, and crossed her long, tan legs. She was wearing a denim skort and a sleeveless white collared shirt with a green alligator on it. Darby thought she looked as if she'd just stepped off the ninth green at the golf course.

"Whew, sure is hot." Helen glanced at her watch, a no-nonsense analog with a tan leather wristband. "My new business partner is coming over any minute now, and before she arrives, I want you to know how much I appreciate your coming down to help me make this transition."

"I'm happy to do it," Darby said. She sipped her Mojito and gave Helen Near a grin. "Don't forget that you're helping me as well by finding someone to buy out my aunt's share. I've got my hands full with my clients in California, and with Jane's death I have her business in Hurricane Harbor, too. I'm sure Serenidad

Key is a great place to sell homes, but I can't handle another location."

"I'm not so sure about that," Helen said. "Seeing you in action in Maine, I think you could sell a house just about anywhere." She uncrossed her legs and leaned closer to Darby. "You know, when your aunt and I started Near & Farr Realty, we were the first women business owners on the Key."

"Really?"

"There were husband and wife, mom-and-pop type businesses, and one widow who managed a grocery store owned by her son, but we were the first women to run our own show." She smoothed the front of her skort. "It wasn't always easy, and we ran up against some pretty tough criticism. Rumors circulated about our sexuality, that kind of thing. That probably hurt the most."

Darby glanced at Helen, but the older woman was looking down and did not see her face.

"But Jane was always a rock. 'Don't let them get you down,' she used to say. 'They can't stand that you just closed a deal, that's all!'" Helen's eyes flashed with excitement. "She was right, Darby. Real estate was one of the few professions where women could get equal pay for equal work. A commission's a commission, no matter who earns it. Of course, we lost out on some listings because we were gals, but we got some because of it, too." She chuckled. "We had a damn good time."

"Until my aunt had to leave …"

Helen nodded slowly. "I'll never forget the day Jane called and said your parents were missing at sea. She sounded so—well, I'd never heard her like that. Bewildered, like all the air was knocked right out of her. She adored your father, and couldn't believe he

17

was gone." She took a long gulp of her Mojito and surveyed the slim Asian beauty before her. "She did the right thing, your aunt. Moving up there to be with you, starting an office on Hurricane Harbor—she did what she needed to do, and I know that she never looked back." She raised her well-shaped eyebrows. "She was very proud of you, Darby. She may not have said it to you, but she told me so—many times, in fact."

Darby met Helen's gaze. "Thanks." Her feelings for her Aunt Jane were still complicated, even after her passing, but Darby appreciated Helen's kind words. "Now why don't you tell me about this new business partner of yours?"

Helen nodded and glanced at her watch. "She must be running a little late—which is unusual." She thought a moment, seeming to choose her words with care. "Kyle's in her early forties, good looking, and a very sharp agent. She's worked with Barnaby's International Realty at their Sarasota office for five or so years now, and is easily their top producer each year. She's brokered deals in the multimillions up and down both coasts of Florida, and has a star-studded clientele that includes all the big movers and shakers in this state, as well as names you'd recognize from overseas." She paused a moment. "Kyle reminds me of Jane back in our early days. She's an unbelievable go-getter, very driven, a real force to be reckoned with. She's also totally scrupulous."

There goes the comparison with Jane Farr, thought Darby. At least in her real estate dealings in Maine, Jane had been known to bend a rule or two. Or three.

Darby took a sip of her Mojito, savoring the clean, pungent taste. Once upon a time, Helen Near and Jane Farr had run successful businesses both in Florida and Maine, but neither had been the kind of star performer Helen was now describing. Near & Farr Realty was a small operation, with one or two brokers and one support person—if that. Barnaby's International Realty, on the other hand, was a world-wide franchise, each office outselling and outperforming hundreds of small brokerages. Comparing Near & Farr with Barnaby's was like comparing a chickadee and an eagle. Both were birds, but one twittered from branch to branch, while the other devoured small mammals in a single gulp.

Darby swirled the mint in her glass before bringing it to her lips for a final sip. She didn't ask the obvious question: why in the world would someone like Kyle Cameron want to work with Helen Near?

The older woman wagged a finger at Darby. "I know what you're thinking, and believe me, I wondered myself. And then I flat out asked Kyle whether she was thinking straight, wanting to leave Barnaby's behind."

"What did she say?"

"She gave me a little smile and said that she had other plans for herself, plans that wouldn't mesh with her position at Barnaby's. I didn't push her on it, because I didn't think it was my business."

"Maybe she'll tell us today," said Darby. She rose to her feet and asked Helen for the location of her powder room.

"Little door to the left just before the kitchen."

Darby walked through the dining room to the bathroom, thinking about Helen's decision to make Kyle Cameron her business partner. Whether Kyle was uber-driven or laid back, a millionaire or middle class, didn't matter to Darby, as long as she treated Helen with honesty and respect. Still, her decision to leave the fast track was curious, and Darby knew she'd need to ask Kyle for an explanation.

Helen's powder room was clean and spare, painted a light, turquoise blue reminiscent of the Caribbean. Darby checked her appearance in the bamboo-framed mirror, releasing her ponytail and freeing her silky black hair. A smooth oval face, with almond-shaped eyes the color of cappuccino, gazed back at her. Her mother's face, the Japanese features softened and rounded by her Caucasian father's genes, the eyes framed by the same thick black lashes she recalled rimming his blue eyes. She was a mixture of their heritages, a true American mutt.

Darby washed her hands and used some of Helen's coconut-scented lotion. Off in the distance a phone rang and Darby heard Helen say hello.

She switched off the bathroom light and went back to the living room. Helen was standing at the window, her back to Darby, her tall body rigid and still.

"Helen?" Darby sensed something strange with the woman's stiff posture. She reached out and touched her on the shoulder. "Anything wrong?"

The older woman turned slowly, a look of horror etched on her tanned face. "That call was from my friend Mitzi. She told me the most awful news…" She swallowed, attempting to regain her composure. "She told me that Kyle—Kyle Cameron—is dead."

TWO

Jack Cameron opened his third can of Budweiser and took a long swig. He wiped his mouth with the back of his hand and surveyed the mangrove-dotted shoreline. The fish weren't biting, not even the snook, and he contemplated trying another spot further down the bay. He shook his head. It was too hot, the mercury still in the high nineties, and he knew fishing in the heat of the day was basically a waste of time. He took another pull from the can and finished the beer, tossing the empty into a corner of the boat. Catching fish wasn't high on his list of priorities today. Avoiding the phone and the mounting piles of bills on his desk, drinking beer and forgetting the past twenty-four hours—those were the reasons he had taken the aluminum skiff, a six-pack, and a bag of Doritos and headed into the mangroves.

"A guy needs to be alone with his thoughts," he said aloud, the words slurring a little, but, he decided, not noticeably so. He watched as a snapping turtle surfaced two feet from the bow of the boat, turned its ancient reptilian head from side to side, and sunk slowly back into the water.

If only those thoughts weren't poisoned by the image of Kyle.

He groaned, feeling the pain take hold of him again, and closed his eyes. Her face, with those perfect lips parted just slightly, and her cruel, mocking eyes, seared through his beer-induced buzz like headlights slicing through fog. He clenched his teeth, opened his eyes and welcomed the harsh glare of the sun. Why couldn't he stop thinking about her? She was some kind of evil spirit, what his Cuban grandmother would have called a *mabuya,* and nothing he did—nothing—could keep her taunting visage at bay. Dead or alive she would haunt him until he himself was dead, and who knows? Maybe even after that.

He reached for another beer and flipped the top. It wouldn't totally dull the pain, but until Jack had something much stronger, beer would have to do.

———

Darby steered the black Mustang through downtown Sarasota, past the shopping and hospital districts, and into an established neighborhood of wide streets shaded by towering red maples. Helen sat silently beside her, motioning only occasionally for Darby to turn. Finally she shook her head, gave a sigh, and spoke.

"The Camerons' house is on the left," she said, "down this drive."

Darby turned where Helen indicated and started down the gently winding drive. A gate with a small gatehouse and a security camera loomed before her, and she slowed the car. Helen waved at the camera and the gate lifted.

Magnificent old oaks lined both sides of the pavement, their arching limbs reaching out and over the flat, grassy lawns. After four hundred or so yards, the drive ended in a neat circle surrounding a marble statue of the Madonna and outlined with magnolias and flowering shrubs. Darby pulled up before a handsome plantation-style estate and turned off the ignition. She could see the Gulf just behind the house, the setting sun beginning to turn the sky a soft pink.

"Here we are," Helen said flatly. "Casa Cameron. Nearly one and a half acres of land with 220 feet of direct frontage." Her voice was mechanical. Sighing, she pulled the visor down so that she could see herself in the mirror. "God, I look as bad as I feel." She reached in a small purse and pulled out a lipstick. Pursing her lips, Helen applied a swipe of coral frost. She pinched her cheeks and turned resolutely toward Darby. "Let's go."

They followed a twisting stone walkway to a large black door with a massive brass knocker. Darby watched as Helen let the knocker fall with a loud clang. She seemed to have added a decade to her looks—although, when the door opened, Helen transformed into the energetic person she had been before the shocking news.

"Harold, terrible thing, can't believe it." The butler, a portly man with a red-splotched face and kind eyes, nodded and moved aside so that Helen and Darby could enter. "This is Darby Farr, the visiting niece of a dear old friend." She gave the man a penetrating look. "Where is Mitzi?"

The man brought his hand to his mouth and cleared his throat. "In the front room, Miss Near. Allow me to show you there."

"That won't be necessary, Harold, but thank you."

Helen led the way through the grand entrance hallway, dominated by a curving stairway and enormous crystal chandelier. Darby's sandals clicked on the cool tiles and echoed off the quiet hallway's walls. Helen opened a set of French doors and indicated for Darby to step into the room.

It was a sunny, spacious living room decorated in shades of cream, with cream-colored marble tiles and overstuffed cream furniture. One whole wall was glass, overlooking an emerald green sweep of grass, beyond which lie the placid Gulf of Mexico; another was floor-to-ceiling shelves holding porcelain figurines and hardcover books. Thirty or so people could sit comfortably in the room, and Darby imagined it was often used for entertaining. She glanced to the opposite side of the room. A marble hearth and fireplace, flanked by brass sconces, dominated the wall. It was crowned by an imposing oil portrait of a stunning young woman wearing a bright blue ball gown, her black hair piled high upon her head. The subject's coy smile was captivating.

Darby heard Helen suck in a quick breath and saw her dash to the far corner of the room. Seconds later, she, too, was hurrying toward a wheelchair holding a lifeless-looking figure. Darby glanced at the slumped woman's timeworn face. Despite the sagging skin and creased lines, she could see it was the beauty from the painting.

To their relief, Mitzi Cameron had merely dozed off. Helen's gentle touch awoke her friend and they regarded each other silently for a long moment. Helen stooped and hugged Mitzi, and when the two had finished embracing, Darby saw Helen wipe her eyes with a slow gesture.

"A serial killer." Mitzi Cameron's voice was husky, tinged with a hint of a Latin accent. "A monster who preys on real estate agents. Kyle was the third victim."

Helen sighed. "It's unbelievable."

Mitzi shook her head, her black hair still lustrous, although now she wore it in a demure bun at the nape of her neck. "From what the police say, she was a random choice. He saw her notice for the open house, and decided to kill her. That's one possibility. Or he chose her months ago, put her on his list of victims, and waited for his opportunity. If that is the case, he may now have other innocent women in his sights." She sighed and seemed to notice Darby for the first time. "Nell, you're forgetting your manners."

Helen clasped her hands together and turned toward Darby. "So I am. Mitzi Cameron, meet Darby Farr."

Darby shook the small, chilly hand of Mitzi Cameron. "I'm sorry for your loss," she said.

The older woman's face hardened. "Thank you." She then added, in a softer tone, "And I for yours. I didn't know your aunt well, but I know my friend Nell thought the world of her."

She wheeled herself away from the window and Helen and Darby followed. "Let's go into the study," she said. "I'll ask Carlotta to bring us some tea." She stopped and turned to face Helen. "Or would you rather join me in a cocktail?"

Helen appeared to think about the offer. She shot a look in Darby's direction and then back to Mitzi Cameron. "I've got a designated driver. Why the hell not?"

The study was a cozy, sunny space, a small part of what Darby was beginning to realize was an enormous house, perhaps ten thousand square feet or so. It was down the hall from the grand living room, adjacent to a large den where Darby glimpsed a pool table, shelves of brass trophies, and mounted game fish.

"This is my favorite part of Casa Cameron," said Mitzi, maneuvering her chair into the study. "It reminds me of the little living room in Miami, back in my family's home in Coral Gables. Do you remember it, Nell?"

Helen nodded, moving toward a table on which an elegant array of crystal paperweights was displayed. "Yes, and I recall your collection as well. I've always loved this one the best." She picked up a small glass oval and held it up to the light. "That tiny little pink shell…"

Mitzi laughed, a silver sound that belonged to a much younger woman. "Helen Near, you *always* tell me you like that paperweight. You're so damn predictable!"

"I can't help it. I'm drawn to this one." Her voice was defensive.

"And you never seem to remember that you're the one who gave it to me on my sixteenth birthday!"

Helen's booming laugh joined Mitzi's and Darby smiled. It was obvious that these two women shared a special bond of friendship. Little wonder Helen had moaned in anguish when the car radio's news report described the details of Kyle Cameron's grisly murder. *Multiple stab wounds…identical to two murders on the East Coast…* It was not only the tragic death of her new business partner and colleague: it was the pain this fatality caused her oldest and dearest friend.

Mitzi rolled her chair to face a chintz-covered couch and indicated that they should sit. Moments later a trim, dark-haired woman wearing a white uniform arrived with a tray of drinks.

Mitzi and Helen took martini glasses filled with an orange colored liquid. Darby accepted a glass of sparkling water and lime.

"Thank you, Carlotta," said Mitzi, and the servant retreated from the room. The hostess held aloft the cocktail and regarded her friend. "I thought we should have one of Kyle's favorites in her honor." She gave a sad smile. "To Kyle."

The three clinked glasses and drank.

"Delicious," said Helen. "Say what you want, but the Florida Cocktail is one good drink."

"Hard to go wrong with Triple Sec, cherry brandy, and gin," murmured Mitzi. "Of course, it's the lemon and orange juices that really give it a punch."

The older women giggled and Darby couldn't help but smile. "How long have you two been friends?"

"Too long!" said Helen. More peals of laughter.

Mitzi's gaiety was short-lived. She sighed and regarded Darby. "I'm not usually this animated, even around my best friend Helen. I think I'm somewhat in shock." She set her drink down on the coffee table. "That poor girl. Alone and at the mercy of a maniac. She was stabbed more than two dozen times. I just pray she died quickly, without too much pain." Tears began to roll slowly down her thin cheeks and Helen handed her an embroidered handkerchief. She looked as if she was ready to cry as well.

"How is Jack taking all this?"

"Not well. At first we couldn't find him ... he was fishing somewhere south of the city. And then, when we did, well, he was not in good shape." She gave Darby an apologetic look. "My son's been having a hard time. He's depressed, and—" she took a deep breath.

"Dr. Menendez came over right away and gave Jack a sedative. He's resting in his room now."

Darby glanced at Helen. Did Jack—who had to be in his forties—still live at home?

Mitzi continued. "The police told us that Kyle's murder follows the pattern of two others on the East Coast. One was in Stuart, I think it was, and the other somewhere by Daytona Beach." She shuddered. "The press is calling this maniac the 'Kondo Killer.' All of the murders have taken place in condominiums during real estate open houses."

Helen placed her drink on the coffee table and gave her friend a shrewd look. "I'm worried about you."

Mitzi waved her hand with a dismissive gesture. "Nell, you know I'll survive. It's Jack I'm worried about. He was crazy about that girl." She sighed. "I called Alexandra, and she's due to arrive any moment." She paused. "She's taking it hard, too, but she's tough like her mother, and I think she'll rally to help Jack."

Helen picked up her drink and gulped the last of it down. "Was Jack still trying to win Kyle back?"

Mitzi nodded. "I don't know whether it would have worked. Kyle had changed—we all saw it—and sometimes I think she saw reconciliation with Jack as a step backward."

Darby sipped her water and listened. The family dynamics at Casa Cameron were tangled, much as hers had been until recent memory. She wondered what the change had been in Kyle Cameron, but an interruption stopped the flow of conversation.

Carlotta appeared in the doorway. "Señora, a car has just driven in. I believe it is Alexandra."

"Thank you. Please show her to us." Mitzi smoothed her hair with her hands, an unconscious gesture Darby had noted earlier, and frowned at the glasses. "I should have asked Carlotta to take our drinks. You know how Alexandra is around alcohol." She lowered her voice. "Since she became a nutrition fanatic, it's even worse."

Helen raised her eyebrows. "For goodness sake. Your daughter-in-law was just stabbed to death. You go ahead and have a drink or two if you want."

A bustling sound in the hall announced the arrival of Alexandra Cameron. She strode into the study, a tall, slim woman with the same beautiful bone structure as her mother, and the same mane of thick, lustrous, hair, although hers was a deep brown, abundantly streaked with blonde. Her eyes, accentuated with eyeliner, flashed as she looked around the room, noticing Darby but then just as quickly dismissing her.

"Mother," she breathed. Her lips were full and red. She kneeled at Mitzi's chair, putting her head in her mother's lap. Great sobs wracked her body.

"There, there," Mitzi smoothed her daughter's hair and shot Helen a mournful look.

Alexandra lifted her head. "I just can't believe it. Kyle—taken from us—it's too horrible." She wiped her eyes with a sweep of a graceful hand. "Where's Jack?"

"In his room."

"And Dad?"

Mitzi's face hardened. "Out."

Alexandra rose to her feet, swinging her hair off her shoulders. She was in her early forties, wearing jeans and a white tee

29

shirt, with a thin, turquoise-studded belt and flat sandals. Her figure was slim through the hips like a model's. The resemblance to her mother was remarkable: in an elegant dress and with slightly darker hair, she was a dead ringer for the portrait of Mitzi Cameron in the salon.

"I'm going up to see Jack. He's got to be devastated."

"He may be sleeping."

"I won't wake him."

The three watched her stride from the room. Mitzi turned to Darby. "Forgive me for not introducing you. I'm not thinking clearly." She added in a softer voice, almost to herself, "It's so awful. Alexandra and Kyle have known each other for years. They were like sisters."

Darby was about to reply when she heard the staccato thumping of someone running down stairs. Alexandra's voice rang out. "Mother!" she cried. Moments later she bounded into the room. "Jack's not there."

"What do you mean?" Mitzi snapped. "Dr. Menendez gave him something to sleep ..."

"I mean he's gone. I can't find him anywhere upstairs."

The women looked at each other in confusion.

"She's right, Señora." A breathless Carlotta appeared in the doorway. "I went upstairs to see if he needed anything, and I could not find him either. Should I call the police?"

"No," said Mitzi. "Heavens, not yet. He's probably just wandered somewhere." She looked up at Helen, her eyes pleading for help. "I pray he hasn't gone outside ..."

Helen glanced at Darby. The situation called for a cool head and quick thinking, qualities which the young agent was fortunate to possess.

Darby looked at the concerned faces and formulated a plan. "Let's get out there and search the grounds as quickly as we can." She pointed toward the doorway. "Carlotta, you check the rest of the upstairs rooms, closets—anywhere he could be. Mitzi, you do the same for the downstairs. Helen, you check with the security staff to be sure no one has left the property. Alexandra, you and I will take the grounds." She thought a moment. "I'll ask the butler—Harold, isn't it?—to check the length of the driveway and stop in at the gatehouse." She looked up and saw relief etched on Mitzi Cameron's face. Darby continued. "If anyone sees anything, they call Helen on her cell." She read out the number. "Everyone got that?"

Hurried nods answered Darby's question.

"Good. Now let's go and find Jack."

———

The searchers spread out inside Casa Cameron and around the property, with Harold heading away from the Gulf and toward the gatehouse. Darby suggested that Alexandra comb one side of the house, while she would take the other.

"I'll check the northern part of the property," Alexandra Cameron offered. "If you go that way, I'll meet up with you at the boathouse." She pointed toward the setting sun. "You can't miss it."

Alexandra hurried off, her hair swaying as she ran. Darby surveyed the southern end of the grounds, forming a quick plan.

She'd scan the beach and pool first, then, provided she hadn't located Jack, head to the Cameron's massive boathouse.

The air was still humid although the sun's slow sink into the Gulf had lowered the temperatures a few degrees. Darby sprinted across the grass, keeping her breathing even to conserve her energy. The pool lay before her, an undulating swoosh of brilliant blue surrounded by a low wooden fence. Darby swept her gaze over the pool's tiled bottom. Nothing. She opened the door of a small beach cabana and a bright green anole skittered out. She saw a stack of clean towels and a bottle of suntan lotion, nothing more.

The beach looked empty as well. Darby glimpsed a trio of porpoises swimming by the setting sun, their fins black and shiny as they crested the surface. She turned toward the boathouse and ran.

The structure was impressive. Tall, shingled, with a beautiful laurel oak framing one side, the boathouse jutted partially into the Gulf. Built to store a vessel at least sixty feet long, Darby knew it was one of a handful of such icons that remained intact. Once common for members of the leisure class living along the coast of America's oceans and bigger lakes, boathouses were now a rare sight, the few still standing relics of history and objects of conservation.

Inside it was dark, the only sound that of water lapping gently against the boathouse's sides. The odor of gasoline mingled with the smell of old wood and the tang of salt water. In the gloom Darby could see the outline of a large powerboat. She approached it, her heart starting to beat faster.

Ever since her parents' disappearance in a sailing accident when she was fourteen, Darby Farr reacted adversely to watercraft. Anxiety in the form of a racing heart, clammy palms, and rubbery legs gripped her whenever she climbed aboard any kind of vessel, from ferries to rowboats.

Nevertheless, a man's life was at stake and Darby knew she could overcome her body's reactions. With trembling hands, she gripped the side of the boat and climbed aboard.

It was a sleek sport fishing boat of fifty-five or so feet in length. Darby could make out a tall fly bridge rising into the darkness, equipped, no doubt, for serious fishing. Darby willed her legs to stop shaking and surveyed her surroundings. A wide deck, with two swivel chairs and what appeared to be a dive platform. Slowly she searched the area for any signs of Jack Cameron, but found nothing.

Next Darby turned her attention to the bow of the boat. Crawling along the side of the vessel, she held on to the metal rails and felt for anything out of the ordinary. The deck seemed to be empty.

The center of the boat was dominated by a large cabin that appeared to be all glass. A door led into the cabin, and to the right was a ladder leading up to the fly bridge. Darby tried the door and to her surprise it opened. She listened for sounds but heard nothing but the background rhythm of the waves.

Inside the cabin it was even darker, and Darby let her eyes become accustomed to the gloom. She noticed a faint, spicy scent lingering in the air—pipe tobacco? This was the salon, a cozy space with cushioned banquettes and a few tables. A sconce was to her left. Hoping it ran off the boat's battery, Darby tried it.

Light flooded the cabin and Darby sighed in relief. Quickly she scanned the salon, three staterooms, the galley, and two heads, but there was no sign of anyone.

That left the fly bridge.

Darby exited the cabin, turning the light back off as she left. It wouldn't help her on the bridge, but it had made searching the boat's many rooms quicker. She began climbing the ladder, her sandals slapping against the metal rungs. Perhaps Jack had already been located on the vast Cameron property, and in the excitement, calls to the other searchers had been forgotten.

The fly bridge appeared to have a large banquette plus two chairs equipped for steering. A roof overhead provided protection from the sun, but also appeared to house some sophisticated electronics, no doubt having to do with finding schools of game fish. Darby circled the bridge slowly. She felt the seats of the chairs, touching nothing but upholstered cushions. As she approached the wheel, she paused. Something was huddled on the deck.

It was a man.

Quickly Darby checked for a pulse. At first she couldn't locate anything, but then she felt a faint throb, very weak. As she whipped out her cell phone, a voice called in the darkness.

"Darby?" It was the lilting speech of Alexandra Cameron.

"On the fly bridge," she yelled. "I think I've found Jack."

––––––

"You're late." Chellie Howe unlocked the door of the hotel suite and stepped aside, allowing her husband to enter.

"Am I?" Foster McFarlin checked his Rolex with a diffident air. "I thought I was right on time."

Chellie watched as he passed her, his suit tailored perfectly to his well-muscled body. How was it that the simple action of his striding across the room could still arouse her, bring color to her cheeks and a longing in the pit of her stomach? She closed the door and made her voice light.

"The least you can do is zip me." She strode to where he stood and pivoted on her stilettos, hands on her hips, waiting. She felt him touch the small of her back and linger a moment too long.

He guided the zipper up slowly, and turned her around.

"You heard the news."

Chellie nodded. She'd been expecting this. "Which development was she in?"

"Esperanza Shores." His voice was tired. "I can't believe it. Some maniac jumped her in one of the units. She was stabbed repeatedly." Chellie looked at his face and saw agony etched on the handsome dark features. *He's in pain*, she realized. *In pain over Kyle Cameron's death.*

Anger began to rise in her, and she willed it away. *It doesn't matter anymore,* she thought. Kyle was a mutilated corpse lying on cold steel in the morgue. *She won't come between us again.*

"We'll catch the guy who did this," she said forcefully. "I've got police units working around the clock on it."

McFarlin nodded. His cocoa brown skin had a slight sheen, as if polished, and she remembered how the feel of it could drive her mad with desire. She tried to make her voice sound sincere. "My heart goes out to Kyle's family."

He barked out a laugh. "That jackass Jack Cameron? Don't waste your time. And you know your pal Alexandra isn't sorry."

Chellie counted silently to ten. She was not going to lose her temper, even though all she wanted was to scream at him, throw something, and kick the bastard between his muscular legs. She was glad—yes, glad!—to know that there was one less female on her sex-addicted husband's radar screen. She wanted to yell that she wasn't sorry Kyle was murdered, but he would never forgive her for that, and if she had any prayer of winning him back, she had to stay calm.

Instead she grabbed her clutch and forced herself to smile. "Not to change the subject, but I'm happy you're coming to this dinner, Foster. This is the perfect demographic for me." Indeed, the wealthy donors to the Trust for Public Lands were exactly the voters Chellie needed to court if she were going to sew up the gubernatorial nomination come fall.

"Glad to be of service." Foster let out a breath of air and regarded his wife. Her gown was stunning: light lilac against her pale skin and golden blonde hair, thin straps that showed off her toned arms and torso, a clingy material that made her look like the knockout she was.

"You look good, Chellie. Real good. Your lunch—how did it go?"

She ignored his question and made a motion with her hand. "Dammit, Foster, we've got to fly." Chellie Howe hated to be late for anything, especially when she was the one giving the keynote address.

They hustled out the door and into the hushed hallway where a petite brunette with a pixie-looking face and severely short haircut hovered by the elevator. "Take the stairs," Chellie snapped at her press secretary, and Mindy Jackson turned with a resigned look on her face and did as she was told.

As Chellie and Foster waited for the elevator, Foster turned to her with a rueful look on his face.

"The whole place's covered in blood," he said.

Chellie's temper flared. Enough was enough. She was just about to reply when Foster shook his head and continued. "It's gonna be impossible to sell that unit, and now the whole place will be under a cloud. Christ, I'll have to *give* those Esperanza Shores condos away."

The elevator arrived and its doors slid open. Foster ushered her in and Chellie bit back a smile. Her husband hadn't changed after all. His lover was lying in the morgue with more holes in her body than a pincushion, but his thoughts were on the salability of his precious condominiums.

"You know," she said lightly, "Kyle's murder may win you some sympathy down the line in court. We'll have to think about the best way to present it." She was referring to the growing number of lawsuits filed against her husband's company by irate investors in his multiple real estate developments, most of which had now tanked in the soured economy.

He nodded, handsome and confident no matter what the situation. "God knows I could use a little sympathy," he muttered.

She was glad she had kept her cool, glad they were nearly at the dinner where she would charm the pants off the room. She allowed herself a secret smirk as the elevator doors opened into the hallway. Foster McFarlin still needed her. She was in charge, and that was just the way Chellie Howe liked it.

———

Helen ran a hand through her short silver hair. She poured Darby a glass of Chardonnay and sank into a chair. "What a day. Thanks for making us a little snack, Darby. I'm not sure how much I can eat, but that omelet looks delicious."

"Eat what you can, Helen. My feelings won't be hurt. I'm sure you must be exhausted."

"I am. I can't believe it's only nine o'clock." She lifted her glass and took a sip. "I hate to say it, but it feels good to be away from Casa Cameron. I'll go back in the morning, but I did need a break."

"What's the latest on Jack's condition? "

"Stable. You found him just in time."

Darby took a bite of the fluffy egg dish and chewed thoughtfully. After locating the unconscious Jack Cameron on the fly bridge, she and Alexandra had alerted the others and called an ambulance. At the hospital, the emergency room technicians had pumped his stomach in an attempt to rid his body of the bottle of sleeping pills he'd swallowed earlier.

"Do you think Jack's overdose was intentional?"

Helen ran a hand through her short silver hair. "I do. I know Mitzi would never admit it, but that man has real mental problems. Kyle didn't cause them, but when she left it made things worse. I think Jack always thought they'd get back together, even after two years of living apart. Now that she's dead…"

"He has to find another reason to go on living."

Helen shrugged. "Something like that." She let out a big sigh and shook her head. "I love my friend Mitzi, God knows I do, and I never had children of my own, so maybe I shouldn't pass judgment. But I'll tell you what, that is one screwed up family."

"You've known them for years."

"Forever! Mitzi and I go way back. We were just kids in Miami when we became best friends."

"How did you meet?"

"We met at a city waterskiing competition. We were twelve or thirteen, I think, and both pretty good. Well, I was pretty good, Mitzi was very good." She smiled. "She was a looker even then, and that didn't hurt with the judges."

"Waterskiing. I thought golf was your big sport?"

"It is, now. But back then I lived to get out on the water and strap on my slalom ski."

Darby pictured Helen as a teen, cutting her way through the water on one ski. "Did you do tricks, too?"

"Of course! All kinds of things. It was such fun. I'll show you some old photos later."

"I'd love to see them." She took a sip of the Chardonnay, the taste clean and with a hint of oak, curious about Mitzi's family and their Miami roots. "What made Mitzi's family move to this coast?"

"Her father and his brother had some kind of huge fight. Mitzi was seventeen, just graduating from high school. The next thing you know, her Dad had sold their house and brought the family to Sarasota. This was in the '50s, probably 1954 or so. Quite a change, especially for a Cuban family, but Juan Carlos Rios was a stubborn man. He owned several companies that made air conditioning systems, and he just transferred the whole operation closer to the Gulf."

"Rios is Mitzi's family name?"

"That's right. Her full name is Maria Magdalena Rios Cameron. Her parents called her Maria Magdalena, but to me she's always been 'Mitzi.' I think she saw it in the movies or something." Helen smiled at the memory.

"How did she meet her husband?"

"I can't remember. It was a few years after she'd moved. I was still in Miami, but we saw each other as much as we could. I remember she called, all excited, said she had met a dashing and wealthy man and that they were engaged. I met John Cameron once before the wedding. I was not impressed."

"Why not?"

"I thought he was a phony." Helen took a drink of her wine. "That Chardonnay's not bad, is it?" She set down her glass and continued. "John has everyone believing he's a smart, rich guy when he's nothing of the kind. He's one of those superficial, charming sorts of fellows. I think Kyle saw right through him, too."

"What makes you say that?"

"She'd give a look, kind of an amused face with her eyebrows way up, whenever he named-dropped about famous Floridians. You've heard of the Ringlings?"

"As in Ringling Brothers Barnum and Bailey Circus?"

"Yes. They're a big name in these parts. Here's the short version: John Ringling and four of his brothers started their operation in the late 1800s, and bought Barnum and Bailey in the early 1900s. A few years later, John Ringling jumped on the Florida land boom and bought a big chunk of the Sarasota Keys. Eventually he and his wife Mable owned nearly a quarter of Sarasota's total area. They built a Venetian Gothic mansion on the water during the roaring twenties, plus a museum to house their art collection. When John Ringling died in the late 1930s, he left it all to the state." She took a breath and waved her hand in the air. "I used to volunteer at the Ringling Art Museum in case you're wondering how I know all this."

"It's interesting. How does John Cameron fit in?"

"He claims to be a distant cousin of Mable Ringling, but I have my doubts. I think he married Mitzi because she has a fortune. I'd never say this to my friend, but I don't think John Cameron ever loved her."

Darby ate a few bites of omelet in silence, thinking about Mitzi Cameron's loveless marriage. "Why is she in a wheelchair?"

Helen rose from the table and cleared her plate with a shaking hand. Darby listened as it clattered against the countertop. The older woman poured herself more wine and sat down with a sigh.

"The accident happened when Alexandra was two. John and Mitzi were out on the Gulf, just for a few hours, you know? Mitzi decided to go skiing. There was no spotter, and they crashed with another boat. Mitzi was badly injured. She lost the use of her legs and sustained some internal damage, as well."

"God, what a tragedy."

"Yes. She was unable to have more children, and that was a real blow. The next year they adopted Jack, and he seemed to give Mitzi a new outlook on life." Helen's face brightened. "That's the year I moved to Sarasota. He was such a cute baby and Alexandra loved him from the start. They made a beautiful little family: the dark-haired mother and daughter and the blonde boy and his father. If only John could have been happy, they might have had a chance. But Mitzi's condition was not something he could accept, nor could he unconditionally love an adopted child. If their marriage was shaky before the accident, it was in shambles following it."

"And yet they have stayed married?"

"Mitzi is a devout Catholic. He'd have to commit some major crime for her to divorce him." She finished her Chardonnay and sighed. She looked exhausted.

"I guess that explains the enormous estate," Darby said, clearing the remaining dishes from the table.

"Yes," Helen said sadly. "Casa Cameron is a big, empty, black hole of a house. John and Mitzi can avoid seeing each other for days, even weeks."

———

After doing the dishes and saying goodnight to Helen, Darby retreated to Helen's cheerful guest room and checked her phone and e-mail messages. Two calls from Maine, but none from California, where she worked as a top-selling broker for Pacific Coast Realty. She checked her watch and figured the time difference. Enrique Tomaso Gomez, her capable West Coast assistant, would be relaxing in front of one of those home decorating TV shows, a glass of Napa Valley Zinfandel in hand. She smiled, thinking of the man who had served as her assistant for nearly three years. *He deserves his off time*, she thought. *I'll call him tomorrow.*

The messages from Maine were also not pressing, and Darby found her thoughts straying back to Casa Cameron and Kyle's murder. Helen's stories about Mitzi and her early life with John Cameron had whetted Darby's interest in the family. Where did Kyle Cameron fit in? What had she seen in Jack Cameron, and why had she wanted to be a part of the dysfunctional Cameron clan?

Darby climbed into the comfortable bed and willed herself to stop thinking about the day's events. In the morning she would help Helen to figure out her next step with the business, and on Wednesday she would fly back to California. In the meantime, she needed rest. She rolled over on her side and visualized herself running through the woods behind her childhood home in Maine. In minutes, she was fast asleep.

THREE

Tuesday morning dawned reliably hot and sunny. Over a breakfast of freshly squeezed orange juice, poached eggs, and grapefruit, Darby asked Helen whether Mitzi or any of the other Camerons had known of Kyle's plan to join Near & Farr Realty.

"I don't think so," Helen said, handing Darby a plate of buttered toast. "Mitzi has never said anything about it, so I think Kyle kept it quiet. These things can be so sensitive. I never felt it was my place to talk about her plans. Now that Kyle's dead, I'm still not sure if I should say anything." She glanced at Darby. "What do you think?"

"I agree that it is tricky. When I'm in doubt, I keep my mouth shut." She paused. "Had Kyle told Barnaby's that she was leaving?"

"I don't know for sure, but I think so. A man named Marty Glickman is in charge of the office, and he gave me quite a glaring look when I saw him on Friday at the County Clerk's office. Kyle represented a very big chunk of that office's sales, so I wasn't surprised at his reaction."

A knock at the front door startled Helen and Darby. "It's only 8:30," Helen said, rising from the table and looking at her watch. "Who could be coming by this early?"

Darby listened as she spoke with someone with a deep, slightly Southern drawl. A moment later Helen was back in the kitchen with a tall man wearing tan pants and a light jacket.

"Darby, this is Detective Jonas Briggs," she said, wringing her hands as she spoke. Darby had often noticed that the very appearance of a police officer was enough to make even the most law-abiding citizens nervous.

"Briggs, Ma'am," he said politely. He turned to Darby and nodded. "Good morning. I'm sorry to intrude on your breakfast."

"Please, sit down," Helen said. "Can I get you something? Eggs? Orange juice? Coffee?"

"A cup of coffee would be nice. Thank you, Mrs. Near."

Helen poured the detective a cup of coffee and indicated the cream and sugar. "It's Miss Near, Detective. I'm not married."

"Excuse me, Miss Near."

Darby thought all of the politeness was a bit excessive, but this was, after all, the South. She wondered what information the Detective hoped to glean from Helen. With Kyle Cameron's murder part of a serial killer's pattern, there probably wasn't much local questioning to be done.

"I'm here as part of a routine follow-up into the murder of Kyle Cameron," the detective explained. "As you've no doubt heard, we have good reason to believe that Ms. Cameron was killed by the same person responsible for two murders on the east coast of the state. Nevertheless, I have to ask a few questions."

Helen licked her lips and nodded. "Of course."

"When was the last time you saw Kyle Cameron?"

Helen thought a moment. "Saturday morning. I was at my office downtown—that's Near & Farr Realty, on Main Street—and Kyle dropped by. She told me she was excited about a new listing, and that she'd tell me more about it when we got together here—at my house—on Monday afternoon. She said she was looking forward to it."

"Was that unusual for her to drop by your office? You did work for competing companies."

"It wasn't unusual. Kyle was leaving Barnaby's and coming to work with me. She was prepared to buy my late partner's share of the company from Darby."

The detective glanced back at Darby. "I see. Did Barnaby's know about her plans?"

"I'm not sure. I think she was planning to tell them this week."

Jonas Briggs made a note on a small pad. "Thank you, Miss Near. We saw your name in her calendar for 4:30 on Monday. She had two appointments before yours, and a cocktail party out on St. Andrew's Isle, none of which, obviously, she made." He turned to Darby and frowned. "I'm sorry you won't get to meet Kyle Cameron. She was quite a star around here, wasn't she, Miss Near?"

Helen nodded. "Yes, I was looking forward to working with her."

"She sold me a house a few years back," the detective remembered. "Nice little place over on Palm Ave. I still live there, love it. Of course, that was before she became such a big shot." He thought a moment. "St. Andrew's Isle. That's where that famous golfer lives."

"Tag Gunnerson," Helen offered.

"That's right. The very same. Do you think she was going out there for business or for pleasure?"

Helen smiled. "I don't know. But with Kyle Cameron, it was usually one and the same."

———

Helen huffed indignantly as she cleared away the breakfast dishes. "I don't think much of Detective Jonas Briggs," she said, shoving a plate into the dishwasher. It clattered against another plate as if to reinforce her annoyance.

Darby laughed as she put away the orange juice. "Now why is that, Helen? He seemed like he was trying to be a perfect gentleman."

"Perfect gentleman, my eye. He didn't once ask about you. Here you are, a guest in my home, and he doesn't even inquire as to your family. No manners whatsoever."

Darby laughed again. "But Helen, he was here to ask questions about a murder! It's not exactly a tea party."

"Doesn't matter. Pretty little thing like you sitting here and all he can talk about is Kyle Cameron selling him his house. Like he was sweet on her! This is the South. Manners are important." She poured herself another cup of coffee. "Let's go out on the patio a moment. There's something I'd like to tell you."

Darby nodded, pouring herself a glass of ice water and following her friend through the dining room and out to the shade.

Helen pulled up a patio chair and sank gratefully into the green and white striped cushion. "Whew, it's getting hot already, isn't it? I tell you, this is about the only time you can sit out here this time of year."

The shade was welcoming, but Darby could tell that it would only be bearable for another hour or so. She inhaled the sweet scent of citrus trees, and took a sip of her water, wondering what it was the older woman had to say.

Helen gave a soft chuckle. "What I said about Detective Briggs maybe being attracted to Kyle, that's because she had that kind of effect on men. They couldn't keep their eyes off her, even as she got older. She had curves in all the right places, you know, and she could be kind of a flirt." She paused. "Did you know she was Miss Florida back in the late 1980s?"

Darby shook her head.

"You should see the photo Mitzi has of Kyle in her evening gown. She looks like someone from the cast of that old television show, *Dynasty*. Did you ever see that program?"

"No, but I've seen the styles of that time. Pretty over the top."

Helen smiled. "They were. I remember your aunt and this get-up she had. A purple jacket with these big padded shoulders like she was colonel in the army or something. She wore it with these flowered gaucho pants…" Helen's thoughts were far away, but she took a sip of her coffee and returned to the present. "Anyway, back to Kyle. The last few times I saw her, she gave me the impression that something more was going on in her life. Something besides real estate, I mean."

"Like what?"

"I'm not sure, but if I had to guess, I'd say it was a new relationship."

"Why is that?"

"Well, she teased me once about dating, said I should try on-line dating profiles. "They really work," she said. She told me she

47

had met a really nice guy on some millionaire matching site, and that they'd had a few dates. Another time, she said she was clearing out the bad things in her life—the negative energy, as she put it— and making room for something new and positive." Helen swatted at a bee that buzzed too close to her cropped gray hair. "I think she finally met someone who cared about her, not just her beauty queen looks." She looked down at her hands. "And I think I know what she meant about negative energy."

Darby waited for Helen to explain. The scent of the citrus trees floated like a light perfume on the ever-thickening air.

"Mitzi told me last week that Kyle asked Jack for a divorce. He was heartbroken, apparently, even though they've been separated for two years." She sighed. "I love that boy, always have, but I can see why Kyle Cameron wanted to move on. Talk about your negative energy. That Jack is like a storm cloud on a clear blue day." She gave a guilty glance toward Darby. "I can't believe I just said that. He's my godson, for goodness sakes." She took a gulp of coffee. "Who knows what was going on in Kyle Cameron's life? It's hard to know what anyone is really going through." She looked down at her watch and rose slowly to her feet. "I have to go into the office for a bit, and then I thought I'd stop and see Mitzi. You're welcome to stay here or come with me."

"Actually, I'm going to throw on my sneakers and go for a quick run before it heats up much more."

"Now is the time," Helen agreed. "If you wait too much longer it will be dangerously humid."

She reached out and gave Darby's shoulder a squeeze. "Help yourself to anything you need. How about if you come to my office at noon and we'll go out for lunch?"

"Perfect." Darby said goodbye to the older woman and went to her little room for her sneakers. She smoothed some sun block on her nose and cheeks and grabbed a baseball cap and a little can of pepper spray which she shoved in a pocket. Moments later, she was out the door and running.

———

Her sleek black ponytail swinging in the sun, Darby Farr pounded down the streets of Helen's neighborhood. She ran for about a mile, past stately homes lining some of Serenidad Key's oldest streets, before turning around and heading back. A turn toward the water took her by a small park, where young mothers were out pushing strollers, and several artists stood at easels, painting the Gulf. Darby glanced at her watch. She'd been running for a half-hour, and although she was not tired, the heat was beginning to get to her. She turned and headed back toward Helen's house.

After rounding the corner of the park's perimeter, she was back in the tree-lined commercial district, running past a set of swanky designer clothing shops and expensive-looking boutiques. She'd passed a children's clothing store just opening for business when the rank odor of burning debris assailed her nostrils. Slowing and turning toward an empty lot where the odor seemed to originate, she ran smack into the solid form of Detective Jonas Briggs.

"Why Ms. Farr," he said, smiling. "How nice to see you."

Darby wiped the sweat off her brow and nodded. "Likewise, Detective Briggs." She gestured at the blackened debris. "What's going on? Smells like a fire."

"Correct. The building behind me burned to the ground last night. It was a fancy restaurant called Belle Haven. You ever hear of it?"

"No. But I'm not a local."

"That's right. I kicked myself after I left Miss Near's property this morning, because I realized how impolite I'd been. I didn't even ask you where you're from."

"Don't worry about it, Detective Briggs. You were investigating a murder, and I'd say that takes precedence over small talk."

"Still, that's no excuse for bad manners. My mother would be appalled."

"Then we won't tell her." Darby glanced at the smoldering remnants of the building. "What caused the blaze?"

Detective Briggs pursed his lips. "The Fire Marshall's office is still investigating. I'm here because of the building's owner, Jack Cameron."

Darby whistled under her breath. "This belongs to Jack? The poor guy. First his wife, and now this …"

"Hmm." Jonas Briggs squinted in the sunlight. "Getting too hot to be out here jogging, Ms. Farr. How about if I give you a lift home?"

"Only if you'll stop calling me 'Ms. Farr.' My name is Darby."

Jonas Briggs smiled and pointed toward a navy Volvo parked a few spaces away. "And I'm Jonas. A pleasure to meet you." He opened the door for Darby and she slid in. It was impeccably clean, without as much as a ballpoint pen out of place.

Detective Briggs climbed in and started the engine. "The air will be on in a second," he said.

Darby buckled her seat belt. "You car is spotless. Is that a department regulation?"

The detective chuckled. "I like a clean environment," he said. "Helps me think. I'm in here so much that I don't think I could take it if it got sloppy." He adjusted the air conditioning and smiled. "You let me know if you get too chilly." Backing out of the parking space, Jonas Briggs eased the car onto the main street.

"Do you always work homicides?"

"Nah. Whatever comes my way." He scanned the streets and turned down the leafy road where Darby had been running only minutes before. "Generally, this is a pretty boring jurisdiction. White collar crime, your occasional crime of passion, but none of the random violence you find in Tampa or Miami." He glanced over at Darby. "The murder of Kyle Cameron is very unusual. A first in my fifteen years with the department."

"How did you know it was part of a series of killings?"

"We relayed the information to OSI—that's the Office of Statewide Intelligence, a fusion center for data—and they got a hit. The guy's MO is the same. He preys on attractive real estate agents, ambushing them at an open house just before it begins. His weapon is a long, thin, blade. The victims are stabbed multiple times in the throat and chest area, and there is no sign of sexual assault. All three have been found by clients coming to look at the property."

Darby shivered and Jonas Briggs adjusted the air conditioning, although her shiver had nothing to do with the temperature.

"How will the investigation be handled?"

"I'll work with the guys on the East Coast through the Department of Legal Enforcement," he said. "The pressure is on to solve it quickly, before a statewide panic sets in. But these are the crimes that generally take a while. You're not dealing with someone who's jealous of a co-worker, or mad at his ex-wife. You're dealing with a psycho, and getting into their mindset is pretty tricky."

Darby nodded and Detective Briggs turned into Helen's neat little driveway. "Here you go. I hope you're being careful about jogging alone around here. It's pretty safe, but still…"

Darby held up the palm-sized can of pepper spray and smiled. "I bring along a friend." She didn't tell the detective that she was a graduate of San Diego's coveted Akido Academy and had competed in countless martial arts competitions.

"Good." Jonas Briggs put the car in park and opened his door. To Darby's amazement, he came around the Volvo and opened hers with a flourish. "There. I hope I've in some way made up for my rude manners this morning."

"Yes," Darby said, emerging once more into the heat. "Your mother would be proud."

———

After a shower and a check of her e-mails, Darby drove the black Mustang to Helen Near's office on Serenidad's main street. She found Helen on the phone, an intense look of concentration on her face.

"Tomorrow morning will be fine," she said, jotting something down on a yellow pad of paper. "Nine a.m., and I'll bring my partner."

She hung up and gave Darby a huge smile. "You will never guess who I have been talking to."

"Tag Gunnerson."

Helen's smile turned to incredulity. "Yes! Well, not Tag exactly, but his assistant. How in the world did you guess?"

"You have that 'I just spoke to a celebrity's assistant' look on your face."

Helen shook her head back and forth in slow motion. "You've got some kind of sixth sense, Darby Farr. How in God's good name…"

Darby could not contain her laughter any longer. Pointing at Helen's legal pad, she said, "I don't need special powers to see that you've doodled the word 'Tag' with dollar signs all around it."

Helen glanced down at her handiwork and gave her booming laugh. "Well, so I have," she said. "Talk about your confidential conversations! Come on, girl, I've got a lot to tell you."

"Where are we headed?"

"A little place called the Dive. Best grouper sandwiches in Sarasota County." Her lips tightened as she hauled up her purse. "It's Jack Cameron's *other* restaurant—the one that didn't burn to a crisp."

———

The Dive was a cozy place, right on the water, with a large dock holding fifteen or so small tables under an awning strung with seagull netting. Artifacts from shipwrecks—the prow of a boat, several rusted compasses, a huge wheel—constituted the majority of the décor.

"Let me guess—Jack's a diver," Darby surmised. "And he likes to dive wrecks."

"That's right. He got the diving bug back when he was a teen, and it's how he spends his free time, along with fishing." Helen looked around the restaurant's full tables and waiting line. The smell of grilled burgers wafted on a slight breeze. "This place is always busy, and Mitzi says that Jack makes a good living—not that he or his sister really have to work, but don't get me started." She lowered her voice. "His other place—Belle Haven—was a flop from the get-go. Can you believe it burned last night? Mitzi called and told me after you left for your run."

"Why did the restaurant fail? Seems like it was in a good location, downtown by the upscale shops."

"Yeah, that's true, but it just never took off. The chefs kept quitting and the menu kept changing. It was too expensive for some people and not pricey enough for others. I think it was doomed from the beginning."

"Why's that?" Darby put up two fingers to answer the hostess' question about how many people were in the party. She and Helen then followed her to a table in the center of the room. Helen took a seat, examined a basket of bread, and resumed her explanation.

"Jack's heart wasn't in it. He started Belle Haven to impress Kyle, that's what I think. He thought he could win her back with a fancier place." She looked around The Dive. "Now, this place is Jack Cameron. That other restaurant was him trying to be someone else. Someone like Foster McFarlin."

"The developer of Esperanza Shores?"

"That's right. Kyle and McFarlin were having an affair. I'm sure they thought they were discreet, but everyone in the state knew. Nobody thought it would last, but it broke Jack's heart and spirit to see her hanging on his arm."

Darby looked up as a pert woman with a notepad materialized at their table. "Do you need more time?" Her pen was poised to write their order.

"Nah." Helen looked at Darby. "We want grouper sandwiches, right?"

Darby nodded. "And an iced tea."

"I'll have the same," said Helen. "Except bring me a beer."

The waitress nodded, her blonde ponytail bobbing, and turned her attention to a family just taking their seats nearby. Overhead a frustrated seagull shrieked, hoping to swoop down on an unsuspecting diner's French fries.

"Foster McFarlin is married to the lieutenant governor of Florida, right?" Darby asked. "I think I read that in the morning paper."

Helen nodded. "Chellie Howe. She's got her eye on the governor's mansion, if you ask me." She gave a weary sigh. "I heard her on the radio pounding home her tough-on-crime routine, using Kyle's death as the prime example of why we need new state leadership." She shrugged. "If a real estate agent can get butchered just for holding an open house, maybe Chellie is right."

Their beverages arrived and both took a long drink. "How are the Camerons holding up?" Darby asked.

"Mitzi is exhausted. I'm worried about her. Alexandra stayed at the house to keep an eye on Jack, who seems to be coming to grips with the whole thing. Poor Jack. He's a mess, but he's planning Kyle's service for tomorrow afternoon." She lowered her voice. "Tell you the truth, I'm kind of surprised that this place is open for business. Maybe there was some reason Jack couldn't close."

Helen took a quick sip of beer, then gave a quick intake of breath. "Shoot! What time did I make that appointment with the golfer?"

"You said 'nine,'" reminded Darby. "You also said you'd bring your partner." She raised her eyebrows expectantly.

Helen gave Darby a sheepish grin. "Yeah, I was going to bring that up." She looked up as the waitress delivered their sandwiches. "First, taste your lunch. You're going to love it."

Darby lifted the sandwich. Lettuce poked out of a soft, sesame-seed sprinkled bun, and Darby could see a slice of tomato and a white sauce slathered on a generous wedge of broiled fish. She inhaled. "Smells delicious." Taking a bite of the delicately seasoned fish, she nodded. "Yum."

"Your Aunt Jane is up in heaven smiling," Helen said. "She loved a good grouper sandwich. She told me once that the lobster rolls up in Maine were pretty darn good, but that nothing could beat this."

They ate in silence for a few minutes, enjoying the simple but satisfying flavors. After wiping her mouth with her napkin, Helen gave Darby a frank look.

"Okay, now I've got to come clean. I really need your help tomorrow. Let me tell you the situation, and then I hope you'll agree to stay in Florida a few more days."

Darby regarded the older woman over the table. "I'm listening."

"Kyle Cameron told me she was going to be signing up a new listing. She wanted to wait until we'd finalized our partnership and she was no longer an agent with Barnaby's. She was thrilled about the property, said it would be quite an achievement to sell it, never mind the commission. I didn't know where or what it was, but I knew it was big."

"When we set up our appointment for Monday, Kyle mentioned that she was going for cocktails somewhere that evening. She hinted that it had to do with her big listing. She laughed and said, "You'll never believe this, Helen, but I may already have it sold!" Again, I didn't press her for details. That's not my way, and I trusted her. Heck, I've known the Camerons for years."

"This morning, Tag Gunnerson's assistant, a fellow named Bernie Shultz, called. He said he was sorry to hear of Kyle's death. He said that her passing hadn't influenced Tag's decision to list with

56

Near & Farr Realty. He said that from everything Kyle had said, Tag knew Near & Farr was the right agency."

"Darby, he was talking to me as if I knew all about Kyle's business, and I confess that I played along. He set up a meeting for tomorrow at nine, and asked for my business partner to come along."

"I don't see why you need me, Helen. You're perfectly capable of landing all kinds of listings without me around. How could I possibly help you?"

"Tag Gunnerson will be there."

"So? You'll charm the pants off the guy."

Helen smiled. "Thanks. Can't say that I wouldn't mind doing that." She paused. "Darby, aside from the fact that two agents always look more powerful than one, there's another reason your presence would help."

"And what's that?"

"The buyer for the property—the one Kyle hinted at—may be there as well."

"So?"

Helen looked around the restaurant quickly and lowered her voice. "I was thinking you could represent him if he wants to make an offer."

"One small problem: I'm not licensed in Florida."

Helen shrugged. "We can work on that."

Darby took another bite of her sandwich and chewed thoughtfully. "Why do I feel there's something else you're not telling me?"

The older woman squirmed in her seat. "Okay, okay." She let out a sigh. "It's the buyer. He's from—well, he's Asian."

Darby sat back in her plastic chair. "Tell me you're kidding." She folded her napkin and gave Helen a level look. The older woman shook her head.

"Afraid not."

"You're playing the Japanese card, Helen Near. That's totally unfair, not to mention discriminatory."

"Come on, it's no different than wearing a designer suit or driving a Lexus to impress your clients. It's tailoring your presentation to fit the customer, that's all."

"You call choosing an agent to accompany you based on her race the same as picking out a skirt and jacket? It's profiling, that's what it is."

"Obviously I want you along for more reasons than your ethnicity," huffed Helen. "It's just that—"

"I get it." Darby toyed with her grouper sandwich as if deep in thought, keeping her companion waiting for several seconds. She wasn't really annoyed, but it had been entertaining to watch Helen think about the implications of her words. Finally, she blew air out of her mouth as if arriving at a tough decision.

"I'll tell you what. I'll check with my office assistant back in California. If he can handle things without me for a few more days, I'll change my flight and keep working on my Florida tan."

Helen clapped her hands. "We're going to make a pile of money, Darby Farr. You just wait and see." She took a swig of beer and smiled. "Fifty acres. Three pools! Oh, I absolutely cannot wait."

———

Jack Cameron sat on the floor of the storeroom, his back against the door and his head in his hands. Restaurant supplies—canned and paper goods, jars of tartar sauce, rolls of aluminum foil, boxes of bagged potato chips—were stacked on shelves around him, and his knees were up against a large plastic container of mayonnaise.

There was scarcely room for anything else in the cramped space, which truthfully was little more than a glorified closet. Overhead the fluorescent light buzzed, a steady drone that seemed to Jack like a drill honing in on his skull.

Kyle would not leave his thoughts, would not stop laughing at him. He pushed his thumbs into his temples trying to make her disappear, but she was there, her head thrown back, laughing at him so hard tears were running down her face. "I know about Belle Haven," she was saying, her voice high, singsong-y, like a girl doing jump rope. Jack wanted to scream at her to stop, to leave him alone, but he knew she wasn't going anywhere.

She was dead, he knew that, he'd seen her lifeless body, but she was the type of evil spirit that would not disappear. *Mabuya*. A spectre that never left, that would haunt his soul until he joined her in the underworld.

Kyle had once been pure and good. They had enjoyed an innocent love, a desire to live a simple life, raise a family, run a business. But she had changed—rotted like a peach left too long in the sun, and it was her career that was to blame.

Jack heard a movement outside of the storeroom. It was only a matter of time before one of the wait staff tried the door, and then he'd have some explaining to do. He rose slowly and blinked a few times. Acting normal was the key. No more crazy Jack if his plan was to succeed.

He opened the door to the storeroom. Stepping cautiously into the hallway, he hoped the voice in his head had finally stopped, until he heard a high-pitched giggle that he knew belonged to Kyle.

———

Helen gave the waitress her credit card and waved away Darby's thanks. "With all you're doing for me, lunch is the least I can do." Finishing her beer with a gulp, she suddenly gasped in delight. "Jack! I didn't know you were here? Get over here and give me a hug!"

Darby followed Helen's gaze to the sturdy, tanned man making his way to their table. He had sandy blonde hair and deep blue eyes, and his grin revealed a set of perfectly straight white teeth.

He hugged Helen tightly. "It's good to see you," he said.

"You sweet boy. You haven't been properly introduced to Darby."

Jack turned his blue eyes on Darby and she saw a flash of fear flit across his face, but it was quickly replaced by his boyish grin.

"It's the winner of the Jack Cameron treasure hunt," he said. "I understand I have you to thank for finding me yesterday."

Darby nodded. "I hope you're feeling better."

"Much. Thanks to Dr. Menendez and the miracle of pharmaceuticals, I'm back to my old self." His eyes grazed over Darby and once more she felt an undercurrent of powerful emotion beneath his benign charm.

"What brings you to Sarasota?" he asked.

"A visit with Helen."

"Remember my partner, Jane Farr?" Helen pointed in Darby's direction. "Darby is her niece."

Jack nodded. His eyes strayed over the tables, still full of diners enjoying the noonday heat. "Did you hear about the fire at Belle Haven?"

"I did," Helen sighed. "Jack, I'm sorry."

He shook his head and Darby thought he might cry. Instead he shrugged his shoulders. "Probably for the best. With Kyle gone ..."

He looked over the water and swallowed. "With Kyle gone I have to rethink everything." He clenched his hands. It seemed to take a tremendous effort for Jack Cameron to converse. "Please excuse me, ladies, I'm needed in the kitchen."

Darby and Helen watched him weave through the tables. Moments later he had disappeared inside the restaurant.

"That is one hurting man," Helen whispered. "I can't bear to see him like that."

Darby nodded. She knew the pain of losing loved ones in a sudden and random way, and recognized Jack Cameron's agony. She looked into her friend's concerned face. "He needs professional help."

Helen gave a sad nod. "I know."

"Aren't Mitzi and Alexandra concerned?"

"They are doing what they can. But John ... he blocks every effort to help that boy."

"Why?"

"Darby, I have asked myself that for years." She picked up her purse. "Tell you what. Let's stop at the office, then head to Casa Cameron and pay that family another visit. It's high time you met John Cameron."

Darby grabbed her pocketbook and prepared to follow Helen. As she walked around the tables and past the bar, an angular man in a black baseball cap swiveled slightly in his seat and snapped her photograph, but Darby, deep in thought, did not see.

––––––

From his vantage point on a stool at the Dive's bar, Clyde Hensley put down his camera and watched the two women as they wove between the tables and out of the restaurant. He turned back toward the bar and motioned to the bartender for his tab. Plunking down a twenty-dollar bill, he forced a casual tone to his voice. "I know that woman who was here with the Asian girl," he lied. "But I can't for the life of me remember her name."

"Helen?" the bartender offered. He wiped the counter with a dingy rag. "That's Helen Near. She's a regular here. Old family friends with Jack." He took the money and lowered his voice. "I didn't know the other one. Quite the looker, huh?"

Clyde licked his lips and nodded. She was attractive, if you were into that kind of foreign scene, and plenty of guys sure were. He himself liked the more traditional all-American girl, with blonde hair and blue eyes, a little on the plump side. He was pushing sixty-five years old and wanted no part of that exotic stuff. And yet, he knew from experience that unusual looks paid top dollar.

The bartender lifted the twenty. "Let me get you change," he said.

I should hope so, thought Clyde. He'd only had two beers, and the guy hadn't quite told him what he wanted.

Like the name of the dark-haired Asian girl. Not that it was important in the scheme of things. He let his thoughts drift to Kyle Cameron, another good-looking piece of ass, and shook his head. Dead, just like his best plan to date. *Shit.*

Clyde waited for his change and pictured Darby Farr once more, this time without her clothes. He groaned and nearly laughed aloud. Yesirree, she could very well be the ticket.

———

Half an hour later Clyde Hensley was at a marina by one of the large bridges spanning the Intracoastal Waterway. He spotted his customers right away, with their sunburned noses and annoyed looks. He hustled up to them and attempted a smile.

"Thought you might be here," Clyde said, sizing up whether they'd be trouble or not. "I was waiting for you at the pier like we discussed, but people always get confused and show up here instead."

The girl's annoyance turned to confusion. She squinted up at him, her blonde hair framing a face that was round and dimpled. "We're in the wrong place? I thought you said to come to the Causeway, take the first right …"

"Hey, hey," he soothed. "It's not a problem. You ladies aren't known for getting directions one hundred percent correct now, are you?" He winked at the loser standing next to her, probably just a boyfriend by their ring-less fingers, and the guy gave a complicit chuckle.

"Shit, Lisa, he's got your number right. You couldn't find your way out of a paper bag if you had to."

Lisa scowled but decided to let the matter go. "Who cares? He's here now and we can have the ride of our life." She reached for her boyfriend's arm and gave it a squeeze. "I can't wait."

Clyde Hensley gave his sunniest smile. "Let's get the paperwork out of the way and get you up there." He handed them a standard release form and a pen. They scrawled down their names without reading the papers and handed them back.

He checked over their signatures.

"Okay, so you're Lisa and Dylan, right?"

They nodded.

"I'll just need your payment and we'll get you on the boat and up into the great blue yonder." He moistened his lips with his tongue. "That'll be one hundred and forty dollars."

"You said one hundred on the phone," Lisa said, her voice wary.

"That's right. It's an even hundred if you want to go up nine hundred feet. I thought you wanted to go up to twelve."

Lisa crinkled up her nose at Dylan. "What do you say, babe? Want to go even higher?"

"Sure." He pulled out his wallet and counted seven twenties. He handed them to Clyde as if he expected some sort of reward.

Clyde nodded and stuffed them into the pocket of his shorts. "Great. Higher the better, is what I always say." He hustled them down to the dock and into the speedboat. Moments later, they were rumbling away from the shore and heading under the bridge.

"Hey sport," Clyde called over the hum of the engine. "Want to steer while I get them harnesses set up?"

Dylan lurched to the front of the boat and took the wheel. Clyde made sure the harnesses were connected to the cable and motioned for Lisa to come to the stern where a dive platform was set up.

"Here you go, sweetheart," he said. "Fasten on a life jacket and then climb into a harness." He waited to see if she needed assistance, noticing that her thighs were rapidly becoming a rosy pink. She did as he asked and waited expectantly. "Now let's get that boyfriend of yours saddled up."

Clyde took the wheel back from Dylan. "Go on back there and get a life jacket on, then step into the harness like Lisa." Dylan nodded. He licked his lips nervously and Clyde had to suppress a smile.

Once the two were secured, Clyde let the boat idle while he connected the giant orange parachute. "Now once I start the boat again, she's gonna take off and it won't be long and you'll be lifting up too," he said. "You just relax while you're up there and enjoy the ride. Okay?"

Dylan lifted a hand as if he were back in elementary school. "How're we going to get down?"

Clyde gave a patient nod. "Same way you're getting up. I'll lower you back down and you'll come right back on the platform. Done it a million times."

"Shouldn't you have another person here? To watch us? You know, a spotter?"

Clyde snorted. Why were the men always the scaredy cats? Lisa was itching to get up and see the view, while Dylan was thinking of every reason in the book why they should abort.

"I've done it both ways, Dylan, with spotters and without." He nodded as if he were giving the matter some thought. "I find that if it's just me, I can really concentrate on my customers, give them the kind of personal service they really deserve. If I've got another guy, we're liable to start chatting about the Marlins game, what kind of beer we like, you know, guy stuff. Alone I am much more focused on you, my valued customers." He paused and gave what he hoped was a convincing smile. "Trust me, you are going to enjoy yourself."

He slammed the boat into gear and it leapt forward. "Ready?" he yelled over the roar of the motor. He sped into the center of the channel, enjoying the wind on his short silver hair. It was a beautiful day, the sky a clear blue to match the sparkling water.

Clyde Hensley heard the winches releasing more cable. Out of the corner of his eye, he saw his customers, sunburned legs dangling, rising slowly into the sky.

FOUR

BACK AT NEAR & Farr Realty, her grouper sandwich now a pleasant memory, Darby used her cell to call Enrique Tomaso Gomez, or "ET" as she called him. Her assistant answered the phone with a smooth, "Pacific Coast Realty, Darby Farr's office," and gave a loud exclamation when he heard his boss' voice.

"Darby! How lovely to hear from you. How are things in the Sunshine State?"

Darby explained what had happened to Kyle Cameron and ET made a tsk-tsking sound.

"How often have I told you, those open houses are dangerous. That poor woman. Do the police have any leads?"

"I don't know. I ran into one of the detectives this morning and it didn't sound like they had anything just yet." She paused. "ET, Helen has asked me to stay a few more days and help her land—and hopefully sell—an amazing listing."

"How intriguing. Tell me more."

Darby described what little she knew of Tag Gunnerson's fifty acre island property and explained that a buyer was already interested. "The buyer is Asian, so Helen thinks I'm the perfect person to work with him." She paused. "I read her the riot act on that one, but the truth is, if it all works, we'll make some good money. Helen hasn't valued the estate yet, but from what I know of waterfront property, it's worth at least thirty million dollars, possibly more."

ET was silent for a few minutes. Darby was about to ask if he was still on the line when he cleared his throat and spoke.

"I know you are anxious to come home," he said. "But this opportunity brings up an issue I've been struggling with for some time now." Darby heard him swallow. Obviously this was not an easy conversation for her friend.

"A family member is in trouble, and I need money. I know it's a lot to ask, but perhaps if this sale goes through, we might talk about a loan."

"There's nothing to discuss, ET. You know I'm willing to help you out, whether this sale happens or not. How much do you need?"

There was a sigh. "It's quite a large sum. Half a million dollars."

Darby did some quick math in her head. If indeed the St. Andrew's Isle deal did take place, Darby would make more than enough money to lend her friend the amount required.

"Listen," she told ET. "You and I can do this if we keep all the bases covered. What's going on there? Is there anything I need to know?"

He exhaled. "The O'Hara estate. I'm close to getting an offer, and I hope I will have good news soon. Everything else is moving along."

"That's great. Here's what I'm thinking. See if you can find out how I can get a license to work with a buyer here in Florida. I'll do my best to land this deal and get you what you need. Even if the sale doesn't work out, you can count on me."

He thanked her, and she could hear emotion in the usually calm man's voice. What was going on? Why such a huge sum of money? Darby wasn't going to pry. She trusted ET implicitly. Whatever he needed, she would get him—no questions asked.

———

Clyde Hensley cracked open a beer and took a long swig. The sun was merciless and the humidity still high, but the cold pungent taste of the beer never failed to help. *This isn't such a bad way to spend the time*, he thought, *in between higher paying jobs. Gets me out of the house and away from my computer.* He gave a half-hearted glance at Lisa and Dylan, still soaring hundreds of feet in the air. *Time to bring them down*, he thought. *As soon as I finish this beer.*

One led to another and Clyde decided he'd better start the process of bringing the couple down before he fell asleep in the sun or ran out of gas. He hit the button on the automatic winch and the machine began grinding its motor, pulling the parachute and the couple closer to the boat. They had certainly gotten their money's worth, Clyde thought. What with the sun and the pleasure of drinking a few beers, he'd left them up there for longer than usual.

Clyde's thoughts drifted to food. He was hungry, and the wad of twenties in his pocket meant he could treat himself to something good for dinner. Snapper, maybe. Grilled with a little butter on his neighbor's gas grill...

Over the groaning sound of the winch, Clyde heard a loud ping—the unmistakable sound of snapping cable. "Shit!" he spat, glancing up toward the sky. Yes, the cable had snapped like the string on a kid's balloon, and his customers were already floating away from the boat, carried now by the currents of a stiff breeze toward the shore.

Clyde yanked the wheel of the boat hard. The broken cable was now slithering towards him like an angry water moccasin, and Clyde turned off the winch and hauled it in. He gunned the engine as fast as it would go, racing back toward the pier where he had left the trailer earlier in the day. His mind was a whirl of questions: Would he have time to get the boat out? Would he find anyone to give him a ride? Had he left anything, other than his vehicle, at the marina? He opened the cooler where two beers remained. The release form Dylan and Lisa had signed was in the corner, a soggy mound of disintegrating paper. He exhaled with relief, ripped it to shreds, and threw it in the water.

Still blasting through the water with the motor at top speed, Clyde rummaged in a compartment and pulled out his lucky Dolphins cap. He shoved it on his balding head and used one hand to hold it secure. The pier was only minutes' away, and he was starting to feel calmer. He could figure this out, just as he had before. He took a deep breath. Plenty of time.

———

Near & Farr Realty was a pleasant storefront office on the main street of Serenidad Key, next to a bakery and a travel agency. Tropical plants bloomed in the small waiting area, and Darby smiled as Helen absentmindedly picked a few spent blossoms from a flowering hibiscus. A petite woman with short black hair rose from a desk as Helen entered.

"*Hola*, Helen," she said in a lilting voice. She wore a short sleeved white blouse and a red skirt that draped to just above her knees.

"*Hola*, Maria." She nodded her head toward Darby. "This is Jane Farr's niece, Darby. Darby, meet Maria Iglesias. She works at the travel agency next door and babysits this place when I'm not here."

Darby shook hands with the small woman. "*Hola, como estas?*"

"*Muy bien, gracias.*" Maria raised her eyebrows. "Your accent is very good. Where did you acquire it?"

"I live in Southern California," Darby explained. "My assistant is from Ensenada and is kind enough to practice with me." As she mentioned ET, she flashed back to their earlier conversation, wondering what troubles had prompted him to ask for a loan. She hoped her promise to lend him the money had been a comfort.

Maria Iglesias gave a nod. "I've always wanted to go to San Diego. Working in a travel agency, I see many wonderful places to visit, so it makes it hard to choose." She smiled and rubbed her hands together. "I'll head back to the agency now. Nice to meet you, Darby." Her skirt swirled as she went out the door.

Helen beckoned Darby to the back of the office, where two large oak desks commanded most of the space.

"This was going to be Kyle's desk," Helen said, her voice heavy with sadness. "You know, I think it's all just starting to sink in. I was looking forward to working with her. She had such a wonderful energy, a vivacity that would have really perked this place up."

She looked around and sighed. "I've been thinking about what I'll do. I'm not sure if I have the energy to recruit someone else."

"Don't make any decisions now," Darby advised. "It's too soon." She reached over and put a hand on Helen's shoulder. In a softer voice she added, "Grief isn't something you can rush through, my friend. Give yourself some time."

Helen nodded. "I suppose you're right." She checked her watch. "Want to work on Tag's property before we head over to Casa Cameron? I can start Kyle's computer for you."

"Sure. I wouldn't mind taking a look at my e-mails on a bigger screen than this." She held up her Smartphone and watched as Helen started the gleaming new computer and punched in a password.

"There you go," Helen said.

"Did Kyle ever work on this machine?"

"Not really. It came last week and I showed it to her on Saturday. She sat down and fooled around a little, but I don't think it was more than that."

"Who bought it?"

"I did. It was a welcome gift." Helen sighed and walked back to her chair, her shoulders sagging.

The two women worked quietly for a half hour, Darby replying to some clients in California before turning her attention to the extensive St. Andrew's Isle property. The barrier island paradise seemed to have it all: a nine-hole golf course, a landing strip for small planes, a palatial main house with three pools and a guest house, as well as a small café where Tag and his golfing buddies could enjoy a few drinks before or after their tee times. Darby shook her head in admiration.

71

"Helen, this isn't a listing, it's a small village!"

The older woman let out one of her booming laughs. "No kidding!"

"I wonder if Kyle did any work to value the property."

"I don't know." Helen thought a moment and pointed at a drawer. "Check in there. When Kyle came by on Saturday, she had a manila folder with her. I remember because I told her I'd order a file cabinet this week. I think she stuck it in there."

Darby opened the drawer. It was empty except for a single file. She pulled it out and looked inside.

"Well?" Helen asked. "Come on, the suspense is killing me."

Darby rifled through several pieces of paper. "There's a listing sheet on a sold property in South Africa." She scanned the details of a forty-acre island retreat located in South Africa. As with Tag Gunnerson's estate, there was a landing strip, a large main house, and several guest buildings. "No golf course," she noted. "But this property boasts a ten-acre wildlife park, complete with gazelles and ostrich." She looked closer. The property had sold the previous year for $30 million.

"I can't imagine having ostriches running around my front yard," said Helen. "Leaving their droppings all over the place. Who handled the sale?"

"Barnaby's," commented Darby. She looked at the remaining pieces of paper. "Here's another comparable sale: Jupiter Island, Florida. That's over on the Atlantic side, right?"

Helen nodded. "I remember that trade. Twelve acres, couple of houses, forty million bucks, right?"

Darby nodded. She rifled through the file and found one more piece of paper. Handwritten columns of numbers, headed "subject property" and "comparison property one," and "comparison property two" were written neatly across the page.

"Take a look at this," said Darby. "Kyle actually did a comparative market analysis—by hand."

"I'm not surprised," said Helen. "She was an extremely thorough broker." She leaned in and looked at the paper. "Wonder why she didn't do it on the computer? I'm from the dark ages and even I don't do CMAs on paper."

Darby scanned the columns of numbers and Kyle's adjustments for dissimilar features, such as number of bedrooms and bathrooms. She could see Kyle's mind working: adding, subtracting, and accessing the value.

"What did she come up with?" Helen asked. "I'm dying to know."

Darby lowered the file and regarded Helen's eager face.

"I'll tell you, but you're not going to believe it."

"Just try me."

Darby shook her head in amazement. "Forty-five million dollars. Kyle valued Tag Gunnerson's estate at forty-five million."

"Mother of God," breathed Helen. She picked up her purse and keys. "Let's hightail it back to my house before we go see Mitzi. I need a Mojito and quick!"

———

The front door of Casa Cameron opened and Darby and Helen stood before Carlotta. Her angular face registered surprise.

"*Buenas tardes,* Carlotta," said Helen. "Where's Harold? Day off?"

She nodded, her eyes darting toward the back of the house. "Señora Cameron is resting," she said, unwilling to move aside to allow them entrance. "Perhaps you would like to come back later…"

"Nonsense." A booming voice cut through the house's silence like a knife through a ripe melon. Darby heard a door slam and brisk footsteps followed. "I haven't had the pleasure of a visit from my old friend Helen in years." A tall, gray-haired man strode toward them and grasped Helen's arm.

"Hello, John," Helen said stiffly. Darby noted the erect posture of the man, his hearty greeting. She had the impression of vitality and strength, a worthy match for Mitzi Cameron, who exuded the same qualities.

"And you must be Darby Farr," he said, his voice filling up the entryway and echoing off the parquet floors. "Met your aunt a few times at Nell's little dinner parties. She was a shrewd one."

His face was relaxed, the very picture of amiability and welcome, and yet Darby thought she could see a certain hardness in his eyes. In a moment, the impression was gone. Had she imagined it, or was John Cameron's cheerful demeanor at odds with his true feelings?

"Mitzi's having a little lie-down, and I was just contemplating a swim in the pool, but I'm glad you stopped by. Let's go to the den. Carlotta will get us something—tea? Coffee?" His eyes narrowed and a smirk played at the corners of his mouth. "Or something stronger?"

Helen shot him a look and squared her shoulders. "Tea would be fine," she said.

"Very well." John Cameron turned and led the women down the hall and past the living room. Darby glimpsed the sunny study where she and Helen had sat during their last visit. Now they were ushered into the adjoining den, her host's expansive "man cave."

Dominating the room was a long pool table with ornate mahogany feet. On one wall hung a huge flat-screen television, flanked by speakers for optimal sound. Large burgundy-colored leather club chairs were positioned in front of the screen, and Darby imagined this was where John watched sports and the news. Heavy drapes obscured the windows, no doubt to provide a darkened atmosphere conducive to television watching.

She took a quick glance around the room. Several mounted trophy fish—Darby recognized a sailfish and a striped marlin—watched from the paneled walls, while gleaming brass awards and collections of leather-bound books adorned a wall of built-in shelves. The faint yet familiar aroma of pipe tobacco lingered in the air while underneath Darby's feet the carpet was thick and plush.

John Cameron indicated that they should sit down on one of the leather sofas before the built-in bookshelves. He hit a button on a nearby phone and spoke to someone—Carlotta, presumably—regarding afternoon refreshments. Walking past the pool table to join them once more, he grabbed the black eight ball and rolled it across the smooth green surface, where it found a corner pocket and disappeared.

"Do you play pool, Darby?"

"Not really," she answered. "It is a skill I admire, however. The precision of a good player is always impressive."

"Yes," John Cameron agreed. "If only life were as easy as pool. Choose the correct angle, make the shot, and in it goes." He strode back and sank into the couch opposite the women. "Take my son, for instance. Bouncing like he's trapped in a pinball machine, instead of focusing on something worthwhile in life."

Helen sucked in a breath. "Sometimes I can't believe you, John," she said sharply. "Jack's had an enormous blow. Two enormous blows: Kyle's murder and now the fire at Belle Haven. I should think you would have a little more compassion."

An amused look came over John Cameron's face. "I love it when you're spunky, Helen. I get to see your fiery temper so infrequently nowadays."

A discreet knock at the door signaled Carlotta's arrival with a tray of tea, coffee, and cookies. She poured for each of them and slipped out of the room, her face expressionless.

"Care for a snickerdoodle, Darby? These are Mitzi's favorites."

"Thank you." Darby took the sugar cookie and bit into it. She remembered making the same cookies with her mother, forming the dough into small balls and then rolling each one in cinnamon sugar. She felt a familiar pang of sadness constrict her throat.

"I'm sorry for the loss of your daughter-in-law," she said.

"Poor Kyle. I haven't really thought of her as my daughter-in-law for quite some time. Still, it's a tragedy."

Darby shot a look at Helen. She had not touched her tea, and sat with her hands clasped and trembling in front of her chest. *She's literally shaking with anger,* Darby realized.

Helen seemed about to vent some of that anger when Mitzi Cameron rolled into the den. "Good afternoon, everyone." She put up a hand to stop Darby and Helen from rising from the sofa.

"Please, don't get up on my account." She turned her head toward her husband, her face noticeably more lined and weary than the day before. John returned her gaze without making any attempt to rise and greet his wife.

"Darling, join us for some tea," he said, the lightness of his voice sounding hollow to Darby's ears. "We've been having such a wonderful chat."

Mitzi gave her husband a cold stare and said nothing. She turned to her old friend. "Forgive me, Nell, for my tardiness. I didn't sleep last night and I'm exhausted."

Concern knitted the brow of Helen Near. "Of course you are." She rose and went to Mitzi's side and gave her friend's narrow shoulders a heartfelt squeeze. "Please, Mitzi, tell me what I can do to help you."

Mitzi glanced toward John, who seemed to comprehend his wife's desire to be alone with her friend. He rose and gave a diffident wave. "Ladies, I'll leave you to your tea and crumpets," he said. Pausing at the door he turned and looked at Darby. "It was a pleasure to meet you. I have a feeling we'll see each other again." Once more Darby saw cold steel in John Cameron's penetrating gaze.

While Helen and Mitzi murmured in low voices regarding Jack's condition and the plans for the services for Kyle Cameron the next day, Darby found her thoughts wandering to the investigation surrounding Kyle's murder and whether any progress had been made in finding the killer. She thought of Jonas Briggs, the detective on the case, and wondered if he'd been working with the lead investigators on the other side of the state. In the distance, a phone rang.

Carlotta was at the door moments later, motioning to Mitzi Cameron.

"It is the police," she said softly. "Detective Briggs."

Darby nearly choked on her last bite of snickerdoodle. Hadn't she just been thinking of the detective moments before? *Get a grip,* she told herself. *He's the lead investigator of a murder and you're sitting in the living room of the murdered woman's family. It makes total sense he would call here.*

Helen stood by Mitzi, one hand on the back of the wheelchair. She glanced at Darby, both of them wondering what the call could mean. Mitzi took the cordless phone, said "Hello," and listened for several minutes.

"Thank you, Detective," Mitzi said. "That is good news indeed." Darby noted that her voice sounded empty of all emotion.

Mitzi let the phone fall into her lap. "The police in Stuart have found the man who killed Kyle," she said. "They tracked him down and stormed his house. They have enough evidence to prove that he is the Kondo Killer." She exhaled. "Thank God."

Helen returned her friend's weary gaze. "It will be some relief to Jack, at least. Don't you think so, Mitzi?"

"Perhaps." She rolled away from Helen and into the center of the room. She turned the chair sharply as if in frustration and glanced down at a cell phone on her lap. "I have no idea where Jack is. He doesn't answer when I call." She closed her eyes. "He needs to know about this before he sees it on television or hears about it at his bar."

"Try the Dive," Helen suggested. "Darby and I were just there and spoke to him."

Mitzi nodded and punched in a number. She asked to speak to Jack and then hung up once more. "He left forty-five minutes ago."

"Could he be at Kyle's condominium?" Darby asked.

"Whatever makes you say that?" Mitzi had an edge to her voice.

Darby rose to her feet. "A hunch. It's obvious that he's deeply upset over Kyle's death, and in a strange sort of way he might find it comforting to be among her possessions." She paused. "If you'd like, I'll head over there and see if my guess is correct. I can go by the restaurant as well."

Helen regarded her friend. "Darby could be right," she said softly. "Someone should check it out. We could call Alexandra …"

"No. She's counseling clients today." Darby detected pride in the older woman's voice. "I'd appreciate your help, Darby. There is one problem: I don't have a key to Kyle's condominium, and I have no idea where to find one."

"Just give me the unit number and I'll figure it out." Darby gave Mitzi what she hoped was an encouraging smile. The poor woman was in need of some encouragement—that much was obvious. "I'll know if Jack is there," she assured her. "I'll call you as soon as I can."

———

Darby was sure that Jack Cameron was seeking solace at Kyle's condominium. Something about his haunted demeanor hours before, the hollows beneath his eyes and his furtive glances led her to believe she would find him at Somerset Sound, the development where Kyle Cameron's condominium was located. Seated in the Mustang, Darby consulted a hand-held GPS that Mitzi had pressed into her palm back in John Cameron's study. She typed in Somerset Sound and began following the device's directions.

The route took her past a series of strip malls and big box stores, before coming once more into a residential section at the edge of Serenidad Key. Darby waved at the gatehouse keeper who smiled back with a nonchalant wave, then began surveying the numbered buildings.

She passed a pool and two tennis courts before locating Kyle Cameron's building. Her condo was a ground floor corner unit with landscaping identical to its neighbors'. A red pick-up truck with Florida plates was parked in Kyle's parking space. Whose vehicle was it? Jack Cameron's?

She parked the convertible and walked quickly down the winding path. Late-blooming azaleas graced the front of the unit and a few geckos skittered beneath them as she passed. She paused at the front door. Should she knock, ring the bell, or simply enter? She tried the door. It pushed open noiselessly.

Darby stepped into the cool interior. The air conditioning was still doing its best to keep the inhabitants comfortable, even though there was no one at home. Or was there? Darby listened intently. She heard nothing except the usual hum of plugged-in appliances.

A pristine white carpet in a plush pile prompted Darby to slip off her sandals and leave them on a small sisal mat by the door. The walls were white as well, but creamy, so that rather than seeming sterile and cold, the effect was clean and somehow warm. Strategically placed artwork helped: Darby noted that Kyle seemed partial to tropical landscapes in vivid colors.

Darby stepped quietly into the living room. Two oversized love seats, slip covered in a nubby white material, were flanked by warm wood tables. A few books were piled on one of them and Darby glanced at the subject matter. *Pre-War Poland, Warsaw, City of Survivors,* and *The Poles of Warsaw. A little light reading material,* she thought wryly.

Darby left the large living room, glancing at the kitchen and dining area. Nothing stirred and nothing seemed amiss. The theme of white on white was repeated, with only occasional bursts of color to enliven the serene surroundings.

She entered the immaculate kitchen, wondering if Kyle was a cook. No appliances on the counters; no dishes draining in the sink. Opening the oven door, Darby saw that it was spotless, as if Kyle Cameron had never turned it on.

Just outside the kitchen, a crystal bowl filled with water and a small goldfish caught her eye. The creature was swimming in circles, his scales flashing against the cut glass. Had Kyle been the last one to feed him? If so, he was probably hungry.

The bowl was on a delicately carved table with a single drawer. She opened it and saw a small box of fish food.

Darby had never owned a fish but knew they required only a pinch of food. Sprinkling it at the surface of the water, she was surprised to note the creature's acute awareness of her actions. Instantly he darted upwards toward the flakes, but to her surprise, did not take any.

Darby replaced the box. Perhaps he didn't like to be watched while he ate.

She was about to close the drawer when she spotted the gun. It was a small revolver, a Smith and Wesson by the looks of it, black and very practical looking. Darby opened the drawer further and was stopped by a man's voice.

"What the fuck are you doing?" It was Jack Cameron, holding a bottle, weaving unsteadily on his feet in the doorway of what Darby imagined was the master bedroom.

Darby caught her breath. *Why didn't I hear him? More important, why didn't I check to see if he was here before I started feeding Kyle's pet?*

"I said," he bellowed, his voice becoming thick and dangerous, "What the fuck are you doing?"

Darby closed the drawer and turned to Jack. "I'm feeding the fish, Jack, and looking for you. I'm Darby Farr. I met you a few hours ago, at the Dive. I ordered the grouper sandwich with your godmother, Helen Near."

Jack licked his lips and seemed to consider her response. He lifted the bottle to his lips, took a drink, and wiped his mouth with the back of his hand.

"That's Buddy," he said, pointing toward the fish. "Buddy the goldfish. You're going to have to take him with you 'cause he's all alone."

Darby nodded. "Your family is looking for you, Jack. Can I give you a ride home?"

He barked out a laugh. "Home? You mean Casa Cameron? Shit, yeah. Give me a ride back to the bosom of my loving family." He looked around the condo, swaying unsteadily on his feet. "This was Kyle's place. She got it after she left me." The bottle dropped to the carpet but Jack Cameron did not seem to notice. "She bought all new things. Didn't want anything except her precious bowl over there." He pointed toward Buddy and shook his head. "She bought that goddamn goldfish."

Darby wondered whether she would be able to get Jack Cameron to leave the condo. Would he turn into a combative drunk if she tried taking him out of the building? *Thank God he doesn't know about Kyle's gun.* She took a step closer to him.

"Jack, you need to come with me now. I'll come back and get Buddy later on."

"You're the one who found me yesterday, aren't you? Who are you, my little Japanese guardian angel?" He barked out a chuckle and kicked the bottle with his toe. "Ah, shit. Her fucking carpet's dirty, and I forgot to take off my shoes." He covered his face with his hands as if to shut out his surroundings and began to cry.

Darby went closer to Jack, wary, but wanting to help. She knew from her training in martial arts that the most dangerous situations were the ones involving people under great emotional stress or those who were impaired by drugs or alcohol. Jack Cameron was both.

"I know, Jack. I know how much you miss her." She reached out and touched his arm, felt him stiffen at the touch.

When he pulled his hands away there was an ugly sneer on his tear-stained face.

"Miss her? Is that what you said?"

Darby nodded.

"How can I miss her? She's inside my head! That bitch won't leave me alone!"

Darby swallowed. She had Jack's psychosis all wrong. Quickly she tried to correct what could prove to be a fatal mistake.

"I see," she said. "Kyle—she's tormenting you, is that it?"

The sneer left Jack's face and his features slowly crumpled into despair. He gave a slow, hopeless nod. "I can't get rid of her." Darby could hear desperation in his voice. "She's talking to me all day long, laughing at me, telling me to end it all …" He stopped. "She won't shut up. I know she's dead, but not really. Now she's an evil spirit, like a zombie only invisible." He spoke rapidly, his tongue darting out to lick his lips, his eyes moving quickly from side to side as if he expected Kyle Cameron to appear at any moment.

"Come with me, Jack, and we'll get her to stop."

"How will you do that? She's smart, you know. She's probably the smartest woman you'd ever meet."

Darby thought quickly, knowing she was dealing with a mental condition akin to schizophrenia. "She is smart, but I think we can get her to leave you alone."

Jack Cameron nodded and shuffled closer to Darby. Her heart was thumping in her chest but she tried not to show her fear. "That's it," she coaxed, not wanting to touch Jack for fear she'd affect his docility. He walked with his shoulders hunched, like an old man, a person who was fighting demons and was damn tired of the battle.

Jack followed Darby through the living room and down the carpeted hallway. She held open the door for him and closed it behind them. He climbed into the back seat of the Mustang without comment and lay down on the seat. As Darby started the car and before Jack Cameron passed out, he reminded her to get Buddy's food when she went back for the fish.

"Careful when you get it out of the drawer," he cautioned. "There's a goddamn loaded gun in there."

FIVE

HELEN, MITZI, AND JOHN Cameron met Darby and her sleeping passenger at Casa Cameron's massive front door. Helen and Mitzi wore looks of concern; John Cameron, a sneer of disgust. "My son, the drunk," Darby heard him mutter under his breath.

Darby and Helen helped John and together they managed to settle Jack on one of the living room's couches. "Are you sure you don't need me to stay?" Helen asked Mitzi.

"No," she said wearily, smoothing her hair with one hand. "I have Carlotta, and John..." her voice trailed off. She took a sudden breath and lifted her chin. "We're fine, really. Thank you both for your help."

Helen gave her friend a hug. She and Darby climbed into the Mustang and motored past the statue and down the winding driveway. When they were barely a stone's throw from the main house, Helen shook her head in frustration.

"What a mess. The only good thing is that you found him alive. I wasn't too sure that would be the case."

"What do you mean?"

"He's got a death wish, that boy."

Darby sensed Helen was right. She knew Jack needed more than just a sleep-it-off session on his parents' couch. He needed serious medical attention.

She remembered the loaded gun, how close she'd come to a serious confrontation, and grabbed her phone to report it. She had begun dialing when she remembered her vow.

"What are you doing?" Helen asked, as Darby pulled to the side of the road and put the Mustang in park.

"Calling Detective Briggs."

"Yes, but why did you pull over?"

Darby pictured the accident she'd witnessed on the San Diego Freeway only two weeks earlier. An SUV driven by a young lawyer had veered into the breakdown lane where he'd hit and killed a fifty-year old woman inspecting a flat tire. At the time of the crash, the driver was talking on his cell phone, discussing an upcoming trial with an associate.

"I didn't see her," he reported to the police when asked what had happened. "I just didn't see her."

Darby put up a finger as Jonas Briggs came on the line. Later, she'd explain to Helen that witnessing the accident had led her to stop her own distracted driving habits. Although she was still tempted to make a quick phone call or check an e-mail while behind the wheel, she was determined—in honor of the poor victim of the freeway accident—to leave that behavior behind.

Darby told Jonas Briggs of her encounter with Jack Cameron and the gun still present in the condo. "What were you doing there?" he asked, a briskness in his voice that was new.

"Looking for Jack. His family couldn't reach him, and I guessed he might be at Kyle's place." She paused, wondering how much she should tell the detective. "He was in the master bedroom, drunk, and obviously distraught. I convinced him to come with me and brought him home." She glanced at Helen. "I'm not a psychologist, but his behavior seems to me to be way beyond normal grief. I suggested to Mitzi Cameron that they get him some medical attention immediately."

Detective Briggs was silent. Darby wondered whether he was taking notes, or checking his e-mails, when he finally answered. "That was good advice." He took a moment more before continuing to speak. "Are you attending Kyle Cameron's memorial service tomorrow?"

"Yes."

"I'd like to talk with you after the service, if that's possible. Some new information has come to light and it affects you. I'll look for you outside the church?"

"Fine."

"Thank you, Darby." His Southern twang was noticeable when he said her name and she found herself smiling. She was about to hang up when she remembered Buddy.

"Oh! There's one more thing. Kyle Cameron had a fish—a goldfish—and no one is taking care of it."

To her surprise, the detective didn't chuckle or give a patronizing sigh. "I remember seeing that fish. Cute little guy. I'll make sure he's given a good home."

"Thanks." Darby disconnected and glanced at her passenger.

Helen raised her eyebrows. "What was that all about?"

Darby pulled back into the stream of cars, relaying Jonas Brigg's request to meet the next day and the emergence of new information.

"Now what in the hell could that be?" Helen shook her head. "I swear to God, you think you've got one thing settled and something else comes in to complicate it. Like a phone call I have to make when we get back to the house."

"To whom?"

"Marty Glickman, the broker in charge of Kyle's old office at Barnaby's. He left a message at the office saying he needs to speak to me immediately."

"Any idea what it's about?"

"Oh, yeah." Helen looked down at her nails and gave a short grunt. "I've got a good idea. I think he's steamed over Kyle's leaving Barnaby's and coming to work for me. He's worried about her listings and whether she'd told her clients she was jumping ship and coming to Near & Farr. I know Marty and he won't want to lose a single one of those properties, especially Foster McFarlin's cadre of listings. Did I tell you that girl had literally thousands of his lots for sale?"

"Seriously?"

"Absolutely. He owned ten developments in South Florida alone. Most of them were financially troubled but that wasn't anything that Kyle had to worry about. She just had to hang on to the listings, hope the economy improved, or wait for a big investor who wanted to scoop up some distressed dirt."

"So Esperanza Shores wasn't the only one in trouble?" asked Darby, as she negotiated the turn onto Driftwood.

"Esperanza Shores was just the tip of the McFarlin iceberg. He's got a nineteen-hundred-acre property inland from here designed to hold eight hundred homes. Only forty-five houses are in there, and it looks like a ghost town. No clubhouse, no pool, and no fancy five-star restaurants like Foster promised his investors. Another two are in bankruptcy. One's got house lots for nine hundred houses; Kyle sold one hundred and fifty or so of them before things soured. I'll tell you, it's a mess. Foster put so much money into these residential golf resorts, and now there aren't enough people with enough dough to play golf! He's got investors who are suing him, people who can't pay the course and association fees, and regulators looking into his sales practices. It's a bad situation."

"Where did Kyle fit in?" Darby pulled into Helen's driveway and turned off the Mustang's engine.

"Well, she made a pile of money when times were good, that's for sure. She told me once that they sold three hundred and fifty lots in a single day during the heyday. Imagine that! McFarlin would have these splashy parties, with champagne and caviar, and invite way more people than he had available lots. A kind of feeding frenzy would develop and folks would start tripping over themselves to sign on the dotted line."

She gave Darby a guilty grin. "I went to one of those parties and saw Kyle in action, working the room in her short skirt and high heels, doing the Miss Florida thing whenever she needed to woo one of the golfers." She opened her car door. "Didn't do her much good in the long run, though, did it? It didn't keep her from being some psycho's final victim."

Darby walked around the car and joined Helen on the bungalow's front porch. "Speaking of that, I wonder how Jack will take the news of the capture of Kyle's killer? He's not a well man, Helen. He's hearing voices, perhaps hallucinating."

"I'll call Mitzi and make sure she's contacted somebody with a few more initials after his name than Menendez. I hate to burden her with anything else, but this is serious. Jack could be in big trouble."

"Yes," Darby agreed. "He strikes me as a man dangling at the end of his rope."

———

Chellie Howe regarded the notice on the granite countertop with disgust. It was another lawsuit against her husband's real estate development company, McFarlin Enterprises. This one was a class-action suit alleging that Foster and his partners had schemed to sell properties based on fraudulent appraisals. She snorted. *That's a new one*, she thought. *At least this team of lawyers has some creativity.*

She left the notice untouched and made her way to the liquor cabinet. Years ago, she'd decided to let Foster and his legal advisors solve their problems without any input from her. She had too much at stake to get involved in anything that could sully her reputation or lose her votes. As it was, Foster's untimely investing decisions had cost them millions; but more to the point they'd cost Chellie in credibility with the voters. She'd adopted an innocent response, claiming that Foster was a victim of the economic downturn just like everyone else in Florida, and so far, it had worked. She frowned. This new lawsuit would not be so easy to explain away. Maybe it was time to cut Foster McFarlin loose.

And then there were his extramarital affairs.

If Chellie Howe still had any close girlfriends, they would have asked her long ago why she'd stayed married to a man who couldn't keep his hands off other women. She pondered the question in an abstract kind of way. *I'm not the only woman married to a sex-addicted man* (for that was what it was, she was sure of that) and she wasn't the first wife to turn a blind eye to the trysts. Certainly one had to look no further than the many political wives who stood by their cheating spouses. She reached into the cabinet and retrieved a bottle of single malt scotch. Did she still love Foster? She had been in love with him once, back in their college days when he'd been the star running back on the football team, but could she honestly say that she still cared for the man who wounded her to her very core?

She poured herself a glass, inhaling the pungent aroma, and sipped it slowly, letting it burn on her lips. She didn't need his money, although it had come in handy years ago. She made enough on her own now, and could easily become a high-paid consultant when her political career was over. Thank God, because Foster was going through their funds like there was no tomorrow. They had no children to keep their marriage together, no pets, and very little personal property. There wasn't much they did together, save for their public appearances for charities and political functions, but those occupied nearly every night of the week. Was that why she remained Foster McFarlin's wife? So she'd have a lousy date?

Chellie gulped the last of the scotch and got up to pour more. She knew why she stayed, and could articulate the answer because she'd asked herself the question so many times before. *The reason I put up with the humiliation year after year after year comes down to one simple word: power.* Foster had it. It emanated from his pores, hovered around him like an aura, driving Chellie mad with desire. He teetered on the edge at all times, a man totally unafraid of risk, whether it was in business or pleasure.

Chellie took a gulp of her second glass of whiskey. Foster would do just about anything to remain in control of his life. Maybe Kyle Cameron hadn't known just how ruthless he could be.

———

Mojito in hand, Helen Near strolled from the living room to the kitchen, where Darby was preparing filet of sole and a green salad. "Just spoke to Mitzi about Jack's mental state. She'll have Dr. Menendez talk to him tomorrow, after Kyle's funeral. Depending on what he thinks, they may see a specialist." She took a piece of cucumber from the salad bowl and munched on it. "Now I think I'll call Marty Glickman at Barnaby's, see what he's all annoyed about."

Darby took a sip of her Mojito and smiled. "You get your work done, girl. Don't worry about me."

Helen smiled. "It's so nice to have a visitor. I almost feel like the old days, when Jane would come by and we'd raise hell." She sighed. "I still have a hard time realizing that she's gone."

Darby watched Helen retreat to the living room and thought about the last time she'd seen her Aunt Jane. It had been only a month or so before, in Maine, that she'd stood beside her comatose body in the hospital, yet it seemed like a lifetime ago. So much had happened on that trip, and now this one was proving to be just as eventful.

Squeezing some fresh lemon on the sole, Darby carefully patted it with flour and set it aside. She'd wait to see how long Helen's phone conversation took before cooking the sole in butter and olive oil. Meanwhile, she chopped some parsley and prepared a light, lemony sauce. *Sole meuniere*, she said to herself, realizing that without meaning to, she was making a version of a French classic which her mother had often prepared. She smiled, remembering her petite Japanese mother bent over the stove, preparing yet another of Julia Child's recipes. Jada Farr had lived her passion for creating fine food, and Darby and her father had been the lucky recipients of that passion.

Darby's thoughts were interrupted by the sound of Helen's voice in the next room.

"Go ahead and try, Marty, but you won't get anywhere!"

Darby didn't want to eavesdrop, but it was impossible to ignore Helen's words and angry tone of voice.

"Don't you threaten me. Look, as far as I'm concerned, this conversation is over." The phone receiver hit something hard. Moments later Helen stormed into the kitchen, her short hair standing straight up like the bristles on a boar's head brush.

"That man is such a jerk! No wonder poor Kyle wanted out of there. He's an absolute ass, that's what he is. Ugh!" She stomped back into the living room and returned with her Mojito. After taking a gulp, she explained.

"You probably guessed that was Marty Glickman. He claims that Tag Gunnerson's assistant—the guy I talked to—consulted with a Barnaby's broker, Peter Janssen, about a year ago. They discussed the listing of St. Andrew's Isle. He says that Peter then referred the listing to Kyle, and that she had promised to pay a hefty referral fee. He's just found out about our appointment for tomorrow, and needless to say, he's enraged. He says that listing belongs to Barnaby's."

Darby regarded Helen thoughtfully. Unfortunately, disputes over clients were common everywhere, although she'd managed to avoid getting tangled up in any conflicts in California. Not that Darby Farr wasn't competitive: she hadn't risen to the top of the ladder in the lucrative Southern California market by being a pushover. It was more that Darby was a consummate professional, and to her, these disputes brought up the seamier side of real estate: the side consumed by greed.

Helen let out a big sigh. "I hate these kinds of things, but Darby, I know that Kyle would have mentioned any referrals to me. Something about this just doesn't make sense."

Darby heated the oil and butter in a pan. "Is this referral agreement in writing?"

Helen nodded. "So Glickman says. He's sending it to me tomorrow." She watched as Darby began to gently sauté the sole.

"Kyle told me about this listing. Not in so many words, but she told me she was getting a fabulous property once she left Barnaby's. I'm sure it was St. Andrew's Isle, and I know she didn't want them having any part of it."

"Who is the other broker?"

"Janssen? In his sixties, fairly successful. He's nice enough, although too much of a salesman type for my taste." She shook her head. "Why in the world would he have given Kyle the listing in the first place? I mean, you don't just give away a forty- or fifty-million-dollar property, now do you?"

Darby watched as her friend took a deep breath and made an effort to calm herself.

"That fish smells absolutely delicious. I'll be damned if I'm going to let that idiot Marty Glickman ruin my dinner. We'll

straighten the whole thing out tomorrow when we meet with Tag."
Helen sat down at the table and giggled. "Listen to that, Darby!
The best golfer in the whole damn world and I just called him
'Tag', like I've known him my whole life."

Darby brought the platter of *sole meuniere* to the table and
took a seat.

"You know how it goes, Helen. Once you sell his house, you'll
be his new best friend. I wouldn't be surprised if you get to play a
few rounds with him."

Helen picked up her fork and grinned. "That would be great,"
she said, scooping up a piece of the sole. "I'd like to talk to him
about his chip shot. Seems to me he's turning his wrist."

———

Chellie Howe got the call from her press secretary just as she was
preparing for an infrequent night at home with order-in Chinese
food and a movie.

"What is it?" she snapped, wishing for the hundredth time that
she could unplug all the devices that kept her wired to her staff all
hours of the day and night. She was alone—Foster was in Miami
at a baseball game and wouldn't be back until tomorrow—and
craving some quiet.

"The Stuart police have the Kondo Killer in custody," Mindy
Jackson said. "They got him just an hour ago. A guy named Cyril
Shank, ex-con with a long list of priors. I'm at Esperanza Shores
with the gathering multitude. Thought you'd want to get over here
and say something."

Chellie rose to her feet. "Damn right. Who's there?"

"WCVB and WLKZ are on their way. I'll get the rest of them, don't worry. Your statement is already written. Want a car?"

"No, I'm planning to walk, Mindy! Of course I want a car." She strode toward her closet and glanced at her clothes. "E-mail me what I'm saying. I'll be ready in two minutes." Chellie grabbed a few hangers with dry cleaned suits and chose a flattering but conservative charcoal gray jacket and pants in a light summer silk. She dressed quickly, and then grabbed her make-up bag and Smartphone and bolted down the stairs.

The car was waiting outside the townhouse. Chellie yanked open the door and slid across the seat. "Go ahead," she ordered, snapping open a compact and brushing her nose and chin with pressed powder. The rest of her make-up application took only minutes, as did her review of her statement. She changed a word or two and took a deep breath as the car pulled up in front of the condo unit where Kyle Cameron's mangled body had been discovered the day before. She glanced at the news vans and crews and gritted her teeth. "Showtime," she said softly, opening her car door.

Mindy Jackson was at her side like a shadow. "You're on right after Detective Briggs," she said, guiding Chellie toward a phalanx of camera crews and reporters. "Tallahassee said to say the usual." She paused, frowning. "Don't take any questions."

Chellie flashed her aide a look. She knew Mindy's concern stemmed from her ever-present worries about Foster and his inability to keep his pants on. "I can handle the press," she said.

Mindy shrugged. "Do what you want. You're the one who thinks she's going to run for governor next fall."

Chellie bit back a retort as they arrived at the cluster of cameras, reporters, and curious onlookers. Jonas Briggs, one of the hunkiest cops in Florida, was standing next to the Sarasota Police Commissioner. Chellie caught Briggs' eye and gave him a hint of a smile, then pursed her lips and listened as the Commissioner cleared his throat and began.

"At fourteen hundred hours today a task force from Stuart, Florida, raided a property and apprehended a suspect in the stabbing deaths of three real estate agents." He looked up from his notes and fixed the cameras with a somber stare. "A warrant to search the property was issued only an hour before the search, using intelligence gathered by departments on both coasts, as well as the Florida Office of Statewide Intelligence. Evidence found inside the home was sufficient for the law enforcement officials present to apprehend the occupant. The suspect was alone and taken by surprise. He is now in custody in Stuart and awaiting charges."

"I'd like to recognize and commend the collaborative work by all of the Serenidad Key police and homicide detectives and Stuart and Daytona Beach detectives and prosecutors in their efforts to track down and bring to justice the person believed to be responsible for the death of three young women, one of them our very own Kyle Cameron of Serenidad Key. I hope this arrest provides in some small measure a level of relief and comfort to her family and friends."

Jonas Briggs stepped up to the microphone as the Commissioner moved aside. "I believe Lieutenant Governor Chellie Howe has some words before I take your questions," he said.

Chellie nodded and moved smoothly to the microphone. Ever the gentleman, Jonas Briggs was letting her go first.

"Thank you, Detective Briggs and Commissioner Conrad," she said. She fixed the cameras with a steely gaze. "Let this be a message to anyone who would use deadly violence on our streets. The state of Florida will spare no effort to identify you and we will use our finest forces to catch you. The hardworking men and women who worked this case did so around the clock to achieve this goal, and they will continue those efforts until we bring justice to the victims' families." She paused. "Both Governor Harris and I wish to thank our law enforcement departments, as well as the OSI, for their thorough and timely work."

The reporters shouted questions and Chellie could not resist staying in the camera's bright glare for a few moments more. "I'll take your questions," she said, pointing at Dan Hughes, one of her favorite reporters. He began to speak when another voice, brash, insistent, and several decibels louder, drowned him out.

"Any truth to the rumor that your husband, developer Foster McFarlin was having an affair with the deceased, Kyle Cameron?"

She tasted bitter bile in her throat and fought to keep her composure. "No comment," she snapped, stepping aside and giving Jonas Briggs a quick glance. He had read the situation and was already grabbing the microphone and assuming control.

"Let me tell you what we do know, Ladies and Gentlemen."

Chellie felt the arm of Mindy, thin but surprisingly strong, yanking her through the crowds and back to the waiting car. She bent and sank gratefully onto the leather seat, heard the noise of the crowd abruptly cease as the car door slammed shut. Mindy's advice to avoid questions had been correct. Chellie closed her eyes and fumed. *I should have listened.*

———

The capture of the Kondo Killer led the stories on the ten o'clock news. Helen had gone to bed, exhausted from a long day dealing with Mitzi, and complaining of an all-over achiness in her chest and shoulders. Darby made herself a cup of organic chamomile tea and listened to Sarasota's police commissioner laud the work of the various law enforcement agencies responsible for capturing the Kondo Killer, now identified as Cyril Shank.

She watched as a petite blonde woman took the microphone and began speaking in a forceful manner, gesturing with a pointed finger toward the crowd.

"Chellie Howe," Darby read aloud from the title underneath the woman's image. So this was the woman who held the position of Lieutenant Governor of the state, and was Foster McFarlin's wife, too. Darby listened as she emphasized the need for a tougher attitude on crime in Florida. "There are other Kondo Killers out there," Chellie warned. "We've got to get them where they live."

Darby switched off the television and headed down the hall to her room. Grabbing her cell phone, she called ET and was pleased to hear his melodic voice.

"I figure you're just settling down to watch 'Stage My House,'" she teased. "Am I right?"

He gave a low chuckle. "Close. An intriguing series on how to renovate the classic American split-level. Who knew a raised ranch could look this good?"

Darby laughed. "Any luck on my Florida license?"

She heard the rustle of papers. "Yes, and luck is the operable word. Just this year the Sunshine State decided to include California as one of the ten states for which they offer mutual recognition of licenses."

"So what does that mean?"

"You need to take—and pass—a Florida-specific real estate law examination. Forty questions, each one point in value. A grade of thirty points or higher and you're licensed."

"Good work. Any idea where and when I can take it?"

"Again good fortune has smiled on you, Darby Farr. There is a test on Thursday in Sarasota."

"And—"

"And you are already signed up." ET was quiet for a moment. "I want to thank you again for offering to help me. You can't imagine what the loan of this money means to me—and my family."

"Listen, ET, we're a team. Thanks to you, I'm able to go jetting off on these trips. How else could I manage my clients and their deals?" She stifled a yawn. "I'd better get some sleep. I've got to study for my test."

"You will ace it." His voice grew husky. "I do hope you are taking your safety seriously."

"I'm not in any danger," Darby replied. "The murderer has been captured." The image of Kyle Cameron's pulverized body flashed into her mind and she shuddered. The serial killer was in police custody; she and other real estate agents across the state were out of harm's way. And yet why did ET's admonishment give her the chills?

SIX

DARBY FARR WAS STEPPING into her sneakers for an early morning run when her cell phone rang. She answered it quickly, before it could rouse Helen, and was surprised to hear the voice of Detective Jonas Briggs.

"Sorry to phone you at the crack of dawn, Darby, but I know you are an early riser. I'm wondering if we could meet sometime this morning, before Kyle's service. I've got a lot on my plate but I'd really like to speak with you."

"I'm just about to head out for a run. Would you like me to meet you somewhere now?"

"That would be super. How about where I spotted you last time, in front of the Belle Haven. Sound okay to you?"

"Sure. I'll be there in fifteen minutes."

"Fine." He paused. "As a police detective, I can't resist telling you to be careful."

"Thanks." She hung up, wondering at the note of anxiety in Jonas Briggs' voice.

Darby pounded down the streets surrounding Helen's little bungalow before cutting over toward the heart of town. It was already hot and humid, and she marveled that Floridians could take the sultry heat day after day. She remembered her aunt Jane, adjusting to her first few Maine winters, and smiled. Cold or hot, it wasn't easy to reset an internal thermometer. Little wonder Jane Farr had favored thick wool sweaters year round in Hurricane Harbor.

Belle Haven—or rather the site where Belle Haven had been— looked even more forlorn than before. Trash was piled in a corner of the lot and a pile of bricks that had once comprised the chimney spilled onto the sidewalk. The smell of burnt timbers and the odor of grease mingled and hung rank in the still air. Darby wondered if Jonas Briggs was any closer to figuring out how the destructive blaze had begun.

A touch on her elbow caused her to jump.

"Are you waiting for Detective Briggs?" It was a uniformed police officer in her twenties, with curly red hair and freckles. She smiled and held out her hand. "I'm Kelly McGee from the department. Detective Briggs was held up a few moments. He asked me to take you around the corner to his favorite breakfast place and he'll be along very shortly." She smiled again. "It's a quick walk and they have fabulous sticky buns. He asked me to order him one."

Darby smiled at the police officer's enthusiasm. "Sure. Sticky buns are high on my list of favorite foods as well."

On the walk to the restaurant, Kelly McGee told Darby about her childhood in Philadelphia, her years at the Police Academy, and the admiration she had for Detective Jonas Briggs. "He's just one of those guys who is so nice, you know what I mean? He doesn't need to be Mr. Macho all the time, and that's refreshing, especially in a cop."

Darby nodded, but Kelly wasn't finished.

"He's a hard worker, too. The way he cracked this condo murder case? Really impressive. He worked with some other departments, but I know he was the one who pulled it all together." She blushed. "Here he comes now."

Darby looked down the street and saw the muscular figure of Jonas Briggs jogging to meet them. He was wearing tan pants and a white shirt with a navy jacket zipped halfway up. The nautical style seemed to suit him.

The detective stopped in front of them, removed his jacket, and wiped his brow. "Whew. It's hot already." He pointed at the restaurant's façade. "You two didn't get that far. Was she late for our appointment, Officer McGee?"

The redhead shook her curls and blushed more deeply. "No, sir. We were having a little chat as we walked here." She smiled at Darby and gave Jonas a shy glance. "I'm headed back to the station for the Wednesday department meeting. Enjoy your um … sticky bun."

Jonas Briggs thanked her and turned to Darby, oblivious to the young officer's parting glance.

"Thanks for coming down. Let's grab a table and some coffee."

Briggs ushered Darby into the restaurant and chose a table in the corner. The scent of cinnamon was so strong she could taste it. The detective placed an order, and, when the waitress had left, reached into the pocket of his jacket and pulled out a photograph.

"Ever seen this man?"

It was a mug shot of a man in his sixties, with a haggard face and gray streaked hair badly in need of a trim. Darby looked at it carefully but did not recognize the face.

"No."

Detective Briggs nodded as if he'd been expecting Darby's answer. "This is Clyde Hensley," he said, waving the glossy image, "He's on parole from a prison in Texas. We suspect he's been involved in quite a few illegal activities over the years, but the one the guys on the panhandle finally nabbed him on was running an unlicensed tourist business. You see, Mr. Hensley's got himself a boat, some cable and a parasail. Our friend here had a good thing going—he'd get money up front, take people up for thirty minutes or so, and then drink it away in a bar that night. Just one problem: once in a while his cable—which of course he never inspects—snaps. And then it's good-bye parasailors." He looked up as the waitress arrived with their coffees and sticky buns. "Last time his customers just got roughed up. This time, they weren't so lucky."

"What happened?"

Jonas Briggs' face grew sober. "Young girl, twenty-one years old, here with her boyfriend having some fun in the sun. They take a ride with Hensley, his cable snaps, and the couple drifts—right into some electrical wires. The young lady was killed."

Darby put down her coffee cup. "That's horrible."

"For her as well as her boyfriend. She was electrocuted before his very eyes." Detective Briggs spooned two heaping teaspoonfuls of sugar into his coffee and sighed. "Luckily he was able to give us a description of Hensley. This time, we'll be able to put him away for a long time."

"So he's still at large?"

"Unfortunately, yes. The incident—ah heck, the tragedy—happened Monday."

Darby was silent. She felt for the young couple whose only mistake had been to choose the wrong parasail operator. She sipped her coffee and waited for the detective to resume his story.

"Now, where does Darby Farr come into all this?" Jonas Briggs took a gulp of his coffee. "I'll tell you after you have a bite or two of that bun."

The pastry was flaky and studded with cinnamon and raisins and covered with a light glaze. "Fabulous," Darby commented after taking a bite. "I'm going to have to run all day to work it off, but it is delicious."

Jonas Briggs laughed. "Life is too short to worry about sugar," he said. "That's my motto." He took another gulp of coffee. "I wanted to speak to you because when we searched Hensley's apartment we found some photographs." He reached in his jacket. "This one I think you will recognize."

Darby picked up the glossy black and white and saw herself. She had her sunglasses on, head down, pocketbook on her shoulder, and was walking past two or three café tables. She didn't need to look at the image for more than a second before she knew the time and place it was taken. "That was yesterday, at Jack Cameron's restaurant. Helen and I went there for lunch, around twelve o'clock." Darby looked at the photo again. "This was taken when we were leaving. I'd say the photographer was seated at the bar."

"That's right." Jonas Briggs reached for the photograph. "The question is, why did he take a photograph of you?"

Darby frowned. "I have no idea."

Jonas Briggs took another bite of his sticky bun and chewed thoughtfully. "The bartender confirmed Hensley was sitting at the bar while you and Helen were having lunch. When you left, he asked who you were, but the bartender—his name is Marco—didn't know." He spread his hands on the checkered tablecloth. "There's more to the puzzle. In Hensley's apartment we found dozens and dozens of photographs of another person—Kyle Cameron."

Darby felt a chill come over her. She searched the detective's face to see his reaction but his expression was impassive.

"Kyle? What was she doing?"

"Everyday life. Running errands, going to work, meeting people for dinner... Looking at the images, I estimate that Clyde Hensley spent a good part of his day—for several weeks—following her around and snapping pictures."

"She never knew?"

"Nah. We found his lenses. Telephoto, so chances are she never even saw him."

"So what's the connection between Kyle and this man?"

"Now you're asking the million-dollar question." He took another bite of his sticky bun, chewed some more, and wiped his mouth with a napkin.

"What is the link between them? So far, we haven't been able to establish anything. Hensley gets out of jail in Texas, comes to Florida, establishes his fly-by-night parasailing operation, and starts taking pictures of Kyle Cameron. She gets killed and a day later he takes photos of you. Why?"

Darby shook her head. "I wish I could help you. I don't have any idea."

Jonas Briggs signaled for the waitress to bring the check. "I'll be keeping an eye on you while you're here. We haven't found Hensley yet and perhaps he's not finished shadowing you. I owe it to the family of that poor girl to find him as quickly as possible."

Darby nodded. "At least the Kondo Killer is in custody. That must be a relief to your department."

Jonas Briggs gave the waitress his credit card and waited for her to depart. "That brings us to the last thing you need to know. I'm telling you something in strictest confidence." He paused. "I do not believe Kyle's murder has been solved."

"You mean the Kondo Killer wasn't captured?"

"Cyril Shank? Oh, he was captured alright. And there is little doubt he committed two murders on the East Coast, and possibly more." Jonas Briggs paused. "But in my opinion, he was not the man who killed Kyle Cameron."

"What are you saying? Someone else murdered Kyle?"

Jonas Briggs looked off to the side then back at Darby. "I'm afraid I can't give you all the details. But there are certain elements of the crime—certain signature elements—that have made me suspicious from the beginning." His face hardened. "My superiors don't share my point of view, but I don't think the Kondo Killer was Kyle's murderer. I think she was intended to look like one of his victims."

"A copycat?"

"Exactly. Which means—" he looked directly into her face and his expression was grim. "Kyle Cameron's killer is still out there."

"Clyde Hensley?"

"I don't know. It doesn't fit what we know of his profile, but he was obviously following Kyle for several weeks. Could he be the killer? And if he is, are you his next target?"

———

Helen Near steered her Lexus onto the causeway to St. Andrew's Isle, paused at the gatehouse, and gave a low whistle. "Holy cow," she breathed, slapping Darby on the shoulder. "Take a look at this approach. Is this incredible, or what?"

Darby smiled at Helen's enthusiasm, happy to shake the feeling of foreboding she'd felt since speaking with Jonas Briggs. Before them was a palm-tree lined drive, perfectly landscaped, curving gently around undulating acres of lush green grass.

"Would I ever love to play this private course," Helen whispered, as the gatekeeper verified their appointment and waved them on. She stepped on the gas and started down the winding drive. "Course we don't have time today, with Kyle's funeral and all, not to mention the fact that you've got to hit the books and study."

The Lexus' wheels hugged the road as they curved around a bend. Before them was a lovely terra-cotta colored home with an orange tiled roof, set back from the links and bordered by beautifully landscaped pools. The turquoise water sparkled as a casually dressed man in tan pants and a golf shirt sauntered up to the car.

"Justin," he said, giving them a smile. "Justin Fleischman. I work for Mr. Gunnerson here at the guesthouse."

"Guesthouse," said Helen, shaking her head. "And here I thought it was the main residence."

Justin Fleischman laughed. "You're not the only one to think that," he said. "Even Mr. Gunnerson admits it's a little on the large side." He pointed at the driveway. "The main house is further up the road. Don't worry, you'll know it."

Helen resumed her slow drive up the roadway, coming around a bend bordered by huge bougainvilleas in brilliant shades of red. Before them was a magnificent Mediterranean-style home, similar in appearance to the guesthouse, only many times its size.

"It's the little place on steroids," commented Helen, climbing out of the Lexus with an admiring grin. "Check out that fountain. The tile work alone is unbelievable."

Darby followed her gaze to a curving tiled wall holding a shallow pool from which a spray of water cascaded. It was placed squarely in the center of the circular drive, a beautiful backdrop for visitors as they parked their cars.

"My goodness," Helen exclaimed, slamming her car door. "This is going to be one fun listing."

They walked toward a massive front door made of weathered, wide-planked wood, which was opened almost immediately by a small man with a receding hairline and wire-rimmed glasses. "You're here," he said, allowing them to enter the cool foyer. Arches framed a wrought-iron stairway that contrasted with the bleached stucco walls. "Tag!" he yelled up the stairs. "The real estate brokers are here."

He gave a quick nervous smile. "I'm Bernie Schultz. Tag will be down in a minute."

He led Helen and Darby to a grand living room with rustic wooden beams against white-washed walls. They sat down on a worn leather couch with vibrant red and yellow pillows while Bernie Schultz looked anxiously toward the door. "He's got appointments all day," he confided. "It isn't the easiest thing to keep him on track."

"Keep me on track? Are you complaining again, Schultz?" The tall, larger-than-life persona of one of the world's most recognizable golfers filled the room, and both women found themselves rising to their feet.

"Ladies, ladies, no need to get up," Tag Gunnerson boomed. He was tanned and boyishly handsome, with a full head of thick blonde hair and wide shoulders. He had an athlete's trim but powerful physique, and the muscles in his arms and thighs rippled under his well-tailored clothes. He was bigger than Darby imagined, and, as he reached out to shake both their hands, the force of his grip was strong and confident. *Magnetic*, Darby thought.

Tag Gunnerson cocked a thumb in Bernie Schultz's direction and grinned. "I keep him around because he reminds me of that old World War Two show, 'Hogan's Heroes.' Remember Schultz? The fat guy with the mustache?" He chuckled.

Bernie Schultz gave a shrug as if he'd heard the joke many times before. "Tag, these are the brokers from Near & Farr Realty."

"Yes, yes," Tag said, motioning for them to sit. "Kyle Cameron's friends."

Helen nodded. "Yes, I was quite fond of Kyle." She smoothed her skirt, and Darby knew she was composing herself. Meeting an idol didn't happen every day, but Darby could tell she was determined to remain professional.

"I'm Helen Near, and this is my colleague, Darby Farr. Unfortunately, Darby didn't get the opportunity to meet Kyle." Helen tried to give a bright smile. "Your home and grounds are beautiful, Mr. Gunnerson."

"Please, call me Tag." He gave an affable smile and looked around. "It is a pretty place. Thanks for saying so."

"May I ask why you are interested in selling?"

Tag nodded. "Sure. It's no secret that I've been helping care for my nephew Charlie since he was born. He's got a rare form of leukemia, and it's a lot for Gretchen—that's my sister—to handle. As much as my schedule permits, I like to help out." He raised his eyebrows, all mirth gone from his demeanor. "I want to be closer to them, and they live outside of Phoenix. Long story short, I'm relocating to Arizona."

Bernie Schultz gave a small cough. "Tag's career allows him to live anywhere as long as there are challenging golf courses nearby."

"Which there certainly are in south central Arizona," said Helen.

"Have you played there?" asked Tag.

"Several times. I love the Scottsdale courses, especially Whisper Rock, Troon, and the Desert Mountain Club."

"I'm impressed," Tag said. "None of them are easy holes."

"I'm not a big fan of easy."

Tag laughed. "Me neither." He turned to Bernie. "Go through the paperwork with Helen, Schultz, and take her on the grand tour of St. Andrew's Isle. Anyone who knows Arizona golfing like she does is the one for me." He turned to Darby. "I understand you may be helping Mr. Kobayashi should he decide to buy this place."

Darby nodded. "I've got to get some licensing requirements out of the way, but once that's done, I'd be happy to represent him. Is he in Florida now?"

"He will be here on Friday and asked if I might set up a meeting with you. He's pleased to work with someone who shares his ethnicity."

"I'm sure Helen told you that I'm only half Japanese, on my mother's side."

"Half's a whole lot more than nothing is the way I see it." Tag Gunnerson turned to Bernie. "Give Darby the details on Kobayashi's flights and set up a convenient time for them to get together." He smiled his expansive smile and rose to his feet. "Now, if you'll excuse me, I need to speak to my agent about some upcoming tour dates." He grinned and pointed a finger at Helen, cocking it as if it were a gun. "I very much look forward to working with you."

"Likewise, Tag." Helen lifted her briefcase. "We'll discuss pricing options some other time?"

"Nah." Tag Gunnerson grinned. "That's what I've got old Schultz for." He glanced at his watch and waved. "*Adios*, ladies. Hit 'em straight and long."

They watched as he strode out of the room.

"Well," Bernie Schultz said, giving another of his delicate coughs. "Tag has spoken, so let's get the show on the road. I believe you met Justin Fleischman. He's waiting to take you through the houses and grounds." He eyed Helen's briefcase. "Have you brought the listing papers?"

Helen nodded and pulled them out.

"And what price are you suggesting?"

"Forty-five million," Helen said. "We may adjust that after we see the property, but I think you'll find our analysis to be quite thorough."

"Very good. I'll go over everything with Tag and call you tonight or tomorrow." He handed Darby a disk. "Hideki Kobayashi's itinerary as well as some background information that may be helpful." He rose to his feet. "You ladies will see that Tag is a very hands-off client. He'll trust the number you've come up with and will expect the transaction with Kobayashi—if indeed he decides to go forth—to be a smooth one." He gave a condescending smile. "I doubt that many of your sellers are as easy to deal with."

Helen and Darby both stood. Helen extended her hand and smiled.

"I look forward to working with you, Bernie. Call me and we'll get the show on the road as you suggested."

Darby thanked him for the disk and his time. She paused as they were heading out of the room.

"Bernie, I have a quick question. Was this property ever offered to Barnaby's International Realty?"

He stopped and thought a moment. "Last year I called Barnaby's and a gentleman—Peter? Paul?—came out to meet us. He was nice enough, but Tag wasn't quite ready to sell, so that's where it ended."

"Did you contact Barnaby's recently? When Tag decided it was time to list the property?"

"Yes. I called them to get in touch with Kyle Cameron. She was the one Tag wanted."

"Had Kyle contacted Tag?"

"He met her at a charity dinner a few months ago, and asked me to set something up. She was supposed to come to a little cocktail party Tag hosted Monday night. Of course, given what happened, she didn't show." He shrugged. "She must have told him she was joining your agency, or he wouldn't have asked me to call you." He gave them an expectant look, clearly ready to be done with all the questions. "And now if you're through, Justin is waiting…"

"Yes," Darby said, following Helen back into the tiled foyer. "We're ready to take the tour."

―――――

When they were back in Helen's Lexus and zooming away from St. Andrew's Isle, Helen looked at Darby and gave her big, booming laugh.

"Can you believe that place? What about the movie theatre? Pretty nifty!"

"I'd rather watch Hitchcock movies than endless rounds of golf, but it was cool." Darby glanced up at the canopy of palms that lined the roadway. "The house is magnificent, but I really loved the gardens. The way they were so private, as if they were little secret hideaways."

Helen gave another booming laugh. "The whole place is amazing. A killer listing, that's what Kyle would have said." She glanced over at Darby, her eyes dancing. "Tag doesn't even want to talk price! So I have to put up with that prissy assistant Bernie, but who cares?"

Darby agreed. "Tag's whole focus is on his game and getting to Arizona. Wouldn't it be nice if all our clients were that uncomplicated?"

"No kidding." Helen's look turned shrewd. "I've been thinking about how we can handle your representation of Mr. Kobayashi. Do you really have to go to all the trouble of taking that exam?"

Darby laughed. "Yes! If I want to stay on the right side of the Florida Real Estate commission, I have to play by the rules." She grinned. "It's no big deal, Helen. I'll study after the service and take the test on Thursday morning. Believe me, I do not want to pass up the chance to help Mr. Kobayashi buy St. Andrew's Isle."

"Gotcha. Hey, how about that whole discussion regarding Barnaby's? It certainly doesn't sound like they had any real client relationship with Tag."

"I agree. Maybe Marty Glickman is posturing, hoping to end up with some of the money. It would be interesting to talk to the other broker—what did you say his name was?"

"Peter Janssen. I'm sure you'll get your chance, Darby. I'm betting he'll be at Kyle's service." She checked her watch. "We've just got time to get dressed. I'd have a quick sandwich, but Mitzi will have plenty of food at Casa Cameron. She always puts out a big spread."

Darby glanced out the window. Coconut palms had given way to large slash pines.

"It's not going to be an easy time for Jack," Darby noted, watching a blue heron swoop over the roadway, a small fish in his beak. "Maybe once the service is over, he'll seek some professional help."

"Maybe," Helen said darkly. "If it isn't already too late."

———

"You've got to pull it together, hear me, Jack? Two hours of your precious time—that's not a lot to ask. Then you can go and drink yourself into oblivion, if that's what you want." John Cameron's handsome features were contorted in a sarcastic snarl. His hands, balled into tight fists, were on his hips. He tapped his foot, impatient to rejoin the guests gathered to remember Kyle Cameron, one of whom was a very pretty and very well-endowed sales associate from Barnaby's.

"Yeah, yeah," Jack muttered, rising from his prone position on the bed. His eyes darted to the bedside table, looking for the bottle of antidepressants Dr. Menendez had prescribed. Gone. No doubt his mother had removed them earlier in the day.

He waved a heavy arm in his father's direction. "Go on, I'm coming." His voice was flat, but if his father cared or noticed, he said nothing.

"Fine. I'll tell your mother you are on your way."

Jack watched the tall man turn and leave, his suit impeccably tailored, face tanned and healthy looking. Not like his own, blotched and bloated with grief.

Kyle was gone. She was really, truly, gone, and he would never have the chance to say goodbye, much less tell her how sorry he was that he had ruined everything. Now that the voices in his head had stopped, he could sense the raw pain of her death just below the drug-induced numbness. She was not coming back, not ever, and he knew that was a truth he couldn't face.

Tomorrow, he thought. If I can make it until tomorrow...

He lurched up from the bed and loped to a mirror to adjust his tie. He finger combed his hair and slapped some color into his face. He looked like hell, but it would have to do. One more day, he promised himself. Just one more day.

———

"Are you Ms. Farr? Ms. Darby Farr?"

A pleasant-looking man in his early sixties approached Darby as she stood by a table laden with salads, cold-cuts, and trays of sliced fruits.

"I am," she answered, surveying the man. He wore a navy suit with a crimson tie, and held what looked to be a glass of whiskey. "And you are …?"

"Peter Janssen, from Barnaby's." He held out his hand and gave a brief smile. "I am—I was—a friend of Kyle's."

"I've heard your name, Mr. Janssen. I'm sorry for the loss of your colleague."

He swallowed hard and the pleasantness left his face. "Thank you. This is—very difficult." He sighed and seemed to collect his emotions. "Won't you call me Peter? I was headed for the verandah, and I'd love it if you'd join me."

Darby threaded her way through the groups of people, amazed at how many mourners had come out to Casa Cameron for the reception following Kyle's funeral. "She was obviously well-known," Darby commented, as Peter stopped in a relatively quiet spot on one end of the porch.

"Well-known and well-loved," said Janssen, pausing to indicate even more clusters of people assembled across Casa Cameron's verdant lawns. "Everyone liked Kyle. You couldn't help it. She was sunny, energetic, and a hell of a real estate broker." He pointed at a wrought iron bench. "Care for a seat?"

"Thank you." Darby sat down, her glass of Chardonnay in hand. She took a sip and regarded Peter Janssen.

"How long did you work with Kyle?"

"Six years at Barnaby's, but we knew each other before that. You know how it is in real estate. You end up doing deals with other brokers, some of whom you like and respect, others whom you keep an extra sharp eye on. Kyle was one of the best. She was thorough and communicative. Working with her was a pleasure."

"She certainly had her hands full with all of Foster McFarlin's properties."

"Indeed. But she wasn't daunted by the prospect. Kyle enjoyed a challenge, and she would have weathered this economic downturn just fine. If only she had had the chance."

He shook his head sadly and took a sip of his cocktail. "Why she insisted on doing open houses alone is beyond me. I'd offered to help her, numerous times, but she always said she'd be fine. You know that real estate can be dangerous, especially for women. Maybe it's different in other markets, but down here it's a gamble." He paused. "I wish to hell I had been there, so I could have protected her from that psycho." He drained his drink and the bitterness left his voice once more. "You're from Maine, right? Here to help out Helen Near?"

"Actually, I grew up in Maine, but my home is Southern California now." She took another sip of her wine. "Helen is an old friend of my family's, and we reconnected a short while ago after the death of my aunt, Jane Farr."

"You're Jane's niece?" Peter gave a broad smile as Darby nodded. "Well, I'll be damned. So you're the one she went to Maine to take care of." He grinned again. "Tell you what. Let me refresh our drinks, and then I'll tell you some stories about that rascally aunt of yours."

Darby smiled, wondering whether she had a choice in the first place. A few moments later he returned, new drinks in hand. He passed her another Chardonnay, which she placed on a nearby planter. Peter Janssen took a swig of his whiskey and turned to Darby.

"I met Jane Farr when I was first starting out in real estate," he said, smiling at the memory. "I had some young clients looking to buy their first house—a tiny little place over in Bradenton. We put in an offer, and Jane flat out refused it. I'll never forget what she said. 'What's the matter with you, Janssen? Don't you want to make even a little money here?'" He laughed, throwing back his head to reveal rows of perfectly white, capped teeth. "And that was my first introduction to Jane Farr." He shook his head. "She was quite something."

Darby gave a rueful grin. She was becoming used to the stories about her aunt's prowess as a broker both in Maine and in Florida. It seems everyone who'd worked with the wolfish Jane Farr had some sort of story, and usually more than one, and they often highlighted her aunt's less-than-flattering qualities.

"What about Kyle?" she prompted, searching Janssen's lightly creased face. Like everyone in Florida, his skin was bronzed and he radiated sunny good health.

His manner changed from playful to somber in a flash. He tilted back his head and downed his drink, and when he looked back at Darby, his brown eyes were sorrowful.

"What can I say? Kyle was my friend as well as my partner. We worked together very closely for six years, and I'll miss her more than I can say." He rose heavily to his feet. "Forgive me, Darby, but I think I need to pay my respects to the Camerons and go home. I've enjoyed meeting you and reminiscing about your aunt. How long are you here in Sarasota?"

"Just a few days more," she said, rising to meet him. "Good bye, and again, I'm sorry for your loss." She watched the older man walk slowly away, his shoulders hunched in grief. A moment later, there was a tap on her elbow.

"Miss Farr?"

A short, stocky woman with a stylish short haircut stood before her. She held out her hand. "I am Sassa Jorgensen. I was Kyle's massage therapist."

Her words were accented—German? Scandinavian? Darby watched as she bit her lip, as if holding back her emotion.

"How nice to meet you."

She nodded. After a few moments she took a breath and said in a soft voice, "I must speak to someone. It is information about Kyle."

"You need to speak to the police. Detective Jonas Briggs—"

"I saw your name in Kyle's appointment book."

Darby raised her eyebrows in surprise and the older woman nodded. "I know she was going to meet with you and Ms. Near. When I came to her house on Monday, she asked me first to read her afternoon appointments. She wanted to have them in her mind so that then she could relax for the massage." She paused. "I'm not sure if this is information for the police, or not. Maybe you could tell me."

Darby exhaled and steered Sassa Jorgensen to a nearby corner of the verandah that offered some privacy. "I'm willing to listen, but I will go to the police if it is information they need to know."

She nodded. "I visited Kyle every Monday. Every single Monday, unless she was on a trip somewhere. I have given her massages for two years. I know her—knew her. I knew her body."

Darby listened, wondering what the older woman was trying to say.

"I mean, I would know if some change in her body was happening."

"Like an illness?" *Perhaps that was why Kyle had decided to leave Barnaby's.*

"Yes. Like an illness. Or something that is not an illness, but that creates changes..."

Darby grasped the massage therapist's meaning.

"Pregnancy?"

Sassa nodded. "Yes," she said softly. "I have noticed changes for several weeks now, and this week I was certain. The glow of her face, the new roundness of her hips and breasts... I have seen it before, many times, and I know the early signs. I am sure Kyle Cameron was going to have a baby."

Darby swallowed. Pregnancy could certainly have accounted for Kyle's decision to leave the fast-paced Barnaby's International Realty and go to work for Helen.

"Kyle never actually told you she was pregnant?"

"No. She didn't have to. I knew without her telling me." She nodded, remembering. "My first clue was a few weeks ago. Suddenly she was sensitive to the scent of a lotion, something we had used for months and months. I had to find another kind, it bothered her so much." She sniffed and said matter-of-factly, "That is very common in the early parts of pregnancy. Women become very sensitive to odors."

Darby nodded, still absorbing the masseuse's news.

"Next, her body started changing, as I have already said. I was convinced she was going to have a child. And then, on Monday, I used her bathroom. There in the corner I saw a book—a new book. It was a manual for expectant mothers." She leaned back, satisfied.

"You didn't ask her about it?"

Sassa shook her head. "I nearly did. But she was already sick of my meddling and asking questions about that man McFarlin…" her face darkened.

"Foster McFarlin?"

She nodded. "Kyle knew I did not like McFarlin, didn't trust him. 'You don't need to worry,' she told me. 'I am through with him.'"

"Do you think she had broken up with Foster McFarlin?"

"The night before. He had flown her in his fancy airplane somewhere for dinner. She said they were finished with each other. She said that McFarlin wasn't angry, but I didn't believe her."

"Why not?"

"Because I heard her arguing with him on the telephone, just before I came in. She was saying that she didn't need his help, that she would be fine without him." She paused. "I think now that perhaps she told him about the baby."

Darby looked the other woman in the eye. Her face was calm, nearly unlined, but she had a set to her jaw that was defiant.

"You think Kyle's baby was fathered by Foster McFarlin?"

"Yes," Sassa Jorgensen said, nodding. "I feel certain of it. And that is not a man who wanted the burden of a little one, I am sure." She stood and placed her hands on her hips. "Is this information for the police, Darby Farr? If a crazy man killed my Kyle, does it even matter?"

Darby thought about what she knew of Jonas Briggs' suspicions concerning the Kondo Killer. "I think your information could be very important," she told Sassa Jorgensen. "I am going to tell Detective Briggs, and chances are, he'll want to follow up with some questions."

"That is fine." She gave a quick nod and Darby thought she saw relief in her eyes. "Thank you for your time. I am sorry you did not get to meet Kyle. I know she would have liked you."

Darby watched the massage therapist slip back into the crowd. Could Kyle Cameron have been pregnant at the time of her death? And would that have been a reason for her to die?

———

Jack Cameron threaded his way through the throngs of guests, stopping to hear the many murmured condolences, words to which he'd bow his head, nod it somberly, and move slowly along. After leaving his room, he'd found the bottle of Valium in his mother's medicine cabinet and had taken several, so shuffling through the crowd felt like being underwater, away from the sharp sounds and bright lights of the surface. He smiled at his own metaphor, thankful that he'd had the good sense to call Tank Webber about diving tomorrow. Jack paused before a group of women that included his sister, Alexandra. She looked at him with concern, but Jack gave what he hoped was a confident nod and moved on.

Munching a sushi roll from one of the several uniformed wait staff, Jack recalled his conversation with Tank only a half hour or so before. "You want to go on a wreck tomorrow?" Tank had been puzzled, knowing full well about Kyle's murder and probably knowing about the service, too, but he'd listened as Jack mumbled something about needing to escape, to get on a wreck, to forget about his grief for a while.

Tank had been silent for a few moments before speaking. Finally he sighed and Jack knew he had won. "Okay, okay, I get it, Cam. I'll squeeze you onto the ten o'clock charter. It's the *Bay Ronto*. Meet you at the dock at nine thirty, and don't be late."

Jack thanked Tank, the only one in his life to ever call him "Cam." The *Bay Ronto* was a four-hundred-foot British freighter that had lain on the Gulf's sandy bottom since 1919. As wrecks went, it was not a particularly interesting dive. Whatever treasures the old boat had once held had been surrendered to the sea or other divers long ago.

No matter, thought Jack, watching his father flirt with a woman barely out of her teens. It was a wreck, a nice deep one. He grabbed a beer from an ice-filled chest and drank it down. Any wreck would do.

———

"Peter Janssen told you a story about Jane, huh?" Helen Near was in the kitchen, fixing herself a Mojito and offering one to Darby. "I don't remember any deals they did together, but I do recall that Jane didn't really care for the guy." They were back at Helen's bungalow, about to relax on the patio before dinner.

"No, thanks," Darby said, refusing the minty drink. The glass and a half of Chardonnay had given her the beginnings of a headache, and she didn't think a Mojito would help. "Why didn't my aunt like him?"

"Who knows? She had her little quirks like that. Maybe she picked up on some resentment of her success. That happened to us, especially with some of the male brokers."

Darby considered Helen's words as she poured a glass of water.

"Peter Janssen also said that he and Kyle Cameron were partners."

"Partners? In what way?"

"I took him to mean real estate partners. Did they ever co-list any properties?"

"Not that I know of," Helen sniffed. "Why wouldn't Kyle have mentioned that to me?" She sat down at the kitchen table and frowned. "All of a sudden things are cropping up, things that Kyle Cameron never disclosed to me. This partnership with Janssen, and the referral agreement on St. Andrew's Isle..." She grunted. "Marty Glickman sent me a copy of it. It's a standard form, signed by Kyle and Peter Janssen, stating she was going to pay him 25 percent of the listing commission." Groaning, she shook her head slowly from side to side. "Why can't things ever be straightforward?"

Darby thought about Kyle's possible pregnancy and felt a pang of guilt. If Helen felt out of the loop now, the news of Kyle's condition certainly wouldn't help. As much as she wanted to convey the information she'd gleaned from speaking with Sassa Jorgensen, she'd decided to say nothing until she'd had a chance to speak with Jonas Briggs.

"There are some questions that are going to be difficult—if not impossible—to answer," admitted Darby. "We can't ask Kyle about the agreement. But in the long run, it doesn't really matter, does it Helen? You're getting the St. Andrew's listing, not Kyle. You won't owe Barnaby's any of that commission. So what if Kyle and Janssen occasionally worked together? She obviously wanted out of Barnaby's."

"You're right," said Helen. "Kyle Cameron wanted nothing more to do with that place. And you know what, Darby? I'm starting to really see why."

———

While Helen excused herself to take a short nap, Darby headed into the heat of the Florida afternoon to call Jonas Briggs. He answered with a quick hello, his voice softening when he learned it was Darby.

"I looked for you at Kyle's service," he said. "I was hoping we'd get a chance to talk." He paused. "I hope I didn't frighten you this morning."

"No, but I have been thinking about the possibility that Kyle's murderer is still free." She squinted in the sun, realizing she'd forgotten to wear her sunglasses. "Any news on Clyde Hensley?"

"Nothing yet. But don't worry—we'll find him." He paused. "What else can I do for you?"

Darby sought the shade of one of Helen's massive palm trees, and felt the temperature lower by a mere degree or so. "I have some information that might bear on the investigation."

"Yes?" She could hear the interest in Jonas Briggs' voice.

"I met Sassa Jorgensen at the memorial. She was with Kyle Cameron on Monday."

"Right. She's the massage therapist. Quite possibly the last one to see her alive—that is, before the killer."

"She's convinced that Kyle was pregnant. Did any of the blood tests indicate she could be?"

Jonas Briggs was silent. "Hang on, let me get the file." The phone thumped down and Darby heard the sounds of a busy office—phones ringing, the muted murmurs of voices—and felt sweat begin trickling down her back. Was it the heat, or anxiety over new developments in the case?

The receiver was back at Jonas Briggs' ear. "Got it." Darby heard the rustle of paper and his exasperated sigh. "Nothing. It doesn't appear we did a pregnancy serum test, but you can bet I'll have the lab run one now."

"If she was pregnant, is it too late to determine paternity?"

"We'd need a blood sample from the father. In the meantime, I'll ask the lab to hold a sample of Kyle's blood and—if they find it—amniotic fluid." He whistled under his breath. "The autopsy is scheduled for tomorrow. If Kyle Cameron was pregnant when she died, we may be dealing with more than we thought."

Darby pondered the implication of his words as she let herself back into Helen's cool home. *Kyle may have been pregnant.* It made sense, really, when she considered the lifestyle changes the driven agent had begun to set in motion. She'd broken off whatever romantic relationship she'd had with Foster McFarlin. Ditched Barnaby's for a calmer, quieter agency and schedule. She'd been about to embark on a new life ...

Darby sighed and pulled out her booklet of Florida real estate laws and regulations. Opening it up, she forced herself to stop thinking about Kyle Cameron. The following day she needed to take and pass an exam. Right now, she had to study.

———

Thanks to Mindy Jackson, it was widely reported that Chellie Howe attended Kyle Cameron's memorial service because they were old college friends—sorority sisters, no less—not because

Kyle's father-in-law, John Cameron, was one of Chellie's largest donors. By the end of the day, the story was spun even farther, with the late night news showing a sorrowful Lieutenant Governor Howe explaining that the murderer had taken "not only one of Sarasota's finest realtors, but also one of my best friends." Chellie had been careful to extol the virtues of the serial killer's other two victims—one was a newly licensed agent with a two-year-old—and promised to work for a stiff sentence, a pledge that meshed neatly with her conservative, tough-on-crime platform.

Foster McFarlin did not attend the service, although a huge flower arrangement sent by McFarlin Enterprises adorned the table holding the condolence book. Chellie had noted the size and choice of flowers: Casablanca lilies, orchids, and roses. The bastard had spared no expense, but at least he'd had the good taste to stay away from Casa Cameron.

Chellie had spoken only briefly with Alexandra Cameron, offering quick words of sympathy before Alexandra had moved on to the next mourner. And yet Chellie had felt those gray eyes linger a little too long, as if she had more to say about her sister-in-law's death…

Chellie sighed and leaned back in the upholstered seat of one of Florida's state planes. Although she often made the 286-mile trip from Sarasota to Tallahassee in a chauffeured limousine, tonight she was glad Mindy had arranged for the plane. She was exhausted, her eyes too heavy to read the briefings for her morning meeting. She let her eyelids close for just a few moments.

She was back at Florida State, cramming for a Poli Sci exam, knowing that a good grade in the course was essential for her hopes at law school. She checked her watch. Dammit! She was late!

Quickly she began gathering up her notebooks and papers. A sudden gust of wind sent them flying around the dorm room, and frantically she tried to scoop them up. Suddenly she sensed someone standing in the doorway. "Shut the door," she yelled over the wind, which had now become tornado-like. Frantic to get across campus for at least part of the exam, she sprang to her feet and ran. But Kyle Cameron was blocking the exit, her head thrown back in laughter, knowing full well she was dooming Chellie's chances at success...

She woke with a start. A typical anxiety dream, brought on by the day's events, but nevertheless her heart was racing, her breathing fast and shallow. Chellie inhaled deeply, then opened the shade of her window and peered into the darkness. What was it Alexandra had called Kyle when they lunched? Poison? *None of it matters now*, she thought, watching as the lights of Tallahassee twinkled below. *I'm the second most powerful person in the state, soon to be governor, and she's dead and gone. My problems are over, and so are Alexandra's. Who's laughing now?*

She gathered up her papers and stowed them in her briefcase. The pilot was beginning his approach to the airport, where a limo would be waiting to whisk Chellie to her condo. And Kyle Cameron? She was history.

SEVEN

On Thursday morning, Jack Cameron arrived at the dock at eight forty-five a.m. He unloaded his diving equipment and put it aboard *Seeker,* Tank Webber's dive boat. The vessel was empty— Tank was no doubt across the street grabbing donuts and coffee. Jack looked around at the assembled gear: tanks, flippers, wetsuits, weight belts, and buoyancy compensators, and felt the familiar excitement diving always engendered. The mystery of the unknown, the vastness of the ocean floor, and the ability to survive underwater, thanks to Jacques Cousteau's incredible invention. He had loved diving ever since he'd first tried it at eleven years old. It was a world of peace, beauty, and yes, danger. A world where you could experience life as well as lose it.

He sat down on one of *Seeker's* gunwales and waited for Tank. He was early, but that had been a conscious decision, one of the first he'd made in days. The pills were history. They didn't really help and besides, he needed to be firing on all cylinders to carry out his plan.

"Hey, Cam." Tank Webber, tall and sunburned, swung his long legs over the side of *Seeker* and came aboard. He handed him a coffee and the bag of donuts. "Two jellies. Help yourself."

Jack reached in the bag and found the jelly donuts. He took the plastic cap off the coffee, inhaled the bitter aroma, and took a few gulps. Cream and two sugars, just the way he liked it. He managed a small grin.

"You're the best."

Tank shrugged. "Hey, it's the least I can do after ..."

They both knew what the "after" meant, and Jack felt an intense stab of grief knife him hard, right between the ribs. He tried not to wince.

"Yeah." He looked out over the water and changed the subject away from Kyle's death. "Pretty smooth today. How many we got diving?"

"Four. A couple from the hotel and two guys who came last week."

"Business good?"

"Fair. I need to do some more advertising, make calls to the hotels. There aren't as many tourists, what with this stupid 'staycation' stuff."

"Staycation?"

"You stay home and have your vacation where you live instead of visiting sunny Florida." Tank snorted. "Tell me, what kind of a vacation is that?"

A car arrived and a couple emerged carrying dive bags.

"That's a good sign," Tank commented. "They own some equipment." He gave a cheerful wave. "Good morning. You the Jensens?"

They nodded, approaching the boat. Tank introduced Jack and asked the couple what equipment they'd require. A few minutes later, a shiny red pickup truck drove up and two men in their late twenties or early thirties joined the group.

Tank's customers began slipping on wetsuits and donning equipment while Tank readied the boat for departure. Jack hopped on the dock and untied the lines, waiting for Tank's signal to push away. He gave the bow a shove and jumped nimbly onto the stern, then coiled the lines, removed the fenders, and stowed them.

Tank flashed him a look that said "thanks" and Jack nodded. He sipped his coffee, remembering the morning three years earlier when he and the tall diver had met. It was on the wreck of the *Hydro Atlantic*, a 320-foot freighter lying in 172 feet of water off the Boca Raton inlet. Both men had been captivated by the experience, and had become more and more drawn to the world of wreck diving.

Jack closed his eyes and saw the familiar images he'd encountered on dozens of dives. The ghostly bulk of a ship, encrusted in coral and seaweed, lying on the ocean floor; the fish, large and small, meandering through the portholes and emerging through passageways; the dark rooms, each with a history, now silent and waiting. He opened his eyes and looked out at the sea. Tank's passengers were chattering among themselves, but Jack barely heard them. His thoughts were on the dive ahead, his last dive, the one that would finally bring him peace.

———

"Any news?" Darby had finished her morning run and was standing in the shade of one of Helen's enormous palm trees, her cell phone in hand, talking to Jonas Briggs.

He made a noise like he was blowing air out from his mouth.

"Yeah, in fact there is some news. Kyle was pregnant—about two months along. Just got the tests back from the lab."

"Does this mean you reopen the case?"

She heard him sigh. "Not until I can show Shank's not the killer. In the meantime, I'm working on it on my own time." He sighed again. "The last thing Police Commissioner Conrad wants is a complication. He and Lieutenant Governor Howe are tripping over themselves to take credit for catching Cyril Shank. Reopening Kyle Cameron's murder would be a major embarrassment."

"But if the murderer is still out there—"

"He—or she—*is* still out there. Every cop instinct I've got tells me that." He exhaled. "So here's the deal. The department's not going to look for more suspects, and I've been told not to spend any more time on it. I'm working on the parasailing death, but the Kondo Killer case is officially closed." Darby heard a scraping sound, as if a chair was being pushed back from a crowded desk. "I know you're heading back to California. If you were to stick around a bit…"

"What do you mean?"

"Just that if you were here, you might help me track down some leads. That's all."

Darby thought a moment. It was Thursday. She was meeting the interested buyer for St. Andrew's Isle the following day. Hideki Kobayashi would undoubtedly need some time to put together an offer on the property, so if she was still in town…

"I have to admit that I'm intrigued, Jonas. If Cyril Shank didn't kill Kyle, her pregnancy could have had something to do with her death. Any chance we'll find out who the father was?"

"We have obtained fetal DNA. Once we have a suspect, we can check." His voice became animated once more. "I gotta say, my money's on Jack Cameron. He and Kyle weren't seeing much of each other, but he still had the hots for her, and Kyle could be a softie. Behind door number two is the on-again-off-again lover, Foster McFarlin, conveniently married to our crusading, crime-fighting Lieutenant Governor. Was Kyle in the family way? Supposing she told Jack that she was having Foster's baby, and he went majorly beserk?" He sighed again, this one a long, tired sound.

"You sound exhausted. You getting any sleep?"

"I'm fine, but I'd sure be a whole lot better if you said you'd devote some of those excellent brain cells to helping me with this."

Darby laughed. "I'm not sure why you think I'd be much help."

"I heard about what happened up in Maine. Word gets around, you know."

"I got lucky up there. I'm not some Nancy Drew who can ferret out the bad guys."

"Too bad!" Jonas Briggs laughed. "Look, some people have a knack for this work, no matter what their day job, and you, Darby, have got the knack. You're a natural detective, and I sure could use your help." He paused. "Buy you dinner tonight and we'll toss some ideas around?"

Darby looked back at the bungalow. Helen would be fine without her, would maybe even catch up on some badly needed rest. "Sure. Where and when?"

"Leave the where to me. I'll pick you up at seven."

———

Helen Near smiled when told of Darby's dinner plans. "Jonas Briggs, huh?" She grinned again. "Nice boy, good family . . ."

"Helen, it's not like that. It's business."

"Business?"

Darby bit her lip. "He wants to talk about real estate. You know how it is—everyone wants to talk about the market, their home's value, that kind of thing."

Helen gave her a searching look before bursting into her booming laugh.

"Right!" She gathered up their coffee cups and walked back into the kitchen. In a minute she was back on the patio, a broad smile on her face. "Speaking of business, I'm going to be picking up the listing papers for St. Andrew's Isle later this morning. Your Mr. Kobayashi will want to get the jump on any other interested buyers."

Darby smiled. "As will his agent. Are you driving over there?"

"Eleven a.m. Want to come?"

"No. I'll be there tomorrow to meet Hideki Kobayashi at the guest house, and I don't want to muddy the waters."

"Gotcha." Helen pulled a lemon from one of her trees and sniffed its bright yellow skin. "I'm heading over to the office. Peter Janssen's coming by for a quick chat."

"Is this about the referral fee again?"

Helen shrugged. "Probably. I'll hear him out, but truthfully, I don't think I owe the guy anything."

Darby straightened the patio furniture and looked up at Helen. "If you like, I'll take a quick shower and meet you at the office."

"I'd love to have you there," Helen admitted. "You ask those tough questions so well."

Darby laughed and gave the older woman's shoulder a squeeze. "Thanks. I'll be thinking up some tricky ones while I shower."

———

Crouched in the bushes, his Dolphins cap pulled low so as to shade his aviator sunglasses, Clyde Hensley listened to the water running in Helen Near's shower. He'd seen the old lady leave only minutes before, so he knew it was the Asian girl alone in the house. He glanced around and saw nothing. Pretty quiet neighborhood, everybody's shades drawn against the penetrating sun. He rose to his haunches and removed his hat. With a damp forearm he wiped the sweat from his bare scalp, his long hair now a thing of the past.

Cap back in place, he crept silently to the bedroom where he knew the girl was staying. Gently he eased up the window sash. He took a tiny lens—no bigger than an M&M—and a small wad of putty. Carefully he stuck the putty on part of the window frame where he hoped it would not show, and then pushed the tiny lens inside. He didn't worry about tripping a security system or arousing a large dog. He knew from observing the property that neither of these deterrents were present. The sticker at the front door, warning of an alarm system, was pure bullshit.

Hensley retreated to his car and booted up the computer. He waited with anticipation while she finished her shower, his excitement growing with every minute. His eyes were glued to the laptop's screen, where the image of the empty room waited like a promise.

Finally a figure, wrapped in a towel, appeared at the bedroom doorway. He smacked his lips in anticipation. *Let the show begin.*

She strode across the bedroom floor, the towel cinched around her torso, her long black hair damp against her neck. God, she was beautiful. The heck with the plump blonde girls. This one was special, exotic. Like an endangered puma, lithe and sleek.

She bent and pulled something out of what looked like a suitcase and shook it out. *Her clothes,* he thought. *She's getting ready to get dressed...*

She seemed satisfied with whatever she had chosen from the suitcase and tossed it on the bed. She rummaged in the suitcase again and pulled up a small, lacy thing. He squinted at the screen and than remembered the zoom. Presto! A delicate pair of white lace panties came into clear focus.

Holding them in her hand she reached with the other to locate a matching bra. Clyde groaned in pleasure. This was good, real good, and she hadn't even taken off the towel! He snickered at how easy it was going to be to splice together some footage and make some dough. *My kind of job,* he thought. *Lucrative, easy, and fun.*

He watched as she pivoted and took a step toward the door. "No," he begged aloud. "Don't go back to the bathroom!" Just then she froze, like an animal in the woods, and cocked her head. She turned slowly and stared toward the window.

Clyde Hensley held his breath, wondering what she was doing. She certainly wasn't undressing, that was for sure. *She can't possibly hear anything from me. Perhaps a phone's ringing in another room?*

As he watched the laptop monitor, the girl's image came closer, until her pointed face and quizzical eyes filled the screen. He jumped back in alarm. Christ! She was right in front of the camera! He felt the remains of a chili hotdog coming back up his throat as her hand closed over the lens...

He scrambled to think what to do. She had found the lens, was probably wondering what it was, but he wasn't in any imminent danger. Just annoyed as all hell. That little thing had cost him a pretty penny, and now it would be tossed in the trash. Not to mention that his internet porn footage would be a bust.

Hensley closed the laptop and started up the car, an old Corolla he'd permanently borrowed from a conveniently dead Texan. "Shit!" He muttered, as the rusted vehicle sputtered down the street. He was shaking his head in disgust as he cruised by Helen Near's house, totally oblivious to the toweled figure watching from the door.

———

Kelly McGee tried not to blush as Jonas Briggs brushed by her on his way out the door. "What's up?" called Dave DiNunzio, a new detective some of the officers called "Lucky" because he was such a loser at cards, despite the fact that he played in a weekly poker game.

"Not sure. Could be a break in the parasailing case," he answered, his face a mixture of focus and excitement. Kelly felt her face growing warm as she sensed some of his anticipation.

"Need backup?" she stammered, desperately trying to appear nonchalant.

Jonas Briggs flashed her a look and her heart did a major flop.

"Sure," he said. "Let's go."

———

Darby was dressed and composed when Detective Briggs and Officer McGee pulled up to the bungalow in Briggs' navy Volvo. He jogged across the yard, ducking under one of the enormous palms, his brow knit with concern.

"Tell me again exactly what happened," he commanded.

"I took a shower, and walked into the guest room to get dressed. I picked out some clothes and was about to put them on, when I sensed something wasn't right. I walked to the window and found the camera. I then came to the front door and saw a white Toyota Corolla—probably a '98 or '97—speed down the road. The driver was the same guy at the Dive's bar."

"Clyde Hensley?"

"That's right. He was wearing the Dolphins baseball cap and glasses. I could see his profile clearly."

Officer McGee had remained so quiet that Darby hadn't known she was there.

"Did you get a look at the license plate?" she asked.

"I did. Texas plates, F69 831. I'm not sure about the '3'. It could have been another '8'."

"Excellent." Briggs made a note and nodded at McGee. She took the slip of paper and trotted back to the car, presumably to call them in.

Jonas Briggs shook his head and pulled a small plastic bag out of his pocket. "Okay, let's see what you found."

Darby showed him the tiny object. He opened the bag and she let it fall inside. "Your prints will be on it, but maybe we'll get lucky and his will be, too." He examined it carefully, peering through the plastic.

"It's a small camera, alright, used to transmit images to a remote location. Probably a laptop." He sighed. "This scumbag has his fingers in more pies than I care to bake." He scowled. "But this time we've got the jump on him. Do you think he saw you?"

"Driving by, or naked?" She kept her tone light to show she was joking.

"Driving by."

"No. He was looking down the road. And to answer your unspoken question, he didn't see me naked, either."

Jonas Briggs did smile then, a fleeting one to show he got the joke. "What put you on alert?"

"What do you mean?"

"You said that you sensed something wasn't right. What triggered that feeling?"

Darby thought a moment, remembering the hint of a scent she'd noticed, a scent that was not her shampoo, not Helen's fabric softener, and not the aromatic citrus fragrance of the trees in the backyard…

"Body odor," she said.

"What? You mean you smelled him?" Detective Briggs was incredulous.

"At first I just noticed something out of the ordinary, a scent I couldn't place. I figured it came from the window. So I walked toward it, and saw the camera."

"Huh," said Briggs, shaking his head in wonder. "That's a new one on me." He backed toward the car where Officer McGee was waiting. "Get anything on those plates?"

Kelly McGee nodded. "Neither one was registered to Mr. Hensley. I'm going through the stolen vehicles right now."

Briggs nodded. "Good." He turned back to Darby. "You're going to have to explain this whole odor thing to me over dinner."

Darby laughed. "There's not much to explain. I have a good sense of smell."

"We're still on for tonight?"

She nodded. "Yes. Thanks for coming over."

"All part of the job," Jonas Briggs said, slamming the Volvo's door. Darby gave a little wave as he pulled away, hoping the stricken look she'd seen on Officer McGee's pretty face wasn't directed at her.

———

The *Seeker* dropped anchor thirty miles from the coast, and activity on the boat went into high gear. The two men—work friends from Jacksonville —would be the first ones in the water, followed by the couple and Tank. Jack had volunteered to stay with the boat while the others dove, then, when they resurfaced and chatted about the dive, he'd go down and check out the wreck.

Or that was the plan.

Jack wasn't sure now if he'd be able to go through with it, although he'd played and replayed it so many times in his head. Descend to the *Bay Ronto*. Enter the great hulking mass of the ship. Disengage his oxygen line, tangling it in a piece of jutting steel for verisimilitude. Wait for oblivion.

He knew the reality would be far from simple. Could he really make himself give up his regulator? Would he have the guts to deprive himself of air when every last cell would be screaming for it?

At first his plan had been more complicated. He'd hoped to go on a deeper dive, where nitrogen narcosis could be his final nemesis. He'd known guys who'd died from "Rapture of the Deep"— what serious diver didn't?—and the looks on their faces when their bodies were brought to the surface was never one of horror. Bliss, maybe, but not horror. But planning to get and die from the bends was proving way too complicated. Far easier to arrange to run out of oxygen, and if he did it right and made it look accidental, no one would be the wiser.

Tank was talking to the divers before they did their backward rolls off the boat, instructing them to keep a hand on their masks and one across their buoyancy compensators. Jack busied himself with straightening the spare tanks. In a few minutes they'd descend, and he'd have a little time to himself.

His thoughts drifted to his family. Even as a small boy, Jack had been chided by John Cameron, Senior, for choosing the easy way out, and he knew that this low opinion had been correct. He'd separated from Kyle rather than face the fact that she wasn't happy. He'd let Belle Haven die a slow death (for the place was bankrupt before the fire had come and completely finished it off) rather than figure out how to run something more than a hamburger joint. He'd turned to booze and pills rather than doing the excruciating work of figuring out why he was such a loser. And now, he was choosing what his father would see as the ultimate easy way out.

He could predict his mother's grief when she heard about his "accident." She'd be devastated, but she was a religious woman and might take comfort in her faith. Alexandra would be stunned, but she was strong, more like their father than she cared to admit. And John Cameron? Jack was sure he'd be relieved. The bad seed of the Cameron family, the one who was really only posing as a Cameron, would be out of the picture. His father might also guess that the whole thing was staged.

The only person who deserved an explanation was Marco, and Jack had left him a scrawled note early that morning. Other than his longtime bartender, Tank was the only one he really worried about. No matter what he did, Tank was going to catch his share of shit. If the incident didn't look like an accident, that might freak people out and hurt Tank's business. Even if it was assumed to be an accident, Tank would still be reprimanded for letting him dive alone. Jack frowned. He wasn't happy about hurting his friend, but that was life.

———

Chellie Howe pushed back from the desk piled high with legislative bills and sighed. She'd tried to get through the bulk of them the night before, but somehow the mound of unread documents seemed to have multiplied by morning. She took a sip of her coffee and glanced at her Smartphone. Nearly eight—time to get dressed and leave before the peach-colored walls of the cramped condominium drove her nuts.

The unit was located in one of Foster's first developments, one of the few projects McFarlin Enterprises had undertaken in the capitol city. Chellie rented the condo from a management company, using the space whenever official business took her overnight to Tallahassee. She'd toyed with buying a house, had even looked at a few with an agent, before deciding to bide her time. It was crazy to buy something now, when the gubernatorial race was only a year away. She thought about the Governor's Mansion, a lovely neo-classical home with Georgian columns and stately rooms, and the image of living and working in such a pretty environment made her smile. Not like this place, with its cheap kitchen cabinets and worn vinyl floors.

She rose and grabbed a yogurt and vitamin water out of the refrigerator. She would eat a little breakfast while tackling one more bill.

The sound of a key in the lock made her freeze.

"Foster?" She wasn't expecting him, but that was the way their marriage worked now.

The door opened and he entered, balancing a briefcase and a brown paper bag. His skin was the color of cocoa against his white shirt.

"Hey." He looked almost as if he was going to kiss her good morning, and then thought the better of it. He plunked the bag on the kitchen counter. "Muffins and coffee. I figured you were hard at work."

She felt an emotion akin to hope flutter in her chest. "How did you know I was here?"

"Mindy." He smoothed the front of his sport coat and pulled two coffees from the bag. The scent of warm baked goods filled the room. She knew him well enough to know he'd brought bran muffins.

Foster was wearing a tie she had bought him in Paris: gray silk with a very faint pink stripe. It was one of the few purchases she'd made on the posh Champs-Elysees, and it had cost a small fortune. She walked toward him and took a coffee.

"You look dashing. What's the occasion?"

He frowned and she regretted her question. "A hearing on Bay Isles." He shook his head. "A bunch of the development's buyers have banded together and formed a coalition. They've got a list of demands and deadlines they want us to meet."

Chellie knew more than she would ever let on about the lawsuit. The buyers were protesting McFarlin Enterprises' closing dates, saying the project—which lacked nearly all of the promised amenities—was not substantially completed. "What do you expect will happen?"

His expression darkened. "Hopefully we can reach some sort of settlement." He ripped the cover off his cup of coffee and took a gulp. "I'm not going to lie to you, Chellie. Lawsuits like this are sinking McFarlin Enterprises. One more unexpected expense and I could be through."

She swallowed. "I didn't think it was that bad."

He glowered at her. "It is. Not for you—you'll stay squeaky clean. But me and the company..." His voice trailed off.

She thought of all those expensive dinners he'd shared with Kyle Cameron and bit her tongue. "The economy will rebound and all this will be a bad memory." She put her hand on his arm, feeling the hard muscle beneath the sport coat.

"Yeah, right." He gave a glance at his watch. "I've got to go. Maybe I'll see you back in Sarasota, tomorrow."

"What about tonight?" She hated the shrill way her voice sounded.

"I have an engagement in Miami, and I'll just stay over there." He touched her cheek; let his fingers travel down to the nape of her neck. "Thanks for the pep talk."

She nodded and watched him go, hating him and loving him at the same time.

———

Peter Janssen arrived at Helen Near's office about ten minutes after Darby, his jovial smile warm. "Darby, how nice to see you again," he said, extending a hand. "Helen, are you filling her up with some vintage Jane Farr stories?"

Helen smiled. "Oh, there are only so many of those I can tell before they all start sounding the same." She motioned for him to have a seat. "I'm glad you came over, Peter. I really want to get to the bottom of this St. Andrew's Isle situation."

Peter Janssen nodded. "As do I," he said, taking a folder from a well-worn briefcase. "I know Marty's spoken to you, but my version of the story may be slightly different." He smiled apologetically. "I admire Marty Glickman, and he runs a damn good company, but our values are slightly different."

Darby glanced at Helen. She hadn't yet mentioned the incident at the bungalow, nor the arrival of Detective Briggs and Officer McGee. There hadn't been time, and besides, Helen had enough on her plate without hearing someone had planted a camera in her guestroom.

"Go on," Helen said to Peter. "I'd like to hear what you have to say."

Janssen nodded and cleared his throat. "Two years ago, I was asked to visit St. Andrew's Isle. I met with Tag Gunnerson and his assistant, a man named Bernie Shultz." The women nodded. "After discussing with them what I felt the property was worth, I left and followed up a week or so later. Mr. Shultz thanked me but said Tag had changed his mind about selling. I put the file in a cabinet and there it stayed, until two months ago."

"At that time Kyle came to me and said she wanted to talk. She seemed uncomfortable and I suggested that we have lunch that very afternoon. We did, and it wasn't long before she got straight to the point."

"She told me she'd met Tag Gunnerson at some charity event. He said that he wanted to sell his island property, and he asked Kyle to list it." Peter Janssen crinkled his brow as he spoke, trying to remember the details of the conversation. "I told Kyle I had spoken to Tag's assistant a year ago, but that no commitment had been made. I congratulated her on what would undoubtedly be a fabulous listing."

"Kyle put down her fork and tossed her napkin onto the table. She said it wasn't fair that they'd consulted with me but weren't going to use my services. I reminded her that I was a big boy and that real estate sometimes worked that way, but she didn't seem to be listening. She insisted on writing up a referral agreement, said it was the only way she'd be able to take the listing in good conscience."

"I wasn't sure what to say. I told her a referral fee was unnecessary, that I appreciated her concern but that I could handle it. She seemed to believe me, and we enjoyed the rest of our lunch, chatting about the market, new happenings in the city, and the like. When we got back to the office, I left my file on her desk so she could see the comparables I'd used. Later that day, there was a copy of a referral agreement in my box."

He paused. "That's the kind of girl Kyle Cameron was." The words sounded choked, and Darby felt for the man. He made an effort to control his emotions and continued, lifting the folder in his hands. "But things have changed. It's ludicrous for Marty to think you owe me anything now. Kyle was leaving Barnaby's. She wasn't going to finalize this listing until she was part of your company." He sighed. "She'd seemed happy at Barnaby's, but who really knows for sure? Marty can be tough to work for, and they had definitely had some misunderstandings over the years."

Darby's interest was piqued. "Such as?"

"The usual squabbles over commissions. Kyle was busting her butt on the McFarlin properties, and she didn't want to give Marty half of what she earned. She was a star for the company, and I think she wanted to be treated like a star. Instead, Marty was on her case, pushing her to travel further down the coast and pick up clients in Naples, Venice, and Verona. That girl was already going 24/7. I don't know how she could have given him any more."

"Will you keep working for Marty?" Helen asked.

"If that's a job offer, I thank you but I have to decline," he said. "I'll stay at Barnaby's until the bitter end."

"Does Marty treat you better than he did Kyle?" asked Darby.

"No," he said with a sad grin. "But I don't have the guts to make a change." He rose. "I appreciate your time, Helen, and it's nice to see you again." He turned to Darby. "Good bye and good luck."

Helen saw Peter to the office door. When he had left, she turned to face her friend.

"What an interesting meeting. His story and Marty's are so different."

Darby nodded. "Peter seems to grasp that—Kyle's leaving the agency, and her death, negates any kind of referral agreement, while Marty is pretty insistent that you owe it."

Helen sighed. "I'm going to speak to the state commission, see what they say. Whatever I do, I don't want Marty Glickman on my case."

"Just how much money are we talking, anyway?"

"Well, just say the estate sells for forty million dollars, that's a fifty thousand dollar referral fee. That's not chump change." She pushed the chairs back where they belonged and gave Darby a long look. "This is my take on it. Giving it to Peter is one thing, but I'll be damned if I'm handing anything over to Marty Glickman if I don't have to." She looked at her watch. "I'm off to St. Andrew's Isle and bag that listing. What about you?"

"Off to take my exam."

"Shoot! That's right. Well good luck, girl. I just know you're going to ace it. How about I call you when I finish and we grab a grouper sandwich?"

"Super. Just call and I'll meet you at the Dive."

———

Jack entered the water alone, leaving the other divers chatting and eating orange slices on board the *Seeker*. "Have a good dive," Tank said, looking into his friend's eyes with what seemed like concern.

"Always do," answered Jack.

Now, as he let the air out of his buoyancy compensator and descended slowly to the bottom, he thought again about his plan. Swim to the wreck, find a jagged piece of metal, entangle his breathing apparatus in the metal, and drown. It sounded so easy.

Once at the bottom, Jack adjusted his buoyancy so that he hovered just above the sand. He loved this feeling—the point where he was neither sinking nor rising. It was what being in outer space must be like, he thought, as he watched a huge amberjack swim slowly by. Beautiful spiny oysters littered the bottom, and Jack could not help but be impressed by their symmetry.

The gray hulk of the four-hundred-foot-long freighter loomed through the green water in front of him. Now laying upside down, her back broken in half, the once mighty *Bay Ronto* had been transporting wheat bound for Marseilles when she foundered in a hurricane in 1919. Jack remembered hearing that the entire crew managed to squeeze into two lifeboats before the freighter went down. Collecting rainwater and eating raw fish, the men on the lifeboats had somehow survived.

As wrecks went, the *Bay Ronto* was not particularly exciting. There was no chance of finding china, or a ship's bell, or any artifacts at all for that matter. But it was a wreck, and beginners and more experienced divers alike appreciated the thrill that swimming through its sunken passageways afforded. It was the chance to imagine you'd discovered the *Andrea Doria* or the *Titanic*.

Jack squeezed through a crack in the hull, startling a group of nearly two dozen large jewfish. His eyes roved, looking for the right place to tangle his breathing apparatus, but there was nothing but smooth edges. Perhaps on the outside of the boat, he thought.

Using slow, graceful kicks, Jack swam slowly out of a cleft in the hull and began circling the vessel. Out of the corner of his eye he saw the movements of a school of panicked smaller fish, and idly wondered what was causing them distress. He rolled slowly to his side for a look. In the corner of his mask, at the very edge of his peripheral vision, swam a large gray shark.

He knew instantly from the wedge-shaped head and faint dark stripes that it was a tiger shark, one of the ocean's top predators. Fear clenched his stomach, while at the same time, his heart surged with appreciation for the magnificent hunting machine. The shark was all muscle, all muscle and sinew, and it evaluated him with a sweep of its tiny black eyes.

Jack hung suspended in the water, as still as he could possibly remain. He knew the fish could smell him, could see him, and definitely hear him, but he was not quite sure what it might do. Sharks were primarily nocturnal hunters—everyone knew that—and yet daylight attacks on humans, although infrequent, did occur. Jack tried to stay calm. He heard the pounding of what sounded like jungle drums in his ears, a noise he quickly realized was the beating of his own heart.

The shark turned to face him head on. It seemed to consider a moment, and then, with a sweep of its powerful tail, hurtled directly at him. Jack held his breath as the huge creature brushed by him, rubbing the neoprene of his suit with its flank. The fish was "bumping" him, testing to see what Jack was made of, and possibly what his reactions would be. He'd heard from divers who'd survived encounters with sharks that this type of behavior could go on for hours.

Jack willed himself to stay immobile. Seconds later, the fish turned abruptly and began swimming once more in his direction, the muscular undulations of his body making ripples through the water. Jack was terrified, holding his breath, and yet he felt a sense of exhilaration he had never experienced before. *If I am going to die,* he thought, *let it be at the hands of a magnificent creature like this. If by some miracle I survive, let me take with me some measure of this shark's strength...*

Thud. His hip was smashed by the shark, which seemed to be curious as to what it would take before this dark creature split into pieces. Jack watched as the shark turned again, his vacant eyes boring through him, gathering speed with every move of his body, rocketing toward his gut…

Jack braced for an impact that didn't come. He opened his eyes and saw the shark swimming by, having apparently veered off at the last second. He watched as it disappeared into the shadowy depths, until all he could see was a faint flicker of tail. He took a deep drag on his regulator and got nothing. He was out of air.

Jack fought the panic that threatened to rise in him once more. After all, this was what he'd planned to do, wasn't it? Run out of air and drown on the bottom?

But the encounter with the shark had changed him. He'd faced off against the apex predator of the ocean, and somehow he'd survived. It was the first successful thing Jack Cameron had done in a long, long, time, and he wasn't about to die without savoring it.

Quickly he groped for his pony bottle, an additional small cylinder of air strapped on his back, while kicking upwards toward the surface of the water. Where the hell was it? He reached with his other arm. Had the shark knocked it loose?

Panic stabbed him like a knife. His lungs were burning but still he swam steadily upward. Normally he would be planning a stop to avoid decompression sickness; now he was simply trying to stay alive.

In desperation Jack sucked once more on the regulator. Nothing.

Blackness was dancing around the edges of his vision. A thought drifted into his brain: *I decided to live, but I'm gonna die anyway*. It was the last thing Jack Cameron contemplated before everything dimmed and went dark.

EIGHT

THE DIVE WAS UNUSUALLY quiet for a hot Thursday afternoon. Only a few tables were occupied, and the smiling waitresses Darby remembered from her earlier visit were not present. Darby chose the same table she and Helen had eaten at before and waited for her friend. A tall, lanky man signaled from behind the bar that he was on his way.

"So? How did it go at St. Andrew's Isle?" asked Darby as a flushed Helen collapsed into a chair. "Did you land the big listing?"

"I surely did," she beamed, flashing a brilliant smile.

"What did you sign for? Forty five?"

"Actually, we are listed for a cool forty million. Tag wants a quick sale, so let's hope your Mr. Kobayashi can step up to that plate." She took a sip of water and nearly spit it out. "Jeez—I nearly forgot! How'd the test go? Are you a Florida broker now?"

"Sales associate, but yes, I am now licensed and ready to sell Tag's property." She grinned. "Believe it or not, I actually knew someone else in the class."

"Really? Who?"

"Justin Fleischman."

Helen looked surprised. "Well, you better hope he doesn't bring a buyer for St. Andrew's Isle first, because that property is red hot." Helen gave a wicked smile and looked up as the bartender leaned over them, a questioning look on his chiseled face.

"Hello, Marco. We'll take grouper sandwiches, and two beers."

"Actually, I'll have an iced tea," said Darby.

Marco nodded and turned on his heel.

"I've always thought he was awfully cute," Helen giggled, wagging her eyebrows suggestively. "He's got that sultry Mediterranean look, you know?" She hushed as Marco returned with their drinks.

"Here you go," he said, his dark eyes darting around the restaurant. He straightened up and hit Darby's glass in the process.

"Dammit! I'm sorry." He mopped up the liquid with a bar towel and sighed. "Let me get you another drink. Be right back."

Helen watched him retreat to the bar and frowned. "Marco isn't usually so flustered," she commented. "Wonder what's on his mind?"

He returned with the replacement drink and plunked it down. "My apologies." His cell phone buzzed and he yanked it out of a pocket. Glancing at the number, he frowned and shoved it back.

"Not the person you wanted to speak to?" asked Helen gently.

Marco shook his head. "I was hoping it was ..." his voice trailed off.

"Jack?" prompted Darby. "Were you hoping the call was from Jack?"

He gave her an incredulous look. "Have you heard from him?"

"Not since yesterday," said Helen, her face growing anxious. "Why? Is he in trouble?"

The tall man scowled and shook his head. "Nah." Darby noticed he was shifting the bar towel back and forth between his big hands.

"Marco, we might be able to help," she said quietly. He gave her a long look.

"I don't see how."

"Why don't you try us and see?"

Marco ran a hand through his curly brown hair He exhaled and pulled up a chair.

"I know you're friends with the Camerons," he said, nodding in Helen's direction, "otherwise I wouldn't be talking." He glanced around the restaurant and lowered his voice. "It's this." He pulled a folded piece of paper from his apron pocket. "Jack left it in the cash drawer. I think he's planning to hurt himself."

"What?" Both women were on their feet.

"Why haven't you alerted anyone?" Helen exclaimed. "Every second counts!"

Marco put his face in his hands. "I've wanted to, but it's not that simple."

"Let me see it," Darby said quietly. He handed her the note with obvious reluctance. The paper crinkled as Darby unfolded it. Seconds later, she understood the bartender's dilemma.

"Jack Cameron has written what sounds like a suicide note, Helen, but he's also penned a confession."

"A confession?" she asked. "Whatever the hell for?"

Darby held the note between her fingers and grimaced. "The murder of his wife."

"But Kyle was killed by that maniac, Shank." An incredulous Helen Near grabbed the note and read it herself. She looked back at Darby with fear in her eyes. "What do we do now?"

Darby had already whipped out her cell phone. "Detective Briggs? It's Darby Farr. I've got some news…"

———

Chellie Howe ate a salad at her desk and worked her way through a stack of legislative bills, the toughest of which involved creatures she found repulsive—alligators and snakes. "Ugh," she groaned, feeling as if her very skin was crawling. Reptiles had never appealed to her, not since her brother's lizard had crawled from the warm aquarium where he spent all day sunning under a light bulb to her closet, to where she found him curled inside her favorite pair of Danish clogs. She shuddered at the memory, even though more than thirty years had passed and both her brother and the lizard were history.

Philip. Normally she remembered him as he'd lived the last few years of his life, wandering the streets of Miami in a haze of drugs, but now she pictured him in his lizard-owning stage, happy to show off his pet, even to a younger sister who couldn't care less. They had never really been close as kids, prone to the usual squabbles siblings seemed to almost relish—fights over who sat where at dinner, bickering about bathroom privileges—and his obsession with cold-blooded creatures hadn't helped their relationship. Still, she smiled at the memory of his delight upon finding the lizard, unharmed and alive, while she screamed and pointed at her clog…

A knock at the door. Chellie frowned and shoved the papers to the side. "Yes?"

The door opened and Mindy Jackson entered. "A new development in the Kondo Killings," she announced.

"What? That's done, we got the guy."

"Apparently not. Jonas Briggs has uncovered evidence that seems to suggest Cyril Shank was not Kyle Cameron's killer. He's our guy for the other two, but Kyle was murdered by somebody else."

Chellie hated it when her assistant wore that smug little face like she knew something Chellie did not. "Just tell me the whole frigging thing, Mindy."

"Briggs is on his way to find Jack Cameron and take him in."

Jack? Chellie wanted to exclaim in surprise but would not give Mindy the satisfaction, so she kept her face a mask, a trick she had learned back in law school. "Is that all?"

"Cameron left some sort of note admitting the whole thing, and saying he was killing himself. No word yet on where he is, or whether he's still alive."

Chellie Howe gave a curt nod. "Monitor the situation and give me updates." She gestured toward the pile of bills. "Get me a meeting with Bob Sneed on this exotic reptile importation, and find me one of those vitamin waters. Pomegranate."

She waited for Mindy to retreat before grabbing her cell phone. *Jack Cameron about to be arrested?* The guy was a mess, addicted to booze and who knew what else, but still ... She flipped open her phone and was about to dial when some instinct made her pause. Calls could be traced and she had to be careful. She thought back to her luncheon, only weeks before, and the steely gray eyes of Alexandra Cameron. *She's poison...*

Chellie felt a queasiness in the pit of her stomach. She bent and pulled open her bottom desk drawer, removing a three-by-five inch black and white photograph. Chellie, Alexandra Cameron, and Foster McFarlin, arms draped around each other, all smiled for the camera. In the background loomed the impressive brick structure that was Florida State University's Westcott Building. She flipped the photo over and read the scrawled words. "To my dearest friends. Love always, Kyle."

Chellie replaced the photo and closed the drawer. When Mindy arrived with the vitamin water, she'd take an antacid and get ready to go home. In the meantime, she would try not to think about the past.

———

"Kyle was pregnant?" Helen looked up from her home computer, where a breaking news story regarding the Kondo Killings had just been posted, and shook her head. "First Mitzi's call, then your news about the Peeping Tom, and now this. I need a Mojito, and I don't care if it's only two o'clock."

"I'll make you one," Darby offered, rising from her seat on the couch.

"No, let me. All that muddling will be therapeutic." Helen rose heavily from her desk. "I don't suppose you want one, too?"

Darby nodded. "Sure."

Everything was in the open now, Darby realized, along with the news of Jack Cameron's shark attack and arrest.

First Mitzi had called, livid that the police were waiting for Jack at the dock. "He nearly drowned, and instead of getting him into a decompression chamber, the police stick him in handcuffs for the murder of his wife. You can bet our lawyers are going to have fun with that scenario."

Furious that her grieving son had been subjected to such harsh treatment, Mitzi had sobbed on the phone. "He didn't kill anyone. How could he?"

Once Helen had finished consoling her friend, she'd hung up and logged on to discover what the press was reporting. After seeing that the case was to be reopened, the only thing she wanted was one of her favorite drinks.

Darby heard the sounds of cupboards closing and her friend fetching ingredients. "You sure you don't need help?"

"Well, alright. You can get me some ice."

Darby joined Helen in the cheerful kitchen, where the older woman was already pressing the mint leaves.

"Kyle's being pregnant makes a lot of sense, when I think about it." Helen gave Darby a shrewd look. "She was planning to leave Barnaby's and work in a less crazy environment, one where she could be a good mom."

"I think you're right. Given Peter Janssen's comments about Marty Glickman's management style, it sounds like Kyle didn't want to keep tolerating that kind of stress."

Helen reached for a jar of simple syrup and tried to open it. Sighing, she handed it to Darby who unscrewed it easily.

"I wonder why she didn't tell me," Helen mused. "I would have been totally fine with an infant around the office. Hell, it would have been fun." She smiled sadly and measured out the syrup.

"I'm sure she was planning on telling you very soon. She was still in the early stages, remember?"

Helen shuddered. "It makes the whole thing even worse, you know? Not only was Kyle killed, but so was this little innocent being-to-be. Of course, the killer didn't know she was having a baby."

Darby took her Mojito from Helen. It smelled heavenly, the scent of mint and the rum mingling together in a fabulous perfume.

"The killer may not have had any idea Kyle was pregnant," Darby said. "That's certainly one scenario. But here's another: Kyle's condition may have had everything to do with why she was murdered."

"What are you saying?"

"If Kyle's death wasn't a random act of violence by a serial killer such as Shank, then whoever murdered her planned the whole thing, right down to copying the killings on the East coast. That person may very well have known about her pregnancy, and it could have been a factor in her death."

"You mean the father of the baby did it?"

"Possibly, but he's not the only one with motive. What about a man who was enraged because he was not the father? Or that guy's wife?"

"Chellie Howe? Do you think she—"

Darby couldn't help but laugh. "Helen, I haven't got a clue. But I do know one thing: the fact that Kyle was carrying a baby could be important to the killer's motivation."

"So whose baby was it? Foster's? Some random sperm donor's? Believe it or not, my money is on Jack."

"Really?"

"Sure." She nodded her head confidently. "When that guy's not on drugs or booze, he is irresistible." Helen took a sip of her Mojito and frowned. "Let's hope he keeps himself alive long enough for you to actually see the real Jack Cameron."

———

Thanks to a favor from Jonas Briggs, Helen Near got her wish. An hour later, she and Darby were seated in the holding cell of the Serenidad Key Police Station. Jack Cameron, on the edge of a metal folding chair, sat across from them.

Darby could hardly believe the difference between the childlike addict she'd encountered in Kyle's apartment and the focused man sitting before her.

"Hard as it is to believe, my father showed up to post bail," Jack Cameron said, rubbing his hand on a stubbled chin. He smiled ruefully. "The judge wouldn't allow it. He claims I'm a threat to my own safety, and I can't say I blame him. I mean, I did try to kill myself, and not just once." He fixed a level gaze at Helen. "Believe me, I'm so sorry for what I've put everyone through, especially my mother. She looks like she's aged ten years from all this."

Helen gave a no-nonsense shake of her head. "Mitzi will be fine, Jack, don't you worry about her. She's been through worse than this. She's glad to see you're acting like your old self again. That's what she wants more than anything."

He nodded. "I know. You've heard me say this before, but this time I mean it: I'm done with all of the substances. I'm a changed man, Helen."

Darby watched as the older woman's eyes grew moist. Slowly she rose to her feet and hugged her godson. Darby let them have their moment before clearing her throat and asking the question she'd come to find out.

"Why did you admit to killing Kyle?"

Helen shot her a look. "Darby, Jack has been through so much today, I hardly think ..."

"No, Helen, Darby is right. She's been my guardian angel a few times now, so she's got a right to ask me the tough questions." He rubbed his chin again and seemed to choose his words carefully.

"I did kill my wife. I realized that when I identified her beautiful mangled body in the morgue. Not physically—I wasn't the one who stabbed her—but spiritually and emotionally. I took what was a holy relationship and destroyed it with booze and drugs. Every single time I came home drunk or fooled around because I was high, it was as if I'd ripped out a piece of her heart. I know I'm guilty of that, and when I wrote that note, that's what I meant. I'm to blame."

He looked up at the two women. "Sounds crazy, doesn't it? I know that, but it's the truth."

Darby ignored the question. Certainly Jack's explanation was flimsy, to say the least.

"Did you discuss this—theory—with anyone? Dr. Menendez?"

Jack shook his head. "No. I wrote that stupid note and ..." He sat up suddenly. "Candy. I may have rambled on to her about it."

Helen snorted. "Who's Candy?"

Jack Cameron sighed. "A friend. She used to come to the Dive to visit Marco, the bartender." He gave a shrug, clearly embarrassed. "She's—well, let's just say I was one of her clients initially, but the last few times we were together, I couldn't ... I mean, I didn't want to do anything but talk. I think I may have shared with her my—theory." He lifted his head. "I don't care anymore. I didn't stab my wife, but I feel responsible for her death. And now, more than ever, I want to find out who did kill her."

Darby scribbled the name "Candy" on a small notepad. "What's Candy's last name?"

"Sutton. She lives in Bradenton."

"Will Marco know how to get in touch with her?"

Jack looked around the dingy room and gave a bitter chuckle. "He should. She's his cousin."

Darby rose to her feet. "I'll see if I can talk to her tomorrow. If she backs up what you're saying, that will certainly help." She cocked her head. "Where were you when Kyle was killed?"

Jack Cameron sighed. "Fishing, south of here. I left around eleven, I think, and returned home later in the day."

"Anybody go with you?"

"No."

"Did you speak to anyone while you were there?"

He shook his head. "Didn't even stop and buy bait." He chewed his lower lip. "The family lawyer suggested I plead guilty. Crime of passion, he said. 'The jury will totally understand, Jack. You couldn't stand Foster McFarlin's relationship with your wife, and so you killed her.'" He gritted his teeth. "I had to nearly fire the guy before he agreed to represent me if I pleaded innocent." He looked from Helen to Darby, his eyes wide. "You two believe me, I know it. I didn't do it. I loved that woman. I just screwed up and lost her, before somebody took her for good."

Darby judged Jack to be able to handle her next question, so she asked it.

"Were you the father of Kyle's unborn baby?"

He shuddered and bit his lip. Moments passed before he spoke. "I could have been," he said. "But I don't know for sure."

"But you and Kyle had been intimate?"

"About two months ago, I went to see her at her condo. I brought along her favorite Chinese food and begged her to let me in. She did, and I was—ecstatic. We sat on the floor in her living room and watched that damn goldfish swim around in his crystal bowl. She told me about the work she was doing to find out about her grandmother's heritage…"

"The books on Warsaw?"

"That's right. Kyle's grandmother Slivicki escaped from Poland with only a few possessions. Kyle was intrigued about the prospect of discovering her past." He looked down at his hands. "God, she was beautiful. Happy, and excited…" His voice hardened. "She told me she was through with McFarlin. She joked about the money she'd made from his properties, and said she'd miss that if he pulled her listings, but that it was time to call it quits."

His hands were balled into fists and Darby saw a vein in his jaw quiver. "Talk about killing somebody, I could wring that Foster McFarlin's neck…"

"Knock it off!" Helen stood and faced her godson. "You want to be a changed man? A big part's accepting responsibility for what you did and did not do. You weren't a good husband to Kyle, that's why she strayed. Spending time with prostitutes! Help her now by focusing on finding her killer, not revenge to make yourself feel better."

Jack started to respond when a buzzer sounded and the heavy metal door opened. Jonas Briggs entered, looking a little more rumpled than usual. He glanced at Helen but his eyes seemed to linger on Darby Farr.

"That's enough of a visit, ladies. Mr. Cameron needs to answer some questions."

They nodded and rose to leave. Helen reached for Jack and hugged him, hard. "You hang tough, Jack. Promise?"

He nodded and tried to smile. "I'm not going to let my god-mother down."

Darby and Helen walked through the doorway and heard Jonas tell Jack that he'd be back in a minute. He joined them in the hall-way that led back to the station. "Can we push dinner to eight?" he asked. "I've got some paperwork to finish up here."

"I'm fine with that, unless you're too busy."

Jonas Briggs shook his head. "Never too busy to eat, and be-sides, I'd really like your take on a few things."

Helen raised her eyebrows and was about to speak when Dar-by's phone rang. She glanced at the number and answered. A mo-ment later she had said "yes" and hung up.

"That was Mitzi," she announced. "She's asked us to come to Casa Cameron."

Helen nodded. By now they had exited the building and were at Helen's Lexus. "You drive, Darby," she said with a sigh. "I'm feel-ing like that Mojito I made could very well have been a double."

Darby slid into the driver's seat and started the car. *Precisely why I only drank half*, she thought.

———

Clyde Hensley kicked the front bumper of the Corolla and swore. He was trying to pry off the dented Texas plates, but the damn things were rusted right onto the bumpers. In exasperation he grabbed a set of metal cutters and clamped down, hard. The blades bit into the metal and he nodded. Now he was getting somewhere.

Half an hour later he had both the front and rear bumpers cut off, along with the old plates. He chucked them into the tall grass that bordered the dirt road and peered into the Corolla's back seat. There were the California plates he'd stolen from the junk store in Palmetto. Quickly Clyde wired them on to what remained of the bumpers. There. That ought to buy him some time if the Asian girl or any of her nosey neighbors had noticed the car.

He got back into the Corolla and drove down the dirt road. Nothing but dilapidated old shacks and bayous full of crocodiles. He frowned as the road grew rougher and grabbed the map. The road was supposed to take him through the Everglades, a route he figured was safer than the highway. He slowed down and stopped. Peering at the map, he found his location and decided to continue.

The Corolla bumped and jerked on the rutted surface and Clyde shook his head in disgust. What was he doing in this god-forsaken part of Florida? The Asian girl hadn't seen him, and even if she'd found the camera, that didn't implicate him. He frowned. There was still the matter of the parasailing accident. That girl was dead, electrocuted on the wires, and that was good reason to lay low. No telling how long they'd look for him for that.

A mile passed without sign of any human habitation, and Clyde regarded the thick brush on either side of the road with un-easiness. Bad place to break down, he thought, and then immediately wished he could banish the idea. All bad luck ever needed was a good foothold, he muttered, at precisely the same time that he noticed steam pouring from the engine.

Shit! He looked at the temperature gauge. Sure enough, he was overheating. He slowed to a stop along the road and got out. Billows of white smoke rose from the hood. Gingerly he lifted the metal, yelping as the car belched out a column of hot steam.

He spat into the dry dirt in disgust and looked up and down the road. Not a sign of another car, and come to think of it, he hadn't seen any traffic whatsoever since he'd left the highway. He looked at the sky. The sun was getting lower, and he guessed it was coming on late afternoon. Nothing to do but wait until the engine cooled down. He sighed and climbed into the front seat. An old magazine lay on the floor and Clyde thumbed through it, glancing at a few advertisements for guns. The interior of the car was stuffy, and before he knew it, he'd drifted off to sleep.

———

Casa Cameron seemed to Darby to be waiting for something to happen, its immense windows keeping vigil as they pulled into the circular drive. Even the Madonna wore a watchful expression, her gaze more forlorn than beatific.

"Place isn't as cheerful as usual, now is it?" Helen asked as they approached the front door. It was opened almost immediately by Carlotta.

Her usually expressionless face seemed to soften at their presence. "This way to Señora Cameron," she said, leading them to the formal living room.

Darby's eyes went immediately to the portrait. There, above the mantel, a young Mitzi Cameron looked down with a coy smile, while the real woman was seated in her wheelchair at an immense antique desk, the edges of which were dotted with silver-framed photographs. She turned to face them.

"How is he?"

Helen bent and gave her oldest friend a quick hug.

"Jack is surprisingly well," she said. "He's lucid, and determined to figure out who killed Kyle."

Mitzi nodded. "John said something similar, although it probably killed him to admit it." She gave an exasperated sigh. "Why in God's name did my son write that ridiculous note? He admitted to killing her."

Darby felt a stab of pity for Mitzi Cameron, whose lined face did indeed seem to have aged in the past forty eight hours.

"He was despondent," Darby offered. "Given the anguish that he's been in, that confession has to be viewed in a different light."

"Maybe." Mitzi Cameron seemed almost despondent herself. She reached for a photograph from her desk and handed it to Darby.

"That's Jack and Kyle, just before they were married," she said. "So much in love. How could it all have unraveled? How could anyone think he would have done anything to harm her?"

Darby and Helen were quiet as Mitzi Cameron continued.

"I nearly lost my son. Now his reputation's on the line." She looked from her friend to Darby Farr. "I'll do anything to prove his innocence."

Helen rose and stood beside Mitzi. "The police will find out the truth," she said with conviction. "That Jonas Briggs is a good man, and he's smart."

Mitzi gave a harsh laugh. "Yes, but he's not the one in charge, Nell. It's that damn commissioner and Chellie Howe. They hate that this case has been reopened, and believe me, they just want a warm body at this point." She looked up at Darby and her eyes were like laser beams. "I need someone who can figure this out before they put Jack away, because believe me, that's what they'll try to do. Someone with brains, who can work outside the system. That person is you."

Darby remembered the look of conviction she'd seen on Jack Cameron's face. He was not a man who had murdered his wife, she was sure of that.

"I appreciate your vote of confidence," she said, "but I'm not a detective."

"That's precisely why I need you. You aren't trapped by the bureaucracy like Jonas Briggs. You aren't at the whim of some politician." She curled her thin hands into fists and then unclenched them. "I beg of you, Darby. Help my son."

Darby walked toward the desk holding the framed photograph.

"I promise I'll do my best to find out the truth."

"That's all I'm asking," Mitzi said softly.

Darby leaned over and replaced the photograph. Beside it was an image of Kyle Cameron, holding a bouquet of flowers and wearing a crown. A sash across her midnight blue evening dress read "Miss Florida."

"This is when Kyle won the pageant?"

Mitzi nodded, then pointed at the photo and chuckled. "She had quite the bouffant hairstyle back then, but of course, it was the eighties. All that teasing and hairspray."

"Who is this?" Darby indicated a beautiful woman standing beside Kyle, whose striking dark looks were oddly familiar.

Mitzi Cameron gave an amused little laugh.

"You don't recognize her? To my eyes, she's hardly changed at all." She gave a fond smile as if remembering the long-ago evening. "If Miss Florida should be unable to perform her duties," she intoned, "this contestant shall replace her automatically." She smiled, her imitation of a pageant announcer apparently finished. "That's my daughter, the first runner-up."

Darby looked into the strikingly beautiful face of Alexandra Cameron. Her head was tilted toward Kyle's, her gray eyes cast downward, as if she was noticing for the first time who was wearing the coveted sash. A strange smile twisted the corners of the young woman's face, a smile that made Darby shudder. Was it her imagination, or had the camera caught the runner-up giving her future sister-in-law a look of pure malice?

———

Sensing heat radiating from the parked Corolla, the snake slithered out of the swamp and toward the vehicle. Its cold-blooded body welcomed the warmth, for dusk was approaching and the wet grasses and mud of the mangroves were turning chilly. It wriggled up to a window, seeking entry to the warm metal box, but the tiny crack wasn't sufficient for its telephone pole-diameter sized girth to pass through. The snake continued along the car's side and around to the back, making only the faintest rustling noise as it moved.

At the rear of the Corolla, the snake flicked its tongue and found a spot where a chunk of missing metal revealed a good sized hole. Heat-sensitive organs on his snout measured the higher temperature of the car's interior, prompting the powerful creature to muscle in further, finding small crevices of rusted metal which gave way with the merest push. The reptile's persistence was rewarded when the floor of the car yielded and the snake glided into the Toyota's roomy backseat.

The warmth of the leather was enticing, but the 20-foot long Burmese python sensed something even more appetizing at the opposite end of the car. It slithered between the two front seats and onto the recumbent body of a warm-blooded mammal, larger than its usual fare of rats, birds, and juvenile alligators, but tempting nonetheless. With surprising speed and force the snake used its powerful jaws to strike at the animal's soft skin, sinking in his small, even teeth and encountering the same surprised reactions all prey exhibited: startled noises, futile pushes from paws or hands, and feeble efforts to stop the pain. Screaming assailed the small vibratory bones in the sides of his head, but the snake was not deterred. It kept its vise-like jaws clamped tightly on its prey, diverting attention from the real danger: the powerful coils that were quickly looping around the prostate form.

The python felt its victim flailing and heard him shouting, and yet already it was far too late to escape. Without releasing its jaws, the snake began rhythmically constricting its muscles, squeezing the length of Clyde Hensley in an inescapable embrace. Tighter and tighter it gripped, causing him to wheeze and sputter as air was forced out of his lungs.

The snake constricted until the body stopped moving, at which point it unhinged its jaw and freed Clyde Hensley's bloodied face. For a few moments it contemplated swallowing its kill. Fatigue won out over hunger and the snake uncoiled from its victim. Exhausted from the effort of suffocating such a large and uncooperative mammal, the python slipped to the still-warm seats in the back to enjoy a well-earned nap.

NINE

"Do you really think Jack Cameron killed Kyle?" Darby was buttering a sourdough roll and waiting for her companion's response. She and Jonas Briggs were seated at Luna, a Spanish restaurant overlooking the Gulf of Mexico in old Tampa. The sun had just begun sinking into the sea, with promises of a gorgeous sunset to follow.

"You don't waste any time, do you, Farr?" He thought a moment. "Honestly? No, I don't think Jack's our man. And before you ask me why he's in jail if I don't think he's guilty, let me remind you that I'm not the only one making decisions in Serenidad Key." He glanced around the restaurant and lowered his voice. "I think I've filled you in, as much as I can, on the politics involved. Commissioner Conrad and Lieutenant Governor Howe are all over me to get this thing settled. Needless to say, they don't like the idea of a murderer at large."

He was quiet as the sommelier approached and presented a bottle of red wine.

Jonas Briggs nodded at the label, waited for it to be opened and tasted it appreciatively. "You're going to love this wine, Darby." The sommelier poured them each a glass and withdrew.

"I'm not going to kid you. The case against Jack is substantial. The guy had motive as well as opportunity. I've got the note he left for the bartender basically confessing to the crime, as well as numerous witnesses who saw him entering Kyle's condo plenty of times."

"She wasn't killed at her condo."

"I know," he said patiently, "but Jack's easy and frequent access to her place sets him up as the obsessed jilted husband. I'm sure that if we dig deeper, we'll find someone who heard him in one of his drunken rants, carrying on about Kyle, and that's all a jury's going to need."

Darby took a sip of the wine, trying to block out the image of Jack Cameron in the holding cell. She knew Jonas Briggs was right—it did not look good for Jack, and yet where was the physical evidence? There was none, at least none that she knew about.

"Is there any evidence linking Jack to the crime?"

Jonas Briggs gave her a long, level look. "No. Not yet anyway." He pointed at her glass. "Isn't this delicious?"

Darby took another sip of the spicy red wine. He'd chosen a Rioja from Spain's oldest and most famous vineyard, and she recognized it immediately.

"The Muga Rioja Reserva, right?"

"Exactly! How the heck do you know that?"

Darby smiled. "I have what is called 'exceptional palate memory.' It is an odd gift that comes in handy identifying wines, teas, things like that. Linked to it is a keen sense of smell. It's how I was able to notice Clyde Hensley's little camera."

"You knew he had been there because of an odor, right?"

Darby nodded ever so slightly. "I know it's strange ..."

"Strange? It's freaking amazing!" Jonas Briggs lowered his voice and continued, a smile on his face. "You're like a secret weapon, Darby Farr. And you're going to help me catch this killer."

"I'm willing to try."

"Okay, here goes. Ready for the lowdown?"

She nodded.

"Like many serial killers, Cyril Shank took a souvenir from each of his killings. We kept it out of the press because we hoped it would help us in catching him, and it did. When we arrested Shank we found a small collection of items taken from his victims. Two pieces of 'memorabilia' were from the so-called Kondo Killings, and the rest have yet to be identified."

Darby felt her stomach roll. "I'm listening."

"Shank's particular 'thing' was to slice off the smallest digit from his victims' left hands."

"Pinkie fingers?"

"That's right. Some guys chop off all of a victim's fingers, but often that's to slow down identification of the body. With Shank, I think the one-finger fetish has some kind of sick significance for him." He took a roll and tore off a chunk, popping it into his mouth with a vengeance. "It's pretty common for these wackos to keep a little something. Fingers aren't very original, but there you have it."

"Just one finger?"

"That's right. One pinkie, from the left hand."

"And Kyle?"

"Kyle was missing a pinkie as well." He leaned back and regarded Darby.

"Why do I feel you're not telling me everything?"

"Okay. Here's the thing that aroused my suspicions: hers was cut from her right hand. The two victims on the East Coast were missing their left digits. And yet Kyle's right pinkie was the one that was severed. Why? These guys don't screw up when it comes to their signature moves."

He chewed the piece of bread thoughtfully, and then continued. "I decided it had to be one of two things: either Shank was starting a new pattern, or he was not Kyle's killer. I talked to a couple of experts and they suggested the new pattern could have something to do with the coasts. Left pinkies were the Atlantic; right pinkies for the Gulf. Makes sense in a sort of sick way, right?"

Darby nodded. "But you didn't quite buy that explanation."

Jonas Briggs shook his head. "No. My gut told me that a different guy killed her, a guy who somehow knew about the pinkie, but didn't know which hand."

"And then?"

"And then we got lucky and caught Cyril Shank. Sure enough, there were the missing fingers, tucked away in a plastic Marshmallow Fluff container. They matched the victims on the East Coast alright, but there was no missing pinkie from Kyle."

A waiter appeared to take their dinner order.

"Ready?" asked Jonas Briggs of Darby.

She gave a pleasant smile and looked at the waiter. "Just give me one more minute," she said. He bowed his head and backed away.

"Jonas, you can't expect me to order until I know."

"Know what?"

"Whether you've found it."

"The pinkie? Not yet. But if Jack Cameron has it…"

"He could be the killer," finished Darby.

"I'd say in all likelihood *would* be the killer," said Briggs. They were quiet a few moments, both of them thinking. The waiter returned, eyebrows raised.

Jonas Briggs looked at Darby. The basket of rolls was empty and the poor guy looked famished.

"I'll have the snapper paella," she said. She waited for Jonas Briggs to order and the waiter to leave.

"So this is a copycat crime?"

Jonas grimaced. "Yeah, although how this guy learned about the pinkie, I don't know. I was in the dark about it until Kyle was killed and we started working with the other police departments. It was never in the paper, never in the news. The only thing I can think is that someone close to the investigation leaked it."

"What about Shank himself? Couldn't he have bragged about it to someone? Or put it on a website, or an internet chat room?"

"We thought of that. His computer was checked and nothing like that was found. We've asked him, and he denies it of course, but he can't be trusted to tell the truth."

"What about Clyde Hensley? Where does he fit into all this, and why was he collecting photos of Kyle?"

"I don't know. I do think I have a pretty good idea of what he was up to this morning."

"At Helen's?"

"Yeah. Filming you to add to his collection. We found compact disks in his apartment with multiple images of women undressing. Doesn't seem like he ever progressed beyond the Peeping Tom stage, but who knows."

"Do you think Kyle's murder was one of his little photo shoots gone wrong?"

"No. Kyle's killing was premeditated. Someone wanted that girl dead and went to that open house to do it. Now that we know it was not Cyril Shank, we have to look at those close to her with motive. Was it her husband? Her lover? His wife? Or someone we're completely ignoring?"

"Have you looked into Chellie Howe and Foster McFarlin's whereabouts?"

"Foster was driving between his various developments, speaking with his subs, but there's quite a bit of time unaccounted for. Chellie was speaking at a fundraiser at the Ringling Museum. Her assistant, Mindy Jackson, was with her."

The waiter arrived with their dinners and placed them down with a flourish. Jonas regarded his miniscule portion of *lomo adobado*, a pork dish, and sighed.

Darby slid him some of her paella on her bread plate and he grinned and said thanks. Taking a bite, he chewed and regarded her carefully.

"It all comes down to one question, Darby: who wanted Kyle Cameron dead?"

She nodded and took a sip of the Rioja, the memory of Miss Florida's First Runner-Up lingering in her mind.

———

Chellie Howe left Mindy sitting at her desk and walked the three blocks from her office back to the condo. It was a mild night, the heat of the past several weeks having broken somewhat, and a hint of a breeze was in the air.

Chellie looked at her cell phone, checking her incoming messages with irritation. She had the usual annoying reminders from Mindy, even though Mindy had been only an office away, and a few calls from staffers alerting her to upcoming legislation and concerns of the Governor. She sighed. Nothing important; nothing from Foster.

She swallowed, tasting acid in the back of her throat. Why had she thought Kyle's death would make any difference in Foster McFarlin's behavior? With Kyle safely out of the picture, Chellie had imagined … She shook her head. It seemed so stupid now. Stupid and naïve. She'd imagined he'd return to her and that they'd once again have a real marriage.

Fuck him, she thought with a bitterness born of years of humiliation. *Fuck him to all hell.* She exhaled deeply, trying to rid herself of the sour taste of defeat. *How do I get beyond this? What do I do?* She bit her lip, heard her heels clicking on the pavement, and then another sound …

Wham! It was too late for Chellie Howe to react, too late for her to avoid the handle of the pistol as it smashed into her cranium. She collapsed to the ground, her arms flung wide, waiting for an embrace that never came.

———

Darby lay in bed in Helen's guestroom, unable to sleep. Her evening with Jonas Briggs had not clarified anything: instead, she now had the additional puzzle of the severed pinkie to ponder. Without a sound she rose from the bed and opened a window. There was a slight breeze in the air and the curtains gently billowed.

Darby looked out over the lawn at the street bathed in moonlight. Clyde Hensley had passed her line of vision directly in front of Helen's massive palms, his baseball cap pulled low and his arm extended. Why the outstretched arm, she wondered. He'd pulled it back into the vehicle a second later.

Darby pulled on some shorts and a tee shirt and made her way quietly through Helen's house. She opened the front door and crept across the lawn, looking at the black asphalt with curiosity. Had Clyde Hensley tossed something out the window? And if so, had the police already found it?

In a gutter on the other side of the street, Darby saw a white paper bag with red lettering. She knelt and examined it, using a stick she found nearby to peer inside. A styrofoam cup, its contents most likely coffee, bore the logo of a nationwide donut chain. A few napkins with the same red lettering were crumpled alongside. Darby lifted the bag using the stick, feeling foolish as she carried it back to Helen's house. *My big discovery is a discarded coffee cup. Who knows if it even belonged to Hensley?*

Back at the bungalow, Darby laid the bag on Helen's porch and poked inside with the stick. There was a crumpled piece of paper in the bottom, most likely a receipt. Darby regarded it with interest. There was writing on it.

She grabbed a corner of the paper and carefully opened it up.

Donald Bergeron. The name was scrawled in ink on the back of a receipt dated several months earlier. This was old trash, discarded by Hensley that morning, whether on purpose or accidentally.

179

Darby said the name out loud. It meant nothing, and yet she felt a strange sense of excitement. It was a clue, in a case where there were precious few such scraps.

She carried the bag into Helen's and placed it in her bedroom. Booting up her laptop, she punched in Donald Bergeron and came up with a wide range of contacts across the country. Typing in the name and Hensley's yielded nothing, so Darby turned off her computer and climbed back into bed.

Despite finding no solid information, she knew she would now get some sleep. Hensley had written down a name. Darby felt sure it meant something, and that she would soon discover its significance.

———

Officer Kelly McGee chirped out "Good morning" to Detective Dave DiNunzio, who was slumped at his desk in the middle of a big yawn as she passed. He mumbled something incoherent to Kelly and shook his shaggy head, reminding her of a big bear just coming out of hibernation. He was always exhausted on Fridays, recovering from his weekly poker game the night before. She smiled as he stretched, yawned again, and answered the phone. She saw him swivel in his chair and cup his hand over the receiver, suddenly alert. "Have you seen Detective Briggs?"

Kelly McGee frowned. "Not yet." She thought about his dinner plans with the beautiful Darby Farr and felt the familiar ache in her ribs. *Knock it off*, she told herself. *You've just got to get over it.*

Kelly looked over a pile of papers on her desk and wondered where to begin. The computer queries on ticket data, or the log book? Reluctantly she lifted the pile of queries and pulled out her chair. DiNunzio was at her side, a strange look on his face.

"The Lieutenant Governor was assaulted last night in Tallahassee," he said. "Briggs is over there as part of a new task force she's formed, and he's tied up until lunchtime at least." He shook his head at Kelly, who wore a confused expression. "Hard to believe, some asshole went and mugged Chellie Howe, huh?"

Kelly McGee's red curls bounced as she shook her head. "Is she okay?"

"Yeah. Shook up, and more determined than ever to catch every criminal in Florida. Hence the new task force." He checked the few notes he'd scribbled while talking to Briggs. "He wants us to head over to Driftwood to see that Darby Farr. She found something on her lawn late last night."

Kelly nearly winced at the name Darby Farr, and yet could not contain a shiver of excitement at the prospect of gathering evidence.

"What are we waiting for?" she asked DiNunzio. "My car is in front."

———

Darby showed the scrap of paper to Detective DiNunzio and Officer McGee while a worried Helen, hands clasped in consternation, looked on.

"What does it mean, Detective?" she asked. "Can you tell?"

Dave DiNunizio put a beefy hand on the older woman's shoulder. "Now don't get too concerned, Mrs. . . . ."

"Miss Near," she said, shrugging off his placating hand. "You're new in the department, aren't you, Detective DiNunzio?"

181

He gave a sheepish nod. "Yes, Ma'am. But I'm not new to police work."

"Then you listen up. I'm already concerned. A man installed a camera in my guest room window. He could have harmed Darby. I want to make sure you're taking this seriously."

Kelly McGee fixed Helen Near with a level gaze. "That's why we're here, Miss Near. This name could be a link to a murder suspect. It's very important evidence, and I'm glad Miss Farr found it."

Darby wondered at the previously garrulous officer's sudden formality but did not react. "How quickly can we run it through your database?"

"I'll take it down to the station right now." She gave Darby a curious look. "Would you like to come?"

Darby nodded. "Definitely. I'll take my own car and follow you." She turned to Helen. "My appointment with Mr. Kobayashi is at ten, so I'll head over to the island from downtown. Are you going to be okay?"

"Who, me? Sure, I'll be fine." Helen leaned toward Darby and whispered, "You really want to make me feel better, get your Mr. Kobayashi to write a check for St. Andrew's Isle. Then I'll be peachy keen."

———

Kelly McGee pointed to a plastic chair in the precinct's waiting room. "Have a seat," she said, heading toward the glass door of an office. Darby picked up a newspaper and glanced at the front page. Lieutenant Governor Chellie Howe was featured, discussing her plan to put more patrolmen on the streets of Florida's cities.

Darby looked for a mention of the Kondo Killings, and found several places where the violence of the murders was decried.

Darby was about to put the paper down when a familiar name—the byline of a wire service story covering rebel groups in Afghanistan—caught her eye. "Miles Porter," she said aloud. They'd met in Maine, just a month earlier, and felt a mutual attraction. She scanned the story, hoping Miles was not in danger, but the report gave no indication of its author's whereabouts.

Kelly McGee cleared her throat and Darby looked up, startled.

"I'm sorry," the officer said. "I didn't mean to scare you."

"It's fine. I just noticed this news story. It's by a friend of mine, someone I haven't heard from in a while." She stood up. "Any luck?"

"Yes, as a matter of fact. Donald Bergeron and Clyde Hensley were incarcerated in the same Texas prison at the same time. Not only that, but they shared a cell for a few months."

"Interesting. Do you think Clyde was planning to contact this guy?"

"Well if he did, he came up empty. Donald Bergeron died last year—just about the time Clyde Hensley was released."

"Did he die in prison?"

"No, Bergeron was already out, still in Texas, when he was shot in an alley near his job. His shooting was never solved."

"Maybe Clyde Hensley didn't know Bergeron was dead."

"Could be."

Darby glanced at the clock on the wall. "I'd better take off. Thanks so much for following up on this."

"I wish it had led somewhere," Kelly said.

"Me too," said Darby. "Me too."

Hideki Kobayashi arrived early at the St. Andrew's Isle gatehouse, but Darby had anticipated this and was even earlier. Wearing a perfectly tailored suit and pristine white shirt, the dapper man with black hair going gray at the temples bowed to Darby and she gave a small bow back. With a twinkle in his eye, he greeted her in Japanese. Darby smiled and answered him back.

"I see your command of Japanese is very good," he observed.

"I can manage the pleasantries, but beyond that, I'm afraid I don't remember very much of what my mother taught me."

"And yet your accent is flawless. What part of Japan is your family from?"

"South of Tokyo. A city called Kamakura."

Hideki Kobayashi inclined his head slightly, but said nothing.

"And yourself? Where are you from, Mr. Kobayashi?"

"I now live in Tokyo, but I was raised in Yokohama City. Kamakura is a beautiful old town; I know it well." He gave another subtle tilt of his head. "I believe that our meeting is fortuitous. We shall talk further about our Japanese roots, but first, may I examine this exquisite property?"

Darby nodded. "Of course." She did not believe in omens, but it did seem her relationship with Mr. Kobayashi was getting off to a very auspicious start.

———

Chellie Howe was ready to leave the hospital. Dressed in fresh clothes and sitting in a chair by the window, she pressed a few buttons on her Smartphone and reread her husband's only message:

*Heard what happened and that you're going to be alright. Thank
God. Listen, it's midnight, and I'm not in any shape to travel. I'll see
you late morning.*

That was it. He had nothing more to say, even when she'd been
attacked and left for dead on the street.

She swallowed and tried to steady her hands. This was the marriage she had chosen, this was the kind of man he was, a man with
precious few feelings, a man who had blatantly taken a lover and
showed little concern at the attempt on her life.

A monster.

Chellie closed her eyes. The pain and rage were almost more
than she could bear.

There was a knock on the door and Mindy Jackson entered,
oblivious to her employer's mood. "Detective Briggs called and
said he'd stop in before the task force meeting. Then I've got a
press conference scheduled at eleven on the steps of the ..."

Chellie's emotions needed an outlet and the hapless assistant
fit the bill.

"Get out of my room! I don't care what you've done. Just get
out."

Mindy's face colored and she began backing away.

"Fine," she breathed, her voice sounding high and reedy. "I'll
leave and this time I'm leaving for good. But one more detail you
may want to take care of, Lieutenant Governor Howe. The Sarasota Women's Club called to reschedule your talk—the one you
completely missed at the Ringling Museum? They'd like you to
contact them as soon as possible ..."

"You little shit!" Chellie's face was twisted in anger, but then,
just as suddenly, it melted to a look of pleased surprise.

"Detective Briggs! How lovely to see you."

Jonas Briggs' eyebrows were raised in a quizzical look.

"Everything okay here?'

"I was just saying goodbye to Mindy."

"I see." His blue eyes looked wary. "There's good news regarding your assault last night."

"Such as?"

"Your wallet's been found in a dumpster near where the attack took place. The Chief here in Tallahassee said they've grabbed a couple of kids for questioning, too. You didn't see the face of your attacker, correct?"

"How could I? I was hit from behind, and I've got the welt to prove it." She looked around the room and sighed. "I can't wait to get out of here. Can you check and see what's taking the doctor so long?"

"Sure thing."

Chellie watched as Jonas Briggs left the room, admiring, even in her frazzled frame of mind, the way he swaggered as he walked.

———

Following her meeting with Hideki Kobayashi, Darby stopped at the Dive, looking for Marco. She found him in the storeroom, loading bottles of tonic water and ginger ale onto a small dolly. He looked up as she approached and frowned.

"What are you doing here?"

"Jack sent me. I need to know where your cousin Candy might be."

"Why is that?" His voice wary, tired. "She's not in trouble, is she?"

"No. I'm hoping she can help Jack. She might be able to corroborate his story."

Marco thought a moment. "Candy is a very private person. She doesn't like to draw attention to herself."

"I understand. I only want to speak with her."

He angled the dolly so that it could be pushed to the bar. "Why didn't Jack give you her address? He certainly knows where she lives." He frowned. "She's in Bradenton, downtown. Right by the video palace—I think it's 1280 Pelican."

"Thanks." Darby paused. "Have you heard from Jack?"

Marco shook his head. "No. I don't think I will, except to find out that I'm fired."

"What do you mean?"

"I gave you that note and you went to the police with it. Now he's in jail. I should have burned the damn thing."

"That would have been destroying evidence, Marco, and you would be in real trouble then. Listen, Jack wrote that note because he wanted help."

The tall man shrugged. "I don't know."

"No one does for sure, but I do know that you did the right thing." She touched his shoulder and turned to leave. "I'm going to see if I can find Candy. Thank you, Marco."

———

Forty-five minutes later, Darby drove by a tired brick building at 1280 Pelican. She parked the Mustang, walked back to the building, and muscled open a dingy entrance door. The walls were grimy and gray, and she had difficulty reading any names on the scribbled mail slots. Finally she found "C. Sutton" and pushed a tarnished bronze button.

A buzzer sounded and from inside the building, Darby heard the bark of a small dog. She opened the interior door. Inside it was murky, the air dank and musty. She climbed the stairs to the third floor, not trusting the elevator.

A woman opened the door of her apartment a crack and gave Darby a quizzical look. "Who're you?" She was tall, and very thin, with honey-blonde hair cut in a bob and an even, golden brown tan. Her long, tapered fingers ended in bright red nails that tapped on the door frame with impatience. "I said, who the hell are you?"

"A friend of Jack Cameron's. My name is Darby Farr. Are you Candy?"

"I am. What do you want?"

"A few minutes of your time."

She glanced down the hallway. "Time is something I don't have a hell of a lot of. Are you with the police? I told them I could speak to them tomorrow."

"I'll only be a minute."

Reluctantly she opened the door and Darby stepped into the apartment, bracing herself for more squalor. Instead she blinked in amazement. It was a surprisingly bright, airy space, with sleek tubular furniture and polished wood floors. Abstract paintings in bold colors accented the walls.

"What a beautiful room."

"Thank you. I enjoy the contrast with the rest of the building." She frowned. "My lease is almost up, and to tell you the truth, I'll miss this grungy place." She waved in the direction of her furniture. A small white dog lay curled in a snowy heap, paying only the scantiest attention to Darby. "That's Fang. Another reason this place has worked out well. Anyway, have a seat."

Darby perched on a cantilevered cane chair and nodded appreciatively. "This is a Mies van der Rohe design, isn't it?"

Candy gave a small nod. "That's right. I see you know something about modernism."

"Not much, I'm afraid, but I've always been a fan."

"The man was a genius. Skyscrapers, houses, furniture ... I love his work. I love his whole philosophy."

"Less is more?"

"Exactly." She settled herself on a red velvet sofa shaped like a kidney bean and pursed her lips. "Less is more." Her face hardened. "Let's talk about why you're here."

"Jack Cameron."

"Yes. And how do you know him?"

"I'm here visiting an old family friend, and she is Jack's godmother. I don't know how much you know about what's been happening..."

"Oh, I know everything. The diving accident, his arrest ... I'm well aware of Jack's situation." She leaned forward. "Are you looking for some sort of alibi?"

"For Jack?"

"Well, I thought that was who we were talking about. Look, I've got a very busy day so let's get to the point. I was with Jack on Monday, right up until he headed for home."

"He said he was on a fishing trip."

"He was." She gave a smirk at Darby's quizzical look. "I sometimes make house calls."

"You mean you met him on his fishing boat?"

"Yes, I did, and I listened to him ramble for hours."

"Could you tell what he was saying?"

She shook her head. "It was a long, convoluted story about his wife."

"Why would you drive out to the bayou and sit on Jack Cameron's boat?"

"Why do any of us do anything?" Candace Sutton asked, arching an eyebrow. "Look around this room, my dear Darby Farr. I've got a lifestyle that I value, and to support it takes money. That's why I'd sit for hours in the hot sun keeping a wasted client company. Money. Pure and simple." She rose from the sofa and Darby followed suit. "I'm afraid I must show you out." From his spot on the couch, Fang lifted his head, looked at the door, and yawned.

Darby's gaze lingered on a brochure that was tossed on a hall table. *Barnaby's International Realty.* "Where will you go when your lease is up?"

Candy Sutton pursed her lips. "I've been looking at property."

"Who is your broker?"

"That's none of your business." Candy opened the door. She seemed to study the building's chipping paint for a moment. "Kyle," she said softly. "I was working with Kyle Cameron."

TEN

DARBY LEFT CANDACE SUTTON'S apartment, her head swirling with thoughts. *Candy knew Kyle! And yet I asked her nothing about her.* She reached the parking lot where she had left her car. She thought about Candy Sutton's claim that she had joined Jack on his fishing expedition. It was strange, but perhaps it was possible. No stranger than having looked at property with his estranged wife.

Darby arrived at the lot and found her car. Less is more, she said beneath her breath, repeating the design philosophy of Mies Van der Rohe. The adage did not seem to apply to Kyle Cameron's murder investigation, where precious few clues represented more confusion instead of clarity. *And then I have a good lead, and I blow it,* she thought.

In the corner of the parking lot, a car door slammed. Darby glanced over and saw a tall, powerfully built man striding away from a glossy black Lexus. Something about him seemed familiar, and Darby watched as he exited the lot and vanished around the corner. Finally, she peered into the window of his front seat.

Tossed on the leather cushion was a news magazine, the subscription label clearly visible. "McFarlin Enterprises." Darby sprinted out of the parking lot and peered down the street, just in time to see Foster McFarlin disappear into Candace Sutton's building.

———

Helen was happy to hear that Darby was headed back to Serenidad Key.

"I called Peter Janssen," she said. "I told him I'd pay him a 20 percent referral fee from the listing side of the St. Andrew's Isle transaction when it sells. I know I don't have to, but I want to. He was a good friend to Kyle, and I think it's what she would have done, had she lived."

"What about Marty Glickman?"

"Ugh. Well, he'll get his share of course, but there's no avoiding that. I made it clear to Peter that it was his relationship to Kyle that I was recognizing, nothing to do with Glickman at all."

Darby heard a pan clatter in the background.

"I'm making us some dinner and I'm hoping you'll have some good news."

"Such as?"

"Such as your Mr. Kobayashi is ready to buy St. Andrew's Isle. Come on, Darby, you were there for three hours and he wants to go back in the morning."

"How did you know that?"

"Justin Fleischman. Remember him? He manages Tag's guest house."

Darby smiled. "Of course. The fledgling real estate agent. Okay, Helen, you'll get your report at dinner." She had pulled off the highway, into the breakdown lane, to make her call. Now she surveyed the rush hour traffic and sighed. "I've got to go. See you in about an hour."

———

Officer Kelly McGee and Detective Dave DiNunzio talked about everything they could think of while bouncing down the rutted dirt road—her upbringing in Philadelphia, his favorite type of poker, her undying affection for Philly cheese steaks, his conviction that the fish on Florida's east coast were far superior to those caught on the west. They'd given up trying to understand why they were nearly out of their jurisdiction—practically in the Everglades, as DiNunzio kept saying—on a trip that seemed like a total waste of taxpayer money. "Detective Briggs wants our department to find Hensley," explained Kelly, although her explanation was starting to sound flimsy even to her ears. "If the helicopter did see a car way out here, it could be him."

Finally they both grew quiet, the thick roadside vegetation seeming to muffle all of their words like a dense, green blanket.

"You sound as if you loved the East coast of Florida," Kelly observed. "Why did you transfer?"

Dave DiNunzio gave a harsh chuckle. "I didn't exactly choose to transfer," he said carefully.

"Oh." Kelly wondered if she should change the subject. "Were you involved in the Kondo Killings investigation in Stuart?"

"Not directly. My old partner was assigned to the case. Pretty gruesome stuff."

They grew quiet once more. Kelly, who was driving, slowed the police car as they rounded a bend and DiNunzio craned his thick neck.

"What do you see? The Corolla?" He leaned forward. "Shit, that's it alright. White Corolla. Plates are wrong but he probably changed them."

Kelly put on the flashers and slowed to a crawl. "I'm going up alongside, see what we've got."

"No." Dave DiNunzio's voice was an urgent whisper. "Let me out right here." His hand was at his side, ready to draw his gun. She recognized the look of focused adrenalin on his fleshy face.

"I'm ready to back you up," she said.

"You stay with the radio. That's the kind of back up I'm gonna need." He opened the car door silently and slid out.

She held her breath, watching his crouched approach to the dusty vehicle. The hood was open, all the windows rolled up. Engine trouble, Kelly surmised, hoping that Clyde Hensley was not watching from the bushes with a shotgun trained on Dave. She hadn't much liked Dave when he'd transferred into the department just a few weeks before, but now that she'd grown used to his tuneless whistling, ridiculous nickname, and endless accounts of good poker hands, she couldn't bear to think of his getting injured.

He was at the side of the vehicle and peering into the interior. She saw him glance in the back seat and then turn his attention to the front, recoiling in alarm at whatever he saw. His hand went up to his mouth as if he was going to throw up, stayed there a minute, and then slowly returned to his side. He holstered his gun and glanced at her. Dead, she heard him yell. She nodded as he made a slashing gesture across his throat. They'd driven all this way to capture a dead guy.

Kelly opened the cruiser's door to stretch her legs a moment when DiNunzio gave a startled yelp.

"Get the fuck back, Kelly," he yelled, pulling his gun. He shot several rounds through the back seat car window and waited, watching with a look that mingled horror and incredulity.

"It's a snake as large as a friggin' tree trunk. I think it ate the guy's face off!" He took a tentative step toward the Corolla. "Christ, it's not dead yet!" The sharp sound of the gun firing echoed through the cypress swamps, shattering the late afternoon silence.

Finally it was quiet. DiNunzio took a long, steadying breath.

"Jesus. I've never seen anything like it. Must be twenty feet long." He ran a hand through his bushy hair. "I looked in the back, but I thought it was a rug or something, all rolled up. I don't know what the hell kind of snake it is..."

"Burmese python," Kelly said, suddenly at his side.

"How in the world—" began DiNunzio.

"My cousin Todd had one, until it ate the family cat." She peered over at the body's mangled features. "So that's Clyde Hensley. I think he got what was coming to him, leaving that poor girl to die on those electric wires."

"Yeah," Dave DiNunzio said, wiping his sweaty palms against his pant legs. "The bastard got exactly what he deserved."

———

The ride from Candy's apartment back to Helen's house took Darby into the center of Sarasota, past the office of Barnaby's International Realty. On an impulse, Darby pulled into an empty parking space at the building and headed inside.

A slim woman with a chic, short haircut met Darby at the entrance. "Welcome to Barnaby's," she said. "I'm Jolene Sebastian. What can I do for you?"

"I'm Darby Farr, from Near & Farr Realty. I wondered if Marty Glickman was available."

"You're working with Helen, right? Hang on a second, I'll check." Jolene Sebastian glided out of the entranceway and into a glass-walled office. A few moments later, she returned. "You're in luck, Darby. Marty is free."

Darby followed her to a large corner office. A massive desk presided over the room, its surface completely clear save for a test tube with blue liquid that was placed on one corner. Behind the desk, framed by a huge picture window overlooking the Gulf, was a man in his fifties, with wire glasses and thick brown hair going gray at the temples. He stood up and extended his hand. Darby could see that he was a slight man whose short-sleeved shirt and tan trousers seemed to hang on his wiry frame, although his handshake was firm.

"Ms. Farr, it's a pleasure to meet you. Won't you have a seat?"

Darby looked around the room for clues to Marty Glickman's personality, but the walls were bare. Where was his computer? Paper, books, pens? She glanced again at the glass tube and noticed there was something green growing inside the vial.

Marty Glickman noted her interest. "Riesentraube grape tomatoes," he said, pointing at the test tube. "They're sprouting in a gel. Cool, isn't it? NASA developed it—who knows why—but I swear sometimes I can see the roots growing right in front of me." He laced his fingertips together. "So what can I do for you?"

"I want to ask you a few questions about Kyle."

"May I ask why?"

"I'm interested in finding out why she wanted to leave Barnaby's."

Marty Glickman raised his eyebrows in surprise. "Then this will be a short conversation, because I have no idea." He leaned forward in his chair, his fingertips no longer intertwined. "I don't have to tell you the perks of working for a company like Barnaby's. Superior market share, name recognition... You're in San Diego, right? At Pacific Coast? Then you probably know you're our only real competition out there." He paused. "Look around you. Kyle had an office with an even more spectacular view. She had her own support staff, the latest in equipment. Frankly, why she wanted to leave this for a little mom-and-pop brokerage, I'll never know." He gave an insincere smile. "No offense."

"Did you have a good working relationship with her?"

"Me? Definitely. I groomed her for this place and was her biggest champion. Smoothed some ruffled feathers when she started, made sure she got the recognition she deserved—I did everything possible for that woman. Don't get me wrong—we got into disagreements now and then. Kyle was very opinionated and she didn't like to be told what to do. But we got along just fine."

"You must have been angry when she told you she was leaving. After everything you'd done for her."

"Of course I was! Look, the bottom line in this business is whether you make the deal happen. Kyle did that and more. Did I hate to lose her? Sure. She was a real rainmaker. Was I angry? You bet! But did I stab her to death? No, I did not." He rose from his chair and came around the massive desk. "Now, if we're through..."

Darby rose as well. "Did Kyle have any enemies that you knew of?"

"No. She was a competitive person and there were undoubtedly people who disliked her. Enough to kill her, I don't know."

Helen was tearing up lettuce for a salad as Darby entered the cheerful little kitchen.

"Helen, I'm sorry to be late. I stopped by Barnaby's to ask Marty Glickman a few questions."

Helen groaned. "Now why do you want to ruin a good dinner by bringing him up? I'd much rather talk about something more pleasant, such as your new friend, Mr. Kobayashi." She smiled as Darby took two plates down from the shelves. "Let's eat on the patio. This heat's finally broken some."

Darby carried the plates outside. A fresh breeze off the Gulf ruffled the leaves of the citrus trees, sending the spicy scent throughout the enclosed area.

"Now who's Mr. Kobayashi?" Darby teased, laughing at the startled look on her friend's face. "Okay, okay, I'll tell you that Mr. Kobayashi does find the property attractive." She reentered the kitchen to fetch the bottle of Pinot Grigio that was chilling in the refrigerator.

Helen raised an eyebrow. "Finds it attractive, huh? Darby, you and I both know he flat-out loves the place! You watch, you'll be writing me up an offer by five o'clock tomorrow."

Darby smiled. She wasn't going to let on just how much Mr. Kobayashi wanted St. Andrew's Isle. It was strange, really, how determined the man had seemed about owning the property. He spoke as if he already did own it, a sign, Darby knew, that he was hooked.

She thought back to her time with the courtly gentleman. After they had toured the extensive grounds and buildings, Darby had attempted to find out why her new client found St. Andrew's Isle such a perfect fit. "As your broker, I want to make sure we've explored all the options," she said. "I agree that St. Andrew's Isle is exquisite, but perhaps we should see some other listings for comparison's sake."

Mr. Kobayashi showed the barest hint of a smile.

"Your advice is wise, Miss Farr," he said. "I appreciate the fact that you do not wish merely to make the sale, but that you are thinking of my needs." He paused, and seemed about to say more, when his cell phone rang. He peered at it, frowned, and excused himself to answer.

It had been years since Darby had heard anyone speaking rapid-fire Japanese, and she smiled at the melodic tone of the conversation. There were those who loved the sound of Italian, or Russian, but for Darby, the Japanese language was musical, comforting. She was about to check her cell phone when she distinctly heard two words she was sure she knew.

Nihon Maru. They were rattled off quickly, as part of Mr. Kobayashi's conversation, and yet Darby recognized them. She glanced his way, heard him say goodbye, and watched as he hurried back to her.

"I am afraid I must excuse myself to take an important conference call," he explained as he strode toward her, his normally placid manner slightly ruffled. "If you are able, I would like to meet in the morning for breakfast and to discuss my offer."

"Certainly."

"There is a small café in Sarasota, the Daily Grind. I will meet you there at nine o'clock. If possible, I would like to come back here following that, to speak with the staff. If Mr. Gunnerson is amenable, I will not need your presence for that."

Darby had said she would check and watched as Mr. Kobayashi hurried away.

Nihon Maru. He'd said those words and she'd recognized them, although she had no idea why they held any significance, nor did she have the foggiest notion of what they meant. *Just because you've got some Japanese DNA doesn't make you an expert on the language,* she chided herself.

Her musings were cut short by Helen's booming laugh. "Well look at you, caught in a trance. What are you thinking about, girl?"

"Dinner," Darby answered firmly. She pulled out a chair for Helen and watched her sink into it gratefully. "Have you heard from the Camerons? How is Jack doing?"

"Mitzi cannot believe the change in him. She says he is a rock. Something happened to him when he stared down that shark. It's as if he realizes he was given a second chance."

"Jack looked death in the face and survived," Darby said quietly, having done the same thing a month earlier while in Maine. "He's a changed man."

The phone rang and Darby rose to answer it. The honeyed voice of Jonas Briggs was instantly recognizable.

"I'm sorry to bother you and Helen at suppertime, but I need to meet with you tonight, if that's possible."

"What's up?"

"I think it's time to put our heads together again and really work on this case. I'll pick you up at seven and we'll go to the station. Okay?"

"I'm not sure what I can bring to the table," Darby admitted, "but I'm happy to help." She paused. "Did you get the message I left about Candy Sutton?"

"I did, and we plan to follow up with more questions for her tomorrow."

This time Helen did not tease Darby when she relayed her plans.

"I'm glad you're helping Detective Briggs, and I hope the two of you can solve poor Kyle's murder. When I think of Jack sitting there in that cell, arrested for a crime he did not commit—" she shook her head.

Darby nodded her agreement. What worried her was not so much Jack's confinement as the fact that the real murderer was perhaps still at large, waiting for the right opportunity to strike again.

———

"Cameron may be guilty after all," Jonas Briggs said, handing Darby a cup of coffee from the deli across the street. They were at the Serenidad Police Station, sitting in an empty conference room around the corner from Briggs' office. She thanked him and placed the styrofoam cup on a section of newspaper. The surface of the table was marred with rings and scrapes, but Darby was a creature of habit, even when taken aback by a statement.

Jonas lowered himself into a chair and pulled another coffee out of a brown bag. "Well? Aren't you going to disagree with me?'

"I'm waiting for you to complete your statement. What's he guilty of?"

Jonas wagged a finger at Darby. "You're sharp, Darby Farr, I'll give you that. You didn't rise to my bait, although I did see you do a little double-take." He tossed a few creamers on the table and removed his coffee cup's lid. "We think Jack paid an arsonist to destroy Belle Haven the night Kyle was killed." He ripped the foil wrapper off two creamers and poured the contents into the steaming beverage. "I've suspected arson from the beginning. Granted, I'm no fire expert, but this thing spread quickly, and the point of origin was just behind the back door leading to the alley. Somebody set it and ran. We just needed some proof."

Darby took a creamer and removed the foil lid. She poured it into her cup and stirred it thoughtfully.

"And now you have it?"

Briggs nodded. "Yeah. The State Fire Marshall's office has found a delay device—a cigarette tied to a matchbook—that proves it was arson. We have a witness who saw someone running out of the building late Monday night. This morning we picked up a punk from Miami who's been suspected of setting other fires, and our witness identified him. Our punk promptly turned around and named Jack Cameron as the guy who hired him."

"What does Jack say?"

"He doesn't think he did it." Briggs took a gulp of his coffee. "He says he certainly thought about it, but he doesn't remember taking any action. Hard to believe he was that messed up, but there you go." Jonas Briggs shook his head.

Darby took a sip of her coffee. "So it was purely a coincidence that the Miami arsonist set the fire the same night Jack's wife was killed?"

"That's right. Here's what I think happened that Monday. Jack drank a few beers on his skiff, and then called Ms. Sutton. Thanks to your visit with her, we know she met him and provided a few hours of company while he rambled on and on. She was there from approximately noon until five, getting paid a thousand bucks an hour to sit in the sun. She told DiNunzio on the phone that Jack never left, and that she'd swear to it." He took a look at his notes. "Dave's going to see her in the morning first thing."

"So Jack is off the hook for murder, but on the hook for arson."

"Looks that way." Jonas Briggs grasped his coffee cup and took a long gulp. "Now we move on to Clyde Hensley. A few hours ago we found him, on the edge of the Everglades."

Darby leaned forward. "No kidding. Alive?"

Briggs shook his head. "Most decidedly dead. Killed by a Burmese python, a type of constrictor. The thing crawled in his car and got him while he was passed out, or napping." Jonas Briggs remembered Kelly's description of the mangled face and shuddered. "In the trunk we found some names and addresses of his parasailing clients. Dave DiNunzio gave them all a call. Hensley took two college girls out on Monday, met them at the dock at 11:30. They were on the water for two hours—during the time Kyle Cameron was murdered. There's no way Clyde Hensley could have been over at Esperanza Shores." Jonas Briggs shrugged. "Hensley was a low-life ex-con, responsible for the electrocution of that poor girl, but he wasn't Kyle Cameron's killer."

"Any idea why he had all those photos of her in his apartment?"

"Maybe he was planning to film her."

"And the significance of Donald Bergeron?"

"He was a prison connection. We're not sure if there's more."

Darby opened a black and white composition book she'd purchased earlier at a stationery store. Jack Cameron was no longer a suspect, and neither was Clyde Hensley. Next on her list was Foster McFarlin.

"Kyle wanted out of her relationship with Foster McFarlin," Darby mused. "Sassa Jorgensen, Kyle's massage therapist, says they argued before breaking up. Kyle was pregnant, perhaps mending things with Jack…"

"You think McFarlin didn't want to lose her, so he killed her?" Briggs' face was skeptical.

"Stranger things have happened."

"Like people getting choked by snakes?" Briggs bit his tongue. "I shouldn't have said that. This whole snake thing's got Lieutenant Governor Howe all worked up." He paused. "Is she in your little book, too?"

"As a matter of fact, yes. She certainly had motive. Maybe not opportunity, but motive."

Jonas Briggs held up a hand. "You didn't hear this from me, but apparently the Lieutenant Governor missed the luncheon as well as her speech, and when she did finally show up at the tail end of the Q and A, she was wearing a different set of clothes."

"What?"

"That's right. I confirmed it with the staff at the hotel, as well as the head of the Women's Club. They were annoyed, but accepted her substitute, none other than her assistant Mindy Jackson. Incidentally, it was Mindy who blew Chellie's cover."

"Hell hath no fury like an assistant scorned?"

Briggs grinned. "Something like that." His face took on a more serious cast. "You can understand the delicacy of this situation.

204

Investigating McFarlin is hard enough, but implicating Chellie in any way..." He frowned. "You heard about the mugging?"

"I did. The press is reporting that she's fine."

He nodded. "For once they've got the story right." He leaned across the table. "Darby, I'm prepared to pursue both of them as suspects, but I've got to do it very carefully. You, on the other hand, don't have the same constraints. I want to know Chellie Howe's whereabouts on Monday. Why did she miss that luncheon?"

Darby met his level gaze. She could well imagine the intense political pressure Jonas Briggs was feeling, and knew that it would escalate if word leaked out. "I understand." She tapped on her composition book with her pen. "What about people from Kyle's past?"

"Such as?"

"Alexandra Cameron."

Jonas Briggs looked baffled. "They were sisters-in-law..."

"And they went to FSU, the same school Chellie Howe attended. In fact, they were friends and sorority sisters."

"So what happened?"

"Sassa Jorgensen says Alexandra was angry that Kyle separated from Jack. She said Kyle used to joke about it, never taking it seriously."

"What else?"

"It may sound silly, but years ago, they were contestants in the same Miss Florida competition. Kyle won the pageant, and Alexandra was runner-up." She searched Jonas Briggs' face for any trace of amusement, but to her surprise he nodded.

"I remember that year. Everybody in Sarasota thought Alexandra was a shoo-in." He thought a moment. "What about Helen?

What does she think about the relationship between Alexandra and Kyle Cameron?'

Darby looked into his eyes. "That's just what got me thinking. Helen swears that Alexandra worshipped Kyle. To all appearances, they were the best of friends."

Jonas Briggs downed the rest of his coffee and wiped his mouth with the back of his hand. "Friggin' appearances," he said, shaking his head. "They can definitely screw you up." He gave Darby a shrewd look. "So you're thinking the answer to Kyle's death may be in her past. Something from her youth, or her marriage?"

"Perhaps. I do think we need to focus on finding out more about her everyday life. I could call Sassa Jorgensen and see what else she knows. That woman saw Kyle every week for nearly two years. There's a good chance she has valuable information."

"It seems she was the closest thing Kyle had to a friend, other than her work colleagues." He considered. "Yeah, go ahead and call her, see what you find out."

"Done." Darby gave a quick glance around the conference room. "I spoke to Marty Glickman today, and I think it would be good to interview more brokers at Barnaby's and see where that leads. We need to check out Kyle's hobbies, where she exercised, and the ways in which she spent her non-working time."

"Find anything interesting out from Glickman?"

"Not really. He said he was her champion, that they had a good working relationship."

"Then why'd she want to leave?" Jonas Briggs thought a moment. "I'm going to have Kelly look into the data on Kyle's computer—her work on her grandmother, all that stuff."

"Good idea." Darby glanced at her watch and sighed. "I'd like to see if I can reach Sassa Jorgensen before it gets any later."

"Come on then, let me drive you back."

They headed into the warm summer evening, both of them quiet. The uncertainties about Kyle Cameron's death swirled in Darby's head. So many questions, and precious few—if any—answers.

———

Sassa Jorgensen answered the phone on the first ring. Darby heard a tired wariness in the masseuse's voice.

"Sassa, this is Darby Farr. I met you at the memorial service for Kyle."

The older woman cleared her throat. "I remember you."

"I hope I'm not calling too late, but I had a question for you about Kyle. Did she ever mention any family members? Other than her grandmother?"

"Anna Slivicki was the only family member that mattered to Kyle."

"I understand. But did she ever talk about her parents? Cousins? Anyone?"

Sassa thought a moment. "I'm sorry. I don't remember her saying anything like that."

Darby thanked her and said goodbye. Disappointed, she went into the little kitchen, where Helen was pouring a cup of tea.

"You don't look like your chipper self," she commented. "How about I fix you a cup? It's decaffeinated." She reached into the cabinet and pulled down an orange mug. A moment later she was handing Darby a steaming cup full.

Darby inhaled the aroma and smiled. "Constant Comment. My mother's favorite."

Helen raised her eyebrows. "Really? Me, too." She settled herself down at the table. "I don't care for all the fancy teas they make now. Ginger, ginseng, pomegranate—you name it, they put it in a tea. Last week a client gave me cup of watermelon tea. Can you imagine that? Watermelon! I want to drink something plain and simple, that's what I want."

Darby smiled. She thought of her friend's penchant for Mojitos and wondered whether a mint tea would elicit such surprise.

"My mother had similar sentiments, Helen. She was raised on green teas—her province was famous for one kind—but when she married my father and he bought Constant Comment, she thought it was the best thing she'd ever had." Darby pictured her mother's slim frame, the way she would slowly fill the red teapot with steaming water, and add two teabags. She felt a pang of sadness. It was difficult to think about her parents, even years after their deaths. At least I have memories, she thought. Unlike Kyle ...

She took a sip of the steaming beverage, letting the flavors of clove, cinnamon, and orange rest on her tongue like a wine connoisseur.

"Helen, do you recall Kyle Cameron ever talking about her family? Anyone besides her grandmother?"

Helen leaned back in the chair and thought a moment. "I don't think she knew them. From what Mitzi's told me, her mother disappeared when Kyle was a small child, and she never knew who her father was." She removed her tea bag and placed it on a small saucer. "I did ask her once how she got the name Kyle. I mean, to me, it sounds like a boy's name, and I was curious."

Darby felt a stirring of interest. "What did she say?"

"Her father had the name all picked out before she was born. Didn't matter whether she was male or female, Kyle was to be the name. Had to do with a pro football player."

Darby took another sip of her tea. "A football player?" She rose and went to the guest bedroom, returning with her laptop.

"Yes, that's what she said. Somebody famous, I think."

Darby booted up her computer and punched in a few words. "Let's see. I'm searching for football players with the name "Kyle." She looked over at Helen and groaned. "Unbelievable! There are dozens of sports celebrities with that name—as a first name and as a last name." She typed in more information. "Kyle Cameron was born in 1964, right, so it would have to be someone who played before that." She typed some more and then sat back, satisfied. "Now this is more like it. Only one entry comes up before 1964, and that's an athlete named Kyle Rote. He played running back for the New York Giants, 1951 to 1961. I bet you he's the one."

Helen took another sip of her tea. "So her dad was a Giants fan. It's interesting, Darby, but does it help us find the poor girl's murderer?"

Darby closed the computer and sighed. "No." She sipped the tea again, the bold flavors announcing themselves in no uncertain terms. If only the answers to her many questions about Kyle's murder could be as obvious.

Who had wanted Kyle dead? She'd been a driven business-woman, actively involved on several boards of good causes, on the arm of several of Florida's most eligible bachelors—as well as its married men. She thought again of Foster McFarlin and Chellie Howe. No matter what route Darby tried to follow, the signs kept pointing to them. When would Jonas Briggs actively investigate them? Was there anyone else?

Candy Sutton. Darby thought of the woman's alibi for Jack Cameron. Could she be believed? Could Jack, for that matter? Could anyone?

Darby groaned, forgetting she was sitting beside Helen at the table. The older woman put a hand on her forearm. "Listen, Darby, please don't give up yet. I just know you're going to figure this out. I have a feeling there's a breakthrough right around the corner."

Darby took a last sip of her tea and rose, rinsing the cup and placing it in the drying rack.

"I hope you're right, Helen." She picked up her laptop and was about to head for the guest bedroom when the phone rang.

"Go on and grab it," Helen said. "I'm too tuckered out to chat on the phone."

Darby recognized the melodic accent of Sassa Jorgensen. "Forgive me for disturbing you, but after we spoke I had a thought. I wondered if perhaps I might give you a massage. I know you are trying to help my poor Kyle, and I would like to give you this one small thing."

"That would be lovely," Darby said, thinking that she heard in the woman's voice more than a desire to massage her muscles. *She wants to talk about Kyle.*

"Call me when you have a free hour," Sassa said simply. She hesitated. "There is one thing I have remembered, but I do not think it is helpful. Should I tell you some other time?"

Darby tensed. "I'd like to hear it now, Sassa."

"Kyle made a little mention to me of something strange. This was at least three weeks ago. She said a man called her, asking for money. He said he was her father. She went downtown to meet him."

"And what happened?"

"She said she knew just by looking at him that he was a phony. She told him if he called again, she would contact the police."

"Did she say anything else?"

"No. She tried to laugh it off, but I think she was a little—disappointed." Sassa Jorgensen paused. "Kyle had no blood relations, and yet family was important to her. She was always trying to find out more about her grandmother. I think the baby may have made her vulnerable to someone holding out the hope that she was not alone." There was silence, and then Sassa Jorgensen continued. "That's all. I look forward to hearing from you, Darby Farr."

———

Darby lay in Helen's guest bedroom, knowing that sleep was a long way off. Who was the man who had posed as Kyle's father? Could he have killed her after she refused to give him money? How, after forty years of absence, did she know so definitively that he was a fake?

Darby sighed and stood up. The windows were closed and the air felt stuffy. She crossed the room and lifted the sashes.

Darby felt the cool night air on her face, a welcome sensation. She glanced across the lawn, remembering how Clyde Hensley's white compact car had shot down the street with him hunched at the wheel. Perhaps he had photographed Kyle as part of his plan to pose as her father. He'd tried to extort money from the wealthy real estate agent, but she'd smelled a rat. Had that rat then turned to murder?

ELEVEN

Darby rose at six o'clock, her head fuzzy. Already it felt warm in the guest room, and as she pulled on her running shorts, she wondered again how Floridians could stand the relentless summer humidity. In Helen's bright kitchen she took a long gulp of water, laced up her sneakers, and headed out into the day.

In three hours she was meeting Mr. Kobayashi, hopefully to take his offer on the St. Andrew's Isle estate. The whole thing had happened with lightning speed, but Darby had learned a long time ago not to question the easy deals too much. There were far too many complicated transactions—some of which never worked out—for her to obsess over the calm ones. *Hideki Kobayashi came to Florida knowing he wanted the estate,* she mused, her feet pounding the cement. *It's just a matter of price now.* She found herself hoping for ET's sake that the transaction would close quickly so she could loan him his money.

Her run took her down the streets of Serenidad, into the neighborhood where Belle Haven, Jack Cameron's swanky bistro, had once stood. Darby slowed by the charred remains of the building. Most of the debris had been cleared and the sooty smell was gone from the air, but part of the blackened chimney still stood, along with a portion of the crumbling back wall.

Darby thought back to Jonas Briggs' assertion that Jack Cameron was responsible for the fire. She still wasn't clear why he'd had the restaurant destroyed. If he owed money to creditors, why not try to sell the building? Certainly the real estate was valuable.

And yet, the economy was in a slump and perhaps even a prime piece of commercial property such as Belle Haven would be a difficult sell. Darby sighed and began running again. She found it difficult to understand the crime, but of course Jack's mental state had been one of confusion at that point.

None of this helps find Kyle's killer, she thought.

Virtually no physical evidence existed. The police still had not located the murder weapon, nor the severed finger, and with every day and every hour, the chances that evidence would be found grew slimmer. *Whoever killed Kyle thinks they are pretty damn smart,* she thought. What if he or she was ready to strike again?

———

Helen, clad in her pink bathrobe, met Darby at the door of the bungalow, a worried look on her face.

"Jonas Briggs called for you," she explained, pulling the belt on the robe tighter. "He sounded awful. I hope it's nothing to do with the Camerons."

Darby untied her sneakers and carried them inside. "Did he leave a number, Helen?"

"He said to call on his cell."

Darby removed her cell from the pocket of her Lycra running shorts and punched in his number. It rang without an answer, and Darby hung up before leaving a message. "That's odd," she said to Helen. "He's not answering."

The ring of Helen's house phone startled them. She answered it and turned to Darby. "It's him."

Darby took the phone and heard the sound of street noise and traffic. "Jonas?"

"Darby, I've got some news for you—some bad news."

Barely breathing, she asked, "What is it?"

"Candy Sutton is dead. Bludgeoned to death in an alley by her apartment." He exhaled and Darby could hear defeat in the sound. "We aren't sure if it's random or not, but my gut tells me it's related to Kyle Cameron's killing."

Darby was silent a moment, processing the horrible news. *Candy Sutton was dead. Had she known something that put her in danger?*

"How did you find her?"

"Dave DiNunzio went over there early this morning to question her and found her dog, still on his leash, whining outside the door. He went in and the place was empty. So he took the dog outside and the little guy led him to the alley next to the Video Palace. She'd been dragged behind a dumpster. We're still waiting for the medical examiner, but it looks like she hasn't been dead very long."

"Any evidence at the scene?"

"Nothing yet, but we're still looking." He paused. "Listen, I want you to watch your back. Whoever this guy is, he's getting desperate. I don't know how Candy Sutton knew Kyle…"

"I do," Darby said quietly. "She was Candy's broker. They were looking at houses together."

214

Jonas Briggs whistled. "Now I'm more certain than ever that it's not a random crime. Candy knew something—or the killer thought she did—and she was eliminated because of that fear."

Darby was silent, thinking of the mysterious Candy and her "less is more" philosophy. "Does her cousin Marco know?"

"Yes. He was the one who made the positive ID. Pretty upset, too." Jonas Briggs cleared his throat. "Looks like the examiner is here. I'll keep you posted."

Darby hung up, ready to tell Helen of the latest development, but to her surprise the older woman was not nearby. "Helen?" she called.

A glance at the kitchen made her heart skip a beat. She could see pink fabric on the floor, twisted tightly around a pair of ankles.

Darby ran to the prostrate form of Helen and felt for a pulse. Nothing. She checked the woman's airway, to be sure nothing had lodged in her throat, but it appeared clear. Was she breathing? No expirations from her mouth or nose; no telltale rising of her chest.

Without hesitation, Darby began cardiopulmonary resuscitation. With every chest compression she shouted at the lifeless woman beneath her hands. "Take a breath!" she urged, as she started puffing air into Helen's lungs. "Please, Helen, take a breath!"

Darby knew the quick arrival of the ambulance was critical. Although she hated to stop CPR for even a minute, she whipped out her phone and called 911. Seconds after relaying the address, Darby was back on the floor.

After about a minute, she felt again for a pulse. Was there the faintest flutter?

Darby had just resumed chest compressions when the paramedics burst through the door. "Any pulse?" one of them shouted.

"I don't think so." Darby felt tears welling up in her eyes. "Please be okay, Helen," she prayed. "Please, please…"

One paramedic prepared the electrode patches of a defibrillator while his companion felt for a pulse. "I got one," he yelled. "Let's transport her."

The emergency team bundled Helen onto a stretcher, administering oxygen as they moved her out the front door. "You can follow us to the hospital," one of them suggested.

Darby nodded, grabbing her purse and phone. She didn't trust herself to speak, so she climbed into the Mustang, started the ignition, and prepared to follow the ambulance.

———

An hour later, Helen was alert and telling Darby to get herself home and showered for the appointment with Mr. Kobayashi.

"Don't let a little thing like this screw up the deal," she rasped, her throat raw from the tubes that had been removed only moments before.

"Sshh. Don't talk, Helen. I'll take off in just a few minutes, don't worry." Darby looked into the kind blue eyes and felt her own grow moist once more. "What else can I do for you?"

"Check my calendar at the office. I think I have an appointment at noon with a new buyer. And I was going to meet Foster McFarlin today to discuss getting his listings."

Darby nodded. "I'll take care of it." She gave the older woman's hand a squeeze. "You rest and get better, okay?"

Helen gave a wan smile. "It's a deal." She closed her eyes. "You can bet I'll want a Mojito when I get out of here. And an offer on St. Andrew's Isle."

Darby smiled and whispered goodbye, keeping her eyes on the prone form as she backed toward the door. Helen had suffered a mild heart attack, probably only seconds before Darby had found her. The good news was that her doctor felt she would recover without any heart damage. The not-so-good news was that she'd probably require surgery in the future to remove several blockages.

Without a doubt, the CPR had saved her life, a fact that made Darby shiver. What if she hadn't returned from her run when she had? What if Jonas hadn't called and Darby had been in the shower, oblivious to her friend lying on the kitchen floor?

She shook off the worrisome questions as she climbed back into the rental car. There was no use in revisiting what might and might not have happened. The important thing was that Helen was alive and expected to recover.

Darby looked at the digital time display on the dash. Nearly eight o'clock. She had just enough time for a quick shower before driving to meet Hideki Kobayashi at the café. And then, between Helen's appointments and her own plans, she was in for a very busy day.

———

Jack Cameron wiped down the bar at the Dive and surveyed the empty restaurant. He was free on bail, thanks to Dr. Menendez's expert opinion and his mother's ample checkbook. He scrutinized the furniture. Some of the chairs needed replacing, he noted, and one of the awnings was starting to look a little tattered. In the past, he would have gotten angry about the constant upkeep a business required. Now he smiled, took out a small pad of paper, and made a few notes.

The Dive was a lucrative spot and Jack felt at home among its patrons. Hopefully they'd still support him while he served his sentence for destroying Belle Haven. *I'll need a manager, somebody to keep the place in good shape*, he thought. Maybe Marco would be up for the job.

Jack thought back to his state of mind before Kyle was killed. Had he really done something so stupid as hiring an arsonist to torch his property? *At least no one was hurt*, he reminded himself. But the lack of any injuries had merely been luck, perhaps the first lucky thing that had happened to him in years.

Now don't start thinking like that, Jack, he chided. *Don't go throwing yourself a pity party. Because that's what it is when you blame your actions on bad luck.* Helen Near had been right when she'd admonished him about taking responsibility for his behavior, told him that was the way a real man approached things. She had said the first true thing that anyone had dared say to him, and he appreciated her tough love.

His phone buzzed and he glanced at the display. Marco. He answered and heard his bartender's familiar voice.

"Something bad's happened, Jack."

Jack noted the flatness of Marco's speech. "Yeah?"

"It's Candy. She's dead."

Jack reached for the bar to support his suddenly weak legs. "No."

A sob escaped Marco's throat. "Somebody killed her last night." He was crying now, gulping big heaving mouthfuls of air like a fish on a dock. Jack felt his chest constrict. *No*, he thought. *Not Candy …*

"Marco, I don't believe it."

There was the sound of a long exhale. "Somebody got her in the alley while she was walking her dog." He exhaled again and Jack could tell he was trying to pull himself together.

Jack felt his insides writhing with anger. Candy—dead—it couldn't be. "We'll get the bastard who did this," he vowed. He closed his eyes and said a silent prayer. "You need anything for Candy, you call me, you understand?"

He hung up and narrowed his eyes. It could only be one person, the same person who had killed Kyle. And he would have to pay.

Jack looked down at his hands. He was still holding the damp rag, but it was twisted it into a tight knot.

———

Hideki Kobayashi rose to his feet when he saw Darby arrive. "I hope you have not eaten breakfast," he said.

"No," admitted Darby. "I haven't." She realized suddenly that she was starving, absolutely starving. Between her run and the trip to the hospital, combined with a hurried shower and drive downtown, she was famished, and nearly everything on the cheerful plastic menu looked appealing.

The waitress came and took their order, bringing Darby a much-needed cup of strong black coffee. She sipped it gratefully and smiled at Mr. Kobayashi.

"Before we talk about St. Andrew's Isle," she said slowly, "could you solve a mystery for me? The other day you said some Japanese words that I recognized. *Nihon Maru*. May I ask, what does that mean?"

Mr. Kobayashi nodded his head vigorously. "Ah, yes, *Nihon Maru*, I did mention her the other day."

"It's a person, then?"

He laughed. "Nearly. The *Nihon Maru* is a boat, a beautiful sailing ship owned by my company. She is about to start a voyage

219

from Yokohama to your home port of San Diego. I was thinking that perhaps I would fly to California and meet her."

Darby leaned back in her chair. "Is it an old boat?"

"No. The *Nihon Maru* is a replica, but built faithfully in the style of the old four-masted schooners. She is a training vessel."

"*Nihon Maru.*" Darby said it softly, trying to remember more. "What does it mean?"

"Nihon is an old term for my country. Maru means boat. So it's something like, 'Boat of Japan.'"

Darby took a sip of her coffee, puzzled.

"I can see that I did not solve your mystery. Perhaps a photograph might help." He reached across the table with his cell phone and pointed at the screen.

Darby picked up the phone and looked at the photograph. A lovely schooner with billowed sails filled the screen.

"What a beautiful boat."

"Yes, she is lovely, the *Nihon Maru*," Mr. Kobayashi said proudly. "That was taken just after she won a prestigious award. The Boston Teapot Trophy."

Darby froze. *Boston Teapot Trophy.* She remembered hearing about the famous race, and the tall ships that competed for the prize. She heard her mother's voice telling her what it had been like to sleep under a canopy of stars...

"My mother sailed on the *Nihon Maru*," she said suddenly. She looked at Hideki Kobayashi and pointed at the image. "My mother was on that boat in Boston. That's where she met my father."

He regarded her with a steady look. The waitress arrived with their food and departed in silence.

"Your mother, she is no longer living?"

Darby nearly winced. Was her status as an orphan that apparent?

"She and my father died when I was young." She looked down at her Eggs Florentine, inhaled the aroma of a perfectly cooked breakfast. This was the here and now, this elegant dish of eggs, spinach, and Mornay sauce; her parents were the painful past. She gave her client an apologetic look. "I'm keeping you from your breakfast. Please, let's eat and I'll stop chattering."

Hideki Kobayashi shook his graying head. "No, you mustn't do that, Darby. I am very interested to hear of your family and to know that your mother graced the *Nihon Maru* with her presence." He picked up his fork. "We shall eat while it is hot, and then talk of St. Andrew's Isle, but then I hope you will soon tell me more about your mother and her time on *Nihon Maru*." He reached for his cell phone, glanced at the photo once more, and then put it in his jacket pocket. Picking up a pitcher of maple syrup, he poured a generous amount atop an enormous stack of blueberry pancakes and grinned. "No matter how much time I spend in America, I will never tire of the fabulous food."

———

When their dishes were cleared away, Mr. Kobayashi pulled out a small pad of paper and consulted some notes.

"I am prepared to make an offer on St. Andrew's Isle."

Darby felt a surge of adrenalin. This was one of her favorite parts of real estate: helping buyers come up with their strategy for purchasing a property. No matter how big or small the dollar amounts were, this aspect of the business got her blood pumping.

"Tell me your thoughts," she said.

"I would like to offer full price. I believe St. Andrew's Isle is worth forty million dollars, possibly more." He peered through his reading glasses, an inquisitive look on his face.

"I agree with you." Darby told him of the market analysis she had seen that valued the estate at forty-five million dollars. "We know that Tag is eager to sell. Perhaps we could get a better deal. I'm certainly prepared to help you do that."

Mr. Kobayashi was listening intently. "I understand. But I do not want to offer less."

Darby nodded. "Fine, then let's draw up the paperwork." She pulled an offer form out of her bag and began jotting down details. "I believe forty million is a fair price. In fact, I think Tag could have commanded even more money had he asked a higher price."

"Certainly," Mr. Kobayashi said, his face shiny with excitement. "I was willing to pay him fifty-five."

———

Back at the office of Near & Farr, Darby listened to a message from Foster McFarlin postponing his and Helen's appointment. "Let's reconnect on Monday," his terse, deep voice suggested. Darby couldn't be sure, but she thought she heard agitation in the brief message.

Next she phoned Helen's new buyer, a man named Reginald Carter. The call was answered on the first ring.

"Yeah?" A clipped voice, sounding exasperated, spat into the phone.

Darby explained why she was calling but Reginald Carter cut her off mid-sentence.

"Fine, whatever. Listen, I need information on waterfront prop-erties. Anything up to ten mil. You can bring it by my boat at the Esperanza Shores Marina. You know where that is?"

Darby took a breath. Esperanza Shores was where Kyle had been killed. She wanted this guy at the office, not the other way around. "Yes, but—"

Again she was interrupted. "I gotta go. Bring it by the boat, soon as you can." Click.

Darby looked at the phone in her hand in disbelief. Had he even told her the name of the vessel? She shook her head and pushed redial.

He answered with a grunt. "Yeah?"

"It's Darby Farr, from Near & Farr Realty. I'm afraid I won't be able to help you after all. Good day."

She hung up the phone and grinned. She'd delivered a verbal front kick to the obnoxious Reginald Carter, and it felt good.

———

Darby drove to the hospital just as the sun was beginning to sink in the sky. Mojito time, she thought, picturing Helen drinking her favorite beverage instead of lying in a hospital bed.

She found her friend flipping through a golfing magazine. Af-ter giving Helen a hug, Darby asked, "What does your doctor say about stress? Are you allowed to have any?"

"If you're talking about presenting me with an offer, better hand it over, pronto," Helen commanded. Darby gave her an enve-lope with Mr. Kobayashi's offer. Helen pulled out the papers, saw the amount, and grinned.

"Yahoo! What are you trying to do, give me a heart attack?"

"Very funny. Don't they call that 'gallows humor'?" Darby touched Helen's arm and her voice grew gentle. "Can I help you with this? Want me to call Tag?"

"Heck, no. I am perfectly capable of calling anyone with good news like this. Grab my cell phone from that plant over there, would you?" Darby walked to a large potted palm and found the phone wrapped in a tissue at the plant's base.

"What's it doing in there?"

"They were going to confiscate it, so I had to think fast." She gave a glance to be sure none of the nurses were lurking about. "What happened with Foster? And that new buyer? Did you get in touch with him?"

"Foster postponed and said for you to call him in Monday. As for your new buyer, he was a real piece of work." She told Helen about the phone call to Reginald Carter.

"Bottom fishers," muttered Helen. "I am so sick of them. I'm glad you didn't waste your time." She waved the offer in her hand. "Now this is terrific. And here's another good thing. The doctor says I can come home tomorrow if my stress tests are good."

"That's great news!" Darby stood and gave her friend a kiss on the cheek. "Why don't I take off so you can rest. I'll be back tomorrow, but you call if you need anything, Helen."

———

Jack Cameron twisted the screwdriver between the door and the jam until the metal door swung open. He jammed the tool into the pocket of his jacket and gave a quick look around. Just before dusk and the development of Esperanza Shores was deserted. No construction workers, no condo owners, and certainly no real estate agents. What little activity there had been before Kyle's murder had now come to a screeching halt. The place was a half-built ghost town.

He pushed open the door to the model condo that served as Foster McFarlin's office and stepped inside. The unit was identical to the one in which Kyle's mutilated body had been found, and he knew from a friend who played cards with one of the detectives on the case that the murder had occurred in the same room in which he now stood. The image of Kyle's body, lying in the morgue, flashed before his eyes. His knees buckled like he'd been hit from behind and he grabbed the side of a plush armchair for support. This was beyond excruciating.

He took a deep breath, wiped the sweat from his brow, and shook his head. *Focus,* he told himself. *Focus on finding what you need…*

He crept to the unit's den, set up as a home office and used by McFarlin when he was at the project. A notebook-type computer was in the middle of the desk, a cup of coffee beside it. Jack opened the computer and a job list appeared in front of him. The damn thing was already on.

He pulled out the chair and sat down. Now to search the computer's contents to find something—anything—that would incriminate the developer. He moved the cup of coffee to one side of the desk and paused, puzzled. The ceramic mug was warm.

A faint noise raised the hair on the back of Jack's neck. As he turned toward the door, he felt certain he already knew who he'd see. And he wondered, not for the first time that week, whether he was about to die.

TWELVE

CANDY SUTTON'S MURDER WAS another rallying cry in Chellie Howe's campaign to clean up the streets of Florida's cities. Along with her own attack, the lieutenant governor could point to an ever-growing list of violent crimes the current administration was not preventing. It was a delicate balance, because she was part of the very status quo she was subtly disparaging. She had to beat the drum for reform, while at the same time appear to be doing her job. No one could get the wrong idea that somehow she was a part of the problem.

Her new press secretary understood the approach perfectly, and unlike Mindy, he didn't nag her about appointments or agendas. Fresh out of law school, R.B. Cloutier was quiet, authoritative, but not cocky. He was a Florida boy from the panhandle who wanted to work in politics, and Chellie had sensed right away that he was perfect for the job.

She wondered what the R.B. stood for. It wasn't the kind of thing she would ask him, but she'd find out at some point. In the meantime, she was determined to keep their relationship professional, even if he was good-looking, young, and possessed of the kind of hard, strong body she'd always favored.

Chellie looked down at the stack of newspapers R.B. had placed on her desk that morning. Had she even glanced at them during the day? She leafed through them now, noticing the headlines splashed across the front pages announcing Candy Sutton's death. The woman was an interesting character: the highest paid female escort in Florida, commanding upwards of fifteen grand a night, as well as an art collector, with an impressive array of paintings, sculpture, and modern furniture. She'd also been the muse and confidante of several prominent artists, as well as many of Florida's most powerful men.

She shoved aside the stack of papers and buzzed R.B. in the outer office. "Can you grab me a salad?" He agreed and she stood, her heels adding a good two inches to her height, and thought about her schedule for the next day. She planned to attend a church service somewhere, with the aim of grabbing a little more media attention. Too bad she couldn't head over to the East Coast, where she could remind voters in Stuart and Daytona about the importance of being tough on crime, without, of course, ever bringing up the Kondo Killer.

She checked her Smartphone for messages, straightened the piles on her desk, and flipped through a magazine without stopping to read anything. A rap on the door startled her, and she snapped out a "yes" before remembering it was not Mindy on the other side.

R.B. pushed open the door, a Cobb salad in hand. "I brought you a vitamin water, too," he said. "I understand pomegranate's your favorite."

His voice was so soothing, Chellie noticed, nodding her head as he placed the salad on her desk. "Thanks. You can take off. See you on Monday."

He nodded and backed toward the door. "Have a good Saturday night."

She winced as he closed the door behind him. It was Saturday, wasn't it, and she was here, alone, working at her desk. How pathetic she must look to R.B.! A lonely workaholic woman with a philandering husband, and nothing but a salad to keep her busy on a Saturday night.

Kyle Cameron took Foster from me. Kyle Cameron and her seductive smiles. She felt the old anger well up inside, as familiar as a bad dream, and this time she knew there would be no squelching it down. The rage was molten, rising through her body like lava, turning her red hot with its intensity and fire.

"Kyle needs to be stopped..."

Chellie thought back to her luncheon with Alexandra Cameron. After not hearing from her old college friend in years, she'd been surprised by an invitation to meet at the Serenidad Key Club. "I'm hoping to run some ideas by you regarding school lunch programs and new nutritional guidelines," Alexandra had explained. Normally, Chellie would have declined, but with John Cameron such a substantial donor, she'd agreed on the spot.

They had known their conversation would turn to Kyle. How could it not? Chellie was sipping her second glass of Chardonnay when Alexandra became oddly detached, insisting that her sister-in-law was out of control. "Kyle needs to be stopped," Alexandra had said, her gray eyes slightly out of focus. A moment later, she'd seemingly dropped the subject.

"That serial killer," Alexandra had mused to Chellie. "You know, the one targeting real estate agents?"

"A real monster." Chellie crinkled up her nose. "He chops off one of his victim's pinkie fingers as a little souvenir."

"Really?" The gray eyes flashed with interest. "That's not in the papers."

"Of course not," Chellie had said. "I have the full police report."

Now Chellie pushed the Cobb salad aside and opened her bottom desk drawer. She pulled out the photograph, looked at the image, and read Kyle Cameron's sappy words scrawled on the back. The anger spilled out and over her, drenching her like a torrential rain, and before she began sobbing on her desk she had ripped the photo to shreds.

————

The bungalow was eerily quiet without Helen, and Darby turned on the radio to have something—anything—in the background. She ripped some lettuce into bite-sized pieces for a simple salad and listened to the public radio station report international news, her brain hearing only part of the newscast. *Afghanistan. Reporter. Killed. Improvised explosive device*... She fled from the kitchen to the tiny living room and the radio, her thoughts on Miles Porter.

She held her breath and listened to the story. *A Canadian reporter, Claudette Bouchard, was killed with four Canadian soldiers in the province of Kandahar*... Darby exhaled slowly. *It's not Miles.* While she was relieved to know that he was safe—at least for the moment—her heart ached for the journalist and the soldiers who had perished.

Darby thought back to the last time she'd spoken with Miles. Had three weeks really passed since he flew to the war zone? His job as an "embedded" reporter with a group of American Marines was incredibly dangerous, and more so all the time. Seventeen journalists—reporters just as committed and courageous as Miles—had perished in Afghanistan since the start of the war in 2001.

Darby pictured the lanky reporter she had met in Maine. Why had he felt the need to accept such a perilous assignment? *Because I'm a reporter,* he'd explained, brushing back a strand of her long black hair. *If we ever have a hope of ending these wars, we need people in the trenches telling us what's going on.*

She felt emotion welling up inside. Why was she keeping her distance from him? Obviously he was too far away for a relationship now, but why did it seem she was ignoring the man completely? She bit her lip and faced the truth: her feelings for Miles were strong, and they frightened her. It was far easier to forget he existed than to confront the fact that she could lose him.

She thought of the day she'd learned of her parents' disappearance, the way the whole bottom had dropped out of her life, and the same hollow emptiness filled her as it had when she was fourteen.

I run the risk of losing Miles, too, she thought. But that was life, wasn't it? People died doing dangerous things, yes, but they also perished on sailing outings and hosting open houses...

Darby took a deep breath and figured the time difference between Florida and Afghanistan. It was pre-dawn in Kabul, too early to phone anyone. She sighed and resolved to call Miles Porter first thing in the morning.

———

Jack Cameron stood slowly, looking into the fierce eyes of Foster McFarlin. The developer had his arms crossed in front of him, a hard look on his face. "Figured I'd see you, Cameron," he drawled, "but I never dreamed you'd stoop to breaking into my building. What were you fixing to do, set it on fire?"

"You know damn well why I'm here, McFarlin." Jack slid his eyes over the room, finally settling them on the developer's face. "I'm here to find out why you killed her."

Foster McFarlin remained expressionless. "Then I'm afraid you're going to be disappointed." He cocked his head to one side, as if sizing up his opponent. "I didn't kill Kyle."

Jack Cameron felt the old recklessness welling up inside him, the same wild energy that had driven him to do so many stupid things. "Hell you didn't!" he yelled, flying across the desk at McFarlin, "I'm going to do what you did to my wife …"

Cameron's fist connected with Foster McFarlin's jaw but the developer barely flinched. He seemed to regard the desperate man for an instant before swinging back with an uppercut to Cameron's stomach that caused him to double over in pain. Next came a cross that smashed the side of Cameron's face and sent him crumpling against the wall.

Jack Cameron tried to move but could not get to his feet. McFarlin stood over him, rubbing his jaw where Jack's punch had connected. "Not a bad jab, Cameron. I'm going to have a nice bruise in an hour or so." He strode to his desk and glanced at the computer, pushed a few buttons and seemed satisfied.

"You don't deserve an explanation, but what the hell—I suppose I'm feeling sorry for you." He straightened up from the computer and regarded the bloody heap that was Jack Cameron.

"Kyle and I had dinner together at a little place in Coconut Grove the night before she was killed," he said. "She set it up— asked me if we could take the jet so that we'd be someplace private. I'm not stupid. I guessed she was ready to call our little relationship quits."

McFarlin grew thoughtful a moment, but a groan from Jack Cameron brought him back to his explanation. "We went to the restaurant and experienced what I would call a very awkward meal. Finally Kyle said she didn't want to see me anymore, except in a professional capacity. She had news on that score, too: she said she was leaving Barnaby's to join a small company. When I asked her why, she said her life was about to change and she couldn't take the atmosphere at Barnaby's any longer." He peered down at Jack Cameron and continued. "We talked about my properties. She convinced me that she was still the best broker to handle them, no matter who she worked for, and that she'd continue to make me money, provided we could deal with each other like grown-ups, on a purely professional basis." McFarlin shook his head and folded his hands once more. "I agreed."

Another groan from Jack Cameron, but this time he managed to get himself to a sitting position. He rubbed the side of his face and gave McFarlin a look that was oddly detached.

"Then what?" he asked.

"Then we went back to the airstrip, got in the plane and flew back. I dropped her at her condo, told her to work her ass off at that open house, and that was it." His voice grew softer. "That was the last time I saw her."

Jack Cameron looked wildly around the room. He was trying desperately to keep his cool, and when he spoke it was in clipped words through clenched teeth.

"You're telling me you weren't angry at her? She gave you the brush-off like that, and you weren't ready to bash in her fucking skull?"

McFarlin spread out his hands. "Look, I'd been trying to end our—relationship—for weeks."

"Then why didn't you?"

"I felt sorry for her. She was lonely." He shook his head. "You can believe me or not, I really don't give a shit. I'm telling you I didn't kill Kyle."

Jack Cameron put a hand to his forehead and closed his eyes. "Then who the hell did? Your wife?"

Foster McFarlin's eyes flickered but he kept his face neutral. "Chellie? She's too concerned about becoming governor to do much of anything." He gave a harsh chuckle. "I'm not saying she was any fan of Kyle's—they had a thing going back since college—but I can't imagine her committing murder."

"Doesn't mean it couldn't have happened."

"No," McFarlin agreed. "People do things all the time that don't make any sense." He thought about his former business partner, by all accounts a reasonable, bland kind of guy, the one he could invite to a Dolphins game and know he wouldn't have plans. Not the type you'd think would turn around and sue you for fraud as soon as the market went south. McFarlin felt a sour taste in his mouth just thinking about the web of lawsuits tangling around him like a noose...

He turned his attention back to Cameron. "Chellie didn't do it." He didn't add that a private investigator had assured him of that very thing only hours before. "I'm wondering if the cops have talked to Marty Glickman."

"Glickman? Why?"

"Kyle tried to sound like it was no big deal leaving Barnaby's, but I think they gave her a hard time. She made a hell of a lot of money for that company, and as the franchise owner, Marty did not want to see her go." His eyes narrowed. "I don't know about you, Cameron, but in my experience, people don't like losing money."

Jack Cameron staggered to his feet. He held the wall for support and waited for a wave of nausea to pass. "That's the first thing you've said that makes sense, McFarlin. You're right. Money is the last thing some people want to lose."

———

Darby had just sat down in the patio with her salad when she heard a knock on the door. She peered out Helen's peephole and saw the haggard face of Jonas Briggs.

She opened the door. "Jonas, come on in. What brings you to this neighborhood?"

Briggs entered the bungalow and shook his head. "I'm on my way home. Sorry to intrude, Darby, but I'm really frustrated. This case has got me climbing the walls."

"Can I get you something? I'm having a salad and a glass of wine. Care to join me?"

He gave a sheepish grin. "I've got a sandwich in my pocket. I would love a glass of wine and a few minutes of your time."

Darby led the way to the patio, grabbing a plate and another wine glass along the way.

"I know Helen is in the hospital," Briggs continued. "She's going to be okay, right?"

"Yes. She's hoping to be released tomorrow. She looks great and is in very good spirits."

"Thank God." Briggs sat down and gave a big sigh. He regarded Darby with a wary smile. "You sure you're up to this? Listening to the rantings of a stymied off-duty detective?"

"Absolutely. Let's see what you and I can figure out." She set his plate on the table, poured him a glass of wine, and sat down expectantly.

Jonas put a wrapped sandwich on the plate and took a gulp of wine. "I've learned over the years to trust my gut, you know, that feeling inside that tells you something?"

Darby nodded. "I call it intuition—same thing."

"Yeah, well here's what my gut tells me about this case. The murders of Candy Sutton and Kyle were committed by the same person." He paused and gave Darby a raise of his eyebrows.

"Kyle and Candy spent several hours together last week, looking at properties all the way down to Venice." He took a bite of his sandwich and chewed thoughtfully. "I know that means they were gabbing it up in Kyle's Miata the whole time. That was the way she operated, you know? Made you feel like you were best buddies while you were house hunting."

235

Darby nodded, remembering that Jonas Briggs had worked with Kyle at one point, so he spoke from experience. "You're thinking that Kyle told Candy something significant during that ride. Candy didn't remember it at first, or she didn't think it was important, until the other day."

Jonas' face looked more animated. "Exactly. Candy had no idea how important her piece of information was, so she didn't feel a sense of urgency. She told DiNunzio that she was busy on Friday and that he would have to come today. You don't do that if you think you've got something really crucial to report, right?"

"Right. Keep going."

"Whoever killed Candy knew her routine and that she walked Fang at five thirty every morning."

"Why was she in the alley?"

"Throwing away Fang's—er—droppings. She put them in that dumpster after every walk."

"So the killer was waiting there?"

"Yes."

Darby thought a moment. "Okay, so then we have to ask ourselves, what was that piece of information, and how did the murderer find out about it? Was it a coincidence that she was killed the night before she was due to talk to you? Or had the murderer planned all along to silence her permanently?"

"I've got some thoughts on that," Briggs offered. "I think our suspect found out and had to act quickly, before Candy talked. He or she may not have known Candy, but they did know Kyle. And one more thing—I would bet you that that he or she is left handed."

Darby couldn't help but smile. "You sound like Sherlock Holmes. 'He walks with a limp, my dear Watson …'"

Briggs grinned as well. "Elementary, my dear Darby, and I wish I could take credit for it. Kelly McGee, in my department, worked with the medical examiner on that, and I think she's on to something."

Darby smiled. *Good for you, Kelly.*

Briggs took another bite of his sandwich and frowned. "The thing I can't figure out is, how did the murderer know we were going to question Candy? That seems to suggest they knew each other."

"From what I understand, her list of acquaintances—male, anyway—is pretty long."

Briggs took another gulp of wine. "We have her client database and it is extensive. Plenty of names that you'd recognize, including McFarlin and the Camerons."

"The Camerons?"

"Yup. Father and son seem to have had the same taste in high-paid escorts. John Cameron wasn't one of her most steady clients, but his name appears a few times."

Darby shook her head. "Can this get any more complicated?" She took a sip of her wine. "Jonas, I'm not sure if it will get us anywhere, but why don't I look into Kyle and Candy's appointments last week? See where they went, what properties they saw?"

"Can't hurt." He finished his sandwich and balled up the plastic wrapping in his hand.

"Still no witnesses to Candy's murder, right?"

"Just Fang." He thought a moment. "On the bright side, we do have a confession in the Lieutenant Governor's mugging. Two teenagers, both under eighteen. Not exactly the hardened criminals she wants everyone to believe are popping up across the state." His jaw tightened. "Any luck on finding out where she was on Monday?

Darby nodded. "I made a few inquiries. Chellie was in Miami."

"Doing what?"

"Special meeting of another task force. When I questioned Mindy Jackson, she said the Lieutenant Governor very rarely screws up her schedule. Anyway, her flight back was well after Kyle's murder occurred. It seems impossible that she could have been at that open house when Kyle was killed."

Jonas sighed, rose from the table, and shook his head. Worry had once more settled on his features and he looked drawn and tired.

"Honestly, we're not any closer to solving this thing. We might as well have just found Kyle's body an hour ago."

Darby's face was grim. "It's not like you haven't been trying, Jonas. What we need is a good old-fashioned break in the case."

The detective nodded and headed toward the door. "Order me up one of those, okay?"

———

Minutes after Jonas Briggs had headed out into the warm Saturday night, Darby's cell phone rang with a call from Helen. Grabbing a pad of paper and a pen, she sat on one of Helen's comfortable couches and answered.

"How's it going, Darby?" Helen sounded upbeat, although her voice was low.

"Fine. Jonas Briggs was just here for a visit, but I'm alone now."

"Great. Got a counter for you on Tag's place. You ready?"

Darby listened while Helen rustled some papers. "Hang on, it's here somewhere," she said. "Okay…I think I've found it…" She let several moments pass. "We'll take it!" She let out a laugh. "There are a few minor changes for Mr. Kobayashi to initial, but nothing major."

"That's terrific."

"I'll say. Tag is ecstatic. He likes Kobayashi and wants to close as quickly as possible." Darby heard her speaking to someone in a surprised tone. "I'm afraid I need to hang up, Darby. Seems cell phone use is frowned upon in this hospital. Did you know that?"

Darby smiled and hung up the phone. St. Andrew's Isle was as good as under contract. She gave a slow exhalation and left Hideki Kobayashi a message to call her. Forty million dollars was no small chunk of change, but she knew he would be pleased.

She sat down on Helen's comfortable couch and flipped through a home decorating magazine, trying to clear her mind before she went to bed. Minutes later, fatigue had overtaken her, and she was asleep.

Darby dreamt of her childhood home on the island of Hurricane Harbor, Maine. She was barefoot and running across the grass of the old farmhouse when she spotted John and Jada Farr in the kitchen window. Happiness and gratitude washed over her as she flung open the kitchen door. They were talking to each other, but turned, smiling, and held out their hands.

Darby tried to walk to them. Her legs were heavy, immobile, and she looked down to see why. At her feet was a giant snake, wound tightly around her ankles, and preventing her from movement of any kind. She stretched out her hands and tried to say

"Help me," but the snake was writhing up her body, faster than she could have imagined, and now she could feel the rough scales of its skin against her lips ...

She woke with a start. She was asleep on Helen's couch, a nubby chenille pillow under her head. She sat up and forced herself to think about the dream before she lost recollection of the images. The snake was a frightening memory, but the faces of her parents—their smiles, the graceful way her mother had been leaning against her father's broad shoulders—had been worth the terror.

She checked to see if Mr. Kobayashi had returned her call, but there was no message. *First thing tomorrow,* she thought. She would give him the good news about St. Andrew's Isle, and ask more questions about the *Nihon Maru* and her mother.

THIRTEEN

AFTER A QUICK RUN through the winding streets of Serenidad Key, Darby showered, dressed, and drove to Sarasota's fashionable St. Amand's Circle where Hideki Kobayashi had asked to meet for Sunday brunch. He stood and gave a small bow as she approached the table.

"Ms. Farr—always a pleasure to see you again," he murmured.

"And you." She sat down at the round table, smoothing her skirt over her tanned legs. She smiled up at her client.

"I have wonderful news regarding St. Andrew's Isle," she began. "Our offer has been accepted. There are a few minor changes to the contract, but nothing substantive." She opened up her file and showed him where Tag and Helen had modified the closing date by several days, requested less time for inspections of the property, and inserted language about contracts and the sale.

Hideki Kobayashi nodded, and smiled. "I am satisfied and prepared to sign." He took a pen out of his jacket pocket. "If you would indicate where I do so ..."

Darby went over the documents with him and watched as he initialed and signed in several places. She then called Helen Near and left a message alerting her that the property was now under contract.

"Congratulations," Darby smiled at him. "It is a fabulous estate and really suits you. Will you be living there full time?"

Hideki Kobayashi shook his head slightly. "Unfortunately, not at first. But I will come to the island whenever possible, and I know much of my family will enjoy the estate's grounds and the lovely swimming pools." He smiled. "My granddaughter Momoko has already asked when she can get a slide!" He chuckled. "She is what you might call a 'hot ticket.' My son and daughter-in-law are constantly amazed at her quick little mind." He smiled again, the fond grandfather.

Darby took a sip of her water. Her client pointed at the menu, eyebrows raised.

"Come, let's order our food and something pleasant to drink, and then I will tell you about the *Nihon Maru*."

———

Jack Cameron woke up slowly and painfully, rubbing the places where Foster McFarlin's punches had connected. He groaned. The guy was a hell of a fighter—that much was true.

He'd spent a good part of the evening on his fishing skiff, thinking about Candy and Kyle, and wishing he could drink away the pain caused by their deaths. He took a long swig of a diet root beer and sighed. Alcohol and pills were out of the question. That road got him nowhere, and he wasn't going down it.

A hearing was coming up on his arson case and he'd need to be in total control. He'd discussed his options in an hour-long meeting on Friday with his attorney, and the normally calm professional seemed frustrated with Jack's lack of detail about Belle Haven's fiery end. The truth was, he just didn't remember contacting anyone about torching it. The lawyer had suggested using temporary insanity as a plea, saying a jury would understand taking such a desperate action in the wake of his wife's murder, but Jack had dismissed the idea. He was through with using excuses, no matter what the consequences.

"What if I say I don't remember?" Jack had asked. "What will a jury think about that?"

His attorney had shrugged, a gesture Jack found almost laughable. "It depends on how sympathetic we can make you." He frowned. "We are going to need to talk about Kyle, you realize that. Your separation, her affair with Foster McFarlin—"

"No!" Jack's eyes flashed and sprang up from his chair. "I won't trash her name just to clear mine."

"But it's the truth!" His attorney was frustrated. "You're the one who keeps harping on the truth, not me."

Now it was Jack's turn to shrug. The truth was, he loved a ghost. He loved Kyle Cameron, always had, and probably always would. The fact that she was dead didn't take that love away.

He thought back to his encounter with the tiger shark. What had happened down there, between him and the fish, to set him on this new course in life? People didn't just "snap out" of depression, and yet somehow Jack had. His doctor couldn't explain it—no one could.

Jack got out of bed and surveyed his surroundings. Fishing trophies from his teen years, old diving magazines, and a well-oiled baseball glove still adorned the shelves of his childhood room, although his old twin bed had been replaced with a queen. He'd been here since he and Kyle had separated, enduring the open hostility of his father and his mother's pitying smiles.

Time to leave Casa Cameron, he thought. Time to finally grow up.

———

The waitress cleared away the brunch dishes from Darby and her companion and brought them both more coffee. Hideki Kobayashi leaned closer to Darby. "Now that we have finished our breakfast, I want to show you something." He produced a five-by-four-inch glossy black and white photograph of two smiling Japanese men standing on the deck of what looked to be a large wooden boat.

"This," he said, pointing at the man on the left, "is Denjiro Kanno, the former chairman of my company." He glanced at Darby who gave the photo a closer look. "And this," he said, indicating the other man who wore glasses and was a head taller than the Chairman, "is your grandfather, Tokutaro Sugiyama."

Darby's eyes widened. "My grandfather?"

"That is correct." He watched her face closely before continuing. "When you told me your family name and that your mother had been on the *Nihon Maru*, something jostled in my brain, some little memory of something that I could not quite grasp. I did a little research and came up with this photograph."

"Did my grandfather work for your company? Genkei Pharmaceuticals?"

The older man nodded. "He was a scientific officer. I did not know him, but I know he was regarded as a brilliant man."

Darby looked into her grandfather's face but the photograph was fuzzy and his features were blurred. "This is amazing. I never met him, but my mother spoke of him often." She looked up from the photo. "What is the connection between the *Nihon Maru* and your company?"

"We are the ship's corporate sponsor. It was Denjiro Kanno who got our company to help raise funds for its construction. It is, as I think I told you, a replica of a very historic vessel."

Darby nodded. "I remember you saying that. My mother sailed to Boston on this ship as part of a delegation from the Tokyo Tourism Bureau."

Hideki Kobayashi nodded. "Yes, that part is true."

Darby looked at him sharply. "What do you mean 'that part?' What part is not true?"

Her client gave her a steady look. "I will tell you what I know, but I warn you—the truth is not always easy."

Darby felt a queasiness in her stomach. What was he talking about?

"In the early 1980s, a book was published in Japan that shed light on a shameful piece of our history, a series of events which most Japanese people did not even know." He looked down at his hands as if he was feeling remorse for whatever long-ago actions he was about to describe. "The book described unspeakable crimes that took place at the time of the Second World War, in a part of northeast China. They involved human experimentation."

Darby's heart was beating hard. What did this have to do with her grandfather?

Mr. Kobayashi looked up, a pained expression on his normally placid face. "There was a secret biological and chemical warfare research and development unit of the Imperial Japanese Army called Unit 731. The scientists explored germ warfare by experimenting on more than ten thousand people, most of them Chinese and Korean citizens." He closed his eyes. "Some sources believe that the use of Unit 731's bioweapons and chemical weapons programs resulted in possibly as many as two hundred thousand deaths."

Darby swallowed. "Surely the people responsible for these crimes were punished?"

Hideki Kobayashi inclined his head. "Some were arrested by Soviet forces and tried at the Khabarovsk War Crime Trials; others surrendered to the American forces, but many of the scientists involved went on to prominent careers in academia, business, and medicine." He paused. "Including your grandfather."

"What?" Darby's eyes flew open. "What are you talking about?"

His voice was gentle. "The book about Unit 731 listed your grandfather as one of the scientists conducting experiments."

Darby shook her head, her hair swaying with the movement. "That's crazy. My grandfather would never have been involved in something so terrible." She looked down at the photograph's image of the smiling, bespectacled man. "You are mistaken. My mother—"

"Your mother didn't know, at least, not until the book came out. I suspect she had much the same reaction as you—shock, horror, disbelief."

"Surely she asked my grandfather, and he denied it?"

Hideki Kobayashi shook his head. "I believe that by that time, the old gentleman was suffering from dementia. His mind was not reliable. I believe that this is the reason your mother sailed on the *Nihon Maru*. She wished to find out the truth."

Darby's head was spinning. "I don't understand."

"From what I have gathered, your mother requested the opportunity to sail on the ship. She knew that the highest officials of Genkei Pharmaceuticals would be aboard, and I believe she wished to confront them and clear your grandfather's name of any scandal. I do not know what she discovered while on the ship, but I do know what she found while in Boston."

"What?"

"Your father." He gave a small, tender smile and Darby felt tears welling up in her eyes. This was too much—simply too much. She blinked them back and cleared her throat.

"Mr. Kobayashi, I thank you for brunch—it was delicious. I need to go now and help Helen. I'll be in touch regarding our next step for St. Andrew's Isle." She managed a shaky smile. "Goodbye."

He stood and looked into her eyes. "Darby, sometimes in these situations, there is no easy right and wrong." He cleared his throat. "I am suggesting that perhaps your grandfather did not have a choice."

She gave a small shake of her head, her long black hair shimmering in the sun. With trembling hands, she grabbed her purse from the adjoining chair. "When it comes to the taking of a life," Darby said slowly, "I believe everyone has a choice." She turned, leaving a silent Hideki Kobayashi behind.

———

Kelly McGee took a spoonful of her frosted wheat squares and reached for the Sunday newspaper, turning immediately to the obituaries. For some reason, she loved to learn about the lives of those who had just passed away, especially if they were a ripe old age. She crunched happily on her cereal and read about an octogenarian jazz pianist who had succumbed to Alzheimer's disease, an insurance salesman who had fought a brave battle with lung cancer, and a seventy-eight year old grandmother who had loved making quilts. She sighed. It was a shame anyone had to die, but at least these people had lived a good, long life. Not like Candy Sutton, whose face smiled serenely from her photograph. Sighing again, Kelly began to read the long columns describing the too-short life of the murdered escort.

She finished reading and gave her tortoiseshell cat, Buster, the empty cereal bowl. He winked in thanks and began licking up the leftover skim milk, his tongue a delicate shade of pastel pink. Kelly leaned back against her faded denim couch, thinking about Candy Sutton's last days.

Two days before her attack in the alley she'd called the station and asked to speak to a detective. Kelly gave the call to Dave and he'd agreed to meet with Candy on Saturday. Early Saturday morning, while walking her dog, Candy was beaten with a foot-long two-by-four until her skull was split apart. Dave had found her when he arrived for their appointment.

Kelly took the bowl from the satisfied cat and placed it in the sink. The killer had taken quite a chance surprising Candy in broad daylight. Yes, it was the early morning, before daybreak, but still, people were out and about, delivering newspapers, opening their shops, and heading into work ...

Kelly let it go and thought instead about Kyle Cameron. Her obituary had run in the daily paper, too, but since Kelly's subscription was just on the weekends, she'd never seen it. She reached for her laptop and found the newspaper's website. Scrolling down, she clicked on the obituary for Kyle B. Slivicki Cameron and began reading.

Kyle had been raised by her grandmother, the late Anna Slivicki, and received a prestigious scholarship to Florida State University, where she'd joined Alpha Delta Alpha, an exclusive sorority, and graduated with honors. She'd won the Miss Florida pageant and gone on to represent her state at the national level. Her successful career in real estate, most recently as an agent for Barnaby's International Realty, and marriage to restaurant owner Jack Cameron were all described, as was her interest in World War II history.

Kelly leaned back to pet Buster who was rubbing especially hard against her calves. Kyle. It was such an unusual name for a girl—and what did the "B" stand for? She looked on a website for the State Office of Vital Statistics, but it was not open on Sunday. With Buster hot on her heels, Kelly McGee got up from the couch with a plan.

———

The light on Helen's answering machine was blinking and Darby checked the message, hoping it was Helen saying she was ready to come home from the hospital. Instead, the message was in a strong, slightly-accented female voice that Darby did not recognize, until the caller identified herself as Carlotta Vega, domestic assistant for the Cameron family.

I am sorry to bother you on a Sunday, the message said, *but I need to speak to Darby Farr as soon as possible. Please call my cell phone number.* After relaying the number, Carlotta had discon-nected.

Darby checked her phone to see if Helen had called, and then called Carlotta Vega's cell. A brisk hello came almost instantly.

Darby introduced herself and asked how she could help. The voice on the other end lowered by several octaves and replied, "Please, meet me at the boathouse on the Cameron property as soon as possible." Carlotta Vega paused. "The building where you found Jack."

"I remember." Darby agreed to leave immediately, glad for a reason to stop thinking about Hideki Kobayashi's revelations. She hung up the phone and headed back to the Mustang. Backing out of Helen's driveway, she wondered what Carlotta Vega had to say, and why on earth it was so urgent.

———

Chellie Howe poured herself another cup of coffee and rubbed her throbbing temples. A sleepless night; a night spent replaying the luncheon with Alexandra Cameron over and over again, the lun-cheon at which the idea to kill Kyle had been hatched.

Jack's own sister had done it. She'd met Kyle at the Esper-anza Shores open house with some sort of thin-bladed knife and stabbed her until she'd bled out on the shiny wood floors. She'd cut off her pinkie, exited the condominium, disposed of the weapon and her clothes, and concocted an alibi.

The "why" was easy: she hated Kyle Cameron. She always had, even before the Miss Florida competition. It wasn't Kyle's beauty—Alexandra possessed uncommonly good looks—it was Kyle's con-fidence, her drive to succeed despite the crappy hand life had dealt her. Alexandra's privileged upbringing had somehow denied her this confidence. She flitted from one thing to the next, unsure and unhappy, doubting every choice she made.

And then Kyle had taken Alexandra's prized possession, her baby brother, in much the same way she'd stolen Foster from Chellie. How painful it must have been for Alexandra to pretend to be happy for them! At least when the couple separated, she could quit pretending to like Kyle. But then she'd watched her brother's slow spiral into addiction and madness, a course no one but Kyle could prevent.

Chellie Howe swallowed. She knew the whole story. The question was: how could she be implicated?

———

Darby drove to the boathouse and parked by the entrance, flashing back to a few days earlier when she'd found Jack Cameron's unconscious body on the fly bridge of the sport fishing boat. She entered the building, remembering how dark it became once she stepped inside the old wooden structure. The scent of smoke caught her attention and she heard a small cough.

"Ms. Farr, thank you for coming." Carlotta Vega emerged from the shadows, a glowing Cuban cigar in her hand. "Pardon my vice. I smoke only on weekends."

"I don't mind," she said. "The scent is so much richer than cigarettes."

Carlotta Vega sucked in a breath. "Oh, yes. There is no comparison. My family has worked in Sarasota's cigar industry for several generations, and my Uncle Carlos owns a small plant just north of the city. This is one of his cigarillos." She inhaled and exhaled slowly. "Would you like to try one?"

Darby declined and Carlotta Vega shrugged. She moved out of the shadows, her face hard, her eyes brittle and black. "You're wondering why you are here, and I won't waste your time. I've asked you to come because you are smart, and because Señora Cameron trusts you." She paused. "What I am about to say will come as a surprise. I know you will use your discretion."

Darby nodded. "I won't break any laws or put someone in danger, but you can count on me to keep your confidence." She watched Carlotta take another long drag, exhale slowly, and then crush the cigarillo under the heel of her shoe. She gave Darby a penetrating look, her demeanor a far cry from a subservient maid.

Carlotta crossed her arms and tilted her head to one side. "Let's see. Do I begin with the fact that John Cameron is screwing my daughter, or enlighten you as to his new business smuggling rum with my cousin?"

Darby knew Carlotta was expecting a reaction, but the level-headed agent met her gaze and waited. Compared to Hideki Kobayashi's news about her grandfather and chemical warfare, Carlotta's revelations were on the tame side.

Carlotta gave a rueful chuckle. "You don't shock easily, do you, Darby Farr?" She shook her head. "Obviously, this—affair—that John Cameron is having with Julia is the worst of the two offenses, at least from my perspective. I'd like to say that he seduced her, but I can well imagine it happening the other way around. My daughter is nineteen, Ms. Farr, and believes she's entitled to the finer things in life, things like Casa Cameron and all that it offers." She swept an arm around the boathouse and sighed. Darby could see her brittle aura of self-confidence starting to crack.

"Julia thinks her lover will leave Señora Cameron, an idea that I have told her is ludicrous, but of course, the more I say, the more she retreats from me and into this schoolgirl fantasy."

"How did you find out about their relationship?" Darby's voice was quiet.

"I suspected something, but it was at Kyle Cameron's memorial service that I knew for sure." She looked down at her hands and then back up at Darby. Her dark eyes flashed with anger.

"I would like to crush John Cameron the way I crushed that cigarillo a few moments ago. He has never treated his wife with respect, and now this, with my daughter..." she closed her eyes and gave a big exhale. "Unfortunately, I am not the murderous type. If I were, he would already be dead."

Darby shifted her weight onto her other foot. "Does Mitzi know? What about Jack and Alexandra?"

Carlotta shook her head. "I don't believe so. Señora Cameron's lack of mobility keeps her somewhat sheltered, and the other two have been so caught up in their own dramas that they don't notice anything else around them."

"Tell me about the other issue you mentioned."

Carlotta raised an eyebrow. "Ah, the smuggling. Again my sweet Julia may be somewhat to blame, as she undoubtedly made the connection between Javier and John." She took another breath. "Javier Vega is a second cousin to me. He's always been kind of a street thug, nothing more, but now it appears he is a thug who smuggles Cuban rum."

"And John Cameron? How is he involved?"

"From what I have heard, he provided the start-up funds as well as a place to store and sell their wares." She paused. "Belle Haven."

"How does Jack fit into all this?" Darby wanted to believe that the man was finally on the road to recovery.

She gave a sound of disgust. "You saw him when you first arrived—worthless. His mental state was like mush. He's had no idea what was going on with his marriage nor his properties. Marco has kept the Dive open, but no one cared about Belle Haven. Jack virtually abandoned the building, so his father used it for a little business on the side."

"Why would John Cameron do something so stupid? It doesn't make sense."

Carlotta's chuckle was bitter. "You don't know the first thing about him. You think he's a rich white man with a huge estate. The truth is, he comes from nothing and has conned people his whole life, including his wife. He's smuggling rum because that's the kind of man he is. Greedy. Reckless. And, although he enjoys thinking he is smarter than everyone else, ultimately he is stupid." She glanced at her watch. "I need to get back to the house. Let me tell you why I have confided in you." She pursed her lips.

"I want to get Julia away from here. We have family in South America, and I think I can persuade her to go. But first I need John Cameron out of the picture." She ran a hand through her hair and continued. "I have evidence that Javier set the Belle Haven fire, on John's say-so, of course, and I want to make a deal with Detective Briggs. Javier cooperates, and John Cameron is dealt with quietly, providing he stays away from Julia." Her face hardened. "Forever."

Darby considered Carlotta's bargain. "Why do you need my help?"

"You know Jonas Briggs. Maybe you can persuade him to keep this whole thing quiet." Her eyes softened. "I'm thinking about Señora Cameron."

"I understand, but what about Jack? His reputation has been ruined—first the murder, now the charge of arson—shouldn't he have a chance to clear his name?"

Carlotta nodded. "Yes, but perhaps he can do it privately, or after some time has elapsed. After all, the damage is already done. But if Señora Cameron learns of all this—"

"I may keel over and die? Is that what you are worried about, Carlotta?" Out of the shadows wheeled Mitzi Cameron, her arms pumping to make the chair roll at a surprisingly fast clip. "I may be in this chair, but I am not dead and I am certainly not going to sit by while my so-called husband lets our son take the blame for something he did. And as for Julia—" her voice softened. "I'm sorry, Carlotta. Let me pay for her flight to Chile. It is the very least I can do."

Carlotta looked down at the ground and then back at her employer. "Señora, I apologize for not telling you this myself."

Mitzi drew herself taller in the chair. "I am disappointed in your lack of confidence in me." Her tone softened. "But I do understand." She pointed at Darby. "Shouldn't you be fetching Helen at the hospital?"

Darby nodded. "She'll be ready after lunch."

Mitzi Cameron pursed her lips. "Good." She turned her attention back to Carlotta. "Please help me get back to the house. It is a long distance and I'm feeling rather fatigued." Her voice mellowed once more. "We will call Detective Briggs the minute we arrive."

————

Driving back to Helen's cottage, past the shopping district and through downtown Sarasota, Darby pondered Carlotta's revelations and the fact that Mitzi Cameron now knew the truth—or some of it, anyway. She had accepted it stoically, with the poise of someone used to dealing with adversity. *That's certainly not the way I responded to Hideki Kobayashi's news this morning,* she thought. She pictured the smiling face of her maternal grandfather, Tokutaro Sugiyama. Could he really have been involved in biological warfare against civilians?

Darby thought about what she knew of her mother's family. They had lived in Kamakura, south of Tokyo. Her mother had been the only child of Tokutaro and Ayaka Sugiyama. She could not recall mention of any aunts, uncles, or cousins. Of her parents' only trip to Japan, shortly after their marriage, Darby recalled more stories from her father than her mother. He'd told her of meeting his new bride's parents, of their kindness and hospitality. She remembered him describing Tokutaro Sugiyama's prowess as a student of karate, and the way the elderly man had tried to teach his new son-in-law some of his famous moves.

She pulled into Helen's driveway, crossed the porch, and entered the cheerful home. Helen's computer was in the kitchen, and Darby sat down and typed in "Unit 731." For twenty minutes she read about the chemical and biological weapons the unit had created, and the horrible experiments carried out on innocent people.

She felt her body grow cold. The atrocities were more than disturbing. They were almost unbearable.

She groaned and leaned back from the computer. Her brain felt like an angry hive of wasps, buzzing with question after question. Was this how her mother had felt when she heard the allegations? Was that why she had sailed on the *Nihon Maru*? Had she confronted the pharmaceutical company's management? What had transpired? Had more been at stake than Grandfather Sugiyama's reputation? Had his pension or his freedom been threatened as well?

Darby turned off the computer. She wished she had someone to help her make sense of this disturbing information.

The image of Miles Porter flashed in her mind. Miles! She'd forgotten to call him in the morning as she'd vowed.

It was just a little past noon. Helen would be ready at one p.m., and Darby calculated the nine-hour difference in time zones between Florida and Afghanistan. Nearly ten o'clock in the evening there, but hopefully Miles would still be awake. Darby took a seat once more at the kitchen table, grabbed her phone, and punched in his number.

———

Across the spacious living room at Casa Cameron, Jack Cameron regarded his sister Alexandra. She was closer to their father than he had ever been, the one with whom John Cameron had actually tried to be a parent, and her reaction to their mother's startling news was unpredictable. After a long moment, his sister looked up and met his gaze, her gray eyes stormy.

257

"So what happens now?" she asked, giving a toss of her hair. She was beautiful, this sister of his, beautiful and frighteningly intense. You could picture her doing anything, she was that extreme. "Do we throw him out?"

Mitzi Cameron pursed her lips. "The first thing we do—the first thing I do—is speak with the authorities. I hope Detective Briggs will see me this afternoon, even if it is a Sunday." She paused. "I felt I owed you two an explanation of what is happening, but I do not want you to get involved. He is, after all, your father."

Jack gave a rueful laugh. "Not get involved? When he framed me for arson?"

Mitzi's eyes flashed. "I know you were wronged, but I am asking for the sake of the family that you let me handle this." She turned to Alexandra and the anger left her voice. "I don't want to put you in the middle, Alexandra. Do you understand?"

She nodded, her face a beautiful mask. Rising from the cream-colored chair where she had been sitting, Alexandra took a breath and exhaled slowly.

"I need to go out for a while. I don't want to be here when the police arrive, so I'll be on Alligator Key until I hear from you." She went to Mitzi and gave her a stiff hug. She turned slowly toward her brother. "I'm glad for you, Jack. After all you've been through…"

Jack nodded. "Thanks." He watched her go, long and lean in her jeans and tee shirt. He looked back at his mother.

"She'll be okay."

Mitzi gave a small nod. "I know. Still, it's hard when someone is knocked off a pedestal."

Jack rose from his chair and strode to the window. He looked out at the beautiful tropical plantings, the very picture of perfection, and yet beneath the expertly smoothed mulch were hundreds of crawling creatures feasting on the sodden wood chips. He turned back toward his mother and nearly echoed the words his sister had asked. "What happens next?"

Mitzi Cameron gave a long sigh and shrugged, a gesture so striking in its eloquence that Jack nearly wept. "I don't know," she confessed. "I truly do not know."

———

"You are a feast for tired eyes," said Miles Porter, appearing via Skype on Darby's computer screen. He had not shaved in days, and yet his British-accented voice was chipper and he gave the same lopsided grin she remembered from Maine. "God, it is good to talk to you."

"You too," Darby said. "I'm so glad you are safe. I heard about the reporter from Canada…"

"Claudette." His tone was somber. "She was a wonderful journalist, and a good friend." He paused. "Darby, if I should end up on the wrong end of an IED…"

"You're not going to," she interrupted. "You are going to be fine."

"I daresay you are right. But just the same, let me tell you something, please?"

Darby swallowed. "Yes?"

"I think you are a remarkable woman, one that I could enjoy knowing for the rest of my life."

Darby bit her lip, her heart pounding.

"You know I can't boil water, right?"

She saw him smile and look off to the side. "Yes, you informed me of that fact while in Maine." He grinned again. "I'm not going to get all mushy on you. I know that's not your style, and it's not usually mine, either, except that in a war zone one feels differently about sharing feelings." He gave her a direct look and she felt her face grow hot. "I plan to come out of this in one piece, and when I do, my first destination is wherever you are."

Darby nodded. "Be careful," she whispered, wondering if he could see the tears in her eyes. "Please."

"I shall." He blew a little kiss and smiled. "You be careful as well. No getting mixed up in any murders, right?"

Darby nodded. No need to tell Miles that it was too late. She was already far too involved to retreat.

FOURTEEN

"I AM SO HAPPY to be home," Helen announced, looking up at her little Caribbean-style cottage. She was holding on to the side of Darby's Mustang as she spoke, and Darby watched to see if she was dizzy or lightheaded. But Helen moved purposefully toward the porch, unlocked the front door, and stepped in. She smiled, her lips brightened by the coral lipstick she favored, and looked over the sunny room.

"Thank you for watching my little house, Darby. How rude of me to go and have a heart attack while you were visiting!"

"That's exactly what I was thinking," Darby said as she carried in Helen's bag. "How can Helen be so thoughtless?" Both women laughed.

"Oh, it feels good to be home," Helen sighed. "You have a little experience like that and it sure makes you glad to be alive."

Darby nodded, thinking about Miles and his comments regarding the slain Canadian journalist. Certainly his brushes with mortality were changing him, making him more intentional, at least where she was concerned.

"What kinds of activity can you do today, Helen?"

"I have to take it easy today and tomorrow, and then I can ease back into my routine." She rolled her eyes. "What a giant pain."

Darby smiled. "There is plenty of time for you to run around at your old pace once you're better. Meanwhile, why don't I get you up to speed on Kyle Cameron's case?"

Helen's eyes widened. "Have there been any new developments?"

Darby nodded and told Helen about the slaying of Candy Sutton. "Jonas Briggs feels there's a connection, and I do, too. Did you know that Kyle was Candy's broker?"

"No." she paused. "I don't think I ever met this Candy person, unless she was the woman Kyle brought to see a listing I had over on the Key." She thought a moment. "Tall, very good looking businesswoman? Blonde?"

"That's right."

"Well, that may have been her, then. She didn't buy the place, so I didn't pay much attention." She gave Darby a shrewd glance. "What's going on with the Cameron family?"

Darby described her meeting with Carlotta and Mitzi's surprise appearance in the boat house.

"John Cameron! I know firsthand what a snake he is." She looked up and made a face. "He put the moves on me years ago. But with Carlotta's daughter? That's lower than low. And torching Belle Haven? And letting Jack take the rap ..." She shook her head ruefully. "He was a bad apple from the beginning. Maybe this will mean that Mitzi will finally send him packing."

"No one would be surprised if she did." Darby lifted the tea kettle inquiringly. "Would you like a cup of tea?"

Helen nodded. "Please." She looked around the kitchen. "I was only in that hospital a day but boy it feels good to be home. There really is nothing quite like the place you hang your hat, now is there?"

"No. I've always thought it's one of the more powerful aspects of our job. We help people find homes—not houses—but homes." She filled the kettle and set it on the stove to boil.

"Speaking of homes, what are the next steps for St. Andrew's Isle?" Helen gave a little grin. "That was a fun thing to think about while I was lying in that hospital bed."

Darby smiled. "I'm hoping to set up the building inspection for Tuesday. If that's not possible, I'm planning to fly back from California when it's scheduled."

"Don't tell me you're going home!" Helen looked truly upset and Darby regretted her words.

"I'm not going anywhere for several days, Helen. I'm lucky to have ET who takes care of my transactions so thoroughly. He's assured me that things are going smoothly, so if I can be of help to you, I'm happy to stay." Not for the first time, Darby silently thanked her capable assistant, hard at work back in California.

"What about Maine? Any action up there?"

"The business is on hold for a bit." Darby pictured Tina Ames, tall, thin, and sporting her fire-engine red fingernails. If all went as planned, Tina would have her Maine real estate license by the end of the month.

Helen bit her lip. "My time in the hospital made me so grateful for your presence. You've done wonders for me, and I just know you are going to figure out who killed poor Kyle." She selected a tea bag and handed it to Darby. "The police decided it wasn't the serial killer on the East Coast. But now two people are dead here. Does that mean we have our own serial killer in Sarasota?"

Darby pondered the question long after the older woman had gone to lie down for a nap. Helen had a point. If Kyle and Candy's killer were one and the same, the murderer had proven that he or she was willing to take multiple lives to stay unknown.

The questions were once more swirling in Darby's head, and she grabbed a piece of paper and a pen and began jotting them down. What did Candy know that made her dangerous? What was she going to tell the police? Was it a coincidence that she was killed just before meeting with them, or had someone known about her appointment? Had she inadvertently mentioned something to one of her clients?

She thought about what she knew of as the facts of the case. Kyle Cameron had known her attacker. She was pregnant at the time of her death. She'd been about to leave her position at Barnaby's to join Helen at Near & Farr.

Sassa Jorgensen had said that Kyle and Foster had called off their relationship the night before her murder. As a jilted lover, McFarlin was a top suspect, and yet his claim that he'd been driving from one end of the state to the other made it impossible for him to have been at Esperanza Shores.

Whom else had Kyle Cameron wronged? Darby felt sure that was the real question. She thought about Chellie Howe, and the humiliation brought on by her husband's affair. Could she have been disgraced enough to kill her husband's lover? And Candy as well?

And then there was Alexandra Cameron, and the defeat she had suffered so many years ago because of her future sister-in-law. Could losing a beauty pageant decades earlier cause someone to kill? Darby thought it was doubtful, but what if other indignities had happened since? What if watching her brother suffer at the hands of Kyle Cameron had proven too much to bear?

Finally, there were the brokers at Barnaby's—Marty Glickman and Peter Janssen. Had Marty been angry enough at Kyle's departure that he would resort to murder? Was there more to his involvement in the case, and if so, what did Peter Janssen know?

Darby put down her pen and sighed. The case was no clearer now than it had been the day of the murder. *Maybe it's time for some basic detective work,* she thought. *Putting the old sandal to the pavement.*

She left a quick note for Helen and grabbed her purse and phone. The late afternoon sun was still strong but Darby barely noticed the heat. Starting up the black Mustang, she backed out of Helen's driveway and headed down Driftwood, steering toward the Sunshine Senior Home in Sarasota.

———

The staff at the retirement facility was polite, but puzzled. Yes, records showed that an Anna Slivicki had been a resident, but she was long gone and none of the nurses remembered her. As to the residents, there was only one woman, Clara Lunt, who had been present at the time of Anna, and her memory, warned the head nurse with a stern look, was not always reliable.

Nevertheless, Darby asked to speak with the elderly resident and was shown into a private room cheerfully decorated with cat memorabilia and a brightly patterned chintz chair. An old-fashioned scent hung in the air, and Darby finally identified it as rosewater.

She introduced herself and asked if she could sit down for a visit.

Clara Lunt nodded eagerly. She had a little, wizened face surrounded by a cloud of nearly transparent white hair, and long thin arms that fluttered slightly in her lap.

"Of course I remember Anna," she said softly, her blue eyes dancing with excitement. "She was my best friend."

Darby smiled and nodded. "I understand that Anna had a little girl who sometimes stayed here."

Clara bobbed her head up and down, causing her silver cloud of hair to bounce. "Yes, the little girl was called Kyle. A strange name but a wonderful little thing! She was so sweet and fun, and of course she grew up to be such a pleasant young woman. She visits us quite often, although I haven't seen her in a few weeks." She looked around the room as if she had misplaced something. Darby wondered if she should tell Clara Lunt the truth.

"I'm afraid I have sad news about Kyle. She passed away suddenly last week."

Clara's eyes dulled and her face puckered. "That's terrible," she said. "How did it happen?"

Darby gave a short account of the murder, doing her best not to upset the older woman. She watched as Clara Lunt processed the information.

"Someone killed that girl," she murmured to herself, shaking her head and clasping her hands. "I wonder if anyone has told Sam."

"Sam?" Darby felt her interest piqued.

Clara nodded. "Sam Wilson. He and Kyle were working on a project together. It was a story about Anna—how she escaped the Nazis and came to America." She looked sad. "I suppose that story will never be told if Kyle is dead."

Darby reached over and squeezed the thin hands gently. "I don't know, Clara. I'll visit Sam and encourage him to continue."

Her smile lit up her entire face. "His room is on the other side of the building, by the gazebo. Tell him I said hello."

———

Sam Wilson already knew about Kyle's murder. He rocked back and forth at a large wooden desk covered in books and papers, a small notebook-type laptop computer perched precariously on top of a stack of magazines.

"Lieutenant Governor Howe is exactly right," he fumed. "The streets of Florida are too dangerous! Look at what happened to Kyle at Esperanza Shores! Hardly what you would call a bad neighborhood. The muggings, the murders ..." his voice trailed off and his bright blue eyes grew misty. "I miss her already," he said softly. "She was such a fun, lively person. She would come here and we would work on the project, and she made me feel like a million dollars." He gave a sad grin and Darby's heart ached.

"Tell me about what you were doing," she said gently.

He brightened. "Writing a story about Anna Slivicki's escape from Warsaw, just as the Nazis invaded. It is quite a thrilling tale of survival, and I was helping Kyle with the research and writing."

He pointed at a stack of papers about two inches tall. "That's a copy of the manuscript," he said proudly. "We were trying to find some photographs, but of course that is difficult."

He pulled a glossy photo out of a folder. "Kyle did have this one." It was a studio portrait of an elegant woman in her sixties, seated at a table. Her hands were interlaced under her chin, elbows resting on the surface of the wood.

"This is Anna?"

"That's right. It was taken when she lived here at the home. Kyle wanted to use it because it shows her wearing the ring."

Darby looked more closely at the photograph. Indeed, Anna Slivicki was wearing an unusual looking cocktail ring on the pinkie of one hand.

Sam Wilson handed her a magnifying glass. "Take a look. It's a lovely piece. Not just the diamond, but six exquisitely cut sapphires. Of course, it's how Anna bought her freedom out of Poland." He gave an excited smile. "She had to sell a few stones at various times but she replaced them as soon as she could."

Darby put down the magnifying glass. "Where is the ring now?"

"Kyle has it." He corrected himself. "She had it."

Darby made a mental note to ask Jack.

"Sam, did Kyle ever mention any problems she was having with anyone? Did she ever seem afraid of anyone?"

He shook his head. "No. She was the most confident person I have ever met. She never complained about anything." He thought a moment. "Except for one guy. He called her once when we were working. She was pretty curt with him. You know how you just get fed up sometimes?"

Darby nodded. "Who was that?"

"His name escapes me."

"Was it Foster McFarlin?"

He shook his head.

"Marty Glickman?"

"Yeah, I think that's it."

"Do you remember what they talked about?"

"No. She didn't tell me. We just got back to work on the manuscript." He paused, and gave Darby a puzzled look. "It couldn't have been that bad, because everyone liked her, didn't they?"

———

Driving away from the Sunshine Senior Home and back to Serenidad Key, Darby pondered Sam Wilson's words. *Kyle was the most confident person* … Had that been part of her problem? Had that ebullient confidence blinded her to other people's true feelings?

———

Darby returned to Helen's bungalow and found her friend relaxing comfortably on the patio. "I feel fine," Helen insisted. "In fact, I've never felt so rested in my whole darn life."

"That's terrific. Want to hear what I learned at the Sunshine Senior Home?"

Helen's eyes sparkled as Darby told of meeting Clara Lunt and Sam Wilson.

"What an interesting project! Oh, I wish I'd gotten a chance to know that girl better." She sipped a glass of ice water and frowned. "I figure I can start back on the Mojitos tomorrow," she said. "Limiting myself to only one a day, of course."

Darby grinned. "Leafy greens are good for you, aren't they? Mint must be full of vitamins and antioxidants."

Helen took another sip of water. "That's just what I was thinking." She snapped her fingers. "Hey, I forgot to tell you. Peter Janssen has a client he'd like to refer to you, and wonders if you can meet with her tomorrow."

"Sure. Wonder why he's not choosing someone in his own company?"

"He said he'd explain it in the morning. Asked if you can meet him down in Verona at the property she wants to purchase."

"Verona? What's he doing down there? That's got to be an hour south."

Helen nodded. "I know. Another part of his little mystery, I guess." Her face brightened. "Hey, it may be Sunday night but the Dive is open. I feel like getting out of this house and celebrating."

"What's the occasion?"

"Mitzi called. Jack is free and clear of all arson charges. Thanks to Carlotta's information, that skunk John Cameron will finally get what's coming to him, and I know I couldn't be happier." She clapped her hands and rose slowly to her feet. "Come on, Darby. Let's go get ourselves some grouper."

———

Kelly McGee smiled upon hearing Jonas Briggs' appreciative whistle. Only minutes before she'd called him at his home to explain that she'd figured out why Clyde Hensley was stalking Kyle.

"Her middle initial, 'B,' stands for Bergeron. That's the name on her birth certificate. Apparently she changed it to Slivicki when she turned eighteen. Hensley did time in Texas with Donald Bergeron—Kyle's father—and later tried to pose as him."

"Go on."

"Kyle went downtown to meet someone claiming to be her dad. I think Clyde Hensley showed up wearing a Miami Dolphins cap, and Kyle figured right away he was lying."

Briggs caught his breath. "I'll get the guys in Texas to look into Donald Bergeron's death. Maybe Clyde Hensley was involved." He paused. "Keep it up, McGee. You've got excellent instincts."

Kelly hung up the phone. She scratched Buster between his ears until he purred in delight. She wanted to solve the riddle of Kyle and Candy's deaths so badly she could taste it. The piece that kept nagging her concerned Candy's murder. Who, she asked herself again and again, had known about the escort's plans to speak to the police?

"I knew," she said aloud. "Detectives Briggs and DiNunzio knew as well. Had Candy told any of her clients? Jack Cameron? Foster McFarlin? Or anyone else?"

Kelly shut her eyes and tried to remember the Friday appointments she'd seen in Candy Sutton's calendar. Most had been mundane errands: a trip to the dry cleaner's, a visit to the groomer with Fang, and a short appointment with a nutritionist. That night, she'd escorted a professional golfer to a charity event in Orlando, and had returned to her apartment around midnight. Five and a half hours later, she was dead.

Kelly made a list of Candy's appointments on a new legal pad. In the morning she'd fill in names and addresses. If Detective Briggs could spare her, she'd go out and question everyone on the list.

Darby and Helen arrived at the Dive at sunset. A smiling young hostess clutching menus met them at the entrance and gushed, "You're just in time. The place is filling up fast."

They followed her to a table in the center of the deck. Darby looked around the funky restaurant. Tables were nearly full and a feeling of lightheartedness filled the air, a feeling as fresh as the surprisingly cool breeze wafting in from the Gulf of Mexico.

Jack Cameron was talking to an exuberant family seated in the corner of the deck. He looked up and waved as Darby and Helen sat down. Moments later, he was at their table hugging Helen.

"You think Mom is going to be okay?"

Helen nodded. "Just fine."

He gave a boyish grin, then looked around the busy eatery. "Not bad for a Sunday night, huh?" He waved a hand in the direction of a group of new arrivals. "I guess I never realized I have so many great customers." He ran an hand through his sun-streaked hair. "I wish Kyle was here to see this."

Helen touched his arm. "I know. I miss her, too."

Darby hoped she wouldn't upset Jack by asking him a question. "Do you remember a cocktail ring that belonged to Kyle's grandmother?"

He nodded. "Sure. Big diamond surrounded by emeralds—no, sapphires. Kind of unusual looking. Why do you ask?"

"I was talking with a gentleman from the Sunshine Senior Home in Sarasota. He and Kyle were writing about Anna Slivicki's flight from Poland, and the ring figures prominently in the story."

Jack shrugged. "I haven't started to go through her things, but I'm sure it's with the rest of her jewelry." He clasped his hands. "I've got to mingle. Thanks for everything, both of you."

Darby and Helen watched him depart. "I think he's going to be alright," said Helen.

Even Marco, who gave a small nod as he approached their table, seemed calm and more peaceful than Darby remembered. "Candy's service is tomorrow," he said softly. "She would be happy to know that her friend Jack is a free man." He wiped their table with his ever-present rag and looked inquisitively at Darby and Helen. "Mojito?" he asked.

Helen looked around the Dive and grinned. "Oh, to heck with it," she said. "Two Mojitoes, Marco. Heavy on the mint."

FIFTEEN

DARBY AWOKE EARLY, HOPING to get in a quick run in before driving to Verona. She trotted through the now familiar streets of Serenidad, thinking about her grandfather and the horrible activities of Unit 731. What had her mother discovered about his involvement? Had she abandoned her quest upon meeting John Farr?

Darby pounded the pavement, avoiding the Monday morning traffic, and tried to make sense of the puzzle. Her mother had sailed on the *Nihon Maru* more than thirty years ago. So much time had passed since then. Was there anyone who would be alive to shed light on what had transpired?

The chairman—the man with whom her grandfather had posed in the photograph—would surely be dead by now. But perhaps there were others who might remember Jada Sugiyama, the lovely young woman from the tourism bureau?

Hideki Kobayashi might have some ideas, Darby thought. She was about to round the corner of a particularly busy street when she heard a familiar yell.

"Darby!" It was Jonas Briggs, sticky bun in hand, waving from across the street. He dodged and wove his way through the early morning traffic. "Got a minute?"

She nodded. "Sure. Let's walk up here to a bench."

He offered her a piece of the raisin-studded pastry, but she declined. "Are you going to Candy Sutton's service today?"

He nodded somberly. "Not only to pay my respects, but sometimes we pick up interesting bits of evidence at these things. Did you know that killers often show up at funerals? Whether it gives them some sort of thrill, or they are genuinely curious as to who mourns their victim, I don't know. But I'll be in Bradenton at one o'clock, you can count on that."

She nodded. "Good news about Jack Cameron. Would you have figured it out without Carlotta's information?"

"I don't know. The combination of Jack's memory loss and John Cameron's clever covering of his trail made it nearly impossible to see the truth. Carlotta is a brave woman to come forward and expose not only her employer, but a family member as well."

Darby hadn't thought of it that way, but she agreed with the detective. She pointed at his sticky bun. "Go ahead and eat some of that," she urged. "Aren't they better when they are hot?"

He shrugged. "Yeah, I guess. I like them any temperature." He took a bite and chewed. "We figured out why Hensley was stalking Kyle."

"I'm all ears."

Jonas Briggs told her about Kelly McGee's discovery that Kyle's real name was Bergeron. "That's probably why he took all those photos of her."

"But she didn't buy it," Darby mused. "What gave it away?"

"I'm thinking it was his team allegiance. The one thing Kyle knew about her father was that he was a Giants fan."

Darby smiled. "Tell Kelly I said good work."

"How's Helen doing?"

"Just fine. We went to the Dive last night for dinner and she enjoyed seeing Jack Cameron in his element." She paused. "Did you double check Chellie Howe's alibi?"

Jonas Briggs nodded thoughtfully. "Yes, you were right. She spent the morning in Miami. It all checks out."

———

Darby ran back to Helen's, thinking that yet another suspect had been taken off the list.

She showered, ate a quick breakfast, and said goodbye to Helen. "Drive safely," Helen called. "I'll look for you just before lunch time."

Darby gathered up a map and began the drive to Verona, a beach town about sixty-five miles from Serenidad Key. The Mustang was a quiet oasis, and Darby played classical music and tried to free her mind of the same nagging questions: *Who killed Kyle Cameron? Who killed Candy Sutton? Was my grandfather responsible for atrocities during World War II?*

She navigated her way through the streets of the beach town, easily finding the place where she was supposed to meet Peter Janssen and the buyer. She turned down the road, noticing instantly that although the pavement was in fine shape, the shoulders were weedy and overgrown.

Darby drove slowly down the street. Modest houses, most of them Colonials, with neat little yards and a few young palm trees. Several looked unoccupied, with curtains across the windows and no sign of any occupants. Darby pulled into the neighborhood's most forlorn property and waited.

It was a foreclosure situation, of that she was certain. Florida had certainly been hit hard in the sinking real estate market and there were many such bank-owned properties all over the state. Darby sighed. She hated situations like this. Not only were they depressing, but they were quite frequently disastrous for a house. Unloved and unlived in, houses tended to have increasingly serious problems—rodent damage, burst water pipes, break-ins, mold—the list went on and on. She shook her head. Foreclosures were a part of the market she had long ignored, and with good reason. They depressed her.

The sound of tires on gravel made her look in her rear view mirror. An attractive blonde in her mid-thirties emerged from a red convertible, huge black sunglasses covering most of her face. Behind her was Peter Janssen, driving a gray Buick sedan.

"Hello, Darby," he boomed, emerging from the car with his hand outstretched. "Thanks for coming down. This is Stephanie Woodrow from Ocean City, New Jersey. She's here to buy a house."

Darby smiled at the woman. "How nice to meet you. I'm Darby Farr, from Near & Farr Realty." She handed her a packet of information.

Stephanie Woodrow took it and gave a brief nod. "Certainly appreciate your coming this morning. Peter has told me all about

277

you." She turned toward the house, her sunglasses so large she looked like some sort of insect. "Shall we take a look?"

"Absolutely!" Peter unlocked the front door. "After you, ladies."

They entered the house and let their eyes adjust to the dim, dusty light. Dingy sheets had been stapled over the windows. They hung like drab banners from the moldings to the floor.

"Let me open some of these," said Peter, lifting the sheets and attempting to tie them back. He bunched one up and tucked it under itself, and the blast of sunlight that poured in had a cheering effect. "There," he said. "That's a lot better."

Stephanie Woodrow pursed her lips and moved through the house. "On the bus, you said this house was in excellent shape," she commented, kicking her toe at a piece of the carpet that had been ripped up and rolled to the side.

"That's right." Peter spread out his hands to take in the whole room and nodded. "When you look at as many foreclosures as I have, you know when you've got one that's nice."

The buyer nodded and moved into the kitchen. "Ugh," she said. "This is unbelievable."

Peter Janssen raised his eyebrows. "What is it?" he asked, moving toward the kitchen.

Darby followed, bracing herself for the worst: rotten food, broken cabinets, a dead rat or two. Instead Stephanie pointed at a refrigerator, its doors and freezer compartment propped open. "No icemaker!" she exclaimed. "How can anyone even live without an automatic icemaker?"

Darby bit her tongue and inspected the kitchen. "Appliances are easy to update," she said. "The cabinets are in good shape, and the countertops may not be to your taste, but they are very useable."

Stephanie Woodrow nodded. "I suppose," she said doubtfully.

"Tell me what you plan to do with this property," Darby said. "Is this an investment? Second home? Something you plan to resell when the market improves?"

She noticed Peter Janssen move tactfully into the hallway. He was giving her time to speak to Stephanie alone.

"I want to live here," she said. "I've been coming down here since I was a small girl, and I want to sell my place in Jersey and move."

"Okay," Darby said. "So we'll be looking with your needs in mind." She smiled at the woman and pointed at the hallway. "Let's go see the rest of the house."

After several minutes of exploring the house's three bedrooms, ample basement, and back yard, Darby handed Stephanie Woodrow her card. "What do you think? Is it something you want to act on?"

Stephanie bit the inside of her lip. "I think so," she said. "I liked it the best of any houses we saw on the tour, and I'm ready to make a decision and move forward."

Darby nodded. "What tour?"

"Peter's tour. He's got a bus that takes you around to all the distressed properties. He serves beer, wine, and lemonade. We had a good time and learned about the market down here. He does it every Saturday."

"I see." She looked back at the house. Peter Janssen was locking the front door and closing the sagging screen. "Stephanie, would you like to call me with your decision? I have to head back to my office now, but if you want to put in an offer, either I or my associate Helen will be glad to help."

"I think I do," she said. "But I'd like to think about it over lunch, crunch some numbers, and then make a move."

Darby agreed that they would talk very shortly and headed back to her car. Peter Janssen met her there, his eyebrows raised.

"Well?"

"She likes this property, but she's going to think it over and call me back today." She paused. "She said you have a tour of foreclosures every Saturday?"

He colored deeply and nodded. "I do. It's been a way for me to make some extra money in this slow economy." He coughed and looked back at the house. "I'd like to keep it from the brokers at Barnaby's, if you don't mind."

"Is that why you asked me to represent Stephanie? Because you don't want Marty Glickman to know?"

Peter nodded. "Yeah. It's kind of embarrassing to be driving an old school bus with 'Foreclosures 4 U' in big letters on the side." He gave a sheepish grin. "To tell you the truth, I kind of enjoy it. I meet some great people and I feel like I'm doing a service, matching up these empty homes with eager buyers."

Darby smiled. "I think it's a great idea, Peter. You're reducing housing inventory and helping with neighborhood revitalization. Nobody wants vacant houses on their street." She looked at her watch. "I'm heading back to Near & Farr. I'll keep you posted on what Stephanie decides to do."

"Thanks." He brushed the hair from his eyes. "Are you going to that service today for Candy Sutton?"

Darby nodded. "I am. What about you?"

"Yes. We had some good friends in common, and I thought I'd give them some support." He looked back at Stephanie, who was gazing up at the property. "I'll see you there. Thanks for keeping my little sideline under wraps."

———

Darby started back north to Serenidad Key, wondering if Peter's "little sideline," as he had called the foreclosure bus, was an enterprising endeavor or simply ridiculous. Before she'd decided, her phone rang and interrupted her thoughts. In keeping with her new vow not to talk on her phone and drive, she waited until she stopped for gas to play the message.

It was Hideki Kobayashi's gentle voice, telling her he had some news concerning her grandfather. She called him back immediately.

"I regret the pain I caused you yesterday," he murmured. "Such shocking information delivered so suddenly. Please accept my apology."

"You don't need to feel sorry. What you told me is the truth."

"Yes, but all the same I am sorry that I had to tell you." He paused. "I hope I will not upset you further. I spoke to someone at my company today about your grandfather."

Darby's heart skipped a beat. "Yes?"

"There is an elderly scientist who worked in his department. If you would like, I can arrange for you to talk with him." He paused. "Perhaps today at noon if you like?"

Darby took a deep breath. "Please," she said. "Shall we meet at my office?"

"Yes. I will leave my hotel now." He said goodbye and hung up.

Darby called Helen and told her she would not be home for lunch. "I need to see Mr. Kobayashi at the office," she explained. "Then I'm heading to Candy's funeral."

"Is everything alright?"

"Yes," Darby said, hoping she was telling the truth.

———

Jack Cameron helped Marco load trays full of appetizers and sandwiches from the Dive into the back of a panel truck. "I'll be right behind you," he told the tall man. He looked into his eyes. "Come on, let's get this done."

Marco nodded and Jack watched him climb into the truck and start the ignition. He heard the whirr of the air conditioner against the afternoon's high humidity. Marco was just going through the motions, but at least he was going through them sober.

Not like me, Jack thought regretfully. *I barely remember Kyle's funeral...* The realization sent a sharp stab of pain through his midsection and he nearly doubled over from fresh grief.

It was a week since her death. A week, and the police were still no closer to finding Kyle's killer. And now Candy was gone, struck down in an alley with only her dog as a witness.

He gripped the side of his car with both hands. His legs wobbled and he felt as if he would vomit. He wanted to run, run from Marco and the trays of finger sandwiches, run from Candy's family now starting to gather at the Church of the Sacred Heart in Bradenton, run as far as he could from death, pain, and loss. Instead he took a deep breath, steadied his thoughts, and climbed into his vehicle.

Darby waited anxiously while Hideki Kobayashi dialed Japan, hoping to reach the elderly scientist who had once worked with her grandfather. She heard him speak in rapid Japanese, and then he stopped and put his hand over the receiver.

"This is Dr. Sato. His English is excellent, but his voice may be a little hard to understand. Just ask me for help if you are having trouble."

Darby nodded. She took the phone from Hideki Kobayashi and introduced herself as the granddaughter of Tokutaro Sugiyama.

"It is a pleasure to speak with you," he said, his voice quaking slightly. "I had the good fortune of working with Tokutaro Sugiyama when I was young and just starting my career at Genkei Pharmaceuticals. I found him to be an honorable and intelligent man."

Darby swallowed. "Thank you." She chose her words carefully. "I wonder if you ever heard anything about his involvement in China during WWII. I'm speaking of the atrocities of Unit 731." Her heart was beating fast. She looked over at Mr. Kobayashi who nodded very slightly, as if in encouragement.

"Yes, I did hear of those allegations. All of us at the company were shocked as there were a number of Genkei men named in the book."

"Did you ever speak with my grandfather about the book?"

"No. He was no longer working at that time, and his—" He paused. "His mind was not good."

"Can you tell me anything about his involvement in China? Did he ever talk about his work as part of the unit?"

"I can tell you that he once described to me a toxin so terrible it would poison an entire city. When I asked him how he knew of this substance, he hung his head in shame. He said he was sent to Manchukuo during the war. That was all he would tell me."

Manchukuo. Darby remembered it was the puppet state created by the Japanese government where Unit 731's leaders had built their biological weapons facility. Her heart sank. She had hoped her grandfather had not even been present.

She tried to thank Dr. Sato for the information, but the old man gently interrupted. "I must tell you as well that your grandfather spent his life helping others, trying to make up for whatever bad things he may have done there." He cleared his throat; his voice was growing fainter. "It is the same thing I told your mother."

"You spoke to her?"

"We had one phone conversation. She said she had found something in your grandfather's papers. I don't know, but I assume it was about the war."

Again Darby thanked the man for his time and information. She hung up and turned to Hideki Kobayashi.

"Was the conversation helpful, or did it cause you more torment?" he asked gently.

"It was very helpful, and I thank you for setting it up."

He bowed, and Darby thought she detected a look of concern on his normally placid face. "I shall leave you. Tomorrow we will meet at St. Andrew's Isle for the property inspection. Tell me, if all goes well with that, may I purchase the property sooner?"

"I should think so," said Darby. "But we'll check with Tag Gunnerson and make sure."

"Fine." He bowed again and left the office.

Darby stood for a moment thinking about the phone call. Her grandfather had been a participant, however unwilling, in the inhumane actions of Unit 731. His daughter had discovered this, but something else as well. Some piece of information in her grandfather's papers...

A journal entry? Lab reports? Darby could only guess. Had her mother truly abandoned her quest upon falling in love with John Farr? Or had she continued to search for the truth once they had settled in Maine?

With difficulty, Darby pulled herself back to the present. She called Tag Gunnerson's assistant, Bernie Schultz, and asked him to find out whether Tag was interested in selling St. Andrew's Isle sooner. Then she hung up, grabbed her pocketbook, and headed out the door to Candy Sutton's service.

———

Less is more, Darby thought, sitting in the stark chapel where three dozen or so mourners had come to celebrate the life of the Bradenton businesswoman. It was a far cry from the lavish memorial service held at Casa Cameron for Kyle, but as Darby looked around at the bare walls and simple beauty of the chapel, she felt sure Candy Sutton would have approved.

Someone tapped on her shoulder. She turned and saw that Jonas Briggs was sitting behind her. He lifted his chin slightly in a greeting.

The pews were filling up with more people. Marco was in the front row with Jack Cameron; Alexandra, her hair pulled in a demure bun, sat behind him. An attractive older woman held a tissue and smiled bravely at other adults seated in the front row. From her striking good looks, Darby guessed her to be Candy's mother.

A young priest entered from a side door while soft music played. A noise at the back of the church caused Darby to look discreetly behind her. Just as the priest began to speak, Foster McFarlin stepped into the chapel and took a seat in the back.

———

Jonas Briggs leaned forward as the service's postlude wound down. "Are you going to the little tea?"

Darby nodded. "Definitely. Do you really think Candy's killer could be out there?"

"Let's hope." He looked around. "Who's that guy?" He jerked his head toward Marty Glickman.

"He's the one who runs Barnaby's. Surely you questioned him about Kyle's death?"

Briggs nodded. "Yeah, yeah. I thought he looked familiar. Dave DiNunzio was the one who actually grilled him." He pointed at another man. "What about him?"

Darby peered at the young man nodding to Alexandra Cameron. "Justin Fleischman. He works for Tag Gunnerson."

Briggs stood up and put a hand on Darby's shoulder. "You do some talking, see what you can find out. I'm going to hang back and observe."

Darby followed the crowd to a small room that had been added on to the main building, probably in the 1960s. Tables with small sandwiches and drinks had been set up, and Darby realized she was starving. She was sampling a crabmeat roll-up when Peter Janssen came up next to her.

"Lovely service, wasn't it?" He picked up a small cook platter. "Ginger tea cakes. I haven't had one of these in years." He took a bite and looked around the room. "I hope you don't think I'm being rude, Darby. Maybe I shouldn't be so obviously enjoying a cookie at a funeral."

"Jack Cameron supplied the food and I'm sure he'll be happy to know someone likes it." She scrutinized the pile of cookies as Peter took another and promptly bit into it. "Tell me what is so special about these tea cakes."

"They're an old Southern treat, made with molasses, ginger, nutmeg, cinnamon, and cloves. I love the taste, but they're special for me because of the memories they evoke of an old family friend, Genevieve Walker." He looked thoughtful for a moment. "She worked for my family the whole time I was growing up, and my sisters and I all loved her." He looked down at the platter and smiled. "She knew these were my favorite treats. I'd come home from school and she'd have a plateful waiting." He took another and bit into it. "The peppery taste is the same, although she frosted hers with a mixture of heavy cream and powdered sugar. I can still see her setting them out on sheets of wax paper, and then putting them in this big square tin when the frosting was hard."

Darby took a cookie and put it on her plate. "You've sold me, Peter. I've got to try one of Genevieve's famous cookies."

He grinned. "I'll mention it when I see her."

"She's still alive?"

"No. I help take care of the small African-American cemetery where she is buried. And when I'm there, I talk to her." He laughed. "I'll admit it is weird. It's become kind of a meditation for me."

"That's kind of you to keep up the old graveyard."

"I enjoy it. Pine Grove is tucked in a very quiet corner of Sarasota, sort of a place that time forgot. Back in the city's segregated days, it was one of the few cemeteries where African-Americans could be buried." He thought a moment. "I read about it sliding into disrepair—must have been about ten years ago. I offered to start working on it. One day I was out there weeding and discovered Genevieve's grave."

"You didn't know she'd been buried there?"

He shook his head. "I'd always wondered what happened to her. And when I saw her grave stone, it made the whole thing more important to me. I convinced the city-wide cemetery association to fund a part-time gardener, and we really started to clean the place up."

"Are people still being buried there?"

"No." He took another cookie. "It's a small place, but, like Genevieve herself, very special." He started to smile, but then his face colored and he looked downward.

"Hello," Marty Glickman said. His voice was smooth and silky. "You must really love these cookies, Peter. Have you eaten a dozen yet?"

Peter Janssen slid his eyes away and mumbled something. Darby looked at Marty Glickman and thought, *You're a bully.* She forced herself to make her voice neutral. "Was Candy Sutton a friend of yours?"

"She was a Barnaby's client, so I thought I should come." He suppressed a yawn. Obviously all of this was just a big waste of time for him. He shook his head as if to stay awake. "Candy was working with Kyle to find a house." He looked at Peter once more.

"Refresh my memory. Did you ever work with Candy, or did you know her through another connection?"

Peter's face was nearly purple from embarrassment. "I didn't really know her," he stammered. "I'm here to support a friend."

"Now just who would that be?" Marty Glickman glanced around the reception room.

"Well, I'm—"

"Here with me." Darby had had enough of Glickman's badgering of his flustered employee. "It was kind of you to keep me company, Peter. I think I'll be heading back to check on Helen now."

Marty Glickman gave an amused smirk. "Keeping you company, huh?" He frowned and turned on his heel. Darby and Peter watched him exit the reception room.

"Whew, talk about obnoxious. Is he always like that?"

Peter gave a shaky chuckle. "I just ignore him, but I know he drove Kyle crazy. She couldn't stand working for him. I was happy when she said she was leaving to work with Helen."

"She told you that?"

He nodded. "She told me lots of things. In strictest confidence, of course."

Darby remembered Sam Wilson saying Kyle had been bothered by phone calls. Had Marty Glickman crossed the line from being obnoxious to dangerous?

"I think that Kyle was getting phone calls from Marty. Calls she described to a friend as 'creepy.'"

Peter looked upset. "She didn't mention that. I'm sure Glickman would deny ever badgering her, but I'm not surprised." He frowned and lowered his voice. "Marty is unpleasant, that's true, but do you really think he's a murderer?"

Darby didn't answer. She was asking herself the same question.

———

"Glickman's alibi checks out," Jonas Briggs said, his voice tired and edgy. He picked up his coffee cup and took a sip, regarding Darby from behind the chipped china cup. They were seated in a coffee shop a block away from the Church of the Sacred Heart where Candy's service had just concluded. "I'm starting to rethink the whole thing."

"What do you mean?" Darby regarded the rumpled man before her. Circles beneath his eyes attested to how little sleep Jonas Briggs was getting.

"Say that Candy and Kyle's murders are not related. Candy's is an act of random violence, having nothing to do with who she was or what she may have known about Kyle Cameron. And Kyle's murder—hers is the work of some sicko imitating the Kondo Killer. Again, nothing to do with who she is, other than a real estate agent who happened to be having an open house." He made a tent of his fingers and leaned against them.

"If Kyle's murder was the work of a wannabe Kondo Killer," asked Darby, "Then isn't that person likely to strike again? At another open house?"

Briggs nodded. "Definitely. That's what worries me."

———

Jack opened Kyle's condominium and heard the door click softly behind him. He removed his shoes and placed them on the sisal mat. Kyle had always been a stickler about things like that, wanting to keep her environments as clean as possible. He glanced at the living room, where her pile of books on Poland still remained next to her favorite reading spot. He walked to the hallway, to the carved table where Buddy and the crystal bowl had been, but they were gone. *Good*, thought Jack. *Someone is taking care of him.*

He pulled open the single drawer of the table, checking to see if Kyle's Smith & Wesson was there, but that, too, had vanished. *Darby Farr must have told Briggs about it.* He sighed and headed toward Kyle's bedroom.

The creamy, serene surroundings filled him with a sadness so intense he nearly crumpled to the floor. Instead he perched on the bed and covered his face with his hands. The last time he had come here, it had been with a bottle of bourbon. Now here he was, filled with anguish again, only this time, he was defenseless.

I will be back to take care of your things, he promised softly. Not today, but soon. He rose unsteadily to his feet and waited until he felt stronger. Then he crossed the bedroom to Kyle's mahogany dresser.

He opened a few drawers, looking for her jewelry box, and found the wooden heart-shaped container tucked behind some silky camisoles. He pulled it out and lifted the lid. Moving aside some necklaces and bangle bracelets, he spotted the faded velvet box which held Grandma Slivicki's little ring.

He pulled open the box, expecting to see it sparkling against the satin interior. He stopped, confused. Where the hell was the ring?

SIXTEEN

"So let me get this straight," Helen and Darby were at the office of Near & Farr Realty, sorting out the next few days' plans. "You are leaving on Thursday, after we sell St. Andrew's Isle?"

Darby nodded. "Tag and Mr. Kobayashi can pass papers Wednesday afternoon. Did you realize Tag has already moved out of the house?"

Now it was Helen's turn to nod. "Bernie Schultz told me this morning. Everything will be totally gone by tomorrow. We'll have the inspections, and boom! It's done." She paused. "I know you need to get back to California, but I've really enjoyed your company, and you've surely been a help. I'll miss you."

Darby smiled. "I'll miss you, too. I'd love to come back and visit."

"Definitely." Helen opened the file on Stephanie Woodrow. "This is the buyer Peter Janssen asked us to represent?"

Darby nodded. "Truthfully, Helen, I don't know why you'd want to travel so far. Maybe you can refer her to a colleague closer to Verona."

Helen considered Darby's advice. "Maybe. I suppose if I'm feeling fine, I may just plug away at this business for a few more years." She smiled. "Keeps me out of trouble."

"You and me, both." Darby looked at her Smartphone and frowned. "I have a message from Jack Cameron. Wonder what that is all about?" She listened for a moment and turned back to Helen. "Here's an odd thing. Kyle Cameron owned a ring that had belonged to her grandmother, Anna Slivicki. That ring was part of the story Kyle and her friend Sam Wilson were writing about Anna's escape from Poland. In fact, I saw a photo of Anna wearing the ring." She paused. "Jack Cameron went over to Kyle's condo today, looking for it. He says it's gone."

"Was she robbed?" Helen's face was puckered with worry.

"I don't think so. It's just another piece of this very complex, very frustrating puzzle."

"Your friend Jonas Briggs hasn't made much progress."

Darby shook her head. "Poor guy, he is turning into a haunted skeleton of a man. He now thinks it was a random person who murdered Kyle, not someone who knew her."

"Maybe it was someone who knew the real Kondo Killer? Maybe they were working together?"

"That's definitely a possibility, Helen." There was a rap on the door and the police detective entered. He looked at their faces and widened his eyes. "You two were just talking about me, weren't you?"

"Actually, yes." Darby told him of Helen's theory. "Maybe that's how the killer got the details of the East Coast crimes."

"What details?" Helen asked.

"Confidential information about the methodology of the murders." Briggs looked thoughtful. "You may be on to something there." He turned to Darby. "Meanwhile, a valuable piece of Kyle Cameron's jewelry is missing."

"Her grandmother's ring. Jack left me a message." She lowered her voice as Helen headed to the back conference room, out of earshot. "You don't suppose Kyle could have been wearing it?"

"It's a possibility." The skin on Jonas Briggs' face was slack. "We find the ring, we find the killer."

———

Chellie Howe gave her new assistant, R.B. Cloutier, a stack of policies to read over and asked him to close her office door as he left. She thought a moment and then took a deep breath and made the call. Jonas Briggs answered immediately. "Yes, Lieutenant Governor?"

"Detective Briggs, I have information about the murder of Kyle Cameron." She swallowed. "I need to speak with you."

"I'll be at your place in fifteen minutes."

Chellie hung up the phone and went into the outer office. "I have to run a few errands, R.B." she lied. "If I'm not back by five o'clock, lock up for me."

He nodded. "Do you need a hand? Would you like me to call you a car?"

She shook her head, wishing she could ask the handsome assistant to accompany her. She grabbed her pocketbook and slid her sunglasses on her face. "No, thanks. I'll walk."

———

Helen Near closed and locked Near & Farr Realty and turned to Darby with a mischievous grin. "Four o'clock. Should we have a Mojito before we go to Casa Cameron for dinner?"

Darby smiled. "Actually, I'm going to run over and meet with Alexandra Cameron at her office."

"Way the heck over to Alligator Key?"

"Yes. Her associate sent me an e-mail asking if we could meet. Truthfully, I'm not sure what it's about, but I figured I'd check it out." She smiled. "I'll take a rain check on that Mojito. Should I just meet you at Casa Cameron?"

"Sure. I may very well head over early and spend some time with Mitzi. With all that has happened, I do worry about her. John's out of the picture now, and even though it's for the best, I still think it is hard."

Darby agreed and headed to the black Mustang. Consulting her map, she found the skinny strip of land that composed Alligator Key and the causeway leading out to it. She started the car and headed south.

Darby recalled what she had learned—mainly from Helen—of Alexandra Cameron's career path to date. Unlike her sorority sisters Kyle and Chellie, the beautiful heiress had not graduated from Florida State. Instead, she'd dropped out midway through her senior year to embark on a series of activities and trips designed to help her "find herself." Spread over the last fifteen years, these diversions had done nothing but make her more and more restless and unhappy.

Then Mitzi gave her daughter a session at a spa specializing in wellness. The stay so impressed Alexandra that she returned to her old university, pursued a degree through the department of nutrition, food, and exercise science, and emerged a woman with a purpose. No one was more surprised than her family and friends when she set up a small counseling practice that specialized in eating and depression. Soon she began collaborating with a colleague on a book designed to help people eat for happiness. Together they'd rented an inexpensive office south of Sarasota on a small windy spit of land called Alligator Key.

Darby drove the Mustang across the narrow causeway and slowed at the end of the road. She consulted the directions from Alexandra's website. As they described, she was now passing a swampy estuary. Immediately after, she spotted the low, boxy building where Alexandra Cameron worked.

Darby pulled into the parking lot. It was empty—no sign of any other vehicles. She took a look at her cell phone. Had she misread the time of their meeting?

The office had huge floor to ceiling windows with a drive-through area on the side and was painted a garish yellow and red. It looked like a fast-food restaurant, which was, in fact, what it had been. "We couldn't resist the irony of turning an old hamburger joint into a nutrition clinic," Alexandra had written on her website's home page. "Fortunately the Cameron Foundation provided the means for us to get rid of the smell of greasy French fries."

Darby regarded her surroundings while she figured out her next step. There was very little traffic on Alligator Key. In the time since she had been sitting in the lot, only one or two cars had passed. She checked the time once more, and punched in Alexandra's number.

Her call was answered immediately.

"Darby, I am so, so, sorry I couldn't get down there. I had an emergency with one of my anorexic patients and have just left the hospital. Did you get my message at the office? Please forgive me."

"These things happen. Is your patient okay?"

"Fortunately, yes. We nearly lost her but she's going to make it, at least for today." Alexandra Cameron sighed. "Mom called about her dinner tonight. Are you going?"

"Yes."

"Then I can apologize again in person. See you soon, Darby."

Darby hung up and started the Mustang. When things like this happened, she tried to stay philosophical. *I can either get annoyed, or I can view it as an unexpected opportunity.* She took a deep breath and willed her annoyance away.

Driving by the estuary, her eye was attracted to a large white bird. Heron, she thought, turning to get a better look. A flash of pink made her curious, so she pulled to the side of the road.

The bird was less than three feet tall, with long, stork-like pink legs and bright pink wings. With a sweeping motion, it swung a flattened bill back and forth in the shallow water, presumably looking for food. The bird's bill was oddly shaped—*like a spoon*, Darby thought. She grabbed her Smartphone and did some quick research. She looked back at the mangrove-bordered water. She was gazing at a roseate spoonbill.

So there, she thought, as she turned carefully back into the road. It was as if the spoonbill had been placed there just for her to observe. She drove back to the city limits of Sarasota feeling as if she'd been given a gift.

———

"What's up?" asked Dave DiNunzio, setting a stack of papers on Kelly McGee's desk with a thump.

"Ugh," she groaned. "Not more paperwork!"

"That's right. All for you." Dave gave a wolfish grin. "You're the one who wants to make detective before you're thirty, remember?"

"Hey, I told you that in confidence."

"I didn't tell anyone." He smirked down at her. "Just the guys I play poker with."

"Great. That's just great. Do you tell them everything?"

"Pretty much."

Kelly fidgeted at her desk, annoyed. She had no idea who played in his precious poker game but she didn't like the idea of his discussing her hopes and dreams with anyone. Not for the first time, she doubted Dave's ability to keep his darn mouth shut.

"Where's Detective Briggs?" she asked, as she began sorting through the stack. That morning she'd made it through half of the appointments on her list, but so far, she was no closer to finding anything new in Candy Sutton's murder.

"I think he had a meeting with Lieutenant Governor Howe." He checked his watch. "She called around four and he left to go meet her." He raised his eyebrows suggestively. "Wonder what that's all about?"

Kelly felt her cheeks growing hot. "The task force, I guess."

He grinned and shrugged. "Maybe."

She watched him walk to his desk. Any goodwill she'd felt for him after their shared foray into Burmese python territory was gone. She was back at square one, finding him childish and downright annoying.

Kelly grabbed the first bunch of papers from the pile and glanced at her watch. Was it even worth starting when it was nearly five o'clock? *Don't procrastinate, Kelly! Whatever you get done today is that much less for the morning.* The self pep talk gave her the little bit of motivation she needed, and with a small sigh Kelly McGee started in on the pile before her.

———

Driving through an unfamiliar part of Sarasota, Darby felt as if another gift was thrust her way. She was on a lonely stretch of road, miles inland from the Gulf, in a part of the city that time seemed to have forgotten. An old industrial plant of some kind sprawled across a weedy field, the company's sign so faded she could not make out even one word. Beside it was a small clearing dotted with narrow gray headstones. "Pine Grove," read a small metal marker.

Darby slowed the Mustang. This was the cemetery Peter Janssen had mentioned, the place where African-Americans could bury their dead during the time of segregation. It certainly was in a remote part of the city. On a whim, she pulled down the long, narrow dirt road that led to the back of the cemetery.

She stepped out of the car for a stretch. Huge longleaf pines, more than one hundred feet tall, bordered the tiny graveyard, nearly blocking out the late afternoon sun. She heard the shriek of a bird in the distance, cutting through the silence like a siren. She walked toward the graves to give her legs some exercise.

The cemetery dated back to post-Civil war days, and was very different from the manicured park-like burying grounds of the Euro-American tradition. Trees and vegetation were native. No attempt to landscape had been attempted, and grass was sparse. The headstones were modest, small, and, in some cases, made of rough pieces of wood.

She wandered among the graves, reading the spare epitaphs and names of the dead. Jedediah Owens ... Maybelle Hunt ... Samuel Lincoln Jones ... Some had years carved into the modest stones, and Darby noted that the oldest grave was at the end of the nineteenth century, while the most recent appeared to be in the 1950s or so.

Nothing appeared to have been touched for a long, long time. Strangler figs wound their sinuous vines in and around the gravestones, giving it an abandoned look, and yet hadn't Peter mentioned something about a gardener? Oddly enough, Darby felt the setting was more moving in its forlorn state than the elaborate, artificially landscaped cemeteries dotting the hillsides of California. This place seemed to say that death was inevitable and yet natural, as natural as the pinecones that littered the mounds of dirt and crunched underneath her sandals.

She wondered where Genevieve Walker was buried. She looked at a few more rows of gravestones and then turned back toward the Mustang. It was getting on dusk and time to head to Casa Cameron.

As she made her way back to the convertible, she noticed one grave with a fresh bunch of wildflowers poking out of a blue enameled pitcher. Curious, she walked toward it, and noticed that the name on the stone was indeed Genevieve's.

A small metal box was wedged beside the flowers. Darby wondered what it held and leaned in for a closer look.

"Go ahead, take a peek." The pleasant voice behind her made Darby nearly jump two feet with fright.

"Peter! You scared the heck out of me!" She smiled in relief at the affable man dressed in tan slacks and a navy blue zip-front jacket. "What are you doing here?"

"I come here often," he explained. "I hadn't planned on it today, but here we are." He gestured at the grave. "I was hoping you'd find Genevieve."

Darby looked at the small marker memorializing the woman who had helped raise Peter Janssen. "I see what you mean about this cemetery being remote. I literally stumbled upon it." She looked at the towering pines and noticed that the sky was becoming grayer. "It's a very peaceful place."

"That it is," he said. He had his hands in the pockets of his jacket as if he were waiting for something.

Darby felt her heart rate speed up. Something was off balance. She looked around for Peter's Buick.

"Where did you park?"

He jerked his head in the direction Darby had driven. "Back at the old canning factory. I didn't want to startle you with my engine."

"But creeping up on me by foot was no problem?" Darby croaked out a harsh chuckle. She licked her lips; they were incredibly dry. "Peter, did you follow me?"

He nodded. "Yes."

"Why?"

"I wanted to be alone with you." He smiled. "Did you see the little gift I gave Genevieve?"

Darby turned back toward the box. "Yes, but I didn't want to—pry," she said. "And I really should be heading out." She glanced in the direction of the Mustang, one hundred or so yards away.

"Take a look in the box." His voice had a slight edge. "See what I've given Genevieve, and then you can head out to the Cameron estate for dinner."

Darby felt a chill wash over her. How did he know about her dinner plans?

"Actually, I do need to get on the road—"

He loomed over her petite frame. "Take a look!"

Slowly, she reached for the box.

It was no bigger than a cigarette pack, made out of tin, with small pink rosebuds stamped on the lid. The metal was smooth and cool to the touch.

"I don't want to open it."

"Do it." His voice was low and dangerous. Darby's hands trembled as she pushed up on the lid.

The box's hinges made a soft squeak of protest as the cover opened. Inside, nestled in a bed of cotton batting, was an exquisite little cocktail ring, oval shaped, with an old-fashioned cut diamond surrounded by small sapphires. Her heart nearly in her throat, she raised her eyes to Peter's face.

"This was Kyle's ring," she whispered.

His eyes narrowed and he nodded, slowly, watching as horror washed over Darby like a wave. "This was her grandmother's..."

She dropped the box and bolted toward the Mustang.

SEVENTEEN

Kelly McGee was reading through a stack of pawn shop reports when Dave DiNunzio tapped on her shoulder. "Almost quitting time. How about a pick-me-up cappuccino? My treat."

Kelly shrugged. It was kind of sweet, the way he was trying to be friends, even if he was the most irritating man on two feet. She gave a quick smile. "Sure."

He grinned and walked down the hallway, whistling a tune that seemed familiar.

Kelly groaned and resumed her study of the data. She was comparing the pawn shops' new inventory against stolen property sheets, hoping to find a few matches. Jonas Briggs had asked her to be on the lookout for something specific: an ornate cocktail ring. Kelly circled an entry labeled "jewelry." She added the shop to her list of follow-ups.

As she worked, snatches of the melody Dave had been whistling kept flitting through her thoughts. Why was it, she wondered, that the smallest bit of a song could stay stuck in your brain, even as you willed it to be forgotten? The melody was one she recalled from the radio—and maybe TV, too—although she had no idea when it was recorded. Kelly was about to scream with frustration when a fragment of the song's lyrics came to her. She hummed a few bars and snapped her fingers. "The Gambler." It was a song made famous by that kindly looking country singer with a big white beard. A song about playing cards."

Playing poker...

She felt the same excited feeling as when she'd stumbled upon Kyle's middle initial and knew it would lead to something. Carefully she put down the stack of papers in her hands and glanced toward the office door. It was swinging shut behind DiNunzio, now strolling down the aisle, clutching a tray with two coffees. He was about to give her one when she put up a hand.

"Dave," she began, her mouth suddenly dry. "About your Thursday poker game."

"Yeah?" he asked, shifting his weight to one side.

"Who are the players?"

———

Wham! Darby Farr's face met the driver's side door of the black Mustang, thanks to a hard shove by Peter Janssen. "Nice try," he growled. "But you're not the only one who knows how to run."

Darby's head was up against the window, her cheekbone and nose throbbing from the impact. He relaxed his hold and she felt a wave of dizziness, followed by nausea. She willed them both away and tried to focus.

"Let me go. I'm sure there's a good reason why you've got that ring." She tasted blood in her mouth; his shove had loosened some of her teeth.

He chuckled. "Oh, yeah, there's a good reason. It was on Kyle's finger when I lopped it off." He used both hands to push her back against the car. "Do you have any idea how hard it is to cut off a finger, even a pinkie?" He brought his face in close to hers. "Like cutting the head off a chicken, only tougher. You have to try and get your knife in between the joints."

He pulled back again and shook his head. "Shit, Darby, I thought you were headed back to California, or Maine, or wherever the hell you came from, and you'd leave this little mystery behind." He glanced around the graveyard, his voice and Darby's panting the only audible sounds. "I didn't think I'd have to hurt you."

"I can still do that," she said, her tongue becoming thicker. "Let me go and I'll just get on a plane."

"Oh sure! Right after you go running to your little law enforcement friends. No thank you. Like it or not, you're a part of the problem now." He paused. "Luckily, most problems can be dealt with."

Slowly he pulled something from his jacket pocket. "Get away from the car," he said calmly.

Darby's mind was spinning. Peter Janssen was holding a gun and it was aimed at her heart. At only two feet away, there was no way he would miss. The words of her martial arts teacher rang in her head. "Once you see a gun, the game is over." She tried to stall until she could figure out a way to escape.

"Peter, what's this all about? You and Kyle were friends."

A soft laugh from the older man sent chills down her spine. "Friends? I'm not sure if Kyle had any friends, to tell you the truth. Conniving little bitch." He waved the gun in the direction of Genevieve's grave. "Walk."

Darby shuffled away from the Mustang, trying to judge how she could bolt from Peter without being fatally shot in the head or heart.

"What did Kyle do to you?" Darby's legs felt like lead. She tried to shake them, to get them ready for escape.

"Let's see. She stole from me, for one. She stole from me every single chance she could get."

"Your clients."

"Damn right. It started long before she came to work at Barnaby's. She targeted every single person I worked with and wooed most of them away from me. Can you imagine what that felt like?"

They had reached Genevieve's grave. Darby stopped and turned to face her captor. "You must have been furious."

"I tried to tell Marty what kind of person she was. I warned him six years ago not to hire her, not to let her work at Barnaby's, but he just laughed." He waved the gun as he spoke, clearly agitated.

"And then?"

"I gave him an ultimatum, said it was her or me. If she came to work with us, I was quitting." He gave Darby a look of cold fury. "He didn't even care."

"Why didn't you quit?"

"Don't you think that occurred to me? Where else was I going to go? Barnaby's was my dream!"

He gave her a helpless shrug. "The truth of it was, I couldn't leave. My sales figures were dropping—no one wanted me. So I stayed and sucked it up, year after year after year. I pretended to like Kyle Cameron. I acted like she was the best thing since air conditioning. I offered to help her out when she took her little trips with her husband, and later, McFarlin. I had Marty and everyone else believing that we were good little buddies."

"But you weren't making money..."

"Not enough. She was raking it in, and I was struggling. And then when the economy soured, it got even worse."

He shook his head as if regretful. "I'm not saying she wasn't a good agent. That woman was unbelievable. What a force for the company! But was she happy with the income she was generating? Was she satisfied? Could she leave just a few scraps for the rest of us? No, because it wasn't about the money for Kyle. It was about winning. Everything was a fucking competition. Getting St. Andrew's Isle was just another notch in her belt, another trophy property." He turned to his prisoner, hollow-eyed. "For me, it was survival."

"What do you mean?" Darby touched something hard with her toe. It felt like a rock, about the size of her fist.

"I mean, I needed that sale. I worked to keep him as a client. Tag Gunnerson was mine." His voice was hard and bitter. "And she meets him at a party and works her magic, and the next thing I know he's decided to list with her." His eyes glittered in the gathering dusk. "I was counting on that sale."

"Is that why you started doing foreclosures?" Darby was trying to make a plan of action while seeming to be interested in her conversation with a killer.

"Of course it is. Do you think I want to be driving a neon green bus?"

He gave an exasperated sigh and backed up, keeping the gun trained on her. She watched him bend and pick up a long tool.

"This is a gardening spade," he said. "I ought to know—I'm the so-called gardener around here."

He held it in his free hand and came slowly back to Darby, stopping about three feet from her. He tossed the tool at her feet and commanded, "Dig."

A coldness washed over her. "Where?"

He waved the gun. "Right here, next to Genevieve." His face contorted with rage. "I said, DIG!"

Darby bent over and picked it up. In a flash she had coiled and then spun as if throwing a discus, flinging the spade as hard as she could at Peter. The gun fired but she was already off, sprinting across the parched ground and toward the pines.

———

Kelly McGee listened as Dave DiNunzio recited the names of his poker pals in a flat monotone. She recognized one man, and he had a link to Kyle.

"You were on the force in Stuart," she said. "The Kondo Killer case…"

Dave nodded. He was fingering a small porcelain flamingo that Kelly kept on her desk, rolling it between his index finger and thumb in a jerky motion.

She took a deep breath. "Did you talk about that case on poker nights?"

The look on his face told her everything. Her mind reeled and she forced herself to focus. Peter Janssen played in the poker game; Peter had worked with Kyle. Perhaps this was a break; perhaps he knew something.

"Call Barnaby's," she snapped. "Let's go talk to Peter Janssen."

Already they were leaving the station and jumping into Kelly's car. Dave shut the passenger side door and shook his head. "He's not there."

"Try his house." Dave obtained the number, but again, he came up empty. "Let's go to his office," he suggested. "See what we find."

———

A startled Jolene Sebastian hurried behind Dave DiNunzio and Kelly McGee as they made their way through the offices of Barnaby's International Realty. "It's right here," she stammered. "Peter's desk." She wrung her thin hands, shifting her weight from one foot to the other. "I wish Marty would get here."

Kelly opened drawers and rifled through pens, notepads, a stapler, and paperclips. Dave was doing the same thing to Peter's file cabinets, hunting for anything that might shed light on Kelly's nascent theory. Peter had participated in Dave's weekly poker games, and Peter had worked with Kyle Cameron. Was there more to it than that? Were they simply wasting time and taxpayer money on an innocent man's office space?

The door burst open and Marty Glickman stormed in. "What the hell?" he asked. "What are you doing?"

"Trying to find some tape," Dave muttered. Now that they had left the station, his adrenalin was pumping and he looked fierce.

He fixed the angry broker with a penetrating stare. "Tell me about Janssen and Kyle Cameron."

"What is there to tell? They worked together." Glickman shot a look at Jolene Sebastian. The poor woman was paralyzed with fear.

"What is this all about?" Glickman demanded.

"We need you to tell us more," Dave growled. "What did Peter Janssen think of Kyle Cameron?"

Marty Glickman rolled his eyes. "He resented her success. I'm sure a lot of the old timers did. That's not a crime the last time I checked."

Dave was about to retort when Kelly nudged his arm. "Take a look."

It was an e-mail, addressed to Darby Farr, asking her to meet at Alligator Key, and signed from the office of Alexandra Cameron. "Get Cameron on the phone," he spat.

Kelly called and listened for a few minutes. When she hung up, her eyes were flashing. "Alexandra didn't send any e-mail. She thought Darby arranged the meeting. Fifteen minutes ago she spoke to her. She was about to leave the Key." Kelly whipped around to face DiNunzio. "Janssen followed her down there. Think, Dave, think. Where the heck would he take Darby?"

Just then Jolene Sebastian let out a scream. She was holding a plastic container, the kind for storing leftover food, and inside was a human finger.

———

Darby raced left and toward the grove of longleaf pines, dodging gravestones in the murky light. Crack! She heard the sound of another shot and felt the whoosh of a bullet as it sped by her ear.

Peter Janssen was a good shot, a very good shot. Was there any way she could escape?

She banked to the right, hoping to reach some cover before her attacker fired again. But she was too late. A bullet whistled through the air and found its mark in her right shoulder. She felt a searing stab that radiated throughout her body. She sank to the ground in pain.

Seconds later Janssen was beside her, panting heavily. "Nice try," he breathed. "You get a goddamn A for effort."

He kicked her in the stomach with his boat shoe. "Get up," he snarled.

The pain of his kick barely registered. "I can't."

"Get up right now or I shoot you in the head like an old coon dog."

Darby struggled to her feet, the pain a blinding white blade slicing through her body. She swayed, feeling blood gushing from her wound. *He's hit my brachial artery*, she thought. *I'll bleed out before long.*

"Let's go," Janssen urged, pointing the gun at Darby. "Walk."

She lifted one leg and then another, shuffling as if she wore shackles. Stumbling over a log she nearly fell, and the jarring motion made her cry out in pain.

"Shut up!" Janssen spat. "It's your fucking fault! I didn't even want to use the gun until the very end."

Darby winced. The smell of blood was overwhelming. It gushed from her shoulder and over her elbow, making her forearm slick and wet. She tried to staunch the flow with her left hand and nearly keeled over from the effort.

"How did you know about the East Coast killings?" she panted.

"Let's just say I have a friend on the force."

Darby swooned. Jonas Briggs? He couldn't be involved in this…

Peter Janssen chuckled. "It's not your precious Briggs," he said, as if reading her mind.

"Dave DiNunzio."

"That's right. I play poker with good old Lucky and he loves to be the one with a thrilling story. Of course he 'disguises' the details, but I know exactly which cases he's talking about."

Realization sunk in. "He worked on the Stuart police force. He knew all about the Kondo Killer."

"You bet. Even that sicko's little trophies."

His triumphant smile penetrated Darby's fog of pain. "You screwed up, you know," she panted.

"What are you talking about?"

"You did the wrong finger."

She tried again to put her hand over the spigot of blood that was the gunshot wound. "Why did you kill Candy?"

"Lucky told us he was about to question a witness who would shed some light on the murder. A famous call girl, he said. Of course I knew Candy Sutton was Kyle's client, so his little attempt at confidentiality didn't work with me." He shifted his weight to his right foot. "I don't know what she was going to tell DiNunzio, but I couldn't take a chance."

Creepy phone calls, Darby thought. Sam Wilson said Kyle was receiving phone calls from someone at her office. That someone had been Peter Janssen, not Marty Glickman. Perhaps Kyle had said the same thing—or more—to Candy.

Peter gave Darby a look that was regretful. "I'm not some crazy man, you know. I never wanted to kill you."

Darby knew he was one of the most unbalanced people she'd ever met, and yet her survival depended on winning his trust.

"You don't have to kill me! Cooperate with the police, let me go—that will work in your favor."

"Darby," he gave a pitying look. "I've carried out two premeditated killings, and pretty successfully too. No one is going to look favorably on me." He shrugged. "No, I'm afraid I have to kill you and add one more piece to this confusing riddle."

He pointed with the gun into the dusk. She looked down and nearly fainted. They were back at Genevieve's grave.

———

Kelly pointed her car toward Alligator Key and drove as fast as she dared. They'd called Darby's phone and gotten no answer. Now, swerving to avoid a piece of tire in the road, she barked at Dave to try Helen Near. Dave complied, but again they were out of luck.

A moment later Kelly's phone rang. "Put it on speaker and say hello." She and Dave waited as the inquisitive sound of a female voice broke the tension.

"Hello, I just had a call from this number."

Kelly introduced herself and prayed for an affirmative answer to her next question. "I'm looking for Darby," she said. "May I speak to her?"

Helen's response was not at all what Kelly wanted to hear.

"I'm not sure where she is," Helen said. "She's not answering her phone, and she's late for a dinner party. She was meeting Alexandra Cameron on Alligator Key…" Suddenly the seriousness of

Kelly's call registered with the older woman. "Darby's not in danger, is she?"

Kelly gripped the steering wheel more tightly and tried to make her voice calm. "We hope not. If you hear anything from her, please call me immediately."

———

Peter Janssen held the gun pointed at Darby, but his eyes seemed far away and unfocused. "You know the only person who ever listened to me? Who ever really, truly, cared about me?"

"Genevieve." Darby was gasping with pain now, but determined not to give into it.

"That's right." He looked for a moment like he might break down. "She was a saint, that woman. Cookies every day after school. Hugs when I fell or when the other kids teased me. Wonderful stories every night about forest animals and talking trees…" His mood quickly changed. "Lie down," he snapped. "Lie down on top of her."

Darby hesitated. She was dead if she got on the ground, as dead as a fish in a barrel. "Peter, I beg of you," she whispered. "Let's work something out. You're not a killer, not really." She swooned and her legs buckled.

Instinctively he reached out and caught her. "Oh, yes I am," he said, chuckling under his breath. "I'm—"

Darby used every ounce of strength she possessed to coil up her left leg and deliver a resounding kick to Janssen's groin. It was a move she had practiced many a time at the Akido Academy back in San Diego.

"Ugh," he breathed, crumbling to his knees in agony. "You— little—" he winced as he lifted the gun.

314

Whack! Darby delivered another blow, this one a snap kick, to his chin. His head jerked backward and he sagged to the ground, moaning. For a split second she thought of grabbing the gun, but Peter was on top if it and she dared not stay a moment more. Desperately trying to ignore the stabs of pain slicing through her whole right side, she moved as fast as she could around the graves and toward the woods.

Limping through the cemetery, her shoulder screaming in agony, Darby felt the safety of the pines embrace her wounded body. She forced herself to keep moving, to get as far as she could from Janssen and his deadly weapon. A rustle in the underbrush made her freeze. It was a small animal—a snake, or a possum—and Darby resumed her painful movements. The road dipped sharply downward and she stumbled, her shoulder wrenching with a force that made her gag. She paused, felt blackness around her vision, and sunk to her knees.

I can't go on, she realized. *I can't go any further.*

She heard shouts and then a shot. *Someone else is here,* she thought. *They've wounded Janssen.* Footsteps in the fallen leaves caused her heart to leap with hope. Was she about to be rescued?

A moment later, Janssen was before her, his face a purple mask of rage.

"I tried to treat you with decency, and this is what I get," he spat. "You're no different than Kyle. You really don't care."

Darby was too weak to argue. She was about to die, she knew that, and part of her welcomed the release from her shoulder's blaring symphony of pain.

He raised the gun to her head. "You can rot in the woods for all I care. You and your little police friend." He took a breath. "Good bye, Darby Farr."

The smell of pine was stronger than ever and Darby knew it would be the last scent she remembered. *Here it comes*, she thought, closing her eyes against her assassin's sneering face. *Maybe I'll see my parents and find out what happened to them. Maybe I'll get to meet Kyle Cameron after all.*

A gunshot rang out and Darby was slammed to the ground. She gasped and tried to breathe, but her lungs were collapsed like a pair of deflated party balloons. A huge heaviness was squeezing the life from her body. For just a second, her eyes flickered open.

In that instant, she stared into the vacant eyes of Peter Janssen. She opened her mouth in a long, silent scream.

EIGHTEEN

Jonas Briggs knocked softly on Darby's hospital door. "Good morning. Are you up for a visit?" he asked.

She nodded weakly and tilted her head toward a chair. "Be my guest."

He sank into it gratefully. "The doctor says you had a pretty good night and that your shoulder is looking better. How are you feeling?"

"Stronger and stronger." It was true. Since arriving at Sarasota Hospital and getting some much needed Type O pumped back into her veins, Darby Farr was once again feeling like herself.

"What about your lungs? I heard one was collapsed."

"It's healing. The broken ribs are sore, but they'll be okay." She looked into his deeply lined face. "How about you?"

He sighed. "We lost Dave. I don't know if you knew that."

Darby shook her head. She remembered few details from her rescue the day before: Kelly McGee bounding up and somehow rolling Peter Janssen off her chest; the ambulance arriving and hustling her inside; the noise of the siren as she was raced toward Sarasota Hospital. "What happened?"

"When Kelly and Dave got to the cemetery they saw you running into the woods with Janssen in pursuit. Dave fired off a shot. Janssen returned fire and hit Dave in the head."

Darby closed her eyes.

"Poor Dave."

Briggs nodded. "Got a wife and kids. I'm hoping they'll remember him as a hero."

Darby was getting drowsy but she needed to know another detail. "It was Kelly who shot Janssen?"

"Yeah. Right on the money and just in time." He paused. "She's outside. She'd like to say hello if you're up to it."

Darby nodded and Briggs went to the door. A moment later the redheaded officer followed him to Darby's side.

"You're quite the survivor, Darby," Kelly said quietly. "The doctors are impressed with your stamina."

Darby gave a weak smile. "Thank you, Kelly. You saved my life."

The young officer blushed. "Only because you managed to stay alive as long as you did." She looked down at her hands. "It was Dave who remembered Pine Grove Cemetery. I guess Janssen mentioned it once at poker." She wiped her eyes and glanced around the hospital room. "Can I do anything for you while you're in here?"

Darby nodded. "Yes. I want you and Jonas to have dinner tonight—my treat."

Kelly blushed a deeper shade. "I'm sure Detective Briggs is busy..."

"No, I'm free, but—" Briggs looked flustered. "We can wait until you're out of here, then the three of us can go."

"No. It's all arranged. You've got a table at Luna for seven o'clock."

The police professionals looked at each other in surprise.

"Well—" Briggs began.

Darby closed her eyes. "I'm going to take a very long and restful nap now. You two take off, okay?" She waited until they had tiptoed out of the room and closed her door before she allowed herself to smile.

———

Jack Cameron consulted the guest list his sister had drawn up for the following day's luncheon in honor of Darby Farr. "What about Tag Gunnerson and the buyer for St. Andrew's Isle?"

"Good idea. Why don't I call Helen and see who else should be included?"

They were perched on a plump couch in Mitzi's study at Casa Cameron. Two glasses of lemonade and a plate of snickerdoodles—courtesy of Carlotta—waited on a nearby table.

Jack reached for a cookie and bit into it. "Marco is figuring out the food. Between what he brings and what Carlotta makes, we should be in good shape." He gave Alexandra a concerned look. "You're sure she'll be out of the hospital, right?"

"That's what her doctor said." The realtor's speedy recovery was truly amazing. With everything Darby Farr had sustained at the hands of Peter Janssen—bullet wound, broken ribs, a broken cheek bone, and a collapsed lung—she was due to come home from the hospital the following day. "It's because she's young, and in such good shape," Alexandra surmised. "Unlike some people I know who are starting to get a little paunch because they don't exercise and eat too many snickerdoodles."

"Hey!" Jack Cameron took a pillow from the couch and tossed it at his sister. "I resemble that?!"

She tossed the pillow back as Mitzi Cameron entered the room. "Children, children!" she laughed, happy to see the two siblings smiling once more. "You'll get lemonade all over the rug." She rolled over to the couch. "Need any help?"

"I think we're all set," Alexandra answered. "Just make sure Helen brings Darby over."

"Don't worry about that," Mitzi said. "Helen can't wait."

———

Helen was Darby's only other visitor that afternoon. Wearing her trademark golf shirt and slim navy pants, she marched in and went straight to Darby's bedside.

"You are looking ten times better, my friend," she announced. "Rested and relaxed. How's the pain?"

"Much better. I'm not quite ready to go sell any houses, but I'm getting there."

"Don't you worry, you're selling St. Andrew's Isle without even showing up! We are passing papers in the morning. I'll have your commission check when I pick you up at eleven." She put a small duffle bag on a chair. "Clean clothes. Hope you like what I picked out."

"That's great." Darby thought of ET and the loan she had promised him. Now he would have the money to help out his family.

"Pretty bouquet," Helen commented, looking at a huge bunch of pink roses, white lily-of-the-valley, and stephanotis. "Mind if I look?" She reached in to read the card and frowned.

"Marty Glickman! That figures." Her tone softened. "He must feel terrible knowing that Peter was the one who murdered Kyle. All that anger, for all those years, simmering just below the surface. And to think it was St. Andrew's Isle that set him off."

Darby sat up a little and winced. "He resented Kyle before she went to work at Barnaby's, and having her work there all those years ate away at him. You're right, Helen, losing that listing was the last straw."

Helen took a peek at another bouquet. "Hydrangea. Now there's a pricey flower." She pulled the card out of its envelope. "The Office of the Lieutenant Governor of Florida. Huh. That was nice."

Darby gave a small smile. "According to Jonas Briggs, Chellie Howe was very relieved to know the killer's identity."

"Do you think she suspected her husband?"

"I don't know. Could be."

Helen put her hands on her hips. "I'm taking off. You get some rest and I'll be here to spring you tomorrow at eleven, okay?"

"Sounds great. Thanks for the clothes. I trust I'll look presentable."

"Thank heavens." She gave a fond smile. "See you in the morning. No more adventures for a while."

———

Kelly McGee ordered Luna's snapper paella on Jonas' recommendation and enjoyed every bite. Even more enjoyable was the way the police detective seemed to grow more and more relaxed, right before her eyes, as she told him stories of a Philadelphia childhood shared with four brothers, three of whom were also cops. First, they'd discussed the shootout at Pine Grove in all of its horrific detail. Kelly had needed to process the event and Briggs was a willing and concerned listener. Then the talk had turned light, and laughter had replaced their shared sadness over Dave DiNunzio's death.

Now Jonas Briggs regarded her over his glass of Rioja. "How old are you, anyway?"

Kelly felt a flush in her cheeks. How many times had she wished for this exact moment? She looked at him square in the face with determination in her eyes. "Don't worry, Detective Briggs. I think you'll find I'm just the right age."

———

Darby was showered and dressed when Helen arrived promptly at eleven. "Your Mr. Kobayashi is now the proud owner of St. Andrew's Isle," she announced. "He's ecstatic. Kept smiling and making these adorable little bows at everyone. Tag's thrilled, too—he's ready to take off for Arizona and help his sister and nephew." She grinned. "The only one who didn't seem pleased was Bernie Schultz."

"Why is that?" Darby let Helen help her into a wheelchair for her discharge from the hospital. "Won't he be heading to Arizona with Tag?"

"Turns out our friend Bernie hates the desert."

"What about Justin Fleischman?"

"Funny you should ask. I'm thinking he could come and work for me at Near & Farr."

"No more retirement?"

Helen grinned. "Not when there are deals like the one we just made." She clapped her hands. "Speaking of deals … guess what? Tag invited me out to Arizona to play golf with him once he's settled." She gave one of her booming laughs. "Can you believe it? I'm going to play my best game ever, I can just feel it."

Darby smiled as Helen pushed her down the corridor and out the automatic doors. The humid air hit her like a wall, but Darby didn't mind. She was happy to be out of the hospital and moving on.

Helen's Lexus was waiting and she unlocked and opened the door. "Let me help you. Are you still very sore?"

"Much better. I'm taking over-the-counter pain medicine, and it seems to be working fine."

"I'm glad to hear that." Helen closed the door and hustled to her side of the vehicle. "Because I'm taking you somewhere special for lunch."

Darby smiled at her friend. "What a good idea. I'm starved."

———

The curving drive of Casa Cameron was lined with cars parked all alongside the magnificent old oaks, and Darby turned to Helen with an incredulous look. "I don't know this many Floridians, do I?"

Helen laughed. "You'd be surprised. There are a lot of folks who want to thank you and wish you well." She pulled up in front of the massive front door and Harold hustled out, his face ruddy and kind.

"Ms. Farr. It's wonderful to see you. Let me be of assistance."

Darby allowed the butler to escort her into the grand entry hall of Casa Cameron and its opulent, cream-colored living room. Dozens of people had gathered, all of whom burst into applause at her entrance.

Jack Cameron was by her side instantly. "Darby, welcome," he said. "Have a seat."

Gratefully, she sank into a comfortable armchair in front of the marble fireplace. She glanced up at the portrait of Mitzi Cameron, smiling its coy little grin as always.

Alexandra Cameron, dressed in a white linen sheath dress, appeared and gave her a gentle hug. "Thank you for bringing closure to my brother's pain," she whispered. "It isn't going to be easy, but at least he knows the truth." Her gray eyes lingered on Darby's. "I want you to know, my feelings for Kyle were mixed, but I never wished her any harm."

"I know." Darby heard the hum of a motor and looked up as Mitzi Cameron approached, a drink in her hand.

"I'm using my new wheels to bring you a Mojito," she said. "Helen says it's your favorite. Mind if I sit next to you? You are, after all, the guest of honor."

Darby looked at the elderly beauty who had suffered so much. "It would be an honor." She took a sip of the Mojito and smiled. "Delicious."

A small dog scampered through the guests' legs, stopping at Mitzi's wheelchair and wagging his tail with a passion. "Who are you?" she asked with a silvery laugh.

Darby looked closely at the little dog. "Fang?" He spun in a circle as if confirming her question.

"That's right." Jonas Briggs and Kelly McGee appeared at Darby's side. "I'm afraid I couldn't let this little guy go to the pound." He gave a sheepish grin.

"He's got Buddy, too," Kelly said, looking up at Briggs' rugged face. She turned back to Darby, her cheeks a warm pink. "I tell you, he's a softie."

Mitzi Cameron laughed again. "I remember that fish. Does he still live in that beautiful crystal bowl?"

Jonas nodded. "Yes. Until Jack wants it back..."

"Keep it," Jack said, coming up with a plate of food for Darby. "I'm glad the little guy has a good home." He smiled and handed her a prettily patterned piece of china. "Okay, despite the array of lunch choices here, Marco insisted that I bring you this."

Darby looked down. It was a miniature-sized grouper sandwich. "Perfect!" she said. "It's just what I wanted." She took a bite and grinned. "Please thank Marco for me."

"Done." Jack Cameron looked around. "Don't get yourself all tuckered out, okay? We just wanted to show you how much we appreciate everything you've done for the Cameron family." He took a deep breath. "Including Kyle."

Darby saw the tightness of his jaw and her heart went out to Jack. She was pondering what to say when Hideki Kobayashi touched her arm. He gave his customary little bow and grinned.

"The beautiful St. Andrew's Isle is now mine, and I thank you for your expert assistance. I hear that you are feeling better?"

"Yes. Thank you for the lovely flowers."

"My pleasure." He lowered his voice. "I have something for you." He handed her a photo of a graceful sailboat which she recognized as the *Nihon Maru*. "Remember that although your mother came to Boston with pain, what she found while there was love." He smiled. "The world can work in mysterious ways."

She took the photo and examined it. A lovely boat, its sails unfurled against a brilliant blue sky. Her mother's transport to another world, a world where she'd found hope and joy. "Thank you."

He bowed once more and backed away, as Sassa Jorgensen appeared. "I did not have the pleasure of giving you your massage," she said, wagging her finger. "But I have arranged something even better. My dear friend Sven is a therapist in San Diego, and he is going to phone you very soon. He gives an excellent massage…" she grinned wickedly, "and he is very easy on the eyes."

"Thank you, but—"

"No buts. I insist. My friend Kyle would be pleased." She gave a wizened smile.

The clink of glasses signifying a speech made a hush fall over the crowd. Mitzi Cameron, sitting in the center of the room, looked as regal as any queen. "We are all extremely grateful to our brave friend Darby Farr," she began. "And we present her with this very special bottle and our deepest thanks."

Mitzi wheeled over and gave Darby a dusty bottle of dark brown spirits. Helen appeared and peered down at the label.

"Carto Oro 1903? My goodness, Mitzi, this is pre-embargo! Wherever did you get it?"

"Sshh," she giggled and glanced around the room. "I confiscated it from John's stash." Her voice was a whisper. "Not fit to drink, I'm sure, but as a collector's item, it's quite a find."

"I'll say," Helen exclaimed. "I've seen bottles go for six or seven thousand dollars at auction."

Mitzi produced a cloth bag and motioned for Darby to hide her gift. "I wouldn't let our friend Detective Briggs see it." She gave a fond smile. "We'll miss you, won't we Nell?"

Helen Near looked at Darby with tears in her eyes and nodded. "You've become like family to me, Darby. I do hope you'll visit again." She brightened as an idea came to her. "We can go down to the Keys."

Darby cradled the bottle of rum and looked at Mitzi and Helen. "I've developed a taste for this sultry weather and the warmth of your friendship." She gave a grin, barely feeling the tear in her shoulder. "I warn you two—I'll be back."

© William von Wenzel

ABOUT THE AUTHOR

Vicki Doudera never imagined her career as a top producing real estate agent would lead to her dream job: mystery writing. A graduate of Hamilton College and the author of several nonfiction books, she entered real estate in 2003, joining a firm specializing in coastal properties and becoming one of its most successful brokers. Meeting clients, touring luxurious homes, and negotiating deals prompted her to pick up her pen and create Darby Farr, a gutsy young agent selling houses—and solving murders. Her debut novel in the Darby Farr Mystery Series, *A House to Die For*, won praise from coast to coast.

Vicki is an active member of Mystery Writers of America and serves on the New England board of Sisters in Crime. She belongs to the National Association of Realtors and is a past Realtor of the Year. Currently president of her local Habitat for Humanity, she lives, writes, and sells property on the coast of Maine.